Also by Joanna Nell

The Single Ladies of Jacaranda Retirement Village
The Last Voyage of Mrs Henry Parker
The Great Escape from Woodlands Nursing Home
The Tea Ladies of St Jude's Hospital
Mrs Winterbottom Takes a Gap Year

The
Funeral
Crashers

JOANNA NELL

hachette
AUSTRALIA

hachette
AUSTRALIA

Published in Australia and New Zealand in 2025
by Hachette Australia
(an imprint of Hachette Australia Pty Limited)
Gadigal Country, Level 17, 207 Kent Street, Sydney, NSW 2000
www.hachette.com.au

Hachette Australia acknowledges and pays our respects to the past and present Traditional Owners and Custodians of Country throughout Australia and recognises the continuation of cultural, spiritual and educational practices of Aboriginal and Torres Strait Islander peoples. Our head office is located on the lands of the Gadigal people of the Eora Nation.

NATIONAL
LIBRARY
OF AUSTRALIA

A catalogue record for this book is available from the National Library of Australia

The authorised representative in the EEA is Hachette Ireland, 8 Castlecourt Centre, Dublin 15, D15 XPT3, Ireland (email: info@hbgi.ie)

ISBN: 978 0 7336 5286 8 (paperback)

Cover design by Alex Ross Creative based on backlist design by Christabella Designs
Cover image (lace) courtesy of Alamy
Author photo by Simply Loved Photography
Typeset in 12/17 pt Sabon LT Pro by Bookhouse, Sydney
Printed and bound in Australia by McPherson's Printing Group

MIX
Paper from
responsible sources
FSC
www.fsc.org   FSC® C001695

The paper this book is printed on is certified against the Forest Stewardship Council® Standards. McPherson's Printing Group holds FSC® chain of custody certification SA-COC-005379. FSC® promotes environmentally responsible, socially beneficial and economically viable management of the world's forests.

For Margot

'For love is immortality'

EMILY DICKINSON

1

All creatures great and small

A TOXIC PLUME OF ESTÉE LAUDER YOUTH DEW SEEPED LIKE mustard gas through the cracks around the bedroom door. Martin's handkerchief was no match for the concoction of rose, lavender and earthy moss. He was mid-sneeze when his mother emerged wearing a dead fox around her neck, identification made easier by the fact that the creature's head, feet and tail were still attached. Martin had learned to expect the unexpected where his mother was concerned and simply blew his nose. Only the cat seemed surprised, unsure whether to snuggle up to the moth-eaten carcass or claw it to pieces.

'He is rather spectacular, isn't he?' Edwina flicked the stole's brush tail over her shoulder while admiring herself in the gilt mirror by the front door.

Martin raised a sceptical eyebrow. 'Don't you think it's a little macabre?' The fox's glassy eyes followed him. 'Nobody wears real fur in public anymore. Especially not to a funeral.'

'Cynthia loved animals.'

'Live ones, surely?'

His mother looked him up and down. Here it came. Black pawn takes White pawn.

'No wonder you're still a bachelor if that's the way you dress, Martin. That Oxford don get-up might have been ironically fetching fifty years ago, but you'll never find a wife wearing tweed.'

Edwina was relentless in her quest to see him married off before she died, as though his bachelorhood was the final clue in a tricky crossword. Martin was cautiously optimistic that things were about to change on the romantic front. It was early days; so early that the object of his affections was still unaware. He certainly hadn't mentioned the delectable Mary Blake to his mother yet. Edwina was over ninety and the excitement might prove fatal.

When Martin, the university's expert on Egyptian ceramics, had been overlooked for promotion yet again, he'd announced his retirement in a fit of pique. He'd soon regretted his hasty decision when it was made known that none other than Professor Mary Blake had been appointed as head of archaeology. The selection panel had chosen her over Martin on the basis of her public profile, her vision for the future of the department, and on a glowing reference from Dominic Smythe, the university's vice chancellor. Martin had always admired her work – had always admired her – and when he'd finally met Mary in person at his own retirement party, he'd been charmed into a more gracious defeat. Not to mention instantly smitten.

'How are you getting to the church?' Martin asked his mother, glancing at his wristwatch.

She seemed surprised by the question. 'You're taking me.'

Martin's stomach swooped. 'Me? Oh no, no,' he stumbled. 'Can't one of your friends give you a lift?'

'Cynthia was the only one of us still driving.'

She gave him a pointed look, reminding him of his part in the conspiracy to have her stripped of her driving licence.

'How about a taxi? I'll pay.'

'You expect me to get a taxi to my best friend's funeral?'

'I can call that fancy limousine company,' he said quickly. He knew how to play her.

'Shirley Temple wouldn't take kindly to being driven by a stranger.'

'You're taking the cat to a funeral?'

'Of course. She and Cynthia simply adored each other. It's only proper that Shirley pays her respects.' Hearing her name, the cat looked up from where she'd been sitting on a Victorian brocade cushion licking her private parts.

'Remember to bring money for the collection,' said Edwina, already halfway out the door.

Realising he was beaten, Martin fetched his wallet. Predictably, the task of manhandling the hissing, clawing Shirley Temple into the carrier fell on Martin and his trusty gardening gloves. Her yowls of protest continued all the way to the church.

'Did I know Cynthia?' he asked as they turned into Church Lane. 'The name doesn't ring a bell.'

'Cynthia from Bend and Sip.'

That Cynthia. He remembered now. His mother had become friendly with a group she'd met at hydrotherapy after her hip operation. The women had bonded over their joint replacements and had begun meeting regularly to compare progress. They were a competitive bunch, both in terms of their rehabilitation goals and the number of martinis they could put away at each gathering. They'd dubbed themselves the Bend and Sip ladies and stayed in touch long after they'd stopped bending. Cynthia had always been more sip than bend.

'She was so fond of you, Martin.'

'She used to call me David.'

'She always sent you a birthday card.'

'And she always addressed it Dear David.'

Edwina tutted and traced the arc of each pencilled brow in her compact, signifying the end of the argument. Martin wondered what his mother saw when she stared back at her reflection. She'd always been a glamorous woman, and never, ever underdressed. With the fox around her neck and her earlobes drooping under the weight of a pair of giant earrings, she looked like something out of *National Geographic*.

The church carpark was already full when they arrived.

'There's a space,' said Edwina pointing to a vacant spot.

'We can't park there. There's a Reserved sign.'

'It must be reserved for me.'

There was no time to argue. He'd drop Edwina and Shirley at the door then, if he timed it right and parked sufficiently far away, miss the entire service. His mother refused his arm.

'I'm not an invalid, Martin.'

He hadn't noticed her shoes until now. Watching her totter up the stone steps, he understood why they were called killer heels. An usher, one of Cynthia's red-headed progenies, rushed to Edwina's side. She smiled and took the young man's arm, leaving Martin holding the pet carrier.

'What's in there?' Another towering Celt, who looked more bouncer than usher, pointed to the grey plastic cage.

'A cat.' Spotting an opportunity to escape, Martin turned to leave. 'Don't worry. No animals allowed inside. I understand. No hard feelings.'

'Take the cat to the front,' the Celt instructed, pushing Martin forward.

'She's all yours.' Martin tried to hand over the pet carrier, but at that moment the hearse arrived. Now Martin realised why the reserved sign had been placed outside as the hearse tried to manoeuvre around his mother's car.

'Whose car is that?' somebody called out.

Martin shrugged in innocence. The decrepit vehicle conveniently belonged to his mother and, even though she was no longer allowed to drive, it remained a symbol of the independence Edwina refused to let go.

The hearse finally came to a stop behind the parked car. Six men in black suits got out.

'I'll move out of the way,' Martin said, edging toward the steps and the chance of freedom.

But a hand gripped his shoulder. 'Wait a sec. You can go in afterward.'

'I really should leave. I didn't know Cynthia, so it wouldn't be appropriate for me to attend her funeral.'

Or any funeral, ever.

'I said, wait.'

The usher pinned Martin against the heavy gothic door while the pallbearers lifted the coffin out of the hearse. They marched Cynthia up the steps with a haste that suggested they had another gig straight afterward.

Meanwhile, Martin's lungs constricted until there was no room left for a breath. His bladder joined in and threatened to expel the single cup of tea he'd drunk that morning. His body remembered a long-buried memory and, unable to choose between fight or flight, settled on freeze. Martin watched the coffin pass, so close that he could have reached out and touched its shiny mahogany lid.

'Off you go,' said the usher when the pallbearers had passed.

'I've changed my mind,' Martin tried to say but there wasn't enough air to project the words. A firm pat between the shoulder blades forced them out as a wheeze.

Shirley Temple began to meow her indignation once again. With the only exit blocked by Cynthia's ten-foot-tall grandson, Martin joined the procession behind the coffin. Head down, he tried to fall into step with the twelve shiny black shoes ahead, but his arms and legs had forgotten which was left and which was right. They refused to take turns. No wonder he'd been thrown out of cadets at school.

His mother was sitting near the front of the congregation.

'Over here, Martin,' she stage-whispered at the very moment the organ fell silent. The minister stood expectantly at the pulpit, his beatific smile holding firm while the meowing cat was passed along the pew to Edwina. Martin hid in the wings behind a pillar. Resting his forehead against the cool stone, he tried to compose himself.

The minister welcomed everyone to celebrate the life of Cynthia Louisa Preston. Several mourners were already shedding tears, passing pocket-packs of tissues between them. Edwina sat dry-eyed and attentive.

'As we all know, Cynthia was an animal lover,' the minister said into the microphone, 'and I can't think of a more fitting way to begin our service than with the wonderful hymn, "All Things Bright and Beautiful".'

By the time the organ played the first chord, it was already too late. The thump of the familiar notes that followed unleashed such a harrowing memory that Martin forgot how to breathe, the very thing he'd been doing since he was seconds old. He sucked and blew; sucked and blew. This was it; he was going to die. At a funeral too. It was actually quite funny, and he imagined his friend Andrew having a good laugh as he delivered Martin's eulogy.

One or two braver members of the congregation sang the first line of the hymn.

All things bright and beautiful.

The others hesitated, waiting to see what everyone else would do.

All creatures great and small.

Something swooped overhead. Martin ducked in time to see a large grey bird land on the lectern beside the minister. A parrot of some kind. The bird flapped its wings and squawked, raising a chuckle from two young children standing nearby.

All things wise and wonderful,
The Lord God made them all.

A small white dog began to yap. This excited a large retriever that had been dozing on the cool tiles beneath a neighbouring pew. Not wanting to be left out, Shirley Temple added her unmistakable yowling meow. At the pulpit, the young minister tried to keep in time. And in tune. Martin couldn't believe his ears. He'd heard more melodious dental drills. Was the minister even singing the same hymn?

Then, above the cacophony, a single voice soared. A perfect soprano. The sweet, crisp notes filled the old church. A most glorious sound. A ray of sunlight burst through what looked like a hole in the stained-glass window above the altar, setting Cynthia Louisa Preston aglow. Martin took a breath and hurled it at his vocal cords. To his surprise, it came out as a B, then an A, then a D. He sang a line, then a verse.

Each little flower that opens.

Another breath. In and out.

Each little bird that sings.

In that moment it was only him and the woman he couldn't see, tenor and soprano.

The purple-headed mountain ...

The cold wind in the winter ...

The tall trees in the greenwood ...

He gave us eyes to see them ...

At the end of each verse, the rest of the congregation joined in the familiar refrain. The minister flicked through the order of service, then glanced at his watch. Martin started to believe he might survive this ordeal after all. As long as he could sing, he could breathe. If he kept singing, he could endure this purgatory.

Martin waited for the organ's echo to fade to silence before turning to look for the woman who'd spared him from public humiliation. Who was the mysterious soprano? How would he recognise her in the sea of faces? He was exhausted from the effort of not dying in public and yet the hymn had left him strangely exhilarated. He'd been surprised at how good his voice sounded, too, considering his lack of practice. So why did he feel so guilty in the aftermath? How could something as harmless as singing a hymn have evoked such a visceral reaction? He'd missed singing out loud, for years resisting the urge to hum along to the radio or croon in the shower. He'd done so well, too, until today's slip-up. Once was enough.

A single hymn was all it had taken to resurrect the memories he thought he'd laid to rest. He'd been right. This had been a mistake. He never should have agreed to come in the first place.

When the service ended, the congregation dispersed and once again Martin was left holding the yowling cat. Her protests continued until they were outside in the fresh air once more, and Edwina had donated fifty of Martin's dollars to Cynthia's favourite pet rescue charity.

2

The war on weeds

By seven o'clock, Grace Cavendish had made herself breakfast, unloaded the dishwasher and cleaned the benchtops. Barely twenty minutes later, she'd showered and dressed, made her bed and put on a load of washing. By eight, she'd swept and mopped the kitchen tiles, vacuumed the living room carpet and re-filled the birdbath. Only another eleven hours to fill before bedtime. Perhaps this was why older people slowed down: to stretch out what little they had to do to fill their days. Not Grace. It was important to keep busy, she maintained. It wasn't called the human race for nothing. To slow down even a little was to risk grinding to a halt altogether. The house was immaculate, with everything in its place. If only her thoughts were as easy to organise.

With a fresh cup of tea, Grace sat down with her diary. It was one of those slim week-to-a-page versions, and served as a reminder that she had no social life. Sometimes she wished she had an ailment, something that required regular trips to the doctor. Nothing too serious or life-threatening, more an excuse to talk to other people. She wouldn't mind a trip to the dentist now and then. But apparently, she was too healthy, her teeth too pristine. Even her lovely optometrist had pleaded with her not to return for twelve months. The next entry in her diary wasn't until Wednesday 26th.

11 am. All Souls.

Whose turn was it on Wednesday? The name would be there, in the notices section of *The Chronicle*. Unfortunately, her copy had been tossed from a speeding bicycle and as usual landed nowhere near its target. After a fingertip search of the front garden, she discovered it wedged in the lilly-pilly hedge. Luckily, it was still readable. Turning straight to the Death Notices, her finger traced the individual tales of tragedy and loss until she reached the bottom of the second column.

Sheila Rosemary Webb. Beloved sister, aunt, great-aunt, grand-great-aunt, and friend to many.

Grace tried to picture Sheila while she finished dusting. She was using the brightly coloured microfibre cloths her daughter had insisted were better for the environment.

'You don't need furniture polish, Mum. You can throw out all those nasty, toxic chemicals,' she'd said.

So Mr Sheen had flown on a one-way ticket to the recycling bin. Melody was right, of course. Such a wise head for such young shoulders.

Grace ran the cloth over the photo frames on the mantlepiece, stroking away the non-existent dust on her daughter's faces. Here was a whole gallery of happy smiles from that first wrinkled grimace, taken moments after she was born, through to the young woman in a velvet evening gown centre stage in her first solo performance at the Opera

House. The next thing Grace knew, her cheeks were tight and salty. She mopped her tears with the microfibre cloth.

With nothing in the diary for today, and with the scalloped fair-weather clouds offering a reprieve from last night's rain, Grace decided it was the perfect day to tackle the pesky vine that was smothering a family of she-oaks in the reserve. The path through the reserve was a popular shortcut to Parklea Primary School where she'd been both a teacher and a parent. With petticoats of green ferns, red bottlebrush flowers heavy with butterflies, and spotted gum bark that cracked and peeled like sunburn in spring, this overlooked square of bushland was a haven for wildlife. Melody used to love spotting the tiny birds that fluttered in and out of the tree canopy and could identify each species by their distinctive calls. Sadly, despite numerous letters and phone calls to the local council, years of neglect had turned Grace and Melody's special place into a tangled jungle, choked with weeds. The litter was piling up too with chip packets, chocolate wrappers and soft drink bottles half hidden in the overgrown undergrowth. There was even a garish party balloon impaled on a branch. On one of the tracks that branched from the main footpath, some local kids had piled up the earth to make a bike ramp. While it was good to see children playing outdoors in the fresh air for a change, she was sad to see her little piece of paradise carved up like an open-cast mine.

Grace arranged her things next to a particularly neglected area and set to work. Few people would derive as much pleasure in collecting litter as she did. Most people walked past, oblivious. Melody couldn't have been more than seven or eight when she'd read that a single plastic item could take up to one thousand years to degrade in landfill.

'Plastic never disappears completely, Mum,' she'd said one night while lying awake. 'It only breaks down into tiny pieces that stay around forever.' She'd fallen silent then, tiny creases remaining in her forehead. What followed broke Grace's heart. 'Why can't humans live forever?'

Grace doubled down on her rubbish foraging, not willing to risk losing herself in that memory. Not in public. The biodegradable bin bag was soon full. Her haul included half-a-dozen discarded vapes in assorted colours and flavours, three chewed tennis balls, and a round of mouldy sandwiches, probably jettisoned from a schoolbag days ago. The sandwiches were neatly cut into quarters and still wrapped in cling wrap.

She surveyed the foliage, settling on a tall-stemmed plant with a head of pendulous orange flowers. She waded through the more innocuous undergrowth and grabbed the offending weed by the base. *Gotcha.* The sensation as the roots gave way was pure pleasure, a rush almost. She reached for another plant, a ragwort or was it an African daisy? Either way, it didn't belong. Grace uprooted the trespasser from the soft, damp soil, enjoying the tiny thrill. She continued, raking backward through the undergrowth like a brush turkey building a nest.

'Your turn,' she told a creeper when they came face to face. 'Other people might be fooled by those pretty purple flowers, but not me.'

She yanked and, ignoring the sting of sap on her skin, tried to coil the mass of dark green leaves and winding stems into a manageable bundle. Instead she ended up tangled in the sticky strands. Then she noticed a vine that would have impressed Tarzan. There was no point in simply cutting through the thing with her secateurs. Pruning would only encourage it to grow back thicker and stronger in the future. She needed to dig it out roots and all. After hacking away some of its larger tributaries, Grace traced the stem back to its source and pulled.

'Come on, you bully,' she taunted.

When it wouldn't budge, she splayed her legs and tugged with her entire body weight. The vine gave way without warning, catapulting Grace into reverse. For a minute or two she lay winded on the ground. It was a ridiculous thing to have done. At her age, she could easily have broken a hip. Luckily the ground was soft, and her backside even softer. Her sleeve was snagged on a blackberry bush that was coiled like razor wire, otherwise she was unscathed.

'You're next,' she told the spiky bush.

When Grace stood back to admire her handiwork she was impressed. Tree trunks freed from choking climbers, shy grasses untangled, and glorious sunlight once again streaming through the unclogged canopy. She arched backward, hands in the small of her aching spine. It would be worse tomorrow, even after a hot soak in Radox. Her forearms were covered in dried blood from the many thorns; battle scars from her war on weeds. With any luck she'd removed the noxious plants in time, before the breeze or passing creatures had spread their seeds. It was important to spot them early. Before they'd had a chance to metastasise. Before it was too late and nothing could be done.

Grace wasn't sure how much time had passed when she looked up from her pile of vegetation and noticed a young boy watching her. Her first thought was that he was too young to be walking to school alone. His blue uniform shirt was covered in stains and one shoe was held together with silver duct tape. The boy's unbrushed hair reached his shoulders.

'Why are you picking the flowers?' he asked.

'They're weeds.' Grace held up a thistle. 'This one is called milk thistle.'

'Because it contains milk?'

'No, but some people eat it.'

'What if they're lactose intolerant?'

Grace was thrown. The boy pointed to another plant.

'What's that one called?'

'It's called asthma weed.'

'I've got asthma.'

'Oh, right. Do you use an inhaler?'

'Only when Mum's been paid.' He pointed to a bush covered in tiny black berries. 'What's that one over there?'

'Don't touch it. That's deadly nightshade.'

The boy tilted his head. 'How deadly?'

'Very deadly.'

'Deadlier than a celestial claw rocket launcher?'

'I'm not sure.'

'Deadlier than the Axe of the Black Labyrinth?'

Grace was out of her depth. 'Look, the point is you shouldn't touch any plant you're not familiar with.'

He eyed the pile of weeds, then the red welts covering her arms.

When things got tricky in the classroom, one of her favoured teaching tactics was to pose a new question. She pointed to a white flower on the top of the pile. 'Why do you think that pretty one is called angel's trumpet?'

The boy looked at her as if she was stupid. 'Because it looks like an angel's trumpet.' He wiped his nose on the hem of his shirt. 'Why are you killing them if they're so pretty?'

Fair point. 'Weeds don't belong here,' she explained. 'They've come from somewhere else, from a foreign country most probably. If we don't keep on top of them, they can take over.'

'Like immigrants, you mean? My dad says they should all go back to where they came from.'

An insect flew into Grace's gaping mouth. She accidentally swallowed.

'You'd better hurry,' she said. 'The bell went ages ago.'

The boy kicked at a stone. 'The teacher doesn't even notice if I'm there or not.'

'Don't your parents make sure you get to school on time?'

'It's complicated,' he said, sounding much older than he looked. 'Mum works all the time.'

'What about your dad?'

He shrugged in response.

'Do your grandparents live nearby?' She was being nosy, but he didn't know that.

'Poppy wets his pants and lives in a home for nurses. Nanna Gwen went to heaven because she forgot what day it was.'

'I'm sorry to hear about your nanna.'

'It's okay, she was old, like you. We went to her funeral and sang songs. Then they burnt her coughing.'

'You mean they cremated her coffin?' Grace stifled a snort. 'That must have been very sad.'

'Not really. Mum bought me a Transformer. It had a missile launcher and a blaster and everything.' His eyes lit up as he described his consolation prize. 'What's that?' He pointed to the plastic bag.

'All the rubbish I collected from the bushes.'

'Can I see?' Before she could stop him, he'd rummaged through the bag and found the sandwiches. 'Can I have these?'

'Don't touch them, sweetheart. Somebody dropped them on the ground. Don't you have a packed lunch or money for the canteen?'

'Not really.'

What kind of parent sent their child to school without lunch or a snack?

'Here, have one of these instead,' she said, offering a tube of toffees from her pocket.

His face lit up momentarily, then he backed away.

'Teacher says we shouldn't accept anything from strangers.'

'Well, that is right, but how about we introduce ourselves properly and then we won't be strangers anymore? I used to be Mrs Cavendish when I taught at the school but you can call me Grace.'

He took another look at the toffees, decided it was worth the risk. 'I'm Hudson.' With his missing front teeth, it came out as Hud-*th*on.

'It's lovely to meet you, Hudson. Here, take this for recess.' She tried to give him a few coins for the canteen. He refused, which Grace took to be a sensible move on his part.

'Why are you doing all this?'

'I'm getting rid of a nasty big creeper that's been bullying the smaller plants. It steals all their light and food and they can't grow properly.'

A shadow of recognition passed over his face.

'Do you get paid?'

Grace laughed. 'I do it because it needs doing. It's more of a hobby than a job. You know, like collecting stamps.' Would he even know what a stamp was? 'Or Pokémon cards.'

Hudson tilted his head. 'How do you buy food and stuff if you don't get paid?' Another excellent point.

'The government pays a pension to people like me who are too old to work.'

It seemed a ridiculous concept now when she thought about it. Too old to teach in a classroom but not too old to dig out an enormous vine with her bare hands.

Hudson unzipped his schoolbag. 'Would you like one of these?'

He handed her a sheet of paper. In the centre of the page was a child's drawing of a woman: a large round head on top of a triangular body with scarecrow arms and legs. The woman was smiling and had dark brown hair, drawn as two curved lines either side of her head, with large blue eyes framed by enormous eyelashes. The sun was a bright yellow circle in the top right-hand corner. In the sky he'd drawn another figure, with wings and a halo.

'Who is the lady in the picture?' she asked.

'That's my mum.'

Grace pointed to the figure in the sky. 'And who is this?'

'An angel.'

'And what is your mum doing in the picture?'

'She's talking to the angel. That's what she does.'

Had she heard correctly? 'Your mum talks to angels?'

'Yeah, you know, people who have died and gone to heaven.'

Without thinking, Grace looked up through the tree canopy into the clear blue sky above and wished it was so simple.

'Do you mean she talks to your Nanna Gwen?'

'No, she and Mum still aren't speaking.'

'I thought you said your nanna was in heaven.'

'She is, although Mum says it was a miracle they let her in.'

Grace wanted to smile. She tried to hand the picture back to Hudson.

'Thank you, but I wouldn't want to take your precious drawing.'

'It's okay I have lots more.' He showed her a stack of about a dozen identical drawings.

'Can I ask why you've drawn the same picture so many times?'

'I'm giving them out at school,' he said brightly. 'If you want to talk to anyone in heaven, Mum's mobile is on the back.' He turned the sheet over to reveal a series of wonky numbers. The three and the five were written backward but the sequence was still decipherable. 'She's very good. She has lots of five-star ratings on Tripadvisor and she's quite cheap.'

'People pay your mum to talk to dead people for them?'

'Yes, she's a minimum.'

'You mean a medium?'

'Of course.' Hudson sighed, as if it was obvious. 'She works in the home for nurses. Only talking to people who are nearly dead doesn't pay as much as talking to fully dead ones.'

He sounded so proud of her. Grace didn't want to burst his bubble. 'Does she know you're handing out these flyers?'

Suddenly he looked terrified. 'You won't tell her, will you?'

'Don't worry,' Grace reassured him, yet something felt off about this. 'It'll be our secret, Hudson.'

He stepped backward. 'The teacher says I should report anyone who asks me to keep a secret.'

'Quite right. Let's call it our surprise instead.' How much more complicated the world had become since Melody was a child. 'Thank you for this,' Grace said, clutching the flyer for Rhondda Divine, the five-star medium. 'You'd better hurry to school.'

Hudson turned and went on his unhurried way, making the kind of engine or weapon noises that all boys his age made. Strictly speaking, it was none of her business why he was late for school or why he was hungry so early in the morning. But once a teacher, always a teacher, and that automatically made it Grace's business.

She called after him. 'Hudson, what year are you in?'

He stumbled over his own feet and shouted back, 'Year three.'

Grace watched him zigzag toward the school gate, a knot forming inside her stomach.

3

Checkmates

MARTIN ADORED MAGGIE, THE WOMAN WHO'D BROUGHT his best friend, Andrew, forty-seven years of happy marriage. Tonight, however, he was very pleased that she'd gone to her book club since it gave Andrew the perfect excuse to invite Martin over for a game of chess and a bottle of excellent Shiraz. On days that were neither too hot nor too cold the two men liked to meet at the park in the centre of the city and play on the giant chess set beneath a sprawling oak, sharing a flask of tea and, if they were lucky, a slice of Maggie's famous Madeira cake. But on this occasion, with spring barely sprung and the days still chilly, neither minded the shift to Andrew's cosy fireside.

The two men had met at Oxford as postgraduates and bonded over their equally pathetic attempts to fit in as outsiders from the colonies. They'd both treated the university city as their personal theme park, embracing every ancient custom and bizarre tradition. While Andrew always knew those days wouldn't last, Martin had found it harder to leave them behind.

Andrew was a pure mathematician who eventually found his calling back home with the Bureau of Meteorology after meeting Maggie, a Kiwi, in his final year. He and Martin never lost touch, returning to Australia within a year of each other. Martin had never had a wide social circle; Andrew and Maggie were the only friends he'd ever needed. There was no such thing as an awkward conversation with them, and for all his loyalty and wise counsel, Andrew knew Martin well enough to read between his lines.

While Martin's walls were decorated with framed oils by obscure artists and framed nineteenth-century etchings, Andrew's were a gallery of family life. Everywhere you looked there were photographs of children and grandchildren, giving the place a homely feel and reminding Martin of everything he'd missed out on.

As always, Andrew greeted him with a playful, 'Professor!' and they exchanged hugs and pats on the back.

'Looking trim, old man,' Martin said, holding Andrew's slight frame at arm's length.

'Maggie's gone paleo.' Which presumably meant Andrew had too.

Martin gave him a sympathetic look.

'So, no cheese then?' Martin held up the paper bag from the French cheese shop he'd visited on the way. 'I brought your favourite brie, as well as a Morbier and a wonderful little goat's cheese from Corsica.'

'I won't tell if you don't.' Andrew took the bag, returning from the kitchen a few moments later with a cheese board laden with cheese, water crackers and a small bunch of grapes.

In the living room the chessboard was already set up on the card table. They took their places and got straight down to business. It was Andrew's turn to be White and, predictably, he opened with his king pawn. He balanced a wedge of brie on a cracker and ate it in a single mouthful. Martin mirrored his opponent's move, as well as his choice of cheese, adding a black grape for good measure.

It was never about the chess. The two of them had been playing for so long that neither ever gained the upper hand. Andrew was the more aggressive player of the two, invariably opening with his signature King's Gambit. Martin was the more patient player, favouring a Sicilian defence. The problem was that when a competent yet old-fashioned attack met a competent yet old-fashioned defence, the result was a foregone conclusion. Every game ended in a draw. But the two hours they spent together meant more than that.

Andrew moved his bishop and celebrated with a slice of Morbier. The wine had hit the spot and in anticipation of Andrew's next move, Martin moved his knight. Two moves each and they hadn't even discussed their prostates yet. Their regular 'organ recital' was a standing joke between them and they'd become hyper competitive about the size of their respective glands. According to his urologist, Andrew was now sitting on a sugar plum, while Martin's remained the size of a walnut.

'How was your stress test?' Andrew asked at last.

Martin remembered they hadn't seen each other since his doctor had given in and referred him to a cardiologist.

'All normal.' He sighed.

'You sound disappointed.'

'More frustrated. The doctor told me there was nothing wrong with me. Apparently I am perfectly healthy.'

Martin didn't feel healthy, and far from perfect. He couldn't understand it. No one could explain the odd symptoms he'd been suffering from over the last few months. Not even the steadfast Doctor Lowe, who was too modern to shake hands, yet had the right amount of grey hair to reassure Martin he knew a fistula from a furuncle.

In the early days, Doctor Lowe had been extremely thorough, running tests and arranging endless referrals. Every corner of Martin's anatomy had been scanned, with sound, magnets and an entire spectrum of rays. So much radiation had passed through his body it was a miracle he didn't light up at night. Unfortunately, with each new negative result, the doctor seemed to lose interest in Martin's mystery illness. Meanwhile, Martin's brain had conjured a smorgasbord of potential diseases for which there was a choose-your-own adventure of bad outcomes. At his last appointment, Doctor Lowe barely looked up from his computer when Martin presented him with the latest development.

'I've got worms,' Martin said, rolling up his trouser legs to demonstrate. 'Under the skin. I noticed them last night in the bath.' Martin waited. The doctor gave Martin's unremarkable calf a solid seven seconds of attention. Fortunately, the worms reappeared in the nick of time, making shallow ripples up and down the inside of his calf.

'Look. There. See?'

'Muscle fasciculations,' Doctor Lowe pronounced. 'Usually nothing to worry about.'

'Usually, meaning not always?'

Doctor Lowe gestured to a chair. He looked tired.

'Sit down for a minute.'

Martin replaced his bicycle clips and slid off the couch. Was this it, the moment he'd both dreaded and prayed for? At least if his condition had a name, there might be a prescription for it. He tried to swallow but the saliva had disappeared from his tongue and reappeared as sweat on his palms. When it came, the diagnosis hadn't been what Martin had been expecting.

'He tried to tell me it was all in my mind,' Martin told Andrew incredulously.

'He actually said that?' Andrew looked up briefly from the chessboard.

'Not in so many words. He went on about people storing emotions in their body, leading them to mistake normal bodily sensations for symptoms of something more serious.'

'You, emotions?' Andrew hitched one sceptical eyebrow.

'I know. I tried to tell him I'm not the type.'

'What about stress?'

'I'm not stressed,' Martin snapped, the words ricocheting off a family portrait.

Andrew hitched the other eyebrow.

Martin sighed deeply. 'It's Mother. I only agreed to her moving in temporarily after she broke her hip. She's taken root.'

'Didn't all these symptoms start when she moved in?'

'They certainly worsened.'

Moving the furniture out of Edwina's house hadn't helped his back. He'd left the heavier stuff to the removalists, including the old wooden trunks she insisted must be stored somewhere safe and dry. Martin had hoped that since she'd be downsizing once she was independent again, she'd eventually go through them and cull whatever was inside. As it stood, it was a case of out of sight, out of mind.

Andrew pushed the cheese platter toward his friend in sympathy. Martin consoled himself with a double-decker of Morbier and Corsican goat's cheese.

'Have you suggested a nursing home?'

'You know my mother. She has an answer for everything. She says she doesn't want to confuse the cat by moving again. Looks like I'll have to wait until Shirley Temple dies.'

'How old is she now?'

'Ancient. Positively decrepit. We'd need to send her for radiocarbon dating to be sure.'

'I meant your mother.'

'I was talking about my mother.'

Andrew chuckled and Martin's shoulders released.

'Can't you look into getting her a care package?'

'Only if the package includes a visiting bartender, otherwise I can't see her accepting outside help.'

A sly grin appeared on Andrew's face.

'What?' Martin asked.

'Is she cramping your romantic style?'

Martin smiled wryly. 'The truth is I'm cramping my own style.'

'Aha! So there is someone. Should I be writing a speech?'

'It's a little premature for that. At this rate, you'll be delivering my eulogy before your best man's speech.'

Maybe it was time to face the reality that if he hadn't attracted a romantic partner when he was young and still bore a passing resemblance to Indiana Jones, he certainly wouldn't now he owned a nose trimmer and sat down to pee.

Naturally, he'd had relations with women over the years, although sadly none of them had turned into anything resembling a relationship.

'Is she anyone I know?' Andrew probed.

'Mary Blake.'

'*The* Mary Blake?' He whistled. 'I read in the paper she was married.'

'Recently divorced.'

'What's the problem then?'

'She's an intellectual thoroughbred, Andrew. You've seen her being interviewed. She's gorgeous too. Totally out of my league.'

'You're a catch, Martin. Don't sell yourself short. You're an above average chess player and you have excellent taste in French cheeses.'

Martin laughed. Andrew reached across the chessboard and clamped his shoulder; firm, kind and reassuring. This man knew him better than anyone, including his mother.

'If you really want my advice,' he said, 'relax. Try to get out more. Find a new hobby.'

'Funny, that's what the doctor told me too.' It was hard to relax when he could drop dead at any moment.

'Join a choir,' Andrew continued. 'You used to love singing when we were in Oxford. You and Jane were the Sarah Brightman and Andrea Bocelli of the college choir, back in the day.'

Jane.

Four letters, a single syllable, yet enough to completely derail Martin. One minute he'd been about to intercept Andrew's rampaging bishop with his knight, the next he was lost in the memory of standing in the choir stalls of a 700-year-old chapel, wearing a white surplice over a purple cassock.

The choirmaster mouthed, 'All eyes on me.' A poorly stifled cough broke the silence, then with a single swoop of the baton, twenty-six voices joined in glorious harmony to sing the first note of the psalm. The choir consisted mostly of undergraduates, with an equal split of men and women. Martin knew most of the men by name but was always too shy to strike up a conversation with any of the women.

During the first hymn, he noticed a new female chorister sitting in the stall below him. She was singing the same notes, the same tune, yet somehow the extraordinary timbre of her voice stood out from the others. He couldn't see her face, only the top of her head. Her hair was as dark and shiny as his leather brogues, but when she turned around, her eyes were green and her skin milky pale. A delightful genetic rarity.

During the Lord's prayer, instead of bowing her head like everyone else, she looked up at the angels painted on the ceiling high above. He couldn't take his eyes off her. By the time the choir had sung Parry's 'Long Since in Egypt's Plenteous Land', and Martin had watched her flick her hair over one shoulder, he was a changed man. That glorious mane would be streaked with silver by now, he thought, returning to the present, and Andrew's triumphant grin.

'Checkmate,' said Andrew, sitting back in his chair.

Martin scanned the black and white squares. How could he have missed it? Andrew's queen had his king in checkmate. They shook hands across the board.

'I'm sorry,' said Andrew, sounding genuinely apologetic.

'What are you talking about? It's about time one of us won a game.'

Andrew poured them both another glass of wine. 'Not for winning. I've waited fifty years for that. I'm sorry for reminding you about Jane. I wasn't thinking.'

'Nonsense.' To be reminded implied that he'd forgotten about her. Not a day went by when Martin didn't think about Jane. The joy of recalling each individual memory was always worth the pain that came with it. 'Anyway, I must be going. It's a long ride home in the dark.'

'Don't tell me you're planning to cycle home! Stay the night. Maggie won't mind.'

Martin shook his head. 'Mother,' was all the excuse he needed to offer.

Andrew understood. When the two men hugged their goodbyes, Andrew didn't let go. Next to Martin's ear, he whispered, 'What happened to Jane wasn't your fault.'

Martin pulled away before the tears betrayed him.

'When are you going to let yourself off the hook?' Andrew persisted.

Even if Martin could find a way to forgive himself for what happened to Jane, he'd never forget.

'Well played, my friend. You deserved to win,' Martin said as they walked to the front door.

He squeezed his friend on the shoulder, feeling Andrew's bones. They blinked as a car's headlights shone through the frosted glass in the front door.

'Quick,' Andrew said, suddenly panicked. 'Maggie's back.' He looked genuinely terrified. 'Hide the cheese.'

4

The emperor's new cassock

IN THE DAYS THAT FOLLOWED HER ENCOUNTER WITH Hudson, Grace saw his face everywhere: sleeping in the sheets she pegged on the washing line, on the back of the cereal packet, and trapped within the cobwebs she swept from the eaves. It wasn't hard to find things to worry about these days, the newspaper was always full of helpful suggestions, and yet Grace had precious few people left to worry about. It was as though Hudson had arrived to fill the void. He was the kind of kid who could so easily fall through the cracks. His teacher had given up on him, his father was clearly a bigot, and his mother was more interested in the spirit world than whether he ate lunch or had proper shoes on his feet. A boy like Hudson needed a champion, someone who believed in him. Someone like Grace.

The flyer he'd given her was stuck on the fridge door beneath a double-decker London bus. The magnet had been a souvenir from Melody's first overseas tour and in time was joined by similar magnets from Milan, Vienna and New York. Grace had so wanted to watch her daughter perform in a foreign city but it had been impossible to juggle with term times. There was always 'next year', until there wasn't. Grace couldn't bear to part with the kitsch magnets that now secured business cards for 24-hour plumbers, discount coupons and the All Souls parish newsletter. The trusty Fisher & Paykel was the nerve centre of her home, a handy extension to a brain increasingly unwilling to store important information. She'd always hoped that one day her grandchildren's artwork would have pride of place on the shiny, white surface. Instead, that prime location was dedicated to a directive for the paramedics in the event she was taken ill at home: *Do not resuscitate under any circumstances*. She hated being a nuisance.

The printed instructions also included the contact details for her nephew in Western Australia. The nephew she hadn't seen in years. The nephew who'd been too busy to attend the funeral. Instead, his wife had sent a lovely condolence card, assuring Grace she was always welcome to visit. Unfortunately, return flights to Perth cost the same as a new washing machine so it hadn't been a hard decision to make.

Earlier that morning, as Grace made herself a cup of tea, burnt some toast, buttered and ate it anyway, she'd had an idea. There might be a way to help Hudson. While she couldn't remember her own mobile number, for some reason the ten digits of his mother's number were clear and crisp in her mind. She'd even picked up the landline to phone Rhondda, the five-star medium. However, on hearing the dial tone, slightly above a middle C – concert pitch, according to Melody – she'd thought better of it. She really shouldn't poke her nose into other people's business like an interfering old busybody. But a child's welfare was at stake and that made it her business. What if something terrible happened, and she could have prevented it? She tried to put Hudson to the back of her mind. His welfare was the school's responsibility, not hers and that meant trusting a process she was no longer part of.

With a clean handkerchief in her handbag, Grace double-checked the time. She owed it to Sheila Rosemary Webb not to be late. She locked her front door and, dropping her keys into her handbag, she looked up to see her next-door neighbour Stephanie doing the same.

'Hello again,' said Grace, cheerily.

'We must stop meeting like this,' Stephanie said, closing her handbag. They often left the house at the same time and Grace knew she was only joking but the casual comment stung.

'How are the kids?' Grace asked.

'Good, thanks.'

'Are you all over that nasty cold?'

'Yes, finally.' Stephanie pulled a face. 'Sorry, Grace, I'd love to stop and chat, only I'm crazy busy and I'm running late as usual. You know how it is.'

Grace remembered being a working mother, juggling a full-time teaching job with tutoring in the evenings to make ends meet. Back then she'd craved a day to herself, a whole twenty-four hours to do absolutely nothing. She couldn't have known that the future held days so shallow and shapeless that she'd struggle to fill them. If only she could give some of her spare hours back to that younger self. And Stephanie.

'Remember, my door is always open if you fancy a cuppa and a chat,' Grace offered.

She'd given up offering to babysit Stephanie's twins. When the family had moved in next door, Grace had hoped she might become friends with her new neighbour. Eighteen months later, it seemed unlikely. Stephanie was friendly, though not someone Grace could call an actual friend. She was a nice woman; her husband was a nice man. They were nice neighbours, thoughtful and respectful, with two nice, thoughtful, respectful children. In many ways, Grace counted herself lucky.

There were three cars in the church carpark. The first belonged to Reverend Roderick Steele, or Rod as he preferred to be addressed. After his predecessor's unremarkable saloon, the new minister's Jeep had raised some conservative eyebrows in the congregation. Luckily, one member of All Souls' left-wing faction had rushed to his defence.

'Show me the passage in the Bible that prohibits a servant of the Lord from driving a Jeep. Besides, a 4WD would have been a very practical vehicle for road trips into the wilderness.'

Since nobody could, the matter was dropped. However, Reverend Rod and his choice of vehicle remained a moot point.

The second car, a white sedan, belonged to Moira. Saint Moira was as much a fixture of All Souls as the memorial window in the east wall. Moira arranged the flowers. Moira served the refreshments after the Sunday service. Moira handed out the hymn books and laundered the minister's cassock. Everything that needed doing at All Souls was invariably done by Moira. Few in the congregation had devoted more of their earthly hours to the service of the church than Moira. Even when Grace pointed out that surely Moira must have guaranteed her place in the heavenly kingdom by now, she refused to relinquish any of her duties. Sadly, this included writing the parish magazine.

No one was game enough to challenge Moira about the typo-ridden publication, for fear of hurting her feelings, and presumably also because her bloopers were so entertaining. Grace was keeping a mental tally of her favourites, which included, *When parking on the north side of the church, please remember to park on an angel.* In the last edition there'd been an invitation to an evening of prayer and medication, and a save the date for a drug awareness seminar that encouraged attendees to *become familiar with drugs before your children do.* Despite the amusement those mistakes created, Grace was peeved that the magazine looked so unprofessional. She couldn't help being a pedant and wouldn't apologise for insisting on good grammar.

Recently, Moira had added chief fundraiser to her many roles. After a remarkably well-aimed stone from a nocturnal visitor to the churchyard had taken out St John the Baptist's stained-glass head, Moira had launched an appeal to repair the east window. With the dwindling congregation, the weekly collections from the faithful few barely covered the cost of the tea and biscuits, let alone the fee of a skilled craftsman. So Moira had turned to baking and sewing. Nobody who set foot inside All Souls left without either a home-baked blueberry muffin or a hand-stitched lavender bag. Despite her high-pressure sales tactics, however, the appeal was still a long way short of its target. Unlike the stone.

At the furthest end of the unsealed carpark, the third car was now a permanent fixture. With its four flat tyres, it wasn't so much parked as run aground. Grace often left a little something anonymously on the bonnet: a container of sweet treats if she'd been baking, a spare blanket if it was cold, or sometimes simply a bar of soap and a deodorant stick in a supermarket bag. Everyone deserved their dignity. And safety, since chief among Grace's worries was the large tree that overhung the parked car. The giant beech had been struck by lightning two summers ago and had been slowly dying ever since.

Grace shivered at the sudden drop in temperature as she entered the church and waited for her eyes to adjust from the bright sunlight outside. Who in their infinite wisdom had decided that services should be held in cold, dank and gloomy old buildings, even ones as pretty from the outside as All Souls? How much nicer it would be to worship in the open air, immersed in nature and in full view of heaven!

As usual, the flower room resembled a crime scene with hacked-up stalks and decapitated flower heads strewn across the floor.

'Shall I give you a hand with the flowers, Moira?' Grace asked hopefully.

'There's no need, Grace,' Moira replied in her usual frosty tone.

The message was clear. Grace Cavendish wasn't needed. Here, or anywhere. By anyone. No one would miss her if she simply stopped getting out of bed. If she stopped breathing. Her nephew might notice when the birthday cards stopped arriving. Stephanie, noticing the overflowing mailbox or the hedge disappearing under rolled-up copies of *The Chronicle*, might eventually ring her doorbell. Or maybe not.

'There.' Moira stood back and admired the vase of gaudy chrysanthemums, arranged like poles in a tepee. It was an unimaginative arrangement, even by her standards.

'Moira,' Grace said, trying to sound non-confrontational as she surveyed the discarded plastic wrapping on the floor. 'Are these flowers from the supermarket? I thought there was a budget for fresh flowers from the florist.' What kind of message was this sending to grieving relatives?

'I've decided the money is better spent elsewhere.'

Grace pictured the dusty cobweb billowing in the hole where John the Baptist's head should have been. Now was not the time to suggest a fundraising tea towel or offer to compile a cookbook, two perennial revenue-raising favourites she could organise with her eyes closed.

'I could collect some greenery to pad out the flowers. There's plenty of Boston ivy growing around the churchyard.' That was an understatement. Many of the headstones were completely buried under the stuff. A handful of graves were well maintained by families, with flowers replaced regularly. Sadly, many more were neglected and overgrown, their inhabitants long forgotten, and the paths choked with weeds.

'Ivy?' Moira reacted as if Grace had suggested adding cannabis leaves to the altar arrangement.

'Or how about picking some natives from the side of the road? The wattle is out, and a few flannel flowers would look stunning on the altar.' God's own flowers, rather than these Frankenstein creations.

'I have been doing the flowers at All Souls since Reverend Rimmer was minister. Neither he nor Reverend Rod have ever had cause to complain.'

That's because neither of them would know a gerbera from a geranium, Grace thought. Judging by today's efforts, neither did Moira. The altar arrangement looked more like a sacrificial offering than a table decoration.

'If you want to join a flower roster, I hear St Andrew's is looking for volunteers,' said Moira.

'But All Souls is my church. I like it here.'

Did Moira really have such a short memory that she didn't remember the funeral two years ago, a day Grace struggled to forget?

Rod poked his head into the flower room on his way for his sneaky pre-service cigarette. Today, he was decked out in a traditional tailored black shirt and white clerical collar. On weekdays he preferred jeans and sneakers with a crucifix tied on a piece of leather around his neck. When he'd turned up on the second Sunday before Lent in a Hawaiian shirt, Bronnie Lockwood, head of the church's historical society, had grumbled, 'We'll be handing round the tambourines and singing "Kumbaya" next.'

The point of the exercise, Rod later revealed in his sermon, was that to paraphrase Matthew 15:18, it was not the clothes a man wore but what came forth from his heart that was important. His dressed-down look was intended to put him on a level with the parishioners. It certainly made him more approachable, and with his turquoise eyes and gameshow-host teeth, 'Hot Rod' as he was secretly known to the ladies of the parish, already had quite a following on social media. Sadly, his popularity for Insta-worthy weddings and baptisms didn't extend to his Sunday services. But he'd made death sexy, and despite St Andrew's being handier for the crematorium,

All Souls had become a surprisingly fashionable venue for funerals. There was only one problem. He may be the Anglican Church's answer to Chris Hemsworth, but Hot Rod was no Michael Bublé. The new minister was entirely tone deaf.

The first time she heard him sing, Grace assumed he was having an off day. A middle ear infection, or sinus trouble, perhaps. On hearing his rendition of 'Shout to the Lord', she really hoped he was interpreting the hymn literally. It was only when he began 'Behold the Lamb of God' that her stomach sank. It was terrible. Truly awful. Verging on sinful. Worse, she appeared to be the only one who'd noticed.

Grace bent to collect the discarded wrapping and flower stems off the floor.

'Leave that,' Moira instructed. 'I'll do it later.'

'What about the orders of service?' Grace asked, looking around for another task. 'Shall I put a pile at the door?'

'Already done,' Moira replied.

'How about I open the hall for the caterers then?'

'Done.'

'The Book of Remembrance?'

'Ready to sign.'

'There must be something I can do to help, Moira.' She knew she sounded like a child desperate to sharpen the class's already sharp pencils.

'All right, if you insist. The toilet floor in the church hall needs mopping, and there are dirty nappies in the bin. Reverend Rod is too soft with the play group, if you ask me. Lets them run amok. The mop and bucket are in the storeroom. As for the nappies, well, I'm sure you'll work it out.'

Grace knew better than to complain. Moira had allocated her a task, albeit an unpleasant one. It was a start. She hurried over to the church hall where the caterers were already setting up for the wake, covering trestle tables with white cloths, and stacking cups and saucers next to the giant urn. By midday, the place would be filled with mourners. She set to work, mopping the tiled floor and emptying the stinky bin into a black refuse sack. When she'd finished, she stood back to admire the gleaming bathroom. Grace had never met the recently departed Sheila Rosemary Webb, but her nearest and dearest deserved no less than presentable facilities.

Hearing the opening bars of 'Wind Beneath My Wings', Grace emptied the dirty water and returned the mop bucket to the store cupboard. The mourners would be taking their seats. She'd need to hurry to make it in time for the first hymn, and the most important job of all. She owed it to Sheila, and all the others who passed through All Souls on their way to the afterlife. Because Grace believed in her own usefulness, even if no one else did. She could make a difference without the need for praise or recognition, she realised now. And sometimes, the biggest impact followed the smallest of acts. Like drowning out a minister's diabolical singing.

5

An indecent proposal

AT FIRST, MARTIN THOUGHT HE MUST BE MISTAKEN WHEN he opened the email from Mary. She'd sent it from her official university address too. He read it twice to be sure. Yes, *the* Professor Mary Blake, author, academic and, following her popular television series, 'Lost Treasures', media personality, was inviting him to dinner.

She suggested they meet at the little French bistro around the corner from the university campus. He knew the restaurant well and had enjoyed many a happy lunchtime discussion with colleagues across the starched tablecloths. On one particularly memorable occasion, a lively debate over the political, ethical and intellectual pitfalls of the post-humanist theory in modern archaeological thinking had seen proceedings stretch well into the afternoon. But this would be the first time he'd have been to Bistro Le Boulevard for dinner. She'd signed off her email by saying she was looking forward to seeing him. He replied with the same.

Since his retirement as one of the archaeology faculty's longest-serving members, Martin had made a conscious effort to stay involved by attending seminars, guest lectures and summer drinks with the academic staff. He'd even put in an appearance at last year's student graduation ceremony. This was all to be expected of an Emeritus Professor, although Martin's expectations were more focused on spending time with Professor Mary. To begin with, he'd been treated as an elder statesman, a minor celebrity even given his ground-breaking research in the field of Egyptian faience. Admittedly, his area of expertise was considered niche in the wider world of archaeology, but fortunately Martin had always been content to swim in a tiny pond. As interest in his reappearances waned he'd begun to wonder if he was behaving like the creepy high school graduate hanging around campus. He'd stayed away so far this academic year and assumed no one had missed him. Until now.

The table was booked for six o'clock as Mary would be coming straight from work. He'd allowed plenty of time to choose the perfect combination of shirt, tie and pocket square. Desperate not to be late, Martin arrived at ten to six, leaving enough time to clean his glasses on his tie. He wanted to be able to see Professor Mary in all her glory. There was also time to text Andrew with a teaser.

Taking your advice literally. You'll never believe who I'm having dinner with.

He hardly believed it himself.

The waiters were still setting up, snapping crisp white cloths over the tables, polishing wine glasses, and laying out the cutlery. Martin tried not to look at his watch as he waited, but six o'clock came and went. Other people began to arrive. After a while, in response to the pitying looks from the staff, he splashed out on a bottle of French champagne and made a point of asking the waiter to bring two glasses. But he still looked like a man who'd been stood up.

Martin checked his hair in the shiny ice bucket. The frontal shedding process had accelerated exponentially since his mother moved in and the remaining hair that stoically clung to the back of his head gave the impression he'd been caught in a strong headwind. The upside was that his expanding forehead made him look intellectually well endowed. More professorial. More like someone Professor Mary might consider a worthy suitor. His mother told him it made him look old. In an effort to make the best of what he had, he'd visited the chemist and invested in a pot of expensive goo for his hair although the choice between pomade, paste, clay, wax or putty had triggered an attack of palpitations in the male grooming aisle.

Professor Mary arrived at seven, by which time the sweltering bistro was full of diners, and the ice in the champagne bucket had melted. He had a pre-prepared mental run-sheet of conversation topics for the evening, but when Martin saw her through the window, he went to pieces. In his eagerness to greet her, he sent his wooden chair toppling backward with a crash. Then, in the confusion, he missed the opportunity to kiss her on the cheek and they ended up with an awkward handshake instead. Mary slumped into her chair and, before Martin could offer her a champagne, she'd filled her own glass and downed the contents as if it were water.

'I needed that,' she said.

Martin poured her another.

'How are all things ancient?' he began, aiming for a light-hearted, playful tone.

'Bloody awful,' Mary replied. As if noticing him for the first time, she looked him up and down.

He tried to read her expression. Had he passed muster, or had she noticed his sticky hair? Was the paisley pocket square too much with the herringbone waistcoat? He'd been aiming for smart but not too formal. His mother had guessed he was heading out to meet a 'lady friend' and had offered plenty of unsolicited advice.

'Just don't be too . . .'

'Too what?'

'Too . . . you know how you are.'

So, on his mother's recommendation, Martin was trying very hard not to be himself. He listened attentively to Professor Mary's bloody awful day, making soothing noises when she complained about internal politics and funding cuts. Whenever he had the urge to say anything beginning with 'in my day', he bit his tongue. This was what women wanted, wasn't it? A man who listened rather than talked endlessly about himself. So far, it all seemed to be going to plan. Whether it was his attempts to placate her, or the half bottle of champagne she'd consumed, by the time the waiter approached their table, her mood had lifted considerably.

While they looked at the specials, Mary fanned her neck with her napkin. Thanks to a poster he'd read during a particularly long wait at the doctor's surgery, Martin now considered himself thoroughly educated on the symptoms of menopause. Here was the perfect opportunity to demonstrate his credentials as a sensitive, new age man. At the thought of saying the word oestrogen out loud in a public place, however, Martin lost his nerve. He racked his brain for a safer topic of conversation.

'I'm sorry to hear about your divorce,' he said.

A shadow passed over Mary's face, prompting Martin to order a bottle of Pouilly-Fuissé. When it arrived, he made sure both their glasses were full to the brim. If this was the ground they needed to cover before their relationship could take off, then so be it. He was in no hurry. The temples at Abu Simbel weren't carved in a day. He'd waited a long time for this opportunity. He wanted to get it right. Too eager, too heavy-handed and he could ruin everything. Too tentative and he'd miss his chance. Martin was under no illusion. With her amber eyes and perfect Cupid's bow, newly single Mary Blake wouldn't stay on the market forever. She was a catch, and an entire shark tank of hungry, horny, middle-aged academics were already circling.

Their *Coquilles Saint-Jacques* and steak tartare had barely hit the table when Mary began to cry.

'He told me he was proud of my academic career,' she sobbed. 'I think he secretly got off on having a professor for a wife. But it turns out he couldn't handle my success. He said it emasculated him.'

It did the very opposite for Martin. He wanted to tell her so. Instead, he placed a comforting hand on her exquisite wrist. When she eventually pulled away, a full six and a half seconds later, he noticed the top button of her blouse had popped open. He offered her a handkerchief from his jacket pocket, half hoping she might use it to preserve her modesty. Instead, she wiped her eyes and blew her nose.

'Thank you, Martin. I should have married a man like you. A man who carries a proper ironed handkerchief.'

This would have been the perfect opportunity to say something like, 'Plenty more where that came from. In fact, you should come round and view my handkerchief collection some time.'

If it worked, they would have a date. If not, he could pretend it was a light-hearted quip. Knowing what a sucker she was for Ptolemaic-period gold and semi-precious stones, the actual scenario he'd envisaged was more along the lines of, 'Would you like to come round and see my amulet collection?'

He'd been rehearsing what would happen next, over and over until it was as familiar as a memory rather than a vision of the future. Candles. Flowers. Sultry jazz playing in the background. Dinner featuring his signature slow-cooked lamb. If they hadn't already fallen into each other's arms, dessert would be a homemade sorbet, followed by coffee and Belgian chocolates. Then, by the light of the fire flickering in the grate, he'd bring out his collection. Just the two of them with three thousand years of history to discuss over a bottle of his finest port.

The only minor hitch was that the amulets weren't technically his. They were his mother's wedding anniversary presents from his father and she kept them hidden away in a drawer. The other stumbling block was Edwina herself. In his imagination there was no cat hair on the chaise, no cake crumbs on the Turkish kilim, and no toffee wrappers stuffed behind his hand-knotted Persian cushions.

Since she'd moved in, his once tastefully attired, two-storey Victorian terrace with its original cast-iron filigree balustrades was barely recognisable. He'd tried to make her feel welcome, replacing an entire wall of handsome etchings with a fifty-inch flatscreen TV, and dragging out his beloved red leather Chesterfield to make way for her NASA-inspired orthopaedic bed. Knowing it was only for a few weeks while she recovered from her fall, he'd sacrificed his favourite room to create a comfortable bedsit. He'd tried to draw the line at hanging the nude portrait she'd commissioned of herself for her fortieth birthday, but she'd paid a handyman to hang the painting while Martin was out. It was well painted and surprisingly tasteful for a nude, but there was still something of the Greek tragedy about the whole thing.

Martin asked the waiter for black pepper. When it arrived, the pepper mill was the size of a Celtic war trumpet. Being a gentleman, he offered it to the lady first.

'Shall I grind for you, Mary?'

She responded with an expression that could either be a coquettish smile or a disgusted smirk, he couldn't tell.

After that, he didn't trust himself to speak except to order a hearty Beaujolais to accompany their *plats principaux*. All too soon the waiter returned to clear away their plates.

'Would sir and madam care to order a dessert?'

'*Habet antidotum?*' Mary asked, laughing raucously at her own joke.

Does it contain the antidote? Luckily, the Latin went over the waiter's head.

Mary ordered *tarte au citron*, tucking into its yolky yellow filling with relish. While he liked to see a woman enjoying her food, Martin wished she'd slow down a bit. There was only so long he could draw out his *clafoutis aux cerises*. At this rate their date would be over in no time. The bistro was busy, and the waiters were masters of efficieny in moving the patrons through, whipping away tablecloths and empty plates like magicians; now you see it, now you don't. The candle-lit ambience might be intimate and romantic but in reality, they were being served very expensive fast food.

Their spoons had barely come to rest when the maître d' appeared with the bill. He handed it to Martin.

'This is on me,' slurred Professor Mary, lunging for the slip of paper and missing by a mile.

'No, I insist.' Whatever it cost, she was worth it.

'That's very kind of you to offer, Martin. But this is on the university.' She reached across the table and snatched the bill away. 'Goodness, we've nearly finished, and I haven't even asked you yet.'

It was noisy inside the packed restaurant, and he didn't want to miss a word of what she was about to ask him. He leaned forward and in doing so caught a glimpse of lace through her blouse.

'I'm all ears,' he said. Indeed, at that moment, his ears were throbbing in time with his racing heart.

'I have a proposition for you.'

He'd never been propositioned before but was fairly sure it didn't start like this.

'I've had my eye on you for a while, Martin. The way you turn up to academic meetings and social events. I think I know what's going on. At least, I hope I know what's going on.'

His cheeks joined his ears, flaming, pulsing. 'Has it been that obvious?'

'Look, I'll cut to the chase. I want you.'

Martin didn't hear the rest. If he'd been a fifty-year-old woman he would have called it a menopausal hot flush. But he was a sweaty old bloke on the verge of humiliating himself. He made an excuse and scurried off to the bathroom. After emptying his bladder and splashing cold water on his face, he phoned Andrew.

Andrew answered almost straight away. 'Martin, you dark horse.'

'You have to help me,' said Martin. 'I'm in a bit of a pickle.'

'You sound out of breath. Are you all right, old chap?'

Where to begin? Martin gave him a rundown on the evening so far.

'She sounds keen. What's the problem?'

'It's Jane. I can't stop thinking about her.'

Even here in the bathrooms, with a dripping tap and the faint smell of urinal cakes, all Martin could think about was the woman he was supposed to marry.

It would never work with Mary. Every time he gazed into her eyes he would see Jane's green irises, the colour of Christchurch meadow in spring. Whenever he kissed Mary, he would taste the cinnamon sweetness of the Chelsea buns he and Jane used to buy in the Covered Market. And when they did make love, it would be with the bittersweet memory of holding back from going all the way with Jane, who'd wanted to save herself for marriage. He couldn't betray the love of his life. And yet, Professor Mary Blake had just told him she wanted him. How many men would kill to be in his brogues tonight?

The fingertip drumming on the other end of the phone was a sign that Andrew was working on a solution. He treated every predicament like a mathematical problem. There was only ever one correct answer.

'Your trouble is you think too much. Stop using that colossal brain and let your trousers take over for a change. You deserve to find love and companionship as much as you did fifty years ago. You deserve to be happy again. If you want my advice, *carpe* the *diem* before some other bloke beats you to it.'

'In that case, consider the *diem carpe*-d.'

Martin took a good look in the mirror above the sink. He wasn't a conventionally handsome man. His hair would always be a problem, and he still lived with his mother, but he had so much love to give the right woman. When he returned to the table, the wine bottle was empty and Mary was leaning on one elbow, eyes half closed.

'About what you said earlier,' Martin began, wondering if Mary had actually fallen asleep. 'I want you to know that I'm all yours. In fact, I'm extremely flattered.'

Mary struggled to open her eyes. When she did, they were bloodshot, and what he hoped was a false eyelash was hanging by a thread. 'Good,' she said. 'We've been looking for someone with your credentials to tutor undergraduates in sh-eramic an-al-y-shish,' she slurred. She tried again, giving up after the third attempt.

'Oh.' This wasn't what he'd been expecting. Mary's elbow slipped off the table and he only just managed to rescue the tablecloth.

'We're desperate actually. Your name came up.' She tilted her wine glass to her lips and, surprised to find it empty, tried to lasso the waiter with the strap of her handbag.

'Look, how about I order you a cab and we can talk about this tomorrow, Mary?'

Martin exchanged urgent glances with the maître d' and, minutes later, they were scooping the professor into the back of a taxi. When the driver pulled away, Martin noticed one of the professor's high-heeled shoes lying in the gutter and quickly rescued it from the path of an approaching car.

6

Is there anybody there?

GRACE WAS MORE SHOCKED AT THE SIGHT OF A GENERIC school mum standing on her doorstep than she would have been if Rhondda had turned up wearing a beaded headscarf and large hoop earrings. The woman looked so unassuming, so unexpectedly normal. If she hadn't introduced herself and handed over her business card, Grace might have thought she was a friend of Stephanie's who'd rung the wrong doorbell. The business card itself was reassuring, if a little amateurish, the kind anyone could have made up in bulk at a printing shop.

Rhondda Divine. Psychic Medium & Intuitive Healer. 5.0 on Tripadvisor (12 reviews)

The woman added, 'I'm *RhonddaDivineMedium* on Instagram and Facebook, and there's a QR code on the back to sign up to my newsletter.'

'Were your parents Beach Boy fans?' It was the first thing that came into Grace's head.

Rhondda, who must have been asked the same question dozens of times, laughed indulgently. 'No, they named me after the valley where I was born. It could have been worse, I suppose. I could have been born in Ogmore or Gwendraeth. Imagine that.'

There was something about the lilting accent and the way she rolled her 'Rs' that made Grace think of lush green valleys, stone chapels and choirs. If this was Hudson's mother, she didn't come across as a con artist, nor particularly as an abusive or neglectful parent. The resemblance to Hudson was unmistakable, however. They shared the same grey-blue eyes, inquisitive yet wary.

'You have a lovely home,' said Rhondda as she followed Grace to the living room.

'Thank you. Do you live locally?'

It sounded like small talk, but Grace had a plan. First she would establish a rapport by pretending to go along with this reading or séance, whatever it was. Then she'd admit she'd met Hudson and say what a lovely, polite boy he was. Every parent wanted to hear that their child was polite. Having softened the blow, she'd mention how, as a former teacher at the school, she was worried, no, *concerned*, that he was late. The shoes and dirty shirt could wait for another day, but she'd have to say something about him having no lunch. Hungry children couldn't concentrate in class. That was as far ahead as she'd planned. She had no idea what would happen after that.

'I live not far from here. On the other side of the reserve,' said Rhondda.

'I hope it wasn't too inconvenient to come to my house.'

'As I said on the phone, home visits work well in my experience. The channels are often stronger in familiar surroundings when both parties are more relaxed.'

'Do you have children?'

'One. A boy. I would have liked more.' She seemed to regret sharing something so personal. She checked herself and arranged a neutral face once more.

Grace went to the kitchen to make tea. While she waited for the tea to brew, she watched Rhondda through a crack in the door. Far from snooping, Rhondda merely crossed her legs and glanced about, as any new visitor might. However, if she was looking for sneaky clues, she wouldn't find them. The photos from the mantlepiece were all hidden away in a drawer.

'Here we are,' said Grace returning with a laden tray. 'My grandmother claimed to have the gift of second sight,' she said as she poured the tea. 'She used to entertain the family by reading their tea leaves. That was back in the days before teabags, of course.' Not to mention QR codes.

Grace had watched how the family matriarch used her supposed psychic powers to manipulate her relatives. It had been surprisingly effective too. Grace had been the only one to see through Granny Ruth's party piece, recognising how family members cherry-picked the occasional truth from the generalisations. As a result, she now considered herself a good judge of character and had developed a teacher's ear for recognising balderdash. She would know straight away if Rhondda was pulling the wool over her eyes.

As if reading her thoughts, Rhondda asked, 'Do you believe in the spirit world, Grace?'

The directness of the question unbalanced Grace. The plate of Arnott's Cream Favourites wobbled in her hand as she offered it to Rhondda. She tried to read into her visitor's choice of an orange slice. No one ever went for the orange slice, the dreaded coffee cream of the biscuit world. Was Rhondda trying to throw Grace off the scent?

'I don't know what I believe in anymore.'

After what Grace had been through, she wanted to believe in heaven again, and on some level she was still convinced of the existence of a higher power. When tragedy occurred, people often questioned their faith, asking why a benevolent God would inflict suffering on those he claimed to love. She'd wrestled with the possibilities: that it was part of His plan, or that she was being tested somehow. The harder she looked for meaning in what had happened, the less it made sense. Eventually she'd stopped trying. She still went to church in the hope that one day, like the resurfacing of a forgotten memory, her faith would miraculously return. But no matter how many church hall floors she mopped or how many funeral hymns she sang, deep down she knew she was only going through the motions.

'Relax,' Rhondda said. 'I'm not here to judge. I do this as much for my own benefit as for my clients'. I hear people, Grace. I have done since early childhood.'

She was sounding more and more like Granny Ruth.

'That must have been confusing as a child.'

'It used to frighten me. Now I use my gift to help others.'

This would be a good time to ask how much all this was going to cost. Hudson had told Grace his mother was quite cheap, yet on the phone Rhondda had assured her the first session was complimentary. 'A cup of tea is all I ask.'

Grace needed to make the most of this first session since she was already sure there wouldn't be a second. She had one shot at bringing Hudson into the conversation, which meant going along with this charade until she found a natural segue. It shouldn't be too hard to maintain the illusion for an hour. Besides, part of her was curious to see how this would play out.

'Your business card says you're a medium,' said Grace. 'Does that mean you're not a psychic then?'

'Let me explain. A psychic isn't necessarily a medium, but a medium is always a psychic. A brain surgeon is always a doctor, but not all doctors are brain surgeons. Are you with me so far?'

This woman sure had tickets on herself. Still, she'd made her point.

'My job is to act as an intermediary, a channel through which the spirits of the dead can communicate with the living.'

'I have to admit I'm a little sceptical,' Grace said, playing the part.

'That's natural,' said Rhondda. 'It's hard to make yourself vulnerable when someone you love has passed over. You don't want to open yourself up to that kind of pain again.'

It was a logical assumption that Grace must be grieving. No one invited a medium round for a simple chat. Whether it was the presence of genuine psychic energy or the novelty of having a visitor in her home, Grace wasn't sure, but her body was humming. The feeling was somewhere between fear and exhilaration, and not entirely unpleasant.

'Okay,' she said. 'When do we start?'

'We've already started,' said Rhondda. 'We started the moment you dialled my number.'

'I don't follow.'

'It was no accident that you phoned me. Someone from the spirit world guided your hand to dial my number.'

Reverend Rod had once preached a sermon about guiding hands, admittedly a welcome change from Reverend Rimmer's notorious wandering hands, but the idea of hands reaching from beyond the grave was absurd. The right thing to do would be to save everyone's precious time by coming clean. On the other hand, there was still half a pot of tea's worth of curiosity to indulge.

'Do you talk to her?' Rhondda asked.

Her. A fifty per cent chance of being right.

'Sometimes.'

'Does she answer you?'

Grace shook her head. Other people talked about hearing or seeing their loved one. Not Grace. She assumed there must be something wrong with her, that she must be grieving all wrong. And yet, she couldn't imagine anyone's heart being more broken than hers.

'Do you feel her presence?'

Again, Grace shook her head. In the beginning, Melody had been everywhere in the house, in the smell of her perfume in the wardrobe, the sight of long hairs caught in the vacuum cleaner, and the rattle of her cosmetic bottles in the bathroom cabinet. But Melody was disappearing, one sense at a time, or had age simply left Grace too short-sighted to see her own daughter, too deaf to hear her?

'That often happens,' said Rhondda matter-of-factly, like a nurse who'd seen everything. 'You think she's gone when it's more likely you keep missing each other, keep reaching each other's answering machines.'

Answering machines. Grace remembered a time when they were considered the height of technology. She'd held on to hers, even after Melody had pointed out that nobody used a landline anymore.

'Why not get rid of it altogether and just use your mobile?' Melody had suggested.

'What if I lose my mobile or it runs out of battery? I might miss an important call.'

'From the friendly customer service team at Amazon you mean, or someone pretending to be from the bank?'

Grace had grinned sheepishly.

'Please tell me you hang up on them, Mum.'

'But they were so helpful. They noticed I'd accidentally purchased an expensive laptop and offered to refund me the money if I gave them my bank details.'

'You didn't, did you?'

Grace had paused, stretching out the moment before she broke into a grin. 'Of course, I didn't. I wasn't born yesterday.'

'The fact that you say, "I wasn't born yesterday" makes you a prime target for scammers.'

Grace was glad she hadn't listened to Melody and had kept the old telephone. She didn't need Rhondda as an intermediary. If she wanted to hear Melody's voice again, all she needed to do was play back the many messages stored on the answering machine. There was the call describing the amazing *malakofftorte* she'd just eaten in a Viennese coffee house. The missed call to say her flight had been delayed. Three verses of 'Happy Birthday to You', at midnight, New York time. A pocket call with Melody singing along to the car radio. A quick call to say hello.

Without preamble, Rhondda began to rock backward and forward on the two-seater. Her eyes were squeezed tightly shut. At first, Grace wondered if she was in the grips of a medical episode, but when she realised this was all part of the show, she relaxed and took it all in, finding the spectacle as entertaining as it was unnerving.

'I'm sensing a very strong presence, Grace.'

Then, as if summoned, an ice-cream van drove past. At one time, that tinny tune would bring an entire neighbourhood of children rushing out onto the street, coins in hand. Grace couldn't remember the last time she'd even heard an ice-cream van in her street, let alone on a weekday morning. What's more, it was playing 'Greensleeves', the first tune Melody had learned to play on the piano. Grace's scalp prickled.

'This person has been watching over you.'

Like some sort of supernatural CCTV. Grace shuddered at the thought.

The woman persisted. 'She wants you to know that she loves you.'

As an opening gambit, it was a safe one. Everyone wanted to hear that they were loved. Grace sat up straighter, gathering her resolve. She would not be manipulated.

'She likes what you've done with the garden,' said Rhondda.

This prosaic follow-up didn't ring true. Melody always noticed tiny details. She was more likely to admire the various pinks of the petunias and snapdragons, or remark on the birds and butterflies jostling for the same bottlebrush nectar. Rhondda had walked through the front garden when she arrived, and she could see the neat back garden from where she was sitting. She'd know that a woman like Grace would welcome praise for their gardening skills. So far, there was nothing to persuade Grace that Rhondda Divine wasn't anything besides a complete charlatan.

'She worries you might be overdoing it with the bigger plants,' Rhondda continued. 'She's concerned about your bad back.'

Bigger plants. Full marks for effort, Grace thought, remembering that she'd left the hacksaw and thick outdoor gloves in the porch. As for the bad back, who didn't experience the odd twinge from time to time, especially as they grew older? Grace was about to challenge her when Rhondda said, 'Remember how much she hates weeds too?'

Now, this was uncanny, spooky even. Still, Hudson could have told her about the lady he'd met with the strange hobby of collecting weeds.

Rhondda shook her head, rubbed her temples. 'Goodness. There's so much she wants to tell you. She's giving me quite a headache.'

'Let me make you another cup of tea,' said Grace.

Rhondda laughed. 'Broken leg? Have a cup of tea. Nasty bout of typhoid? How about a cup of tea?' It was an uncanny impression of Melody. She'd always made fun of Grace's belief in tea as a panacea, the cure for all ills. Almost all. It couldn't cure cancer.

In the kitchen, Grace wiped her sweaty brow on the tea towel, grateful for a moment to think. There was no point prolonging this charade. It was time to bite the bullet and say what needed to be said, even if it meant ending the most interesting interaction she'd had with anyone in months.

'She's happy your voice has come back,' said Rhondda, when Grace returned with the teapot. 'Does that mean anything to you?'

Grace touched her larynx, felt it slide under her touch as she swallowed. Only her doctors knew about her voice. Hudson had said his mother worked in a nursing home. But what if he'd made a mistake and she was a receptionist in a medical centre with access to Grace's medical records? If this was some kind of confidence trick, it was an elaborate one, and Rhondda had done her homework.

'She says you could go back to teaching now. She thinks it would do you the world of good.'

Enough was enough. She would not be taken for a fool. It was time to call Rhondda's bluff.

'Tell me who you're talking to. Tell me her name.'

Grace knew how this worked and prepared for the trip down the alphabet until surprise, surprise, she chose the correct letter. Then the random roll call of names. Grace had half a mind to report her as a fake, a quack. But did psychics have a regulatory body like teachers or doctors? Was there a Royal College of Psychic Mediums? Or was it *media*?

'I'm getting the letter M.'

Grace nudged the table in surprise. The cups rattled like chattering teeth in their saucers.

'Melanie. No, not Melanie. Something more unusual. I'm hearing music.'

Time stopped. Grace had always planned to call her baby Melanie, after her mother's French mother, Mélanie. When she'd gone to register the birth she'd changed her mind at the last minute. There was something about the baby's cry that had been different from others on the maternity ward. It was almost as if she was singing for a feed or a nappy change. And when, as a kindergartener her daughter had made even her recorder sound tuneful, Grace knew she'd chosen the right name.

'Her name is Melody.' Any pretence was well and truly over. 'She is my daughter.'

Rhondda covered her ears. 'There's so much Melody wants to tell you, only she's speaking so fast I can hardly make out what she's saying.'

Grace knew that impatience. The little girl who wanted to run before she could walk, who spoke in full sentences by her second birthday and taught herself to read before she'd started school. She was the girl who raced through her music exams, left home at seventeen to study at The Conservatorium, and became the youngest soloist with her opera company. It was as though Melody knew she wouldn't have long on the Earth and wanted to cram a whole lifetime of achievements into those precious years. She'd always been a chatterbox too, so keen to share every thought that she often broke into song when her words wouldn't keep up with her brain.

Was she really here? Grace remembered teaching a year six class that energy can neither be created nor destroyed, only altered in form. All the energy that made Melody – so much energy for one person – must be somewhere. Why not here, in this room? Grace held her breath, scared that if she exhaled she might accidentally blow away her daughter's atoms.

'Is there anything you want to say to her?'

What a strange notion, as if she'd been granted a single wish. There was so much she should have said when she had the chance, but she had put it off. They both thought they'd have more time. Until they didn't.

'Tell Melody I'm sorry.'

Rhondda opened her eyes. 'Why are you sorry?' she asked gently.

Where to even begin? Sorry for not seeing what was in front of her eyes. Sorry for pretending everything would be all right. Sorry for not facing reality. But most of all, sorry for not listening.

'Because I'm still here and she's not.'

7

Teacher's pet

MARTIN HAD WOKEN EARLY TO TRIM HIS EYEBROWS AND
polish his shoes, ready for his first day of tutoring. The ride
to campus was uneventful, rush hour slowing the traffic to a
bicycle-friendly speed on the bridge that divided the city into
two postcodes. Today, a pair of eagles rode the thermals that
rose from the river gorge below. Martin thanked his lucky
stars that he'd been fortunate enough to spend his entire
working life in this lovely place. It wasn't quite Oxford,
but the university brought its own old-world charm to this
unpretentious corner of the southern hemisphere.

A rumour had been circulating that the entire university
would be moving to a disused railway works on the outskirts
of the city. The architect's pencils had already been sharpened
in preparation. While Martin understood the need to attract
overseas students with state-of-the-art facilities, he was fond
of the School of Archaeology and Anthropology. He hated to
think what developers might do with the sandstone building,

given its leaky roof, draughty windows and the pigeons nesting under the eaves. While his dinner with Mary hadn't been a date as he'd hoped, he was excited to be working alongside her at last.

The bell tower had not yet struck nine when he removed his briefcase from the spring-loaded pannier rack. Most of the other academics carried backpacks, especially the ones who cycled to work, but Martin cradled the chestnut leather case like a comfort toy. The handle, made of sturdy English bridle leather, smooth and dark from years of use, was as unique as a fingerprint. Such craftsmanship was rare nowadays, which was why he treasured the ancient over the modern. He owned artefacts dating back millennia that were still fit for purpose. His last mobile phone had died after two years.

His father had once told him that you could tell a lot about a man by the state of his briefcase. Martin was six when his father suddenly died and Martin had prematurely inherited this briefcase. The only clues he'd found about his father were a single unsmoked Camel, and a few grains of Saharan sand trapped between the seams. The current contents – an ironed handkerchief, half a packet of Werther's Originals, and a single black stiletto – conjured a very different man. Martin wondered what would happen to the briefcase after he was gone. He had no descendants to inherit it or any of his other prized possessions. That there was no one to pass judgement on his unremarkable life was both a disappointment and a comfort.

The briefcase wasn't the only item he'd held on to and cherished. His bicycle, a genuine 1940s Raleigh All-Steel gents' cycle with John Bull pedals, was still going strong, thanks to annual servicing at a reputable bike shop. It might seem old-fashioned compared to the electric scooters and carbon fibre bikes that whizzed around campus, but Martin's bike was solidly built and undeniably stylish. He'd bought it second-hand at the start of his fellowship at Oxford. After answering an ad in the paper he'd been pleasantly surprised to find that the bike was not only in immaculate condition, but a vintage model to boot. As he cycled the cobbled streets with Andrew, his small life in Australia had felt like a distant memory. They'd been two young men playing dress-up, seduced by the history and glamour of those dreaming spires. While Andrew had grown up, Martin couldn't help but feel that his life had paused in his twenties, when he'd collided with Jane.

He hadn't been paying full attention as he rounded the tight corner near his college and came face to face with the bicycle speeding toward him. While Martin had managed to brake and swerve, the reactions of the young woman on the other bike weren't as quick. Her front wheel bounced on the uneven cobbles and she crashed hard into the kerb. Martin rushed to her aid, insisting he was entirely to blame. Something caught his eye on the cobbled road. Thinking it must have fallen out of her basket, he retrieved it and was shocked to discover he was holding the skeleton of a human hand, the pale bones held in place by tiny wires. Thankfully the young woman was unscathed, and by the time he reached her, she was smiling.

'Would you like a hand?' Martin said, only realising that he'd made a joke when she laughed. The woman – the very attractive young woman, Martin now noticed – took the bones from him and put them back into her basket alongside a copy of *Gray's Anatomy*.

'Medical student or grave robber?' he asked.

She laughed again, her meadow-green eyes dancing. It was her. The girl in the choir. Martin's toes tingled inside his brogues.

'Medic,' she replied. 'You?'

'Post-doc research fellow.'

'Which field?'

'Egyptology.'

'Mummies?'

'Not exactly, I'm looking into Ancient Egyptian ceramic glazing techniques.'

'Fascinating.' She regarded him, as if trying to decide something. 'You'll have to excuse me, I'm late for an anatomy tutorial.' She had one foot on the pedal when she noticed her front tyre was flat. 'Blast! It must have happened when I hit the kerb.'

'Let me mend it for you,' said Martin. 'It's the least I can do.'

Using the puncture repair kit the previous owner had attached to the back of his saddle, he set to work. While most practical skills eluded him, including catching a cricket ball with his eyes open, or shaving himself without requiring first aid, Martin excelled at puncture repairs. Soon they were both standing back admiring his handiwork.

'As good as new,' he pronounced, checking the firmness between his oily finger and thumb.

'I'm sorry, I have to dash,' the young woman said as she cycled away, lustrous hair billowing behind her in the breeze. No one wore helmets in those days. She called over her shoulder, 'Thanks again, Martin. I'll see you tonight, at evensong.'

She'd recognised him! She even knew his name. All Martin knew about her was that he was already in love with her and that, one day, he was going to marry her.

~

Martin locked his beloved bicycle to the painted railings, ready to step back into his old life in the department. He removed his helmet and ran his fingers through his flattened hair.

Professor Mary greeted him in the tutorial room. 'Congratulations on going green,' she said, gesturing to his bicycle clips.

'I like to do my bit for the planet.' And for his heart. Besides, he needed to stay in shape if he wanted to keep up with a younger woman like Mary.

He was grateful for Mary's ice-breaker remark since he'd been dreading seeing her again after the other night. Fortunately, she was acting as if the whole fiasco had never happened. Or had the alcohol blacked out her memory? Martin was fluent in deciphering hieroglyphics but still found women impossible to read.

'Do you need a hand setting up the IT system?' Mary asked. 'Do you have your own HDMI cable, or would you like to use mine?'

'Thank you but that won't be necessary, Mary. I printed off some handouts at home.'

Mary raised her eyebrows. 'How very old school. I like it.'

He took this as a good sign; perhaps she liked her men 'old school' too. The downside was that clearly she was expecting nothing less than a 3D, immersive, multimedia presentation on ancient ceramics. And that meant, so were the students.

'Anyway, I'll leave you to it,' she said, backing away. 'Do pop in and see me afterward. You know where my office is.'

There it was. The first indication that she saw him as more than merely another tutor on the roster. He was still in with a chance. When she'd gone, Martin hummed while he unpacked his briefcase. Having forgotten to give it back to Mary, the shoe was inside, but there was no sign of the notes and student handouts he'd carefully prepared the previous day. Not quite believing his eyes, he checked and double-checked each compartment. Sure enough, the only piece of paper he found was an article he'd printed out describing a condition called Exploding Head Syndrome. He'd been planning to discuss it with Doctor Lowe at his last appointment but had been derailed by the doctor's instructions to magic up a social life. Even worse than Doctor Lowe remaining ignorant of the rare parasomnia that affected up to ten per cent of the population, Martin now faced the prospect of ad-libbing his first tutorial in some years.

The students arrived in dribs and drabs, chatting among themselves. They barely registered him as they scraped their chairs and flopped down at the individual desks. Finally, when five out of the six were occupied, he began.

'Good morning, everyone,' he said. 'My name is Professor Martin Pottinger. I will be your tutor for the remainder of this semester.'

The reply was unintelligible. Most of them looked as if they were still half asleep. Had the conventions of time in the modern world shifted while he'd been away and all young people become nocturnal without his knowledge?

'Today we'll be discussing the origins of Egyptian faience.'

This was greeted with an unstifled yawn from the blue-haired lad on the right. He had the decency to mouth sorry when he caught Martin glaring.

'Who can tell me what distinguishes faience from the more utilitarian clay-based pottery found in Ancient Egypt?'

Silence. How predictable.

'In that case let me enlighten you. As you will all know from your pre-tutorial reading, faience is a glass-like ceramic art form used for jewellery, amulets and architectural decorations.'

This was apparently news to everyone except a young woman with long dark hair and, oh god, meadow-green eyes. How on earth was he supposed to get through this class with Jane's doppelganger sitting in the front row? A late arrival rescued Martin from his emotional pothole. A lanky young man wearing an oversized leather jacket opened the door without knocking. He dragged his feet across the tutorial room as if his shoes were still in the boxes. Minus any kind of apology, and apparently any discernible skeleton, he slumped into the single vacant seat.

'This tutorial started five minutes ago,' said Martin. 'Punctuality is a basic courtesy.'

'Okay, chillax man,' said the boy in the leather jacket.

Chillax? Martin was sure he was the very opposite of chillaxed. Especially now he'd lost his train of thought.

'You were describing faience,' the girl with the green eyes prompted.

'Ah, yes. Faience is made from a mixture of crushed quartz or sand, powdered minerals like copper or cobalt for colour, and a binder or fluxing agent such as plant ash derived from salt-tolerant plants of the *Chenopodiaceae* family that grow in deserts, salt marshes or coastal regions, or lime.' So far, so good, thought Martin, gaining confidence. 'These ingredients are mixed to create a paste or clay-like substance that can be moulded, shaped, and fired at high temperatures. The firing process transforms the mixture into a vitreous or glass-like material.'

All that off the top of his head. He was more comfortable in the world of unglazed clay pottery but had proved he could rise to the occasion. He looked up to see the tops of heads, all staring at a screen of some kind. The exception was the green-eyed girl who was hanging on his every word.

A hand went up. It was the blue-haired kid seated next to the boy with the leather jacket.

'Yes?'

'Will this be in the final exam?' he asked. 'I mean, do we need to know it?'

Frustration and disappointment bubbled up inside Martin. Luckily neither reached his pursed lips.

'Could you comment on the work of the nineteenth-century French chemist Alexandre Brongniart in the context of reviving the ancient art of Egyptian faience?'

Martin scanned the room to see who'd spoken. It was the girl. Her fountain pen – yes, an actual proper, nibbed pen – was poised above a leather-bound notebook.

She tilted her head, still thinking. 'I mean, would you say there's a role for combining science with historical techniques to bridge the gap between the past and the present?'

Martin was speechless. Not ideal for the one who was doing the teaching. Brongniart's 1844 *Traite Des Arts Ceramiques* was at the bottom of the reading list he'd sent out. In the years that he'd been lecturing, he'd never had a student refer to it. His tear sacs throbbed.

'My dear Sonia,' he began, trying to picture the names on the tutorial list Mary had emailed him. Jane, he wanted to call her Jane. 'I cannot tell you how refreshing it is to have a student who is so engaged with the subject matter, and curious enough to read widely around it. The rest of you could take a leaf out of . . .' Damn, he'd already forgotten her name. '. . . This young lady's book.'

He beamed at her but instead of returning his smile, she looked away, cheeks blazing. Perhaps he'd gone a little over the top and embarrassed her, but the boys could learn a thing or two from Sonia. Or was it Serena?

The room fell silent. Outside in the quad, a lawnmower screeched as it hit a stone. He fumbled for his non-existent notes, cleared the gravel in his throat and carried on.

When the session was over, and riding on the high of having conducted the entire tutorial off the top of his head, he headed to Mary's office carrying the black stiletto he'd saved from the gutter outside the bistro. Her secretary, who was usually posted like a sentry outside, must have gone for a coffee break. Martin knocked on the door and waited.

Moments later, the door opened and Martin recognised Dominic Smythe, the university's vice chancellor standing in front of him. The two men sized each other up. Dominic was a good six inches taller. With his salt-and-pepper hair and cleft chin, he was offensively good-looking. Middle age suited him. His pale strides showed off his long legs, and his brown R.M. Williams boots were perfectly worn-in. Martin remembered he was still wearing his bicycle clips.

Mary appeared at the door.

'Let me put something in writing and I'll have it back to you by the end of next week, Dom,' Mary called after Smythe. 'Come in, Martin.' Mary led him toward a pair of identical blue armchairs arranged conversationally at a bay window that overlooked the quad. 'Sherry?' She produced a bottle and two crystal glasses from the bottom drawer of her desk. It was only lunchtime.

Without making it too obvious, he looked around, taking in all the changes to the office since Professor Emmett Myers had retired and moved to Queensland. It looked like something out of a modern interiors magazine rather than the office of the head of the school of archaeology. The new minimalist furnishings were undoubtedly tasteful yet jarring in such a traditional setting. Although Myers had pipped Martin to the post a few years previously, Martin hadn't envied him the mountain of administration that went with the coveted position. When Myers left, Martin had thrown his hat into the ring one last time, hoping he might finally see his passion project of an on-site museum of archaeology and antiquities through to fruition. It soon became clear that the university was looking for a candidate with a higher profile. They wanted someone younger, more dynamic, and more able to attract the right kind of funding. Someone like Professor Mary Blake.

'How was the tutorial?' Mary asked, handing him a sherry. He exchanged the glass for her stiletto which she hurriedly tossed under her desk as if the night at the bistro had never happened.

'I think it went very well; all things considered. That Sarah is a bright young thing, isn't she? Definitely heading for honours. I'd go so far as to say she's a potential Master's candidate.'

Mary narrowed her eyes. 'Do you mean Shona?'

Martin knocked his own head. 'Silly me. I'm not great with names. I should have remembered given she's the only girl in the group.'

At least he hadn't called her Jane.

'That's not quite true, Martin. Sam also identifies as female.'

Which one was Sam again? 'You mean the one with all the piercings?'

'No, that's Reece, they are non-binary.' Leaning back in the armchair, Professor Mary explored the velvet fabric with a fingernail, a surprisingly long and well-manicured fingernail for an archaeologist. 'A word of advice, Martin. Be mindful of the language you use. The term "girl" is considered very disrespectful nowadays.'

Martin didn't need reminding. This was no longer his day, no longer his age. Like all the other ancient relics in the department, he belonged to a bygone era. The modern world was a minefield. And Martin had huge feet. He'd dug some holes in his career, but it would take more than a trowel to dig himself out of this one.

'I'm sorry, you'll have to excuse me.' Professor Mary skolled her sherry. 'I have a meeting to get to.'

'In that case, I won't hold you up.' Martin skolled his and handed over his empty glass.

'Welcome back, Martin.'

'It's good to be here,' he replied rubbing his hands together. 'I have some ideas for how we can attract more undergraduates to the department.' Now wasn't the time to share his museum proposal. He would keep that one up his sleeve; the perfect excuse to invite her for another dinner.

'Let's see how this trial period goes first,' Mary said, guardedly.

The message was clear: Martin was on probation, his tenure subject to a satisfactory performance review, and the correct use of pronouns for the remainder of the academic year.

'Duly noted,' he said, tugging his forelock and backing away like a courtier. Once he was safely outside, he leaned against the corridor wall. What a bumbling idiot. If he hadn't been wearing his bicycle clips, he would have kicked himself.

8

The second-best biscuits

ASIDE FROM THE DISPLAY OF THE CURRENT YEAR'S STUDENT artwork, the school office at Parklea Primary was exactly as Grace remembered. It was almost as if she'd been away for a long weekend instead of in a circle of hell that even Dante couldn't have imagined. Behind the reception desk, Dee, whose customary warm welcome was sadly unmatched by her organisational skills, was as helpfully unhelpful as always. Even Barry the groundsman was in exactly the same pose as when Grace had last seen him, resting on his broom, chatting to anybody who'd listen.

On the day she'd left, with arms full of farewell flowers and a painting by a local artist, Grace had let the tears flow. There'd been no point fighting them as the school applauded her. Everyone at the special assembly assumed they were tears of joy as she contemplated the life of leisure that lay ahead, tinged with sadness at leaving the school she'd come to love. No one knew the real reason she was retiring in the middle of the school year. Dee's last words, 'I expect you'll be jetting off all over the world to watch Melody perform. Have a wonderful time,' had rung hollow when Grace held back her daughter's hair while she vomited up her first round of chemotherapy. The furthest Grace had jetted was to the hospital.

Today, Dee wore the wary expression Grace had come to know well. Dee would be wondering whether she should offer condolences, or whether too much time had passed and a reminder might make Grace self-combust. As if a moment went by when she wasn't already thinking about Melody. It was up to her to offer the cue.

'Melody would be thrilled that the children are still singing her school song at assemblies,' she said, pointing at the framed copy of the words hanging on the wall. 'Hard to believe she's been gone two years now.'

Dee smiled with relief. 'She was an extraordinary girl.'

Extraordinary didn't even begin to describe her. Grace had learned to play down her daughter's achievements, inventing flaws and boasting about her failings, simply to hide her embarrassment. Melody would have fallen short at some point in her life, because everybody did. But she hadn't lived long enough to fail at anything, besides noticing when the dishwasher needed emptying.

Grace knew what was coming next. People always asked how she was doing, as if they needed to hear that life returned to normal, even after the most tragic events. Nobody wanted to know that, for a long time, she'd kept a stash of pills in the bathroom cabinet, and every day forced herself to find a reason not to take them.

'How are you, Dee?' Asking a question was the best way to avoid answering one.

'Me? Same old, same old.'

There'd been a time when Grace had envied other people's lives carrying on as normal, while hers had come grinding to a halt. She'd resented the birds for singing, and the sun for shining. She stayed awake for nights on end because if she didn't sleep she wouldn't have to wake up and remember all over again. Grief wasn't like an illness or injury that would heal in a predictable time. The pain hadn't dulled and the sadness hadn't lessened over time as people told her it would. Distraction was the only thing that made it bearable, at least for a while.

'Angela's with a year three,' said Dee, gesturing to a plastic chair outside the principal's office. 'Have a seat. She shouldn't be too much longer.'

While she waited, Grace took in the familiar: the trophies and ribbons in the glass display cabinet; the Meet the Teachers photo board with so many old and a few new faces. Once upon a time she'd dreamed of becoming deputy principal. But unexpectedly falling pregnant had changed her priorities. Much as she loved being an educator, she also loved being a mother. Even a single mother. The ambitious and energetic Angela Vine had been appointed instead and had then stepped into the principal's role as Grace left.

At last, the door opened. Grace stood, ready to greet Angela. Instead, a boy emerged. Grace could tell he'd been crying. It was only when she saw the duct-taped shoe that she recognised Hudson. He trudged out, head down, without registering Grace.

'It is lovely to see you again.' Angela wrapped Grace in a suffocating hug.

'Thank you for seeing me,' Grace said.

Angela ushered her in and asked Dee to make them a pot of tea. 'Be a love and open those nice biscuits Aaron Peterson's mother brought in.'

'The chocolate ones for climbing out of the window or the broken toilet seat selection box?'

'Use your initiative, Dee.'

Angela pasted on a smile while Grace lowered herself into the tiny 'naughty chair' that was a punishment in its own right.

'What is it, three years since you left? And you miss us already?' Angela quipped.

'Sort of.' Grace shifted uncomfortably in her uncomfortable seat.

'I'm so, *so* sorry.' There it was. The so, *so* sorry, accompanied by the knitted brows, the deep sigh and the head tilt. Still, it beat those who pretended not to see her.

Grace brushed away the sympathy. 'I came to ask for my old job back.'

The silence that followed was fortunately broken by the arrival of tea and a packet of chocolate biscuits with a note attached.

Dear Mrs Vine, Sorry about the window, from Aaron Peterson.

'Are you sure you want your job back?' Angela offered Grace a biscuit.

'I'm rattling around at home on my own when I know you're short-staffed. I miss teaching. I miss the children.' She longed for their energy, their joy and the unsullied optimism of youth. 'I'm fit for my age.'

'I don't doubt that.' Angela looked doubtful all the same.

It was possible that Angela had heard what had happened to Grace at Melody's funeral. More likely, instead of a highly qualified teacher with a wealth of knowledge and experience to offer, she simply saw Grace as past her use-by date.

'I can cope, if that's what you're worried about.'

Angela bit the head off a chocolate-coated teddy bear. 'Things have changed,' she said through a hail of crumbs. 'It's not the kids that are the problem, it's the parents. They're so entitled. Some are here every day, interfering or threatening to sue the school for this or that. No child is allowed to be average anymore. Every parent expects their child to be gifted and talented. Then there's a handful who expect us to bring up their child for them. The boy who was in my office when you arrived, for instance. Eight years old and already going off the rails.'

'Tricky. What are his parents like?'

Grace knew she'd crossed a line and was expecting Angela to do the same. At her first reading with Rhondda, Grace had been too exhausted to start grilling Hudson's mother like she'd planned.

'We never see her.'

'Perhaps she does shiftwork,' said Grace trying not to sound too defensive.

'The boy is completely out of control in the classroom, and violent to the other kids. None of my teachers can handle him. It's almost a relief when he plays truant. And he's only in year three. Can you imagine what he'll be like in high school?' Angela offered the biscuit packet. 'Go on, have a chocolate bear.'

Grace pictured Hudson as a forlorn Paddington Bear.

'What did he do today?'

'Tried to flush another boy's head down the toilet.'

'Why?'

Angela looked surprised, as if this wasn't relevant. 'The kid told him Santa Claus wasn't real.'

Some might argue that the punishment fitted the crime, thought Grace. But condoning Hudson's behaviour wouldn't help her get her old job back.

'Look,' said Angela. 'Take my advice. After all you've been through, the last thing you need is the stress of the classroom.'

'I really want to work, Angela.' It wasn't about the money. She got by on her pension and savings. She had no grandchildren to spoil and didn't see the point in spending money on herself. She had everything she needed, and now she wasn't working, she didn't need holidays. What she was really looking for was a sense of purpose, a reason to get up in the morning beyond cleaning her already clean house, and weeding the reserve. That was something money couldn't buy.

'How about relief teaching?' Grace persisted. 'I know how hard it can be to get staff at short notice.' She'd checked and they couldn't discriminate on age alone. 'I've kept up my Working with Children certificate.'

Angela tapped her chin with a ballpoint pen. 'If you really want to help, you could always volunteer for reading groups. Most parents work during school hours now so we're always short of volunteers to listen to the children read.'

'I'd like that.' It was a toe in the door at least.

'In that case, good to have you onboard. Now, come with me. I'll show you round.'

It was strange to be offered a guided tour of the place she knew so well. She followed Angela out into the playground where the sun was high overhead. Grace had forgotten how much heat radiated up from the concrete surface. On the other side of the fence in the reserve, the air beneath the trees was cool and breathable.

'We're in desperate need of new playground equipment,' said Angela. 'We had two broken arms, a fractured collarbone and a concussion last term on those monkey bars.'

'That sounds serious.'

'It is considering that kids don't break bones anymore, not like we did when we were young. In our day no one survived childhood without a broken arm to show for it. Nowadays they're all inside on their screens instead of playing outside developing their coordination and gross motor skills. I shouldn't say this,' said Angela anyway, 'but in a way, we're doing them a favour by giving them an opportunity to injure themselves.'

'How come?'

'We're giving them stories they can tell their own kids when they grow up.'

Grace hoped Angela was only joking. 'What about that soft-fall rubber surface?'

Angela smiled ruefully and rubbed her thumb and index finger together. It always came down to money.

'As you can see, the canteen is still a hazard to public health.' She laughed as she pointed out the school's many faults like a building inspector on commission. The shade cloth over the benches where the children ate their lunches was ripped to shreds.

'Have I put you off?' Angela asked when they finished the tour at the school gate.

'Not in the slightest,' said Grace. 'I can't wait to get started with the reading groups.'

'Excellent. Do you have a preference for a particular year?'

Grace thought of Hudson. 'As a matter of fact, yes. I'd like year three, please.'

9

Pride and prejudice

MARTIN'S MOTHER'S FRIEND PAT'S HUSBAND'S SISTER'S funeral took place on a dull and overcast morning. There'd been no getting out of this one. It was like reliving the game of chess he'd lost to Andrew, only this time it was his mother intercepting his every move. Finally, when Martin had run out of excuses, he'd laid down his king and resigned. He would drive her to All Souls, and stay for the wake.

'How well did you know this Sandra what's-her-name?' Martin asked while they were stopped at traffic lights.

'I never met her,' Edwina replied.

'What?' Martin put the car into third gear by mistake and stalled when the light turned green. 'Excuse the obvious question, but why are we going to her funeral?'

'To support Pat.'

'You haven't seen Pat in years.'

'Exactly. That's the beauty of funerals, Martin. They're perfect for reconnecting with long-lost friends. There are plenty of families who only get together at funerals too.'

'Couldn't you send a condolence card instead?'

Edwina looked at him as if he'd suggested she take up knitting.

'If you must know, I'm conducting some important research.'

He'd noticed a spiral-bound notebook poking out of her handbag and wondered why she needed it at a funeral. Having little experience with women's handbags and the mystery of their contents, he'd not inquired.

'Research for what exactly?'

'My funeral, of course. How else am I going to decide what does and doesn't work unless I see what's on offer? You see those wedding expos advertised all the time, but you never see a funeral expo, do you?'

Martin agreed he didn't, though he was quite certain he'd be attending plenty in his nightmares from now on. His panic was already on standby as he helped Edwina out of the car. He'd survived Cynthia Preston's funeral because of a woman he'd heard and not seen. How was he going to get through this one?

Once again, All Souls was at capacity. Martin had never attended a sports match as a spectator, other than supporting the school's 1st XV, and then only because attendance was compulsory. Today was his first taste of being packed in with spectators wearing team colours, since the mourners were all dressed in pink. Edwina had donned a salmon-coloured lace and chiffon dress that made her look like a toilet-roll doll. The only pink garment Martin owned was a pair of old white socks that had ended up in a coloured wash. He drew the line at wearing sportswear with a suit. Adding to the stadium atmosphere was the segregation of supporters: family in the left-hand pews, friends on the right. Martin wondered out loud where friends of a friend's husband's sister should sit and was shushed by a 94-year-old elbow.

As more and more mourners squeezed into the tiny church, Martin felt the familiar pressure building in his chest. His adrenal glands had been on high alert all night and his bladder was already sending out warning signals. He sat between his mother and a woman wearing a hat so wide that he needed to lean his head to one side to accommodate its brim. The pews were filled like garden beds, with every shade of pink, from soft pastels through to Pepto Bismol. It was enough to bring on a migraine.

'Please be seated,' said the same minister who'd officiated at Cynthia Preston's funeral. Martin had been too busy trying to stay alive to take much notice of who was delivering the sermon. What Martin did remember, however, was how embarrassed he'd been at the minister's awful singing. The prospect of a repeat performance did little to steady his nerves.

The minister welcomed everyone and congratulated the congregation on adopting so many interpretations of Sandra's favourite colour. So far, so good. The mention of a collection for a well-known cancer charity was the cue for Martin's brain to start overthinking. What if Doctor Lowe was mistaken and his recent endoscopy result was the wrong one? What if that little camera had missed something, rushed blindly past a corner of his duodenum where the unmentionable was growing? What if the throbbing inside his skull wasn't a migraine, but a brain tumour? And hadn't he noticed a funny-looking mole on his chest that morning?

His rib cage clamped his terrified heart. He tried to think nice positive thoughts, but it was no good.

'What's the matter?' Edwina hiss-whispered beside him.

'Nothing.'

He needed to get out of the church.

Everybody stood for the first hymn and Martin saw his chance to escape. When he counted how many bodies he'd need to squeeze past to reach the aisle, then how many tip-toed steps to the door, he realised it was no good. He was trapped. Suffocated by thousands of giant pink marshmallows. The pounding in his ears heralded that something much worse was on the way. It was too late to stop it now. He closed his eyes and waited for the inevitable. This time, he *was* going to die.

Then. That voice. Clear and crisp above the organ.

Blackbird has spoken, like the first bird.

It was her. Not a blackbird, but a nightingale singing.

He scanned the crowd until he found her, a woman standing two rows back on the other side of the aisle. She was dwarfed by the tall men on either side of her, but she stood tall and proud. Sunlight shone through the stained-glass window above the altar illuminating her face in a jewelled glow. Such an ordinary, unremarkable-looking woman, but here, in this church, she looked ethereal.

Martin reached for his order of service though he already knew the words and the tune.

Praise for the singing ...

The notes erupted with such force that his mother flinched at the sudden burst of sound. Several others who had been mumbling into their hymn sheets now straightened up and joined in. With each line, Martin collected voices and added them to the woman's. Together they were the pied pipers of All Souls. This hymn was the perfect tribute to Pat's husband's sister, Sandra somebody. A celebration of her life. Of life itself!

Praise for the morning . . .

Martin attacked the chorus with gusto, and not a little gratitude, given the mess the minister was making of it. With every breath, a delicious warmth spread through him, soothing every jangled nerve. Each note he sang was deeper and fuller than the last until, on the final verse, his voice was as glorious as it ever had been. He held the final note *fermata* long after the organ fell silent, as though he could carry on forever.

'What a wonderful hymn to begin with,' said the minister, clearly optimistic for the rest of the service. 'And sung with such conviction too.' He looked straight at Martin, then at the woman, then up at heaven. 'I hope you enjoyed that one, Sandra.'

Everyone appreciated the light-hearted touch. Unfortunately, the minister's caterwauling did not improve over the course of the next three hymns. If anything, Martin and the mystery woman's efforts to drown him out only roused the pastor further. There was relief all round when he announced the final hymn.

Later, at the wake, Martin shadowed his mother as she worked the room. It was a full house for the buffet, and the cacophony of voices echoed off the high, varnished ceiling and exposed brick walls of the church hall. He caught snippets of conversation as they skirted the various cliques, each a variation on how lovely the service was, or how somebody really should try the carrot cake. A group of young men stood wide-legged in a circle nursing beer bottles, laughing and joking now that the serious part of the day was over.

Edwina exhibited Martin to her friends and acquaintances as if she was auctioning him off.

'This is my son, Martin. He's single.'

Martin smiled graciously and indulged in the small talk that invariably ended with him parroting the same answers.

He was a retired archaeologist. No, not an architect, an archaeologist. Yes, a bit like Indiana Jones. No, he didn't like snakes either. Mummies weren't really his area of expertise. Clay pots were.

'I wish you wouldn't keep telling people I'm an archaeologist,' he told his mother between encounters.

'It's the only interesting thing about you, Martin. Everybody is fascinated by mummies.'

'Sorry to disappoint you, but I'm an expert in pre-dynastic unglazed ceramics, remember? Not mummies, Mummy. I know you'd like all your friends to think that I'm Australia's answer to Howard Carter, but I was always more interested in the lives of the ordinary people. Not everyone could afford to be buried in a gold coffin.'

She looked as though she was about to say something, then thought better of it. He'd mentioned Carter but Martin could tell she was thinking about her glamorous life with Doctor Henry Pottinger, the respected Egyptologist. It was curious that she rarely mentioned his father's name or spoke about him, considering she'd been married to and had a child with him. Growing up, Martin had been left to fill in the blanks as best he could.

Martin remembered the hushed voices surrounding his father's death, the sympathetic looks and pats on the head from people he didn't know. He'd been used to his father being away on digs in Syria, Sudan or Egypt. On the rare occasions he was home, he took Martin to museums, explaining in far too much detail for a boy of five or six, the history and meaning of each item. Martin could still feel the cool glass against his forehead as he leaned on the display cabinets, his breath fogging the surface, and the greasy prints left by his eager fingers that longed to touch what was inside. Then one day, his father was gone for good.

At six, Martin had been too young to fully understand death. There were things he'd been too afraid to ask. Without answers, the questions had stayed inside him, throbbing in his head and twisting in his tummy. In the church he'd taken his cue from his mother who'd remained dry-eyed and tight-lipped, and afterward he'd learned not to upset her by mentioning his father. As an adult, he wondered if perhaps his father, a dashing and charismatic man by all accounts, had been a philanderer too. Why else would his mother renounce his memory?

A woman who looked even more like Barbara Cartland than his mother did approached, trailing a middle-aged woman behind her. Edwina introduced the woman as Pat. Pat's-husband's-sister Pat. The reason Martin was enduring this whole excruciating experience.

'Pat, *this* is Martin.' Martin was immediately suspicious.

'I've heard *so* much about you. You must meet my daughter, Sally.' Pat seized Martin in one hand and the middle-aged woman with the other and pressed them together. 'Sally is single too,' she added. They smiled politely at each other.

'Thank you, Mrs Bennet but I'm not sure this is the time or the place for matchmaking,' said Sally, rolling her eyes.

The mothers made a not-so-subtle exit, leaving the two of them alone together.

'For the record, I'm not single. I am a widow,' said Sally. 'My husband had a fatal heart attack while screwing his PA.'

'I'm sorry to hear that,' Martin said. Twenty minutes and his clean handkerchief later, he was very sorry indeed.

'Look,' said Sally checking to ensure the mothers weren't within earshot, 'to be honest, if I was in the market for a hook-up, I'd want a much younger man. No offence, Martin.'

'No offence taken.'

'Take my advice, if it's sex you're after, get on the apps,' said Sally.

'Thank you. I'll bear that in mind. Now if you'll excuse me . . .' He searched for a suitable exit. 'It is a truth universally acknowledged, that a single man in possession of a good fortune, must be in want of a crustless sandwich.'

He lunged for the sandwich platter like a drowning man for a lifebuoy. It was only when he was standing in front of the woman holding the platter that he recognised her.

'May I interest you in something trapped between two slices of bread?' she offered. 'I can't say with any certainty what the fillings are. It's Russian roulette, I'm afraid.'

'How very apt for a funeral,' said Martin.

The woman smiled, then frowned. 'I know your face from somewhere,' she said.

'I was on *Time Team* in 1996. It's still available on YouTube. Perhaps you recognise me from there.' When this didn't ring any bells for her, he came clean. 'More likely you saw me at Cynthia Preston's funeral last week.'

'That's right. I remember now. I saw you arrive with the cat.'

Martin shrugged. 'What can I say? It's so hard to find a proper date for a funeral, don't you think?' He helped himself to a sandwich. Roast beef and English mustard, he guessed.

This time the smile lingered on her face. 'The fox was a talking point too.'

'Yes. I think it was still alive at the start of "All Things Bright and Beautiful."'

The woman laughed. When was the last time a woman had laughed at one of his jokes? Replaying the dinner with Mary, as he'd done ad nauseam, the only time he'd made her laugh was when he tripped over her handbag on his way to the bathroom and crashed into a waiter carrying an armful of souffles. He was glad he'd provided some entertainment for the evening, only it wasn't exactly the way he'd hoped.

'Did you make these?' Martin asked as he polished off another sandwich. This time the sandwich was disquietingly fishy. Tinned salmon, or tuna maybe?

The woman glanced over at the serving hatch and sighed. 'No, that would be Moira. Moira does the catering. Moira does the flowers. Moira hands out the orders of service.'

'She does all that?'

'Yes,' replied the woman through gritted teeth. 'Moira Manners is undefeated in her decade-long reign as Martyr of the Year. She gets very touchy if anyone else tries to help. Especially me, for some reason.' The woman sighed. 'Sorry, you must think I'm a terrible person. I'm Grace, by the way. Graceless Grace, obviously.'

'I'm Martin.' Since three of their four hands were occupied with sandwiches, they merely smiled in greeting.

Apparently in no hurry to circulate the sandwich platter, Grace asked him how he knew Sandra.

He dropped his gaze and wiped his fingers on a napkin. 'I didn't. I've never met her before. I brought my mother. That's her over there. She's the one in pink.'

Grace chuckled.

'How did she know Sandra?'

'A friend of a friend.' It was too tenuous to unravel further. Martin continued the traditional funeral small talk. 'Did you know Sandra well?'

'Hardly, I'd never met her before either,' Grace replied.

'Really?'

'Don't look so surprised. There are at least half-a-dozen people here who wouldn't know Sandra from a bar of soap. Look, over there.' Grace nodded toward a scruffily dressed older man who was piling sausage rolls onto a plate. 'That's Bill. He comes to every wake at All Souls. Always leaves with his pockets bulging. And see that lady over there?' Grace gestured to a well-groomed woman who was squawking with laughter as she helped herself to white wine from a bottle. 'That's Claire.'

Martin noticed now. The hall was filled with people huddled together in conversations punctuated by polite laughter, while others, red-eyed, exchanged hugs with other puffy-eyed mourners. But there were also several people who seemed more focused on the food and the free booze. They were indeed the same faces he'd seen at Cynthia Preston's funeral.

'Are you saying these people have snuck in for a free feed?'

'And for the company, I suspect. There are a lot of lonely people in the world, Martin. Especially when you get to our age. This is the one place you can come where nobody judges. Besides, you don't need to have known somebody personally to celebrate their life. Some poor people have hardly a handful turn up to their funeral. Can you imagine? I like to think I'm performing a community service by swelling the numbers.' Grace's smile faded. 'Even the smallest gestures can mean so much when you're grieving.'

'I noticed you singing. You have an incredible voice,' he said, hoping it didn't sound like a cheesy chat-up line.

'I love to sing, especially the good old-fashioned hymns that everyone knows. Where else can you belt out "Morning Has Broken" on a weekday and not have people think you've got bats in the belfry?'

'The church acoustics certainly beat singing in the shower.' His cheeks flushed as he tried not to picture this lovely, church-going woman showering.

Luckily, she didn't read anything untoward into his comment. 'Most people mumble into their boots at funerals. I think people have become self-conscious about singing in public.'

'You're right. Once upon a time, everyone used to practise in church on a Sunday.'

'What a shame we only get to sing at funerals nowadays.'

'And weddings.'

He looked away, afraid she might see the pain in his eyes. Keen not to lose the one person at this gathering who didn't want to discuss how lovely the service was, how delicious the cake was or, worse still, mummies, he asked, 'You're a soprano, right?'

'Spot on.' Grace tapped her chin, as if deciding something. 'And you're a tenor.'

'All we need is to find a bass and an alto, and we'll have ourselves a choir.'

How much easier it was to talk to a woman he wasn't romantically interested in, Martin thought. As with his mother, conversations with Mary felt like a game of chess in which he needed to plan several moves ahead. They were challenging, exciting and invariably stimulating, but often left him feeling defeated. Meeting Grace felt like reconnecting with an old friend. Comfortable, familiar, playful. Unfortunately, there were only so many crustless sandwiches he could eat.

Grace stroked the sides of the sandwich platter with her thumbs. 'Look, Martin, I know we've only just met, but I was wondering if you'd like to join me?'

'Join you for what?'

'To sing a few hymns. At the next funeral.'

Another funeral? The thought tumbled inside his stomach. He swallowed the remains of his sandwich with difficulty. 'Whose funeral?'

'I don't know yet,' Grace said, brightly.

'You're inviting me to crash a funeral with you?'

'I suppose I am.' She looked as surprised as him at the impromptu invitation.

Martin could think of a million reasons why not, and yet he barely hesitated. 'Yes. I'd like that very much.'

10

Seriously funny

THE GALLERY ABOVE THE WEST DOOR THAT HOUSED ALL Souls' 100-year-old pipe organ was known as the Holy of Holies. Moira had made it quite clear that the organist Bernard's environs were strictly off limits to Grace. That didn't stop Grace from exchanging pleasantries with Bernard, a friendly gesture that never failed to produce a scowl from Moira.

On seeing the back of Bernard's shiny pate above the parapet, Grace called up to him.

'Ready for action, Bernard?'

A man of few words, he replied with a brief thumbs up.

'I'll save you some cake.'

A double thumbs up.

For all the hours he spent supposedly practising, Grace rarely heard him playing a note whenever she popped in unannounced. Bernard's tenure as All Souls' organist was secure, however, not least because he was the only person in the parish who could find the on/off button. Despite the variable quality of his performances, many of which managed to make the historic instrument sound like a fairground Wurlitzer, live organ music gave All Souls a competitive edge over its main rival, St Andrew's, where an elderly pianist with unpredictable fingers plonked away on an equally ancient and unpredictable piano.

As usual, everything was set up and ready to go for today's funeral. There was nothing left for Grace to do except get in the way. Moira wasted no time in reminding her that she was surplus to requirements.

'I would have thought you had better things to do with your time,' she said when she saw Grace.

'I really don't mind,' Grace replied.

Mind wasn't the right word, but it sounded plausible. Altruistic enough that no one would suspect the real reason. It was too hard to make others understand when Grace couldn't understand it herself. Why would she want to return to that day, to the scene of the most unspeakable pain, over and over again? It made no logical sense to punish herself like this. Yet the only way she could live with the haunting memory of her daughter's funeral was to revisit it until, through gradual desensitisation, her mind had created a less painful version. She also wanted to ensure that no other mother, daughter, wife or husband would look back with the same regret. A funeral marked the worst day of somebody's life, and she didn't want anyone else to face it alone.

Today Grace would be smoothing the way for a woman who, according to the notice in *The Chronicle*, would be missed by her Bridge club and all at the Country Women's Association branch where she was secretary. Grace pictured an elegant lady wearing a twinset and pearls, a fine upstanding member of the community, the perfect choice for Martin's first time. If he turned up.

She'd lain in bed the night after Sandra's funeral, blushing in the dark as she recalled her brazenness. To his credit, he hadn't baulked at the invitation. Perhaps he'd been too shocked at the unusual proposition to refuse. Or too polite. He seemed such a gentleman. He had probably come to his senses afterward, and dismissed the whole episode as the evangelical fervour of a Bible-bashing do-gooder. But Grace remained hopeful and took it upon herself to polish the already shiny collection plate at the door, which just happened to be the perfect spot to see people as they arrived.

Catching her reflection in the silver collection plate, she began to have second thoughts about the lipstick she'd worn. Was it trying too hard? He'd seemed like a nice man – decent, and funny too. He hadn't been wearing a wedding ring, so she hadn't seen any harm in suggesting he join her for a few hymns. It was hardly a date. What if Martin got the wrong idea? Martin wasn't exactly her type. Then again, she doubted she was his type. She doubted she was anyone's type these days.

The first vehicle arrived, a bright yellow garbage truck that turned into the church carpark then stopped abruptly. It was late today. The bins had usually been emptied by this time. Mourners would start arriving any minute now, and there was only half an hour until the service began. Assuming the truck would do its business quickly and be on its way again, Grace didn't pay too much attention to it at first. It was only when the engine noise died and a man in high-vis jumped out that she had misgivings. When he scratched his head and reached for his phone, she knew there was a problem. A big problem given the garbage truck was blocking the only entry to the church.

Moira was first on the scene and tried to shoo away the broken-down garbage truck. Reverend Rod joined in but not even his earnestly offered prayers could restart the engine. By now, a line of traffic had formed in the road, and the first impatient horns began blasting. A bicycle appeared, skirting around the side of the truck. The cyclist navigated the narrow gap with ease, dismounted and locked his bike to the metal railing. When he removed his blue plastic helmet Grace recognised Martin, his wiry hair flattened into a sweaty chainmail hood. He trotted across the carpark toward her, apologising as he took the steps two at a time.

'I hope I'm not late,' he said, oblivious to the unfolding chaos behind him.

'Perfect timing,' Grace reassured him. Unlike the garbage truck.

She couldn't help but smile as he adjusted his tie and tidied his hair. He looked very dapper in his herringbone suit and shiny leather shoes. She was constantly amazed by what some people considered appropriate for a funeral. Shorts, thongs and baseball caps; she'd seen it all. How refreshing to see a man dressed properly for a change. Shame about the bicycle clips.

'Some larrikin has changed the No Parking sign in the space reserved for the hearse to No Barking,' Martin said, still fidgeting with his tie.

'That's the least of our worries,' said Grace, pointing to the melee outside. The hearse had arrived, and was trying to squeeze past the line of cars by driving half on the grass verge. It wasn't going to end well.

'I hope the family see the funny side of it,' he added.

'Assuming they make it inside before their mother does.' She handed him an order of service.

'"Thine Be the Glory". Good choice,' said Martin, nodding approvingly as he scanned the inside pages. '"How Great Thou Art". Excellent.'

By the time everyone was seated, Bernard had exhausted his repertoire of entrance pieces and was on his third rendition of 'Ave Maria'. Luckily none of the mourners witnessed the deceased's ungainly entrance as the pallbearers lifted the coffin over the gate into the carpark of industrial units next door, and from there across the crumbling stone wall finally onto hallowed ground.

Ten minutes late, Rod kicked off proceedings with his customary greeting. 'A very warm welcome to All Souls this morning,' he began.

A mini spring heatwave had made the church unusually stifling. Faced with the stink from the garbage truck still stranded outside, Moira had ordered the doors to remain closed. Without a cooling breeze, Rod's welcome was proving an uncomfortably warm one and the mourners were already fanning themselves with their orders of service.

'We're here today to celebrate the life of a unique woman, someone who was well known, or should I say renowned, throughout the community.'

The projector screen flashed on and off briefly. Grace watched Moira tapping fruitlessly at the keys on the laptop computer that controlled the display.

'According to her sons she was a hard-drinking, foul-mouthed chain-smoker who loved her pigeons and her grandchildren about equally. We are not here to judge her lifestyle choices but to rejoice that we knew the real Brenda.'

Rod had clearly been expecting a laugh at his audacious comedic opening. He seemed confused by the silence. The projector screen sprang to life. There was a collective gasp at the cheeky photograph of a heavily tattooed woman winking at the camera. Underneath were the words, *A service of thanksgiving for Brenda 'Birdie' Sullivan* printed in a novelty font.

The undertaker, who was about to leave, turned and cleared his throat. Like a theatre prompt, the undertaker fed the minister his line, *sotto voce*.

'Today is Joan Sweeney.'

'Are you sure?' Rod mouthed.

'Brenda isn't until next week,' the undertaker replied, his voice echoing across the empty pews.

Even from where she stood, Grace could see that Hot Rod was sweating heavily.

'Welcome to All Souls,' he began again, 'as we gather to celebrate the life of Joan . . .'

'Sweeney,' came the pantomime prompt.

The projector screen went blank and Moira could be seen scurrying to the hymn board, replacing the black and white numbers with different ones. She had the decency to apologise when she accidentally nudged the coffin that didn't contain Brenda 'Birdie' Sullivan.

A sound that could have been a sob, but turned out to be a snigger, escaped from a woman in the front pew. Joan's daughter, perhaps. Even from the back of the congregation Grace could see her shoulders heaving. A woman next to her followed suit. One by one, the family started to laugh, stifled giggles at first, progressing to great guffaws. The laughter was infectious and soon the entire congregation joined in. Only poor Rod was able to keep a straight face, mortified at the terrible mix-up.

The rest of the service was as joyous a farewell as Grace had witnessed at All Souls. The mourners sang with such fervour that Rod's contribution was easily overpowered. The eulogy, delivered by Joan's eldest son, was hilarious, as he leaned into the accidental comedy of the occasion.

'My mother would have enjoyed today immensely,' he said. 'Contrary to outward appearances, my mother had a wicked sense of humour. She would have found particular delight in the fact that there was a garbage truck waiting for her outside the church.'

The audience cheered and clapped when he'd finished his tribute to the virtuous teetotaller who had never smoked, and only loved pigeons when they were topped with shortcrust pastry.

'That was quite something,' said Martin later at the wake. 'My mother will be disappointed she missed this one.'

'Really?' Grace filled a teacup from the urn and handed it to Martin.

'Yes, she loves funerals, claims they're the only social life she has these days.'

'That must be true for many folk her age.'

'She's worried that since most of the people she's known are already dead, she'll soon run out of funerals to attend.'

Grace looked around at the different generations that had turned out to mourn Joan. The oldest with looks of stoic acceptance, wondering who among them would be next. The adult children on whose shoulders the arrangements had fallen, and the youngsters for whom death was still an abstract concept. She wondered who would come to her funeral, whether any kindly stranger might turn up to sing a hymn or help themselves to a sandwich or two.

Martin told her about his mother, and their home arrangement. It must be hard for a man of his age to have his mother living with him. She gathered he wasn't married and didn't have any children. That a cultured, immaculately dressed man was still single at his age could only mean one thing. If anything, she relaxed. She'd never had a gay friend before. He asked her about herself. She told him only that she was a retired teacher. This wasn't the time or place to talk about Melody. Instead, they discussed the service over slices of a passable carrot cake which they awarded a cautious seven out of ten.

'Shame about the confusion at the beginning,' said Grace.

'At least everyone will remember this one, even if it is for the wrong reasons.' Martin raised his eyebrows. 'The garbage truck was a bit unfortunate though.'

Grace leaned in closer. 'The pallbearers looked as if they'd been dragged through a hedge backward.'

'Poor Joan literally had!' Martin's face turned more earnest. 'I just hope they double-check the paperwork at the crematorium.'

A beat of silence before they both started laughing.

'Is it disrespectful to find humour in something as sombre and serious as death?' Martin grimaced.

'I think human emotions are complicated, Martin. People laugh at funerals and cry at weddings.' She noticed Martin glance at her ring finger. She covered the bare skin self-consciously.

'Perhaps it's a survival mechanism. It's how people cope with tragedy.'

They lowered their voices, suddenly aware of the strangers around them.

'I hope this hasn't put you off,' said Grace. 'Will you come again?'

'To another funeral?'

A smile grew on Martin's face. 'Are you kidding? This is the most fun I've had in ages.' The smile faded again. 'Does that mean I'm a bad person?'

He was anything but a bad person, thought Grace. He was kind and funny, and she felt comfortable with him.

'No, Martin. It means you're human.'

Was it very wrong of her to hope there'd be another funeral soon?

11

Operation Ponte Vecchio

EVERYTHING WAS SUSPICIOUSLY QUIET WHEN MARTIN returned home. He placed his keys in the ninth-century Luristan bronze bowl he kept by the front door and luxuriated in the silence. The house was at peace, as if it was holding its breath. It had barely exhaled when the silence was broken.

'Is that you?'

It didn't matter whether Martin had been out for the day, or to the mailbox at the end of the path, whether he slammed the front door or nudged it closed with barely a click. The same three words, every time. It was getting harder to remember how things used to be before his life took on a backing track of canned laughter and cooking shows. His mother claimed the television was her only pleasure in life. Without it she'd be bored and lonely.

'It's company, Martin,' she would say. And he wasn't?

Pausing to pre-arrange a smile, Martin opened the door to the snug, the room at the back of the house that was now his mother's bedsit. With French windows, an open fireplace and an original period ceiling rose, the snug had once been his sanctuary, a place where he could sip a glass of port and admire his *objets*. Edwina had specifically requested this room, so she wouldn't be disturbed by traffic noise at the front of the house. Ironic considering her hearing. Over the past twelve months she'd made herself remarkably snug in the snug, and Shirley Temple, judging by the tumbleweeds of matted cat hair and scratch marks on the skirting boards, was feeling very much at home wherever she liked. Martin could now tell the time of day by the position of the dozing cat, who tracked the sunlight around the house like a sundial.

'Oh, it is you, Martin,' Edwina said from the chaise longue, where she was propped up against a throne of scatter cushions like Venus of Urbino.

'Of course it's me. Who else would let themselves in the front door with a key?'

'You hear such stories. Break-ins, robberies, attacks on defenceless old ladies. It certainly wasn't like that in my day.'

'In your day, defenceless old ladies ended up in the workhouse, Mother,' Martin muttered under his breath. 'Would you like a fresh cup of tea?'

As he reached for the untouched cup he'd made before he went out, he noticed what looked like a half-chewed toffee stuck to his 1920s French brass and marble martini table. He tried to remove it, but the sticky mass was welded on, and he needed both thumbs and forefingers to free it. Stepping sideways to drop it into the wastepaper bin, he caught his shin on the frame of the electric bed and released a torrent of Latin swearwords.

'Language, Martin.' Edwina was still as sharp as ever.

Shirley Temple watched on from the top of the bookcase, with an expression of faint amusement. When she was sure she had Martin's attention, she darted her eyes toward the handwoven Coptic panel hanging on the adjacent wall and back again. To find a panel in such good condition had taken Martin many months of research and an indecent portion of his academic salary. The linen and wool fragment depicting birds and dogs had survived fifteen centuries remarkably intact. The cat extended her talons. Martin wondered if the panel would survive the time it took to boil the kettle.

When Martin returned with the tea tray, the cat had vanished and Edwina looked as if she'd fallen asleep. He placed the china cup and saucer on the martini table.

'I've brought you some tea,' Martin said, leaning in close enough to smell her coppery breath. He tried again, louder this time. 'Mother. Your tea.'

When she didn't respond, he placed a hand on her shoulder, surprised by the sharpness of her bones through her blouse. It still shocked him that his mother was so old and that, one day, she would be gone for good. What shocked him even more, was how sad he felt when he imagined life without her.

He leaned in to stroke his mother's hair. Shirley Temple leaped from nowhere in a fit of possessive rage and crashed into the martini table. Martin caught it as it toppled, but not before the cup and saucer had smashed on the floor. The delicate cup, previously a fine example of eighteenth-century bone china, lay scattered in irreparable pieces. The cat was nowhere to be seen.

Edwina opened her eyes to see Martin picking the shards of broken china from the Turkish kilim.

'What a shame,' she said. 'You are a clumsy clot, Martin.'

'Bloody cat,' he hissed.

'That is no way to talk about your fur sister.'

'It was Spode, for heaven's sake. *Spode.*'

Sensing his barely contained rage, Edwina said, 'Sometimes I think you think more of your precious things than you do of me.'

Unfortunately, his mother did not share his passion for collecting and was not in the least bit sentimental. Only last week he'd found her dental plate soaking in a second-century Roman beaker. But her words stung. They hurt because they were true. He found comfort in objects, not relationships. He had chosen to surround himself with antiques and artefacts rather than people, things with permanence that he could preserve and protect from the dangers of the outside world.

'That is rich, coming from someone who insisted on storing all those dusty old wooden packing boxes in my attic. Goodness knows why you hang onto them.'

'One day you'll understand, Martin.'

One day she might understand him too. If either of them lived that long.

Martin cradled the pieces of china as gently as if they'd been broken bones. So tiny and fragile in his palm, too many to mend. He dropped them into the kitchen bin. Along with a little piece of his heart.

'Where have you been all dressed up like that?' Edwina asked when he handed her a fresh cup of tea.

'Nowhere,' he replied, aware of how truculent he sounded.

'Tell me the truth, Martin.'

'Okay, if you must know, I've been to a funeral.'

His mother snapped to attention. 'Whose was it?'

'Joan Sweeney's.'

Edwina looked genuinely hurt. 'I can't believe you went without me.'

'Sorry, I didn't know you knew Joan.'

'I didn't. That's beside the point.' To his surprise she patted the seat next to her on the chaise. 'Come and sit here.' He did as she said, nonplussed by the spontaneous show of affection. She reached behind the cushion she'd been leaning on and produced a notebook. Martin recognised it as the one she'd stuffed into her handbag at Pat's husband's sister's funeral. Edwina opened the notebook and clicked the top of her ballpoint pen. 'Now, tell me everything.'

Martin answered her many questions about Joan Sweeney's funeral. He omitted the details about the various mishaps. Unlike Joan, he doubted his mother would find them amusing. Edwina scribbled notes, dissecting every detail: the hymns, the flowers, the sandwiches and the cake. Had she not inquired about the colour of Joan's casket, they could have been discussing a wedding.

'Fetch my funeral scrapbook,' Edwina demanded when Martin's description of the specific type of flower arrangements did not meet her approval.

'What scrapbook?'

'The big one on the bookshelf.'

He hadn't noticed the A3-sized scrapbook before. If the thickness and weight of the pages were anything to go by, his mother's plans were already well advanced. She had separate sections for music, flowers, food, readings, and a selection of templates for the order of service. There'd been pharaohs who'd put less thought into their funeral arrangements. Next, she'd be telling him she wanted to be buried with all her jewellery and furniture, with cans of pre-mixed martinis and a plate of cheese and bickies for sustenance on her journey to the afterlife.

'Have you decided what kind of weather you'd like on the day?' Martin said facetiously. 'I only ask because in the movies, it's always pouring with rain, and everyone is huddled together at the graveside under black umbrellas.'

He wouldn't put it past her to conjure heaven's tears on her big day.

'These details might seem insignificant to you, Martin, but they are important to me.'

Exasperated, he tried to get up. Edwina grabbed him by the arm and pulled him back to the chaise.

'If I left the arrangements to you, you'd shove me in a shoebox and have the church decorated in carnations.'

'I didn't know you felt so strongly about carnations.' Martin thought back to all the times he'd given her flowers on Mother's Day.

He took the scrapbook out of her hands and began to flick through. She had an entire page devoted to birds.

One company stated that releasing a white dove – or depending on the package, several – was a beautiful tribute, signifying release and letting go. The doves were actually white homing pigeons, he read in the small print, reminding him of the booze-swilling, potty-mouthed, pigeon-fancying Brenda. He found himself smiling as he pictured Grace's horrified expression turning to amusement.

'I've had second thoughts about the doves,' said Edwina, turning the page over his shoulder. 'I'd like to go out with a bit more of a bang. There's a company that turns ashes into fireworks.'

'Now that would be a statement.' And fitting. People had always described his mother as a firecracker.

'Sometimes I wish I'd been born Irish,' she said, wistfully. 'I quite fancy a three-day wake with all that singing and dancing, and loads to drink.'

'Perhaps you'll be lucky next time.'

Edwina let out a rueful sigh. 'Did you know that one hundred and seventeen billion people have lived on Earth since the dawn of time? That's a lot of funerals. I just want mine to stand out from the crowd.'

Behind the pragmatism, he recognised fear. Fear of what lay ahead; not so much the dying, he suspected, as fear of the unknown. Planning her funeral at least gave her the illusion of control. Martin softened. He closed the scrapbook and handed it back to his mother.

There was one thing still puzzling him. 'Why does it say Operation Ponte Vecchio on the front?'

'Because of the Royal Family,' Edwina replied, as if it was obvious. 'Queen Elizabeth's funeral was codenamed London Bridge, Prince Philip's was Forth Bridge. I'm calling mine Operation Ponte Vecchio.'

'I hate to be pedantic, but you've never been to Italy, let alone Florence.'

This was greeted with a look that said, *Do you really want me to spell it out?* She'd never been to Italy because of him. His mother had never hidden her resentment that his inconvenient arrival had clipped her wings at a time when she was just beginning to spread them. Now, in a twist of fate, the tables had turned, and she was clipping his. They were two flightless birds trapped inside the same cage.

A folded copy of *The Chronicle* lay at Edwina's feet. He knew that she'd insist on reading it from cover to cover before passing it on to Martin.

'Mind if I read the paper first for a change?' he asked.

If she thought this unusual, Edwina didn't remark on it. 'Be my guest.'

He took the newspaper into the kitchen and carefully removed the obituaries and death notices. If she asked where the pages were, he'd say he used them to line Shirley Temple's litter tray. The last thing he wanted was his mother tagging along to the next funeral at All Souls.

12

Reading between the lines

THE PERIMETER OF PARKLEA PRIMARY SCHOOL HAD ONCE been marked by a simple post and wire fence. In a sign of the times, the grounds were now fully enclosed by a tall steel fence topped by metal spikes, as much to keep the kids in as to keep the miscreants out. The fence gave the place the feeling of a low-security prison rather than a primary school. In the playground the children were oblivious. They bounced handballs against classroom walls, laughing, shouting, and chasing each other with the raw energy of childhood. In many ways nothing had changed since the day Grace left. And yet she was a different person. Not better, not worse, merely changed by what she'd been through. Much as she found singing at funerals rewarding, and therapeutic, she was looking forward to surrounding herself with children again. They were so alive, so unburdened by guilt or regret.

The first adult Grace bumped into was Sandy, the deputy principal. She remembered Sandy as a student teacher who'd sat in on her class many years ago.

'How lovely to see you again,' said Sandy, stopping to hug Grace as she crossed the playground. 'The year three teachers are so grateful to you for giving up your time like this. It's so brave of you.'

What an odd turn of phrase. Did she mean brave that Grace was risking painful memories by returning to Parklea, or was she letting herself in for more than she'd bargained for?

Grace made her way to the year three classroom where, once upon a time, she'd been the one to allocate pupils to read to the parent volunteers. Back then, there'd been half-a-dozen mothers all keen to help. The children were always so excited to see their parent at school, either helping in the classroom or serving in the canteen at recess. Now, with two working parents in almost every family, she was the only volunteer.

The format hadn't changed. While the teacher conducted the lesson inside the classroom, the students would join her one at a time to read from their current reading book. Grace chose the one shaded bench in the sunbaked playground. Here she could offer a brief reprieve from the oppressive, unairconditioned classroom as well as the precious gift of her undivided attention. While she waited for her first reader to appear, she switched her phone to silent mode. To her surprise and secret delight, there was a text message from Martin. They'd exchanged phone numbers after agreeing to meet at the next funeral. She'd typed her details into his phone under 'Grace All Souls'. He'd entered himself in Grace's contacts as 'Martin All Souls'.

'Like a married couple,' she'd joked. 'Mr and Mrs All Souls.'

He'd laughed.

Afterward, Grace wondered if she'd gone too far, and he'd merely been polite in return.

Checking the coast was clear, Grace opened the message.

> Dear Grace,
>
> I want to say how much I enjoyed seeing you again at the church. May I draw your attention to a notice in this morning's Chronicle, announcing the funeral arrangements at All Souls for a Raymond Samuel Bowen, next Tuesday? I do hope it isn't too presumptuous of me, but given our shared interest in the hearty recitation of traditional hymns, I was hoping we could arrange to meet there.
>
> Yours sincerely,
> Martin All Souls

She couldn't help but smile at his formality. So different from the barely decipherable, punctuation-less messages Melody used to send her. She wondered how long it had taken him to type. Her reply was succinct.

> Consider it a date, Mr All Souls.

Her finger hovered over the send symbol. A date? What was she thinking? Grace deleted the message and retyped.

> Dear Martin,
> I'd like that very much.
> See you on Tuesday.
>
> Best regards,
> Grace All Souls

Her stomach skipped as she watched the message disappear. When she looked up she saw a serious little girl holding a battered reading book.

'Hello,' she said, shoving her phone out of sight. 'What's your name?'

The children varied widely in their reading abilities, as they always had. The first child was very advanced and read her book like a seasoned newsreader from an autocue. The next child, a round-faced little boy, stumbled over each word. She encouraged him to sound out the letters, hoping this was how reading was still taught. Progress was slow, as if he were deciphering an encrypted code, but even in the ten minutes they were together, she watched his confidence grow. This was the type of child Grace most loved to teach. Seeing the sheer exhilaration on their faces when they went up a level, or found a book they really engaged with, was reward enough. In her eyes, there was no such thing as a reluctant reader. Every child wanted to read; some simply needed a little help to get started. Half the battle was matching the right child with the right book, a task that wasn't helped by the paltry selection of reading books.

There was a pause between readers on account of an incident inside the classroom that required a raised voice. Grace remembered how she'd preferred silence as her weapon of choice, how she could bring an entire class of unruly children to attention with a single steely stare. Perhaps Angela was right and teaching was different now. Attention spans were so short, children so overstimulated. She blamed devices. No one should be allowed to have a mobile phone in school. She sneaked a look at hers.

Another message from Martin.

Dear Grace,

Thank you for responding to my message. I am already looking forward to Raymond Samuel Bowen's funeral.

Best wishes,
Martin

He'd added a PS.

Am I the only one who laments the falling standards of punctuation these days? I enclose a photograph of the headline in this morning's paper for your disapproval.

There was a slightly out-of-focus photograph of the front page of the newspaper. In the background Grace could make out the cat he said belonged to his mother.

MAN HELPS DOG BITE VICTIM

Grace replied straight away.

Outrageous! They should sack their entire editorial team immediately.

She saw the green dots bouncing under her reply. He was typing.

Dear Grace,

Finally, proof that correct punctuation saves lives?

Warmest regards,
Martin

Biting her lip in concentration, Grace concocted her response.

If you want more proof of the demise of Western
civilisation, read the parish newsletter. Moira reminded
everyone about Tuesday night's 'bile studies' class.
Grace x

Had she really put a kiss after her name? The phone was growing warm in her hands as she waited for a new message. When one didn't arrive, she feared she'd scared him off. This wasn't Tinder and, even if it was, she might still be barking up the wrong tree. Then, the green dots appeared again.

Grace,

At last, I've found a fellow pedant!

Best,
Martin

No kiss, but she'd coaxed a whimsical exclamation mark out of the man in the suit. Grace held the phone to her chest where her heart was beating unusually fast for a Friday morning. She felt girlish and could barely hide her grin.

'Put that phone away, now,' she heard the teacher shout. 'You know you're not supposed to have it in school.'

Grace froze, then exhaled. The teacher wasn't talking to her. From the front of the class, Miss Michaels couldn't even see Grace sitting on the bench outside under the classroom window. Grace stole another peek at her phone before shoving it back inside her bag. She'd think carefully about her next move. She wanted to come up with something wise and witty, playful but not overtly flirtatious. Something that would keep up the light-hearted banter she was enjoying so much between them.

Hudson was the last reader the teacher sent to Grace. She'd spotted him earlier through the classroom window, noticing how the other children had moved their chairs away as if he was contagious. It broke her heart. No one wanted to risk catching his poverty and disadvantage.

If he was surprised to see the weed lady waiting for him on the bench, he didn't show it. She tried not to give too much away as she studied him more closely, this time taking in the scar on his chin and the bruises on his shins. A result of playground rough and tumble, or something more sinister?

'What are you reading, Hudson?' Grace asked as he settled down next to her.

He showed her the cover. *The Lion, the Witch and the Wardrobe* by C.S. Lewis. She tried to hide her scepticism. It was an ambitious choice. But, given his bookmark was placed halfway through, he was making progress. When he began to read, Grace was astonished. He was not only fluent, but he read with expression too, as though he understood the characters and was following the story. She, of all people, had fallen into the trap of assuming that a boy like Hudson would have learning difficulties. She was curious to know what he made of the fantasy and its religious themes. Did he identify with Edmund, the young wartime evacuee who follows his sister through the wardrobe into the magical world of Narnia? What did he make of the White Witch who plied him with Turkish Delight and promised to make him a prince? Was he hoping to find his own kindly professor who also believed in Narnia?

'That's excellent reading, Hudson. What do you think the author is trying to say?'

Hudson swiped his nose on his blue shirt sleeve and thought before answering.

'I think the book is trying to warn kids about not taking lollies from strangers.'

Grace was taken aback. She'd expected more. 'That's true. But do you think there are other important messages the author is trying to put across?'

'You mean like good triumphing over evil and stuff?' Hudson cocked his head. 'Kids are way smarter than adults think we are. Grownups are always trying to protect us from the big things like war and death, but the scariest stuff is what goes on inside our heads.'

To throw her arms around this skinny little boy and hug away all his fears was against the rules. She did the next-best thing.

Checking that no one was watching, Grace reached under the bench and retrieved a brown paper bag. She knew it was overstepping the mark, but she couldn't let a little boy go hungry.

'What's in here?' Hudson asked, taking it from her.

'Some sandwiches for lunch.'

He peered warily into the bag, then at her. His eyes narrowed.

'What kind of sandwiches?'

'Ham, cheese and tomato.'

'I don't like tomato.'

Grace frowned. 'Never mind, you can pick out the tomato and throw it away if you like.'

This sealed the deal. 'Thanks,' he said.

A strand of hair had fallen across his gorgeous grey-blue eyes and, without thinking, Grace brushed it away. He flinched and leaned away. The bell went. Hudson darted back into class leaving Grace sitting alone.

As the kids came out into the playground, she pretended to search for something in her bag but, really, she was watching Hudson. Her heart ached at the sight of him sitting alone on a bench in the far corner of the playground, eating the sandwiches she'd made for him. His skinny body was in constant motion even as he ate. A group of boys approached him from behind. The tallest of the boys, a year five or six, reached over Hudson's shoulder and snatched the paper bag. Grace watched in horror as the boy emptied the contents into the nearby bin. The others looked on, laughing and jeering.

Hudson leaped to his feet and faced the boy who was a good deal taller and wider than him. Without warning, Hudson punched the boy in the stomach, knocking him off balance. Winded, the boy fell heavily to the asphalt. When he got to his feet again, there was blood dripping onto his shirt from a graze on his cheek. Before Grace could intervene, a teacher swooped, grabbed Hudson by the arm and marched him toward the school office while another teacher comforted the bloodied boy.

Grace's first instinct was to run after the teacher and explain what she'd seen. The older boy had provoked Hudson. It didn't excuse Hudson's retaliation even against a bully. Violence of any kind could not be condoned. Had his father taught him to fight back like that, or had he already lost faith in the world, deciding at such a tender age that he was the only person who could stand up for himself?

Shaken, Grace gathered her things and went inside to say goodbye to the classroom teacher.

'Thank you for coming in,' said Miss Michaels. 'I really appreciate you giving up your time. Even the grandparents are too busy these days.'

'It's nothing,' said Grace. 'Kids keep us young.' Really young, judging by Miss Michaels who looked barely out of school.

Miss Michaels measured her next words. 'I noticed you watching Hudson just now,' she began. 'How did you find him?'

'His reading is excellent. He's obviously bright.'

'As you can see, he has some behavioural issues.' She glanced out the classroom window.

'It seems to me he's acting out his frustrations, that's all.'

'I think you should be aware of his social background.'

Grace swallowed. Where was this heading? 'What do you mean?'

'Hudson is the subject of several reports to Family and Community Services. He has been exposed to family violence. As you know, we as educators have a duty to report any child we feel may be at risk. Reporting is mandatory.'

'I am well aware of that,' said Grace, her dry tongue sticking to the words. How dare she lecture Grace about duty of care.

The young teacher softened. 'The reason I mention it is that you appear to have developed a rapport with Hudson. He seems to trust you. That makes you ideally placed to observe him and report back any concerns.'

'Like what exactly?'

'For instance, if he mentions anything unusual about his home life.'

For instance, if his mother claimed to be in touch with the spirit world, or if Hudson drew pictures of his mother speaking to dead people? If he touted for business on her behalf?

'I'll bear that in mind,' said Grace.

On the way home, she phoned Rhondda from her mobile. Hearing the automated message, Grace debated hanging up. No, this couldn't wait. A young boy's future was in her hands. She had to try again.

'Hello, Rhondda. This is Grace Cavendish. I know I said I didn't need any further sessions. Well, I've changed my mind. Is there any chance you're free to meet again?'

13

A pew for two

MARTIN SNUCK OUT, HOPING HIS MOTHER WOULDN'T question why he was wearing his best suit to a tutorial, nor why his tutorials had mysteriously switched from a Wednesday to a Tuesday. The subterfuge almost came undone when Martin set off on his bicycle without his briefcase. She narrowed her eyes when he returned for it.

'What time will you be back?' she asked.

'Three-ish,' he replied.

Edwina persisted. 'You're usually home by lunchtime.'

He was hoping he and Grace could have more of a chat today and so he didn't want to rush away from the wake. He was keen to see where, as a retired schoolteacher, she stood on Oxford commas. Over the past few days they'd been sending each other examples of poor punctuation they'd come across in the community. It had become quite competitive, and Martin had taken to wandering around the shopping centre snapping shots of adverts in shop windows. There was also a book he wanted to give her. Knowing her frustrations with Moira's fundraising at All Souls, Martin thought she might enjoy reading *The Spire* by William Golding. In the novel, the fictional Dean Jocelin descends into madness as he becomes obsessed with building a 404-foot spire for Salisbury Cathedral. Martin was sure Grace would see the funny side of it.

'I've made you a sandwich and left it in the fridge, Mother,' said Martin. He'd skipped breakfast himself so that he could comfortably consume at least two slices of cake.

Was Edwina on to him? The last thing he wanted was to have his mother tag along today. He wanted Raymond Samuel Bowen all to himself; or rather, he didn't want to share Grace. His mother had always muscled in on his friendships, winning over school chums and academic colleagues alike. She and Andrew were as thick as thieves when they got together. Sadly, Jane never got to meet Edwina. If she had, Edwina might have questioned what a gorgeous, intelligent young Englishwoman was doing with her son.

It had taken Martin many weeks to pluck up the courage to ask Jane out for tea, despite them having stood less than six feet apart at choir practices. Even then, he was only spurred into action when he saw the stroke of the 1st VIII chatting to Jane outside Hall. To this day, he couldn't believe that she chose a dorky academic like him over a hunky rower. They'd talked for hours, ordering pot after pot of tea, until four o'clock when the cafe closed. Martin had walked her back to her room overlooking the main quad and, still assuming she would prefer a rower or a fellow medical student, he'd been surprised when she'd leaned in and kissed him on the cheek. It was brief, barely a butterfly landing, but it was all he'd needed.

Martin took the scenic route to All Souls, cycling through the park where new green leaves on the deciduous trees were almost fluorescent against the sun. He had to swerve as a toddler ran into his path in a hurry to feed the already fat ducks on the pond. The air was fresh and scented with jasmine and honeysuckle. What a glorious day to be alive, he thought, almost forgetting he was on his way to a funeral. With his feet out wide he freewheeled down the hill toward the main gate.

'And did those feet in ancient time walk upon England's mountains green . . .' he sang. There was nothing like a verse of good old 'Jerusalem' to warm up the vocal cords. *''til we have built Jer-u-sa-lem, in England's green and pleasant land!'*

'You're in 'Straya now, mate!' shouted a labourer working on a nearby building site. His workmates roared with laughter. Martin felt a whoosh of air behind him and caught a streak of black and white as a magpie swooped. The next thing he knew, his wheels were wobbling and the ground was rushing toward him. Luckily his landing was a soft one, and his beloved bicycle remained intact. When he picked himself up, he noticed grass stains over the knees and elbows of his suit. His funeral suit no less. The builders were having a field day at his expense.

'Is that green and pleasant enough for you, mate?'

By the time he reached All Souls, Martin was a sweaty, dishevelled mess. He did his best to tidy himself but there was no hiding the green stains. The sight of Grace standing at the top of the steps looking lovely only made him more self-conscious.

'You're bleeding.' She frowned when she saw him. Out of nowhere, she produced a clean, folded handkerchief.

'It's all right,' Martin said, taking out a crisply ironed handkerchief from his jacket pocket.

A smile of recognition and respect passed between them.

'Where?' Martin asked, unsure without a mirror where to dab. Grace gestured to his left ear. He felt it now, the sticky trickle now dried to flakes.

'What happened?'

'A magpie attacked me.'

'In the park?'

'Yes. I'll stick to the main road in future. Much safer.'

'I'd fetch you a band-aid,' said Grace. 'Only problem is Moira hides the first-aid box. And today of all days, she's not here. Some medical appointment, apparently. Let's hope it's nothing too trivial.' Martin wasn't sure whether she was serious or not but risked taking it as a joke. He was relieved when Grace smiled too. 'I told you, I'm Graceless Grace where her ladyship is concerned.'

Inside, the church was surprisingly empty.

'Where is everyone?' he asked taking in pew after vacant pew.

'I don't know.' Grace shrugged. 'They're cutting it very fine if they want to arrive before Raymond does.'

Together, they glanced across the carpark. There was no garbage truck blocking the entrance today, and the roads had been quiet only a few minutes ago.

'Are you sure we have the right day?' Martin asked.

'After the fiasco at Joan Sweeney's funeral, anything is possible.' She handed him an order of service. 'Take a seat, anywhere you like.'

Apart from whoever was playing 'Nimrod' on the organ, and the anxious-looking minister who was pacing at the front, Martin and Grace were the only people in the church.

How peculiar. The hearse arrived on the dot of eleven, and Martin wondered if Grace might tip them off and suggest they drive around the block a few times. Out of the corner of his eye, he noticed a man in a dark suit approach, murmur his apologies, then make his way to the far end of the back pew. He'd swelled the numbers by fifty per cent, but the turnout was still woeful.

There was no way to delay proceedings further. The service had to start. The organ misfired the final chord and fell silent. Unfazed by the paltry attendance, the minister ploughed on.

'I am delighted to welcome you all to the service this morning as we give thanks for the life of . . . Raymond Samuel Bowen.'

He paused to double-check the name. The young minister had a gift for personalising each of the services Martin had attended, making it sound as if he'd known the deceased personally. This wasn't the case for Raymond Bowen. As it turned out, there wasn't much to say about his eighty-four years on this Earth. Indeed, without a single member of his family, a friend or acquaintance of any description to fill in the blanks, his life was a mystery. The minister did his best with what little he had, falling short of his usual entertaining schtick. Even the organ was nonplussed, barely sputtering to life for the first hymn, 'Abide with Me'.

Martin attacked the first line with zeal, Grace matching him with her splendorous sound while the man in the dark suit remained mute. The minister knew the words by heart, never once glancing at his hymn book or the projector screen. The hymn was clearly a favourite. The downside was that the order in which he sang the notes bore little resemblance to the composer's version. Grace nudged Martin and smiled encouragement. *Animato*. Martin took the hint. He squared his shoulders, filled his lungs and delivered the air to his primed vocal cords *fortissimo*. When his note found Grace's, the resonance was palpable. The rousing sound they made together was greater than the sum of its parts. Their duet filled the empty church with a sparkling rendition of the solemn hymn.

When they kneeled to pray, Martin's entire body was thrumming, his breathing ragged. The euphoria was almost post-coital in intensity. He could tell by her breathing beside him that Grace had felt it too. Appalled at himself, he whispered a little prayer of apology for thinking about sex at a funeral. His knees cracked when he tried to stand up again.

All too soon the service was over. The minister offered a blessing and Raymond Samuel Bowen was escorted from the premises to his final resting place. 'You'll Never Walk Alone' was an ironic choice to finish with, Martin thought sadly, or perhaps Raymond had been optimistic to the end.

There was plenty of food to go round at the wake. Martin had been reticent about attending. When the church hall was packed it was easy to go unnoticed as an interloper. With barely a handful of people, however, they were more likely to be rumbled for gate-crashing. But then who was going to complain? The only other guests helping themselves at the buffet were the other crashers, Claire and Bill who, as usual, had materialised in time for the wake.

'Not exactly a great turnout, is it?' Martin whispered to Grace as they sipped from uninspiring white teacups.

'I'll say. At least we sang for our supper. Unlike the others. Where are Raymond's nearest and dearest?'

'I suppose some people get to a point when they've outlived or lost touch with their relatives and friends.'

'What a depressing thought,' said Grace.

'Did I tell you my mother's busy planning her own funeral?'

'How very pragmatic of her.'

That was one word he'd never associated with Edwina.

It wasn't long before the minister drifted into their conversational orbit. Inevitable given there were only six people at the wake and two of them were already drunk. Grace introduced Martin to Reverend Rod. They had a brief three-way chat about the service and the choice of hymns before Rod excused himself and headed back to the buffet. Conversation was even more strained when Grace tried to introduce Martin to beery Bill and glassy-eyed Claire.

'I suppose we can never fully know another person's story,' Martin said when they were out of earshot.

'That's the beauty of occasions like this. Being here reminds us that we're all in this together.' Grace looked around the church hall. As buildings went it was far from beautiful. Built in the 1980s, it was dated yet still functional. 'Everyone experiences loss at some point in their lives. Some people are simply better at hiding their pain.'

Was she hinting at some private tragedy of her own or had she sensed something in him? Either way, she'd touched a nerve, and thoughts of Jane returned like pain in a phantom limb. The sandwich he was halfway through turned to cardboard in his mouth. With great effort, he managed to swallow.

'So, Bill and Claire,' he said, redirecting the conversation.

Grace told him what she knew. Bill was a widower. He lived alone in a single room in a huge house that he couldn't afford to heat or light. The obvious solution was for him to sell up and downsize. For whatever reason, he'd become suspicious of authority, which included the many doctors, social workers and estate agents who'd tried to gain his trust over the years. His wife, Eileen, had been a highly respected member of the church congregation, and when she died, there'd been an impressive turnout of mourners. Eileen had taken care of all the cooking in the marriage and it transpired that the buffet at the wake was the first proper food he'd eaten in days. He'd returned a week later to another funeral where everyone pretended not to notice as he helped himself to second and third helpings. After that, he'd become a regular, and always went home with a doggy bag.

'And Claire?'

Claire's tale was even sadder, Grace explained. She'd fled an abusive marriage with only the clothes on her back. Since she'd been out to a fancy lunch on the day she'd escaped, Claire wore the same Chanel suit to every wake.

Martin watched Claire refill her wine glass yet again.

'Did you see the car parked under the big beech tree in the corner by the graveyard?'

'The one with all the stuff inside? I noticed it the last time I was here too.' Grace told Martin the rest with her eyes. At least Claire didn't have far to go home.

The man in the dark suit had been hovering nearby. He was in his early sixties, wearing thick tortoiseshell glasses and shiny black shoes. No doubt he was a man who also carried an ironed handkerchief in his pocket.

He cleared his throat.

'I'm sorry to butt in like this. I am David Dyer of Bader, Beaver and Dyer solicitors.'

Martin shook the man's hand warily. Where there was a solicitor, there was usually an awkward conversation to be had.

Grace also sounded wary. 'If this is about the mix-up with Joan and Brenda, you'd best speak to Moira. She handles the admin.'

'No, nothing like that.' David Dyer cracked a lawyerly smile. 'I was hoping to collect your names and contact details,' he said, pulling out a notebook and pen from the inside pocket of his suit jacket.

This was it, Martin thought. They'd been caught in the act. They were about to be sued for . . . what exactly? Trespass? Fraud? Defamation? Andrew would have a good chuckle at this, but it would be the end of Edwina.

But what came out of David Dyer's mouth was even more unexpected. 'I have some very good news for the two of you.'

'I don't understand,' said Grace.

'As far as I could tell, you two were the only mourners at Raymond Bowen's funeral service. Correct?'

Martin nodded. 'Sadly, it seems that way.'

'In that case, according to the last will and testament of my client, as legally drawn up and witnessed in the weeks before his death, you two are the joint beneficiaries of Mr Bowen's estate.'

'Us?' Martin was totally confused.

'But neither of us was related to him,' Grace said.

Martin refrained from adding that neither of them had even met him.

David Dyer continued. 'Mr Bowen had no family. I gather he had few friends. Very few, judging by today's turnout. He asked me to visit him in his nursing home a few weeks ago after his stroke. That's when he instructed me to divide his estate between whoever turned up to his funeral.'

Grace and Martin traded silent looks. Was this a set-up? Were they on some kind of twisted reality show with hidden cameras recording their reaction? Nothing would surprise Martin. Honestly, the depths that people would go to for entertainment these days.

'I will send you written confirmation explaining the process in due course. For now I'll need your name, address and telephone number. Email too, if you have it.'

They both nodded mutely. Not knowing what else to do, they took turns writing their details in the solicitor's notebook. Out of habit, Martin used his old university email address. Grace left her email blank.

'If you have any questions, please feel free to contact my secretary.' He handed them each a business card.

When he'd gone, Martin raked his fingers through his hair and exhaled in a whistle.

'I wasn't expecting that.'

'Do you think it's some kind of scam?' Grace asked.

'I don't know,' Martin replied. 'I recognise the name of the solicitors. They handled the conveyancing for the sale of my mother's house last year. We dealt with Bob Bader, but I know there's a David Dyer in the practice.'

'It's hard to know who to trust, isn't it?' Grace said, her forehead concertinaed with worry.

'We all want to believe that people are basically good, that their motives are genuine,' Martin added. It was easy for an honest person to assume everyone was playing by the same rules.

'By the same token, no one wants to be taken advantage of. Nobody likes to be taken for a fool.'

14

Cross my palm with silver

WITH FRESHLY BAKED MUFFINS ON THE RACK AND THREE
spoonsful of Earl Grey in the bottom of the teapot, there
was enough time for a last-minute touch-up before Rhondda
arrived. Today was rinse and repeat for the fuchsia lipstick
Grace had worn for Sandra's funeral. The mirror had seemed
as surprised and delighted as she was at the transformation of
her wan complexion. The injection of colour had emboldened
her too. Grace without lipstick would never have had the
courage to invite a man on not one, but two non-dates. Both
occasions had been eventful, meaning they would have plenty
to discuss the next time they met.

Grace had brought out her best china for today's session.
A pair of side plates and two silver cake forks were waiting
on the coffee table with a stack of paper serviettes decorated
with a chinoiserie pattern. She'd cut a dozen roses from her
garden and arranged them in a vase on the mantlepiece.
The photos of Melody were still hidden away in a drawer

in the sideboard. As far as Grace was concerned, Rhondda's psychic powers were still on probation.

'I'm glad you decided to go ahead with another reading, Grace,' Rhondda said, catching crumbs from the corner of her mouth with a finger. 'My clients have differing reactions to their initial session. For some it's enough to simply connect with their loved one and be reassured they are always with them. Some find closure having said something they should have said when the person was alive.' She ate another mouthful of muffin. 'Others like to have an ongoing relationship with their deceased loved one. An initial catch-up, followed by top-up sessions every month or so. Naturally, I do make a small charge for these.'

This sounded familiar. A few months ago Grace had pulled a muscle in her back while turning her mattress. The chiropractor had bandied around terms like 'tilted pelvis', 'leg length discrepancy' and 'disc bulges', that'd made her sound as if she belonged in a travelling circus. The crunching and cracking noises he'd elicited from her spine had been enough to put her off ever returning. Afterward, however, both her body and her wallet had felt much lighter. For a few days anyway. Then she was back for another round of clicking, cracking and crunching. This maintenance therapy went on for weeks, each costly visit seeing the same adjustments performed in less and less time until she was in and out in under three minutes. When she'd wondered out loud if she really needed to keep coming, he'd warned her of the consequences of not presenting her credit card once a fortnight. Eventually she'd had enough. Was she heading for the same scenario with Rhondda?

For all Grace's initial cynicism, that first session with Rhondda hadn't been the cookie-cutter reading she'd expected. Rhondda had guessed Melody's name on only the second attempt. What were the chances? Then much of what she claimed Melody wanted to say was uncannily relevant. Could Rhondda be playing her? Either way, Grace still had Hudson to think about.

'I'd like to keep going as long as Melody needs me,' she said. This bit was true. Alive or dead, girls always needed their mothers. To brush their hair and kiss their scraped knees. To buy them their first bra, their first pack of sanitary pads. To hold them when their hearts broke. Or stopped. To miss them so badly they wished their own hearts would stop.

'Okay, Grace. Are you ready? Let's see what Melody has to say today.'

Hands resting on her knees, Rhondda began to rock. Grace was used to this by now and wasn't fazed by the theatrics. She waited patiently while Rhondda connected with the spirit world. Grace hadn't needed to understand how a telephone worked to have a conversation with Melody when she was alive. She just needed to have faith in the technology. The magic.

Rhondda's face contorted, as if she were riding some unseen wave of pain.

'Is everything all right?' Grace ventured. This hadn't happened last time.

'There's someone here who wants to talk to you.'

'Is it Melody?'

'No. She's an older lady. There's a large mole on her chin and she's not very happy.'

'Who is she?'

Rhondda opened her eyes. 'I was hoping you could tell me. Something to do with a hedge.'

Older. Large mole. Unhappy about the hedge.

'Mrs Gladstone from next door?' Grace hadn't seen her since the beginning of last year when she'd moved into a nursing home interstate to be near her daughter. The house had been sold and that's when Stephanie and her family had moved in.

'She says you need to cut it. She can't see the goings-on in the road.'

Grace couldn't help but roll her eyes. She and Mrs Gladstone had been neighbours for years, though they'd never seen eye to eye. Mrs Gladstone had complained constantly about Melody's singing and instrument practice. She'd complained to Grace about the bins, the shared nature strip and the hedge that divided the two properties. Grace liked it bushy so that the birds had somewhere to nest. Mrs Gladstone liked to see out from her chair next to the window. Perhaps the conflict over the hedge was what had kept her alive. Now Grace wondered if she'd been simply trying to connect because she was lonely. The same way Grace kept inviting Stephanie in for a chat.

'Tell her I'm happy to trim it a little.'

Rhondda looked relieved. 'She's happy with that.'

'Is Melody there?' she asked.

'Not yet,' said Rhondda. 'I'm sorry. I'm having trouble getting through to her today. There's interference in the channel.'

Grace remembered her parents complaining about having to share a line to the exchange with their neighbours. Since others could listen in, everyone knew their business.

'There's an Alice here,' said Rhondda. 'Young woman, wearing old-fashioned clothes.'

'I don't know an Alice.' Grace was disappointed. She was beginning to believe that Rhondda's knack for landing on salient details in that first session had been purely luck. This time she seemed to be stabbing in the dark. 'Would another muffin help?'

'I think they're what's attracted all these random spirits.'

Grace knew she'd need to pay for today's session and already had an envelope of cash waiting. While she didn't mind paying to supposedly speak to her daughter, she objected to all these freeloading strangers muscling in on the session.

'Wait,' said Rhondda, rocking again. 'I can see her.'

'Melody?'

'Yes. She has someone with her. A little boy. She's holding his hand.'

'A little boy?'

'Oh bless him. He's upset. He can't find his mummy.'

'Who is he? What's his name?'

'It begins with T. Teddy? Tommy? Yes, Tommy.'

'I don't know a Tommy,' said Grace. This was getting ridiculous. If it wasn't for Hudson, she'd put an end to this charade.

'Melody says you've met his mother. You know her.'

Grace racked her brains. Did she know a Tommy from Parklea? Had he read to her? No, if Rhondda was channelling him, Tommy must be dead. Years ago, a girl in year two had been killed in a car crash along with her parents and baby sister. The tragedy had rocked the community. Their names and faces were still etched into Grace's heart. It wasn't as if she'd have forgotten a Tommy.

'Your daughter is very good with children,' said Rhondda. 'She's distracted him and he's stopped crying. They're playing together now.'

Grace looked at the spot on the mantle where she usually kept the photo of gap-year Melody with a group of happy smiling children in a Sri Lankan village. She couldn't have known then that she wouldn't live to have children of her own. If her opera career hadn't taken off, Melody would have become a music teacher. One way or another, she would always have surrounded herself with children.

'I'm sorry, Grace. They've gone.' Rhondda sighed and slumped back on the sofa. She looked exhausted. 'It happens sometimes. Everyone arrives at the same time, causing a bottleneck and no one can get through.'

Grace softened. Rhondda looked disappointed too. Everyone was entitled to an off day and if Grace was too prickly, she might lose her link to her daughter, and to Hudson.

'If you think the spirit world is impatient, you should try parent–teacher nights,' said Grace, only half joking. She saw her chance. 'Which reminds me, I wanted to tell you that I took Melody's advice about going back to work. I went to see the principal and I'm volunteering for reading groups two days a week. Hopefully if that goes well, I might progress to relief teaching.'

'That is good news, Grace.'

'I've already had my first group. Year three.'

Rhondda's eyes widened. 'My son is in year three. Hudson.'

'What a coincidence,' said Grace, who could hardly believe her luck. 'He read to me. He's such a lovely boy.'

'Really?'

Rhondda looked pleased to hear this. 'You and your husband must be very proud of him.'

Rhondda's face fell. Had Grace touched a nerve, or crossed a line? She backtracked into general chit-chat, surprised how quickly the time passed.

'Our time is up,' Rhondda said, without checking her watch.

'Are you available the same time next week?' Grace couldn't lose her now. Not when she was starting to make progress and they'd moved beyond the supernatural small talk.

'I'll have to look at my roster, maybe move a few shifts, but yes, that could work nicely.'

A whole week until she could try again. This time, Rhondda had raised more questions than she'd answered. Who was Alice, and why couldn't little Tommy find his mother?

'What do I owe you?' Grace asked as she gathered up the dirty cups and saucers. She'd been to the bank and withdrawn five crisp twenty-dollar notes in anticipation.

'Let's call it one eighty.'

'One hundred and eighty dollars?' Grace felt as if she'd been punched in the stomach. That was more than the chiropractor charged and would blow her budget for the week. Rhondda's fee would have to come out of her rainy day fund. On the way home from Raymond Bowen's funeral, she'd briefly thought about what she might do with the money from the will, what it would be like not to have to live on such a tight budget. But she quickly put the encounter out of her mind. As long as she was careful, she could live quite comfortably on her pension. Should she ask for a seniors discount?

Rhondda beat her to it. 'I hope I'm not making assumptions but that's my seniors rate.'

Too embarrassed to protest, Grace fetched her chequebook.

'Is a cheque acceptable?' she asked as she opened the blue chequebook.

'Yes, of course. It's still legal tender, isn't it?'

'Not if the banks have their way. Cheques are being phased out because apparently they cost too much to process. I choose to do my banking the old-fashioned way as a matter of principle. An act of civil disobedience, if you like.'

'I admire you for taking a stand, Grace. I bet Hudson wouldn't even know what a chequebook is.'

Grace put on her reading glasses and wrote the date. On the payee line she wrote, Rhondda Divine.

Rhondda peered over her shoulder. 'Rhondda Divine is my professional name. Could you make it out to Rhondda Tucker. T-U-C-K-E-R.'

Ignoring the alarm bells going off, Grace tore along the perforations and handed the cheque to Rhondda, who folded it and stuffed it into her handbag.

'Thank you. Hudson needs new school shoes, so this won't go amiss.'

'They grow so fast at that age, don't they?'

'He's eight, going on sixty-eight.' Rhondda smiled to herself.

Rhondda had handed Grace the perfect segue into an awkward conversation. Surely she wouldn't take offence at a light-hearted comment about the dangers of a 68-year-old walking alone to school. But the words refused to come out. Rhondda looked so genuinely grateful that Grace felt a pang of guilt. She'd thought nothing of handing over the money to someone who claimed he could lengthen her right leg, and yet here was a woman who'd given up an hour of her time to come to her house. Even if she was a charlatan, it had been an enjoyable sixty minutes. Grief was a lonely place. It made a pleasant change to be able to talk about Melody so openly.

She watched Rhondda walk to the end of the road before she closed the front door. Doubts niggled as she washed and dried her best china. Was Rhondda really who she said she was, or was this all part of some elaborate deception? Grace was desperate to trust her, to trust in something. She'd cast her faith adrift after Melody died. Perhaps it was time to start believing again, even if it was in a woman who claimed supernatural powers.

Grace remembered what Martin had said at Raymond Bowen's wake.

We can never fully know another person's story.

Who exactly was Rhondda Divine, and what was her story?

15

One cappuccino, extra hot

AFTER THE FIASCO THAT WAS HIS FIRST TUTORIAL, MARTIN had learned to double check his briefcase before leaving the house. His classes were improving and today, having purchased an HDMI cable to connect his laptop to the audiovisual system, he was confident he could deliver the required course material in a sufficiently interesting and technologically acceptable manner. There was a minor hiccup when he had been unable to work out which end of the cable was which, and had to rope in a passing anthropology undergraduate to help him set everything up. He'd also rearranged the chairs and tables in a horseshoe shape, hoping that the more interactive set-up would win him a few extra points on the student feedback forms. And the takeaway cup of coffee he'd bought on the way was intended to lend him an air of 'down with the kids'. In his final concession to modernity, he'd dressed more casually in an open-neck shirt and a pair of pale-coloured chinos, similar to the ones Dominic Smythe always wore.

The first to arrive was Shona. As always. She was such a pleasure to teach, asking relevant and thought-provoking questions. While the other students were dull and indifferent, Shona was a rising star. The work she'd handed in so far had been thoroughly researched and well argued. It was getting harder and harder for Martin to disguise his favouritism. And to suppress the effervescent memories of Jane that popped like champagne bubbles through the surface of his consciousness without warning. There was just enough time to indulge one while he waited for the other students to arrive.

Emboldened by the success of his first date with Jane, Martin had decided it was time to move on from tea and buns. For their second date Martin collected the enormous iron key to the college chapel tower from the porter's lodge. He'd gambled on the fact that, as a busy medical student, Jane wouldn't have had time to play tourist in her own college. It would be a first for both of them.

The stone stairs were well worn after seven hundred years of use, and the space almost claustrophobically narrow. It soon became obvious that Jane was a great deal fitter than he was, and she raced ahead. Trailing behind, an already breathless Martin tried to impress her with stories about the college's ghosts: the young royalist soldier who'd been executed during the Civil War; the watchful warden who refused to leave his post; and the serene white lady who could be seen gliding through the gardens at dusk. She'd heard them before, she told him later.

The view from the top of the tower was well worth the strenuous climb. Martin watched while Jane pointed out the city's famous landmarks, entranced by the way the breeze lifted her hair away from her face. Her skin was flawlessly pale, courtesy of the hours she spent inside the hospital, but the fresh air had brought a fetching colour to her cheeks. He had the sudden urge to propose to her, to tell her he loved her and couldn't imagine his life without her. Afraid that he might scare her off, or worse, face rejection, he took her gently by the hand, pulled her into his arms and kissed her instead. Unfortunately, the whole thing came to an abrupt stop when the bell chimed the hour. The sound was deafening at such close quarters. When they pulled apart, Jane was laughing.

It was only when he came to descend the steep staircase that he remembered his fear of heights. Surrounded by solid ramparts on the roof of the tower, and preoccupied with exploring Jane's sensual mouth, he hadn't given much thought to how high up they were. Now, looking down, his legs began to tremble. This time he insisted Jane should go first, so that she wouldn't see his fear. He couldn't recall which one of them had started to sing first. All he remembered was how splendid 'Guide Me, O Thou Great Redeemer' sounded with their two voices echoing off those solid stone walls, and how relieved he'd felt when they'd reached the bottom.

Shona interrupted his reverie. 'I said, is everything all right, Professor?'

Had he been staring at her?

'Yes, everything is cool.'

Cool? He took a swig from his takeaway cup and pretended to scroll through his phone one-handed, as he'd watched the students do.

Shona hesitated, then said, 'Do you mind if I ask you something?'

'Fire away.' He was ready. Notes, slideshow, everything was at his fingertips.

'Were you on *Time Team*?'

Martin corrected his slouch. 'Yes, I was.' It was the first time anyone had recognised him from his guest appearance back in the nineties.

'I thought so,' said Shona. She appraised him, nodding her approval. 'Mum introduced me to the show recently. We binged back-to-back episodes together. All twenty-two series.'

'I was only in the one episode,' he admitted. That was thirty years ago. Suddenly he felt his age again. Still, it was nice to have a fan.

'This is a bit embarrassing,' said Shona, blushing. 'I've developed a bit of a crush.'

Martin smiled, equally bashful. He'd never been anyone's crush before. 'Don't be embarrassed.'

'Do you think you could get Tony Robinson's autograph?'

He was saved by the unhurried arrival of the other students. While Martin waited for them to settle, he took a final sip of coffee and opened his slideshow. Everything had connected perfectly, and his computer desktop was now mirrored onto the projector screen. How clever. Hearing a few sniggers around the room, he realised too late that his desktop folders, with titles such as Symptoms of a Brain Tumour, Mole Progress Photos, and Cures for Male-pattern Baldness, were on full display. He tried to open PowerPoint, but his hands were shaking from the caffeine and he clicked the wrong icon and opened his email instead.

Suddenly, his personal correspondence was on full display. The room fell silent. Most were links to update forgotten passwords, but a single new unread email stood out at the top of the list. It was from <u>David.dyer@baderbeaverdyersolicitors</u>. The subject line read: *The Estate of Raymond Samuel Bowen.*

Without thinking, Martin opened the email.

Dear Professor Pottinger,

We refer to the estate of Mr Raymond Samuel Bowen, of which we are the executors. The purpose of this letter is to inform you that you are named as joint beneficiary of my client's estate, with Ms Grace Cavendish. While I appreciate that Mr Bowen was not known personally to either you or Ms Cavendish, as per my client's express wishes, you will each receive the sum of $1,104,334.50. I will be in touch again in the coming days to arrange transfer of the bequest.

A copy of this letter has been sent via Australia Post for your records.

If you have any queries, please do not hesitate to contact me.

Yours faithfully,
David Dyer BA LLB (Hons) Solicitor

The tutorial room let out a collective gasp. One of the boys wolf-whistled. For a moment, Martin levitated outside himself. Reality returned in the form of a warm, wet feeling in his crotch. Before he knew what he was doing he'd shot to his feet, the takeaway coffee cup, minus its lid, still in his hand.

'*Et sanguinem infernum!*'

The Latin speakers sniggered. Shona came to his rescue with a wad of clean tissues. Martin dabbed at his groin, succeeding only in spreading the blooming stain. He excused himself and hurried to the men's bathroom where, straddling the handbasin, he tried a mixture of hand soap and warm water to remove the stain. It didn't help. If anything, his efforts made it look even more as if he'd wet himself.

Gripping the sides of the basin, Martin glimpsed his reflection in the mirror. Instead of a distinguished professor, he saw a round-faced little boy with wiry hair and ugly prescription glasses, cheeks shiny from snot and tears. All at once, the pain and the stinging humiliation came surging back. The wet trousers, the puddle on the flagstone floor. The deafening din of the church organ. A thousand eyes boring into the back of his skull. A cold hard voice from the pulpit preaching hell and damnation. His father in the coffin. His mother stiff with grief. Both parents unreachable.

Martin blotted his wet patch with paper towels, to no end. The hand-dryer was the kind you dipped your hands into. Unless he stripped off and lowered his trousers repeatedly into the hot air, it wasn't going to help. Should he head back into the tutorial room and try to pretend he wasn't wearing cappuccino chinos? If only he hadn't stopped at the campus coffee shop on the way. If only he hadn't opened that email and inadvertently broadcast his good fortune to six young people with social media at their fingertips. How long could he hide in the bathroom before he had to face the world again? Ten minutes? All day? The rest of his natural life? If only the ground would open and bury him so deep in sand and silt that it would take an entire army of trowels to discover him.

The door swung open and he turned to see Professor Mary. If ever there was a time for a cardiac arrest, it was now. *Please Lord, grant me a swift and painless exit from this ignominy.* But his heart refused to spare him from humiliation, and his defiant ventricles continued to pump.

'Martin. Are you all right?'

He tried to hide the stain with his hands, like a defender before a penalty kick. Sensing that an explanation was required, Martin said, 'I received some unexpected news.' An understatement, to say the least.

Martin had put the peculiar incident at the funeral to the back of his mind. He'd come to accept that, as Grace had suggested, it had been a scam after all, or more likely, a family member had crawled out of the woodwork at the last minute to claim the estate of Raymond Samuel Bowen. Where there's a will, there's a relative, as the saying went. Not knowing how much he and Grace had stood to inherit, it was easy enough to move on. Easy come, easy go.

'So I heard.'

'I should get back to my tutorial.'

She glanced at his groin. 'Not until we've dealt with *that*.'

If only they hadn't been surrounded by urinals, hand-towel dispensers and a condom vending machine, this might have been the moment he'd dreamed of. Instead Mary led Martin to her office where she conveniently kept a hair-dryer. While he suffered the mortification of having his groin blow-dried by Mary's secretary, Rita, his thoughts returned to the solicitor's email. He and Grace, for no good reason other than they happened to be in a particular place at a particular time, were now millionaires. It didn't seem right, and yet, according to David Dyer it was completely legal and above board. He was still vacillating between guilt and euphoria when Dominic Smythe walked past carrying a box from a fancy local patisserie. Balanced on the top were two takeaway coffee cups. The vice chancellor smirked at the sight of Rita kneeling between Martin's legs. He knocked once on Professor Mary's door and, without waiting for a reply, strode into her office.

Martin returned to an empty tutorial room. If he'd been in the slightest doubt that he'd imagined the whole inglorious episode, the email from David Dyer was still projected on the screen. The faculty's gossip machine would be well and truly in motion by now, and not in the way he'd hoped. Was there the slightest chance that the students would keep quiet and respect his privacy? He thought back to the essays on faience he'd marked and returned by email at the beginning of the tutorial. Naturally, Shona's essay had earned her top marks. The standard of the others ranged from average to downright abysmal, and he'd not held back in his comments. With hindsight, he wished he'd shown a little more restraint.

16

It's all coming back to me now

GRACE'S KETTLE HAD NEVER SEEN SO MUCH ACTION. FIRST Rhondda, now Martin. Before them, the last person she'd made tea for was the washing machine repair man, and that had been six months ago.

Martin had left a cryptic message saying there was something he wanted to discuss with her, and he wanted to do it face to face, away from All Souls. One simple phone call could have replaced the lengthy chain of text messages that had finally seen them agree to meet for tea at Grace's house. Either he was too polite to call out of the blue or he enjoyed their clever, witty exchange of banter as much as she did. There was something about waiting for the ping of an incoming message, combined with the satisfaction of devising an eloquent response that had seen her uncharacteristically glued to her mobile lately. In their private virtual and increasingly flirtatious world, their relationship was beginning to feel more intimate than that between acquaintances who shared an unusual hobby.

The grandfather clock in the dining room was still chiming when she opened her front door at three. Grace couldn't help but smile. So few people saw punctuality as a basic courtesy these days.

'I hope I'm not late,' Martin said.

'Come in.' There was an awkward moment when neither of them seemed sure whether to kiss or hug the other. They ended up doing neither.

'I'm sorry to bother you like this.'

'No need to apologise, Martin.'

Grace could almost hear Melody laughing in the background. *Pot calling the kettle, Mum!* She was always telling Grace to stop apologising for everything.

'I hope I'm not disturbing you,' Martin said.

'Not at all. I was sorting out my cutlery drawer.' He looked confused. Now she worried she sounded unbelievably dull. She could hardly say she'd been sitting watching the hands of the clock crawl round toward three o'clock.

'Here,' he said, handing over a cardboard container bearing the name of a well-known patisserie. Inside were two equal slices of carrot cake. 'This one is at least an eight out of ten.'

She laughed. Appraising the carrot cake at each wake had become their little in-joke. Like two judges at a country show, they'd discuss the individual merits of the cake on offer, awarding points for appearance, texture, moisture content, and flavour. Martin, being a purist, insisted they deduct points for unnecessary embellishments like flaked almonds or, heaven forbid, sugar carrots. Grace insisted the frosting must contain full fat cream cheese, and reach a depth of at least one centimetre on the surface of the cake.

'Tea?'

'I wouldn't want to put you to any trouble.'

'It's no trouble.'

'Are you sure?' He thrust his hands deep into his pockets as if searching for loose change. His nervousness was making her nervous too.

'I'm certain.'

They'd seemed so comfortable with each other at the church, singing together and then discussing sandwich fillings and carrot cake. She'd found him witty and charming, and he'd led her to believe he thought the same of her. Now she couldn't think of a single thing to say to break the ice.

'I thought we'd sit in the garden,' she said, carrying the tray out through the sliding doors onto the deck. At least here they'd have something to talk about, even if it was only to exchange gardening tips.

When he complimented her on her green thumb, she replied, 'I've tried to keep things suited to the climate and the environment, as nature intended. No exotics. Nothing that might escape and cause havoc.'

They discussed his garden. 'I let nature take over too, with very different and far less pleasing results, unfortunately.'

She offered to give him some pointers if he ever wanted to start a new project. The conversation stalled.

'Was there any particular reason you came, Martin?'

'I take it you've read the email.'

She shook her head. 'What email?'

'The one from David Dyer, Raymond Bowen's solicitor.'

'Not that I recall.'

Grace remembered Melody always reminding her to check her spam folder if she couldn't find something.

'Have you checked your spam folder?' Martin asked.

Tea caught in Grace's throat and she spluttered.

'I've always been wary of spam,' she said when she'd caught her breath. 'I tend not to go looking for it. Besides, I didn't give my email address. Only my home address and my phone number. I'm of the belief that anything of importance always arrives in the post.'

Martin nodded as he licked cream cheese icing off his fingers. 'The letter then? You should have received a letter from David Dyer in this morning's mail.'

'The postman doesn't deliver here until the afternoon. I haven't checked my mailbox today.' How could she have when she'd been so busy twiddling her thumbs while she waited for the doorbell to ring?

Martin handed her a letter, printed on Bader, Beaver & Dyer notepaper. 'You'd better read it for yourself.'

At first, Grace thought an insect might have landed on the numbers. She tried to brush it away.

'Surely there's been some mistake,' she said. 'This can't be legitimate.'

'I've no reason to suspect it isn't.'

If she hadn't been in shock she might have teased him over his use of a double negative.

'This must be some kind of practical joke.'

'It's no joke, Grace. I rang Dyer's office and spoke to him in person. He reiterated that this was what Raymond Bowen wanted. He specifically stated so in his will. Some kind of test for those who knew him, I suppose. David Dyer is very keen to get things moving as soon as possible. I gather he can't claim his fee until the matter is all wrapped up.'

A magpie landed on the fence nearby. Martin quailed at the sight of the large black-and-white beak.

'Don't worry, this one's friendly. I don't know what it is about cyclists that makes them so territorial.'

She noted he was still wearing bicycle clips around his ankles, the hems of his wool trousers neatly folded beneath them.

'Obviously, we can't keep the money,' Grace said, thinking the exact opposite. 'It doesn't seem right.' And yet. The money would come in so handy. It would mean the end of scrimping and saving.

Martin's face dropped. 'Obviously not,' he agreed. 'Only, David Dyer was most insistent we accept it. Apparently it creates quite a headache for him if we don't.'

'A huge headache, I would imagine.'

Grace thought of all the things she could do to her modest little house with a million dollars. She could extend, add another bedroom and bathroom, put in a pool. But she already had three bedrooms and two bathrooms, and there was only one of her. A pool would be nice on hot days, only she preferred to look at water rather than swim in it. All that upheaval for what would be little more than an expensive water feature. As long as she could watch the birds splashing around in their little stone bath, she was happy.

'What about your daughter?' Martin asked. He must have seen the photos she'd put back on display. 'I know how hard it is for young people to afford their own home these days. Perhaps you could help give her a foot on the property ladder?'

'My daughter died two years ago.' Grace inspected her cuticles.

Martin looked mortified. 'I'm so sorry.'

Grace was pleased when Martin accepted another cup of tea and helped himself to more cake. She'd expected him to make an excuse and leave after what she'd told him, a revelation that would send most men running for the hills. Only Martin wasn't most men. He listened whenever she spoke, gave her words full consideration before adding his own. She trusted him enough to share Melody.

'She was a singer; she sang before she could talk. I wasn't to know how prophetic the name would be.'

'It's called nominative determinism,' Martin said.

'What is?'

'When people gravitate toward careers that suit their name.'

She thought about her chiropractor, the aptly named Doctor Krakenbach.

'The other kids at school used to call me Potty. I suppose I was always going to end up in ceramics.' Martin shrugged. 'Tell me more about Melody.'

As Grace opened up, the earlier awkwardness between them evaporated like the sun burning off the morning mist. It was as though they were more comfortable having the big conversations than making small talk. She began at the beginning, with her long-term relationship with an older man, a music producer who'd been married previously and definitely didn't want more children. It should have been a deal-breaker, but Grace was so in love. She'd always assumed he'd eventually come round to the idea of a second family, and focused on her own career. Until it was too late.

'When I missed a period I assumed I was going through early menopause, or it was the stress of the break-up after I discovered he'd been seeing someone else. I didn't believe the doctor when she told me I was pregnant. I was so shocked I asked for a second opinion.'

Though Martin looked mildly uncomfortable with the gynaecological details, he paid attention to every word, his face showing no hint of judgement.

'Was Melody's father part of her life when she was growing up?' he asked.

'No. I didn't want him to be. I did try to contact him. I thought he had a right to know about the pregnancy. Before I'd had a chance to tell him, he made it clear that he wanted no further contact with me. He told me his new partner was pregnant and he wanted a clean break. It turned out that she was further along than I was. It didn't take a genius to work out what had been going on behind my back.

'Naturally, I was hurt and angry. For better or worse, I decided not to tell Melody who her father was. She grew up thinking she'd been conceived by donor sperm. I thought about telling her the truth when she was diagnosed. I didn't know how she'd react. I agonised for weeks and even debated contacting her father myself. The more I thought about it, the more I realised how unfair it would be. I'd feel better for having unburdened myself, but it would've been too late for Melody to have a meaningful relationship with him, and it could have destroyed our relationship at a time when she needed me the most.'

Martin grimaced, though Grace couldn't tell whether it was at her dishonesty, or the fact that she'd used the word 'sperm'. She'd been so busy surviving as a single mother she'd never thought how it might appear to an outsider. Having maintained the lie for so long, it almost felt like the truth. She wasn't proud that she'd deceived her daughter, but all she'd wanted to do was to protect her. If she had her time again she would have done things differently. But it was too late to take it all back.

The sun had sunk behind the silvery gum trees, and the noisy birds were preparing to roost by the time Grace reached the part of the story where Melody had first fallen ill. The tea was cold in the pot and the cake reduced to carrot-coloured crumbs, but Martin had made no attempt to leave.

'I think this calls for something a little stronger,' Grace said, swatting at the first of the evening's mosquitoes. She returned from the kitchen five minutes later with a bottle of brandy, two glasses and a can of insect repellent.

'The funeral was terrible, Martin. So depressing.' Grace cradled her brandy against her heart, as she had with Melody when she was a newborn. 'All funerals are sad, especially when it's for a young person. It's somehow easier to celebrate a long life. That's not to say that losing someone you love is ever easy, whatever their age. But it feels more like the natural order of things, the closing of a loop or the circle of life, whatever you want to call it. It's different when someone dies before their time. You're mourning the loss of a future, and the unfulfilled potential, as much as what they'd already achieved. However much I'd wanted Melody's funeral to be a celebration of her life, no amount of uplifting music and colourful flowers could change the tragic fact that she'd died too soon. I felt like I'd failed as a mother. Failed to keep her alive, then failed to give her the send-off she deserved.'

Grace took a sip from the glass, remembering too late that she didn't like brandy and why the bottle only saw the light of day at Christmas. The dense liquid burned the back of her throat, making her splutter. Martin, who'd so far listened without comment, finally spoke up.

'You shouldn't be too hard on yourself, Grace. You'd lost your daughter. I'm not exactly an expert, since before Cynthia Preston's, the only other funeral I'd been to was my father's . . .' He stopped mid-sentence and took a large glug of brandy before he continued. 'Obviously, I'm no expert on motherhood either. What I'm trying to say is that, as a mother, I'm sure you did the best you could at the time under the circumstances.'

She wanted to believe him, and perhaps what he said was true. She was in survival mode when Melody died, barely more than a ghost herself. She'd put a notice in the paper, phoned her nephew in Perth, and Melody's old school friends had circulated the details on social media. Many who'd wanted to come were unable to at such short notice, and the other musicians from the company were touring overseas and couldn't make it back in time.

'Before she died, Melody tried to talk to me about her funeral. I wouldn't listen, Martin. I was still hoping she'd get better. I wanted her to hold on to that hope too, so that she'd keep fighting. I thought that by being positive, by not talking about death and funerals, that it might magically keep her alive. In the end, she went very quickly. I failed her, Martin, and I must live with that. Afterward I kept wishing I could turn back the clock and do it all over again. Differently, this time. You hear of people renewing their marriage vows, but we only ever get one funeral.'

Martin's eyes glistened. He had kind eyes that sloped down at the corners. People's faces dropped as they aged, which was probably why old people often looked benevolent and trustworthy. There was something about Martin that made her think he'd always been kind and compassionate. She'd come this far, she thought. She may as well tell him the rest of the story.

'I lost my voice on the day of the funeral. I couldn't sing the hymns, and had to ask Reverend Rimmer to read the eulogy I'd prepared. Let's just say that he didn't exude the same warmth and charisma as Rod. It was as though I didn't recognise the person he was describing. He could have been reading the phonebook. Afterward, my doctor sent me to a specialist who couldn't find anything physically wrong. The speech therapist couldn't help either. They called it psychogenic dysphonia. I cut myself off from other people. It was easier that way, less embarrassing. And then one day, about six months later, I watched the paperboy fling my newspaper into the hedge from the passenger window of a moving car and I saw red. I shouted that I was going to report him to the newsagent, and you know what?'

'Your voice came back?'

'No, and the newspaper still lands in the hedge every morning, but the next day I started singing while I was folding the washing.'

'Actual singing?'

'Yes. There I was, folding a fitted sheet, singing "My Heart Will Go On" like Celine Dion. I'd always been able to sing, but when it returned my voice had changed. It was richer, more powerful. More melodious.'

Melodious. Why hadn't she realised it before? Her skin prickled.

It was fully dark now. Moths flitted around the outdoor lights on the deck. Jasmine scented the warm spring air. It was quite lovely.

'I think you're incredibly brave for what you're doing for the community. It must have been very harrowing to set foot back inside a church at all, let alone sing at all those funerals.' There was genuine admiration in his eyes.

'I'm not brave, Martin. Far from it. When the thing you fear most in the world has already happened, there's nothing left to be afraid of.'

There was a glimpse of recognition before he disappeared into his own thoughts.

'I must be getting back to Mother,' he said.

Grace was surprised how disappointed she was at the thought of him leaving. She was about to apologise for prattling on about her problems, then thought better of it. Instead, feeling Melody on her shoulder, she said, 'Thank you for listening, Martin.'

They stood at the same time and he held her arms gently. 'Thank you for telling me. I wish I'd known her.'

I wish she'd known you too.

They were at the front door when Grace remembered the reason for his visit.

'Gosh, I'm sorry, we still haven't decided what to do about the money.'

Martin scratched his neck. He was thinking, or possibly scratching a mosquito bite.

'We shouldn't rush into anything. There's a lot to think about, and many options to consider.'

The thought of all that money sent a rush of blood to Grace's head. Having that sum in the bank would give enormous peace of mind. Her savings were modest and even her pension would run out one day. With no one to care for her in her old age, she'd need to go into a nursing home. And they didn't come cheap.

'Although . . .'

'Yes?' He looked at her expectantly.

'Imagine the mountain of paperwork for David Dyer if we refused it.'

'Positively Himalayan in proportion, especially when the poor chap thinks he's done his job. He's probably already closed the file.'

'Exactly,' said Grace. 'He'd be lumbered with two million dollars.'

'What if we saved him all that bother and disposed of it ourselves?'

'Donations to good causes, you mean?'

'Exactly, Grace. Giving the money to charity is definitely the way to go.'

In her heart of hearts she knew the right thing to do was to give the money away. Most of it, anyway. Plus, she didn't want to seem shallow or greedy in Martin's eyes. Not when he was so honourable and incorruptible.

'The question is, with so many worthy causes to choose from, how does one decide?' Grace asked. Neither of them knew the answer.

After Martin left, Grace checked for the newspaper in the lillypilly where the paperboy had thrown it earlier that day. When she couldn't find it, she collected the solicitor's letter from her mailbox instead. She already knew the contents, but in the dim glow of the streetlight she ripped open the envelope and read the letter anyway. It was true: she really was a millionaire. Grace wasn't as excited as she should be. The money suddenly felt like an extra thing to worry about.

17

Going, going, gone?

THE AUCTION APP ALLOWED MARTIN TO ENTER ANY AUCTION house, anywhere in the world, and bid on an item in real time. Genius. He'd stumbled across the world of online auctions by accident when researching the 1952 first edition of Hemingway's *The Old Man and the Sea* he'd discovered on his mother's bookshelf, sandwiched between *Wuthering Heights* and *Valley of the Dolls*. Her reading tastes were as eclectic as her wardrobe. In fact, the more time Martin spent with his mother, the more of an enigma she seemed. When he asked her about the rare Hemingway, still in its original dustjacket, she'd forgotten she even had it. What other treasures had she simply forgotten she owned?

Researching the book led to a successful bid on a silk smoking jacket that had allegedly once belonged to Noël Coward. Before long he was completely hooked. In his first week on the app, in addition to the smoking jacket, he'd bought a Georgian silver inkwell, a vintage typewriter, and an art deco toast rack. All strictly utilitarian items that happened to be old and aesthetically pleasing to his eye. Nothing too extravagant. Nothing that would break the bank. Much as he loved the convenience of virtual auctions, nothing beat the thrill of attending one in person.

He'd expected to feel different with so much money at his disposal. There'd been the initial euphoria after the bank confirmed the transfer. That night, however, he'd lain awake listening to the hop, skip and jump of missed heartbeats. All those digits, so many digits, weighed heavily on his chest, especially after his conversation with Grace. They could do so much good with the money, and once they'd agreed on a cause, they'd both be free of their moral burden. The more Martin stared at the balance on his laptop screen, the more uncomfortable he felt. It was such an untidy, jarring number – 1,104,334.50. There was no pattern or symmetry to it. Rounded down, 1,000,000 was much neater, so much easier on the eye. To give away a million dollars would still be considered generous. It even had more of a ring to it than the actual sum and he could still treat himself to a little something with what was left over. Nothing too frivolous. An investment of some kind.

He toyed with opening his auction app then remembered he'd ordered a catalogue for an upcoming sale of antiquities at a local auction house. It was hidden under a pile of papers on his desk. Martin tore away the plastic wrapping and came face to face with the Roman god Hercules. The fragment of an early Byzantine mosaic was magnificent, and when he checked the reserve price, well within his range. He flicked through the glossy photographs, filling his mental shopping cart with exquisite pieces. It wouldn't hurt to go along in person. To window shop. To look, not touch.

On the day of the auction, he took the reappearance of the sun as a good omen after a run of gloomy, overcast days. He rarely ventured into this part of the city, and, since he was early, he decided to call into an art gallery he remembered was located on the same street. For once he could browse without feeling like an imposter. He might even treat his mother to something, using it as a handy hint.

'This would look amazing in your new apartment, Mother.'

Unfortunately, the gallery was now a pie shop. Thinking he must be mistaken, he pushed his bike up and down the road several times until he was convinced. Instead of tasteful oils and watercolours, the window now displayed a sign with the unprovable claim that Pete's Pies were the world's best. Martin's stomach growled when he caught the aroma of cooked meat. The flaky golden pastry looked delicious. Not wanting to risk the embarrassment of public borborygmi, or worse still, his digestive juices placing an ill-advised bid, he bought himself a beef and red wine pie. It was possibly the most delicious thing he'd ever tasted, a transformative, almost religious experience. It was only when he finally tossed the grease-stained paper bag and empty foil tray into a nearby rubbish bin, that he noticed that he was wearing half the filling. He managed to remove most of the solid matter, but his scrubbing with a paper napkin succeeded only in spreading the greasy brown stain on his shirt. All that cholesterol! Was it his imagination, or could he already feel the blood clotting inside his fat-lined vessels?

Luckily, his potential heart attack resolved with a red wine–flavoured belch.

A short walk later, Martin climbed the worn sandstone steps to the auction house and collected his paddle in the wood-panelled reception area. He felt remarkably at ease in such a rarefied environment. Once upon a time he'd fancied himself as a bow tie–wearing auctioneer. If only he hadn't been so allergic to adrenaline.

The glass display cases containing today's lots reminded him of those boyhood museum trips with his father. While other kids trailed blindly behind well-meaning parents, or dawdled at the periphery of organised groups, Martin had his very own, real-life Egyptologist.

Martin inspected the lots on display; a bronze statue of a cat dating from the 26th Dynasty, a small alabaster jar, a carnelian hair ring, and a framed letter purporting to be signed by Howard Carter. There was one lot that was either a late entry, or that he'd missed in the catalogue: an intricately carved amethyst scarab that was so breathtakingly perfect he wanted to weep. The purple of the stone was vibrant and spectacular. He'd never seen anything like it. No wonder these gemstones were associated with royalty and high status. Buried with a good luck charm as spectacular as this, who could fail to be protected in the afterlife?

He remembered Professor Mary showing him a picture of a similar one on display in the Louvre, after she'd returned from a trip to Paris. They'd queued for coffee together during the interval at the annual conference of the Antipodean Archaeological Society where she had just delivered the keynote address.

'I won't lie, Martin,' she'd said, after expressing surprise that he still wanted to attend boring conferences now he was retired. 'I would give my firstborn to own that scarab.'

At the time, her firstborn had just dropped out of a prestigious law degree to become a social media influencer, and Martin wouldn't blame her for trading him in. Not that she could afford a piece like this on her academic salary. However, following his recent stroke of luck, Martin could. He imagined her face when she opened the box and saw the stone.

'Is this what I think it is?' she might ask, hand covering her mouth, tears forming in her eyes.

Naturally, he'd make a joke, toy with her a little. 'It is indeed. Middle Kingdom, twelfth Dynasty.'

The daydream leaped ahead. Martin pictured himself on one knee.

'Mary,' he'd begin. 'This ancient funereal decoration symbolises the immortality of my love for you. Would you do me the honour of becoming my wife?'

At this point she'd let out a tiny squeal, tap her toes excitedly and throw her arms around his neck.

'Yes, Martin. Yes, yes, yes!'

Martin returned to reality to find none other than Dominic Smythe looking over his shoulder. 'Lovely, but out of your league, surely?'

'What?' Martin replied, thrown to see the vice chancellor out of context.

'Apparently you and I share similar tastes,' said Smythe. 'Funny, I had you down as more of a clay pot sort of man.'

'I am, but I also know when I've found something special. It's rare to find a piece like this on the open market.'

'Not for long. Precious things tend to be snapped up by those with the deepest pockets.' Smythe smirked.

'Or the sharpest wits.' Blood pounded in Martin's temples.

Smythe raised his eyebrows. 'I didn't realise I had competition. In that case, may the best man win.'

With that, he sidled off, paddle in hand.

Martin considered himself a pacifist but at that moment he felt a strong urge to punch Smythe's supercilious nose. With the auction room filling fast, Martin sized up the other bidders as they took their seats. There were middle-aged men in suits, some with ties, others in open-necked shirts; and couples, some dressed smartly, others casually. One man was wearing shorts and a t-shirt. As far as Martin could tell, he himself was the only one wearing the remains of an excellent beef and red wine pie. People's outfits may have differed, but they were all wearing the same poker face. Martin's heart sank as more and more bidders piled in, including Smythe, who was man-spreading in the front row, paddle at the ready.

'Ladies and gentlemen, welcome to today's auction.'

At the sound of the auctioneer's voice, Martin's paddle slipped and clattered to the ground.

'I see someone is eager to start us off.' The auctioneer's quip was met with polite laughter.

Martin retrieved the paddle, gripped it with both hands and tried to control his breathing. In through the nose, out through the mouth. The woman in the next seat gave him the side eye. He held his breath for as long as he could before the air came bursting out. She inched away from him. By the time Martin had regained his focus, the gavel had already come down on a carved wooden ointment spoon dating from 1000 BCE. He didn't even hear the sale price. The next dozen or so lots sold in rapid succession. Lot fifteen, a necklace made from faience, agate, lapis lazuli and carnelian beads sold to a well-dressed woman.

Martin tried to keep up but the auctioneer was too fast for him. Suddenly he was back at prep school, the one sports day his father had travelled nine thousand miles to attend. When the gun went off he was still tying his laces at the start line. He could still hear the jeers and mocking laughter as he stumbled along behind the other runners.

'Lot sixteen is the amethyst scarab amulet, circa nineteen hundred BCE. Ladies and gentlemen, as I'm sure you will recognise, this is an exceptional piece with a rare provenance.'

Smythe sat to attention.

'I'll open the bidding at two thousand dollars.'

Martin's paddle shot up. The auctioneer nodded. The room came into sharp focus, every sense was heightened. He was off.

Then Smythe raised his paddle.

'Two thousand two hundred.'

Martin thrust his paddle high above his head.

'Two thousand four hundred.'

His paddle hadn't reached his lap before he was outbid again. Three thousand. Three thousand three hundred. The pace accelerated. From two-hundred dollar increments to three hundred dollars and before he knew it, they were at five thousand dollars.

The auctioneer paused. 'Any advance on five thousand?'

The room took a breather. Then they were off again. Five and a half thousand. Six thousand. It could have been sixty thousand dollars for all Martin cared. He wanted that scarab. And so, apparently, did Dominic Smythe. The vice chancellor's paddle alternated with Martin's, the two of them locked in an increasingly expensive game of ping-pong. When the smarmy Smythe showed no sign of dropping out, Martin kept his paddle above his head, supporting his tiring arm with his hand like the class swot who always knew the answer. 'Please, Sir!'

Martin jumped to his feet. 'Ten thousand dollars.' He was sweating profusely as he tried to stare down his rival.

The auctioneer's eyes widened.

'Eleven thousand,' said Smythe, almost inaudibly.

'Fifteen thousand!' Martin could feel the spittle collect in the corners of his mouth.

Out of your league.

Smythe's words had hit a nerve, triggering a painful memory. This was no longer a tiny auction house in a far-flung corner of the planet. This was Christie's in London. Martin was wearing his best – his only – suit, his shoes were polished and his youthful hair newly trimmed.

He'd caught the train from Oxford to Paddington, and walked to Christie's at St James's. The antique diamond halo ring he'd set his heart on would cost him more than he could afford as a young research fellow. He'd be living on bread and jam for the rest of term, but she was worth it. Nothing but the best for his future fiancée. Martin was new to the world of auctions, and it showed. Instead of playing the game, he'd rushed in and was soon outbid. There'd come a point at which he'd known he was beaten, out of his depth. That he couldn't afford the ring should have been a warning, a signpost he failed to heed. He wasn't worthy of a beautiful, kind and brilliant woman like Jane after all. On his way back to the station, he'd called into a jewellery shop and bought a generic-looking solitaire on impulse. Later, it had been surprisingly easy to sell with a simple advert in the paper.

Engagement ring for sale. Never worn. Six words. A lifetime of heartache. If he'd recognised at the start that Jane was out of his league, he could have saved himself the pain that followed.

'Twenty thousand dollars,' Martin shouted before Smythe could enter a counter bid. The room echoed with a collective gasp, followed by the low murmur of voices. He'd outbid himself. Stumbled over his own flailing shoelace.

The auctioneer raised his gavel. 'Any advance on twenty thousand dollars?'

Smythe shook his head. This was it, Martin's victory for the taking.

The gavel hit the wood, piercing the overbreathed air like gunfire. Martin collapsed back into his seat as if he'd been shot. The initial euphoria soon gave way to nausea. His breastbone was on fire and the acidic remnants of his beef and red wine pie threatened an encore. What had he done?

He thought of Grace, lovely Grace. Grace was expecting him at a funeral on Friday. Afterward, he was going to suggest they go for a walk, and brainstorm ideas for donating Raymond Bowen's money. How could he face her again after this, knowing he'd thrown away a ludicrous sum of money, out of vanity, simply to impress a woman? He would have to come clean about his folly. Besides, he was terrible at keeping secrets. One way or another, the truth would come out. His impulse purchase wasn't the only thing he needed to confess. If anything it would be easier to explain why he'd spent an extortionate amount of money on an amethyst scarab than to tell her the reason he'd stolen her newspaper from the hedge.

18

Attack of the killer strawberries

GRACE PACED THE LIVING ROOM. RHONDDA WAS LATE AND it was raining heavily. When she'd seen the weather forecast, Grace almost rang to cancel, picturing the poor woman driving through the deluge. In the end her selfish desire to see Rhondda again won. She'd forgotten how much she enjoyed the company of another woman. It had been years since she'd chatted with a girlfriend over coffee. Normal conversations had become impossible after Melody was diagnosed, with everyone treading on eggshells, afraid to say the wrong thing. In turn, Grace had resented the petty frustrations of their normal lives. It had been easier to cut herself off completely, and concentrate on her daughter. She probably should have invested more in those friendships, she now realised, allowed herself to be vulnerable, and comforted, however clumsily.

With those women misguidedly banished to the corners of her life, Rhondda was the closest thing Grace had to a friend, even if she was paying by the hour for the privilege.

The only other person who qualified as a confidant was Martin. She'd already shared more with him than she had with any girlfriend, shocked by how quickly he'd broken through her defences.

Rhondda was full of apologies when she arrived beneath a wonky umbrella with two broken spokes.

'I was late leaving the nursing home. Then the bus drove straight past my stop.'

'You walked? Don't you have a car?' Grace recognised immediately how privileged and out of touch she sounded.

'I did. The gearbox packed up a few weeks ago. I can't afford to replace it.'

Grace thought of Hudson sitting in class in wet clothes while the other kids remained warm and cosy after being dropped off at the gate by their parents. His life was one long uphill battle. She took Rhondda's sodden coat and hung it to dry over the heated towel rail in the bathroom.

'Here,' she said, returning with a warm fluffy towel. 'Dry off while I fetch the tea. I made shortbread this morning.'

'My son's favourite,' said Rhondda.

'Melody's too. I'll give you some to take home. I'll never eat them all myself.'

They took their customary positions; Grace in the armchair and the bedraggled medium on the sofa with a towel wrapped around her shoulders. Grace had withdrawn the last two hundred dollars from her current account earlier that morning so she could pay Rhondda in cash for today's session. She'd tell her to keep the extra twenty to pay for a taxi home. Grace had thought about the conversation with Martin and their pledge to donate the money to charity, but after reading the solicitor's letter over and over, she'd come to a decision.

The money wasn't hers to give away in the first place. It would always be a millstone around her neck. The only way to clear her conscience would be to phone the solicitor and decline her half of the bequest. It was up to Martin what he did with his share.

'This is delicious,' said Rhondda taking a bite from the shortbread, hand under her chin to catch the crumbs. When she'd finished, she brushed the crumbs back onto the plate and closed her eyes. 'Now, let's see what Melody has to say.'

Grace was no longer alarmed by the swaying and the groaning noises that allegedly summoned the spirits of the departed. When Rhondda claimed Melody had joined them, like accepting an invitation to a ghostly Zoom meeting, Grace felt a change in the room. Not a sudden drop in temperature, the traditional herald of a ghostly presence, more of a change in the energy around her. It began to vibrate, hum even. The memories of Melody, her voice, her laugh, how she smiled, became so vivid that it was as if they were happening in real time. Grace could almost believe her daughter was in the room. Almost.

Rhondda's eyelids twitched, as if she was watching a moving scene behind them. Grace waited impatiently, clasping her hands. Rhondda opened one eye. 'Nearly there.'

'Is everything all right?' she asked.

Rhondda shushed her. A sudden draught whipped Grace's ankles and somewhere in the distance a door slammed. Damn weather.

'She's here,' said Rhondda.

'Is she with anyone?' Grace was thinking about the little boy.

'Tommy is with her.'

'Has he found his mum yet?'

Rhondda shook her head. 'Don't worry. Melody is looking after him.' She was silent for a while.

'Are you okay, dear?' Grace eventually asked.

'I'm sorry,' Rhondda said at last, pushing her bedraggled hair away from her face. She looked as if she might cry. 'This has never happened to me with a client before.'

'What is it?'

'Tommy. It's so sad. He told me he was run over by a car.'

Grace gasped and held her chest. 'Oh no!'

'He got separated from his mother and siblings in the crowd outside the school gates on the last day of term. He was supposed to start kindy the following year and was wearing his new school uniform. With so many kids wearing the same uniform, he got lost in the crowd. He decided to walk home on his own and was knocked down by another parent doing a U-turn in a driveway.'

'That's terrible.'

Rhondda rolled her shoulders and took a couple of exaggerated breaths. 'I don't know why this is affecting me so much. I don't even know this boy. That poor mother. Imagine.'

'It's only natural to be upset. You have a young son.'

'Yes, one who has to walk to and from school alone every day. It breaks my heart but I can't afford before- and after-school care.'

Grace swallowed. How could she have been so judgemental about Rhondda's parenting?

'He always forgets to take the lunch I've packed for him,' Rhondda continued. 'He must be starving all day.'

'What about Hudson's dad? Is he . . . ?'

'In the picture?' Rhondda shook her head and Grace took this as her cue not to pry further.

'It's hard being a single mother,' she said instead. 'I should know. Bringing up a child is difficult enough, and even harder without someone else to share the responsibility, and emotional burden when things go wrong.'

Rhondda worried at a jagged nail. Her eyes were downcast and her hands were shaking. 'I don't know what to do. Hudson is having a hard time at school. He's being bullied by the other kids, always coming home with grazed knees or a torn shirt. And yet he's the one who gets the blame. The teachers have given up on him and it's really knocked his confidence. He's acting out his frustrations, that's all. He's a physical kid.'

There was no arguing with any of that. Grace had loved the raw physicality of the boys in her class, and had often sent the liveliest out of class on invented errands, simply to burn off excess energy.

'Being the smallest in the class isn't helping,' Rhondda continued. 'The doctor said he'll only start growing when he has his tonsils out.'

Grace remembered the bouts of tonsillitis that struck Melody every winter when she was in primary school. All the days spent in bed, the antibiotics and, eventually, the battle to see a surgeon. How much better she'd been after the operation. How she'd grown the following year, going from one of the shortest in the class to one of the tallest. Hudson was so tiny for his age.

'Does he get many infections?'

'All the time. He's had so much time off school. And then there's the stopping breathing at night.'

'He stops breathing?'

'Don't worry, he usually starts again on his own.'

Usually?

'That sounds serious.'

'The specialist says his tonsils are the size of giant strawberries. The largest he's ever seen. At night, they completely close off his airway.'

Grace closed her gaping mouth. 'Shouldn't he have them removed immediately?' *Before he suffocates.*

'He's on the waiting list. Fingers crossed it'll be before the end of this year. Or next.'

'That's appalling,' said Grace. 'All that disturbed sleep must be affecting his concentration too.'

'It's not helping. Everyone assumes he has ADHD. If I could afford it, we'd go privately.' She shrugged.

'How much would it cost?'

Grace swallowed when Rhondda told her the figure. There was no way a single mother, working shifts in a care home, could afford that sort of money. But the longer Hudson had to wait, the worse he would get. There came a tipping point with a child like Hudson. The scales were already stacked against him. Could she in all conscience look away?

'I want to help,' said Grace. 'I want to pay for Hudson's operation.'

'No! You can't do that. I won't allow you to.' Rhondda put up a hand as if stopping traffic.

'I insist. Wait here.' Grace hurried to fetch her chequebook from the drawer in the kitchen dresser. There was enough in her savings account to cover the cost but according to David Dyer's letter, a million dollars could soon be hers. All she had to do was say yes, and she could use some of her windfall to help a little boy who was being slowly suffocated by two giant strawberries. When Grace returned with her chequebook, Rhondda was still protesting, though much less vehemently.

'I feel really awkward about accepting this money,' Rhondda said as she slipped the cheque into her handbag. 'I should never have given you my whole sob story. It's very unprofessional.'

Grace shook her head. 'I won't change my mind so you'd better cash that cheque. I want to help. I know what it's like to bring up a child on your own. And please, Rhondda, you're not to blame.'

As she said it, Grace realised what a hypocrite she was. She still blamed herself for what happened to Melody, could trace it back to the very beginning. Like drinking wine at a Christmas party before she even realised she was pregnant. In her second trimester she'd eaten a shark steak and been terrified that she'd poisoned her unborn baby with mercury. Then there'd been the birth itself, the drugs she'd accepted during labour because she hadn't been strong enough to endure the pain. It was her fault Melody wouldn't eat vegetables as a toddler, and when she'd discovered the bottle of vodka in her teenager's bedroom, she'd turned a blind eye. But her biggest failure was not recognising that Melody was sick when she returned pale and underweight from that last overseas tour.

The endless spiral of 'if only' was no less than the torture she deserved. If only she hadn't tried to feed Melody up with hearty stews and creamy puddings that she could barely swallow. If only she hadn't insisted they wait for the cooler weather to settle the night sweats, or the insect bite cream to shrink the lump on the back of her neck. It was only when the swollen mosquito bite multiplied into several, and Melody had continued to lose weight, that Grace insisted she saw the doctor. The truth was that she'd not wanted to believe what was in front of her eyes. The idea that her only child could be sick was simply beyond her comprehension.

'I will repay the money,' said Rhondda. 'My father is very frail. That's why I work at the nursing home, so I can spend time with him. I know it sounds callous, but I'll be coming into some money soon enough. I have three brothers and a sister, so it won't be much, but enough to pay back what I owe.'

Grace waved away her offer. 'That won't be necessary.' She ran to the kitchen and returned with a tin containing the rest of the of shortbread. 'For Hudson.'

Rhondda hugged her, and Grace realised this was the first real physical contact she'd had in a long time. She tried not to spoil it by soaking Rhondda's newly dry shoulder with tears.

'I must be going,' said Rhondda, pulling away.

'Let me drive you,' said Grace, reaching for her car keys.

They wasted several minutes arguing: Rhondda that she didn't want to put Grace to any trouble, and Grace that it really was no trouble. In the end, Grace conceded defeat, but only after she'd insisted Rhondda take her umbrella in case it started raining again.

'Thanks again,' said Rhondda as she left.

'Wait,' Grace called after her. 'I haven't paid for today.'

'I couldn't possibly charge you after the money you've given me.'

'In that case, let me make it up to you in childcare. I'm free every morning and afternoon. What would you say to dropping Hudson here before school, on your way to work? I can meet him after school too, bring him home with me and feed him afternoon tea. I could help him with his homework too.'

This time, Rhondda's protests were only half-hearted. It was the least Grace could do. Her generosity wouldn't bring Melody back, and it was too late for poor little Tommy. It wasn't too late for Rhondda and Hudson however. Grace had an opportunity to make a real difference to their lives, and it was the most excited she'd been in a long time.

19

Knockin' on heaven's door

Warwick Winthrop OAM had drawn quite a crowd, a veritable who's who of local and not-so-local dignitaries. His funeral entourage included a private security company, a television crew and a celebrity chef to oversee the catering. So many people had turned out to pay their respects that the police were called in to direct traffic, and one woman fainted in the snaking meet-and-greet line.

Martin kicked off the critique as he and Grace headed toward the church hall.

'That eulogy should have come with an intermission,' he said, reflecting on the interminable list of Warwick Winthrop's achievements.

'I'll say,' said Grace. 'It's extraordinary how much one person can pack into a lifetime.'

'He must have had an impressive address book too. Look at all these people.'

'I spotted our MP on the way in.'

'I think he just came for the buffet,' Martin joked.

Grace slowed as she pondered something obviously profound. 'For all that was said about him, I didn't really get a sense of who he was as a person.'

'It was odd that it was his business partner who spoke,' Martin agreed. 'Perhaps he knew him better than his family did.'

'And for all that he'd supposedly achieved, I wonder what Warwick Winthrop will actually be remembered for.'

'Beyond making lucrative business deals?'

'An impressive property portfolio isn't really a legacy, is it?' Grace looked wistful. 'I know it sounds idealistic, but for me, legacy is more about leaving the world a better place, by sharing kindness, wisdom and life lessons. And love, of course.'

Martin swallowed. He liked to think he'd shared his knowledge and experience, and had been kind when it mattered. However, if his legacy was measured in terms of love, it amounted to almost nothing. Apart from his parents, he'd loved only three people in his life. Andrew and his wife, Maggie. And Jane. As for Mary Blake, he was fond of her, but if he was honest, he wasn't in love with her. Not yet anyway. He hoped that, in time, his strong physical and intellectual attraction to her would eventually turn into something more substantial. If he even remembered what being in love felt like after so long. For now, he had everything he needed in Grace: friendship, companionship, intellectual stimulation and fun. Plus, they made each other laugh. She was warm and he enjoyed her company. There was no need to complicate things further.

He steered the conversation about love back to safer ground. Death.

'Fifty-two seems so young to die these days. Cut down in the prime of life. It goes to show that money can't buy extra years on Earth.'

This was the perfect segue to discuss Raymond Bowen's money. The situation had been left up in the air to give Grace time to digest the news. He still didn't know how to explain his impulse purchase at the auction, to himself or to anyone else, especially someone as full of integrity as Grace.

'There was one thing that let the whole event down though,' said Grace. 'On the back of the order of service.'

Phew. She was as reluctant to talk about the money as he was. They were back on safe ground.

'Refreshment's. With an apostrophe.'

'A total disgrace.' Martin was smiling beneath his mock outrage. 'Unforgivable.'

The more he got to know Grace, the more they appeared to have in common. Andrew would like her, Martin thought, and he trusted Andrew's judgement more than his own.

The line outside the hall stretched almost back to the church. Grace's nemesis Moira was making the most of the captive audience.

'Who would like to buy a fundraising lavender bag? All proceeds and donations go to the east window appeal. We accept cash, cheque or bank transfer,' she announced. She thrust a miniature EFTPOS machine under the nose of a well-dressed man. 'It's tap and go,' she said. 'You'll need to enter your PIN for larger sums.'

'I think I've found our first good cause,' said Grace. 'It was staring us in the face all along. Quite literally.'

They both chuckled.

'See if you can attract Moira's attention.' Martin fumbled in his pocket. 'I'll get my credit card out.'

By the time he'd retrieved his wallet, Moira had walked past. She had deep-pocketed prey in her sights. Martin debated running after her. But that would mean losing his place in the buffet queue and, after four hymns, he'd worked up an appetite.

'We probably shouldn't interrupt her. She's on a mission.'

Luckily Grace was equally famished and agreed. She leaned in and whispered, 'Did you notice Warwick's mistress hiding in the wings?'

'Mistress? Where?' Several people turned around.

'Keep your voice down, Martin. I'm talking about the woman in the dark glasses who arrived late and left early.'

He finally caught on to the game. 'I think you've been watching too many *Midsomer Murders*, Detective Cavendish.'

They moved forward a few feet.

'Not great for the property prices,' said Grace.

'What isn't?'

'All those murders. It must be hard to sell a house in Midsomer.'

He laughed. Then pretended to cough. The last thing either he or Grace wanted to do was attract attention. Being escorted off the premises by one of the burly security guards wouldn't be a good look for either of them. When they finally made it inside the church hall, the atmosphere was reminiscent of a cocktail party. White-gloved waiters mingled in the crowd offering platters of exquisite-looking canapés and glasses of champagne. If it hadn't been for the incongruous maroon and mustard decor the guests could be forgiven for thinking they'd stepped into a wedding reception rather than a wake.

'I overheard someone saying they're the colour of the silks his jockey wears,' whispered Grace, pointing to the coloured bunting. They each accepted a glass of champagne from a passing waiter. Claire, the woman Martin had been introduced to at Raymond Bowen's wake, was already exchanging her empty glass for a full one.

In one corner, a harpist was playing 'Can't Take My Eyes Off You'. As he listened to the sultry music, Martin found himself watching Grace. She was people-watching herself and didn't notice. They'd spent enough time together that he was familiar with her overall appearance, but he'd never really studied her in detail. She was shorter than Mary, heavier in the hips, and he guessed silver was her natural hair colour. She had an overbite to Mary's underbite, giving her a softly sloping profile. Her nose was neither too big nor too small, and unlike Mary's full set of porcelain veneers, her overlapping front teeth only added to her genuine smile. Her hazel eyes, which he'd noticed during conversation, were flecked with the colours of autumn leaves. He imagined she'd have been very pretty when she was young. While Mary was blessed with a bone structure that stretched out her wrinkles and made her the kind of woman who grew more beautiful with age, Grace shared his sense of humour. Someone who understood the importance of a well-ironed handkerchief and a correctly positioned apostrophe.

'The family must have spent a fortune,' Grace said. If she was aware of his gaze, she was pretending not to notice. 'They say you can't take it with you, but it sure can give you a fancy send-off.'

Another opportunity to talk about the money. To come clean. And yet . . . No, he couldn't spoil the short time he had with Grace by discussing the money. Not now. Martin deliberately dropped the conversational baton.

'Don't tell my mother about the harp,' he said. 'She'll want one at her funeral.'

'How are her plans coming along?' Grace asked.

'Rather too well, I'm afraid. She's upgraded her scrapbook to a mood board.'

'Perhaps she's trying to make things easier for you, Martin. Her final gift to you.'

'Her idea of a final gift was to buy me a burial plot for my birthday. It's right next to hers.' He sighed. 'It's one thing living with your mother when you're my age, now it looks as though we'll be cheek by jowl for eternity.'

Grace suddenly looked sombre, and Martin realised he'd put his foot in it.

'I'm sorry, that was very insensitive of me after what you told me about your daughter.'

'That's all right, you don't need to apologise.' Grace painted on a brave smile. 'You've made me realise where I want to spend the rest of eternity. I'd always thought I'd end up in a traditional cemetery with a headstone. Now I realise that I want to be buried next to Melody at the woodland burial ground. I quite like the idea of my atoms growing into a native tree in years to come. I've made up my mind. I want to be planted!'

How simple, thought Martin. As nature intended. How different from the complex mummification process of the ancient Egyptians. Were the elaborate funerary customs they employed, not to mention the great expense of golden caskets and carefully placed good luck charms, any more likely to gain them a peaceful afterlife? he wondered. Martin wished he'd been able to ask his father these questions. What fascinating conversations they could have had as adults with a shared passion for the ancient. Momentarily lost in his thoughts, he returned abruptly to the present when Grace suddenly clutched his elbow.

'Don't look now,' she said, gesturing toward Claire who was draining another glass of champagne. 'I think we might have a tiny problem on our hands.'

Sure enough, Claire reached for another champagne and overbalanced into a waiter, almost causing a landslide of smoked salmon blinis. She righted herself by throwing her arms around the neck of a short stocky man.

'Should we rescue him?' Grace asked.

'Best not. He's keeping her upright.'

They watched as Claire tottered away from the man.

'I think we should go,' Martin said. 'We've done our duty in the church.'

They were heading for the exit when Claire completely lost her balance, taking a waiter and a platter of carrot cake with her.

Grace's hands flew to her face.

'What a travesty,' Martin said, trying to lighten the moment. 'The blend of sweet and savoury in that carrot cake was exceptional.'

A crowd formed around Claire, who was sprawled on the floor. Martin hesitated. He'd never been very good in an emergency. In fact, his tendency to panic was more likely to lead to a second casualty than help the situation. Fortunately Grace seemed to know what to do and was soon kneeling beside Claire. Martin's contribution was to remove his suit jacket in an attempt to cover Claire's modesty. Moira offered up a lavender bag in lieu of smelling salts.

While some of the people crowded around were keen to call an ambulance, Martin could see that Claire simply needed to sleep the whole thing off.

'Does anyone know where she lives?' the MP asked. 'My driver could take her home.'

Reverend Rod intervened. 'That won't be necessary,' he said. 'I'll take it from here.'

'Who is she anyway?' asked Warwick Winthrop's business partner.

'I'm Claire,' slurred Claire.

'And how do you know Warwick?' the man demanded.

Martin stepped forward. 'Why don't we let the minister go ahead and minister?'

Another man, who Martin had seen loitering outside with a camera, tried to take a photo of the spectacle. Martin raised his hand to block the shot. He took a step toward the man, and skidded on a patch of cream cheese icing, accidentally knocking the camera out of the man's hand. The sickening clatter on the wooden floor momentarily paused the harpist's rendition of 'Somewhere Over the Rainbow'.

The business partner put up his hand. 'Who are you? What's your name?'

Martin dithered and fumbled.

'Professor Martin Pottinger,' said the man who'd been pointing the camera. Judging by his supercilious smirk, he was a reporter. He retrieved his camera and inspected the lens. 'It's all right, no damage done.'

The business partner moved away while the MP thanked the helpers for acting so promptly, and reminded everyone that if he was re-elected they would install portable defibrillators in every public building. His impromptu campaign speech dispersed the onlookers, leaving Martin and Rod to carry Claire away from prying eyes.

Rod arranged some old cassocks on the floor of the vestry, and Grace fought with Moira over a kneeler for Claire's head. Soon, she was asleep.

The walk back to the carpark was more of a stroll, as if neither Martin nor Grace wanted it to end. They paused to read the inscriptions on the tombstones that lined the path through the neglected churchyard. Many graves were overgrown with brambles or ivy, their weathered headstones unreadable beneath moss and lichen. Bernard, in his informal role as head groundsman as well as chief organist, must have only nibbled around the edges while Mother Nature slowly reclaimed her garden of the dead. Seeing a weedy bush growing in front of one grave, Grace leaned over and pulled it out by the roots.

Martin read the inscription.

Alice Bailey (1867–1896) Died aged 29.

'Old age is a surprisingly modern phenomenon,' said Martin. 'It makes you realise what a privilege ageing is.'

Seeing Grace swoon, he put his arm around her. She didn't pull away.

'Are you feeling okay, Grace? You've gone awfully pale.'

'She was the same age as Melody when she died.'

Martin was horrified. 'I'm sorry, I didn't know.'

'It's quite all right. It's odd though,' said Grace, clearing another handful of weeds from the grave. 'I feel as if I know Alice.'

A willy-wagtail landed on the headstone and danced, a fan of black tail feathers flicking from side to side in protest at the intrusion.

'How did that reporter know your name?' Grace asked, looking sideways at him.

Martin either needed to come clean about the newspaper, or keep digging. As an archaeologist and a coward there was only one choice.

'Perhaps he recognised me from *Time Team*,' he joked. He cleared his throat, unable to look her in the eye. He needed to change the subject, fast. 'I've been meaning to talk to you about the money. Now is as good a time as any.'

'I thought we'd decided to donate the money to worthy causes.'

'Yes, absolutely. Worthy causes.' Martin's eye began to twitch. Was buying an overpriced scarab really a worthy cause?

'The question is, with so many to choose from, how does one decide?' Grace said. 'What a shame we can't ask Raymond Samuel Bowen himself.'

A thought came to him in the nick of time. 'That's not such a bad idea, Grace. Do you remember which nursing home they said he was in when he died?'

'I'm pretty sure it was Ambrosia Lodge. I remember the name because ambrosia is what the Greek gods drank. It's meant to confer immortality, which I thought delightfully ironic for a nursing home.'

'In that case, leave it to me,' said Martin. 'I have a plan.'

20

The elixir of eternal life

WHEN GRACE SPOTTED MARTIN HELPING AN ELDERLY woman out of a car, she understood. Edwina was wearing a full-length purple chiffon dress with an ugly red straw hat, and trailing a cat behind her on a pink diamante lead.

'I like your outfit,' Grace said after they'd all been introduced.

Edwina seemed delighted with the compliment.

'I'm the woman in the poem. You know, the one about the lady who wears a red hat and a purple dres and doesn't give a fig!'

Martin apologised with his cycs. He whispered, 'Jenny Joseph's "Warning". Look it up and you'll understand what I'm up against.'

'It's so nice to finally meet your *friend*,' said Edwina. Her fingers made knotty air quotes around the word friend.

'Mother, please. Grace really is just a friend. She's come along for moral support.'

Grace tried to hide her disappointment at his dismissal. It was the truth. They were platonic friends. Nothing more. So why did her heart feel the tiniest bit bruised?

Edwina sniffed. 'What a pity. It's been so long since you had a girlfriend, Martin. It can't be good for your body, all that . . . you know, building up inside.'

Martin's cheeks coloured. Grace felt hers glowing too. It must be the sun.

'Mother will be hoping Ambrosia Lodge doesn't allow cats,' Martin explained as they headed for the main entrance. 'Even if they do, the odds of her agreeing to move in are infinitesimally small. In her eyes, this is purely a social outing, an opportunity to get dressed up and create mischief. You have been warned.'

Too late. Grace had already taken quite a shine to her.

'Shall we?' Martin offered his arm but his mother ignored him. She strode ahead, a blur of papal purple, dragging the aggrieved kitty behind her.

The golf carts and palm trees lent Ambrosia Lodge the air of an exclusive country club rather than an aged care facility. The grounds were manicured and the staff uniforms starched stiff. Expensive contemporary artworks adorned the walls in the main foyer along with extravagant arrangements of fresh tropical flowers on every horizontal surface.

'We've stepped into *The Truman Show*,' Martin said in a low voice.

'This place must cost an arm and a leg,' Grace whispered as the sales agent introduced herself. 'I'm surprised Raymond Samuel Bowen had anything left over in his will.'

'Do you play bridge, Edwina?' the sales agent asked.

'Too tedious,' Edwina replied.

'My mother has a low boredom threshold,' Martin explained.

'What about ballroom dancing, is that more your thing?' The agent was clearly used to dealing with contrary geriatrics.

'Pffft.'

The woman's smile remained steadfast. 'Well, what do you like doing?'

'I like drinking cocktails.'

Again, the woman's expression didn't change. In fact, Grace noticed that her face hardly moved at all. It was quite unnerving. The penny dropped when they stopped outside the Natural Beauty Centre.

'We have an entire team of resident aestheticians available for all your treatments and tweakments,' the agent said. 'Organic radiance facial. Hydrating facial with hyaluronic acid. LED light therapy to reduce the appearance of lines and wrinkles. IPL skin rejuvenation. Botox. Dermal fillers. Micro-needling.'

'Cryogenics?' Martin whispered, making Grace giggle.

'I think the "natural" bit is used ironically,' she whispered back.

'You're right. Everyone in here looks like they've already been embalmed.'

For an aged care facility, there was precious little ageing on view. The residents who passed by were remarkably spry and, yes, well preserved.

'I wouldn't mind a bit of tweaking,' Edwina announced, helping herself to a brochure from the display. 'I want to look my best for my funeral.'

The agent guffawed. Martin raised his eyebrows at Grace.

As they moved on toward the accommodation section, Grace drew level with the agent. She said, loud enough for

Martin to hear, 'My aunt had a friend who was a resident here. Raymond Bowen. He had nothing but wonderful things to say about the place.

'Friend?' The agent's shiny forehead approximated surprise. 'As far as I know, the only person who ever visited him was his solicitor.'

'Which is why he was so grateful to find so many new friends here at Ambrosia Lodge,' Grace persisted. 'Apparently he loved all the activities on offer.'

A shadow of a frown appeared between the agent's brows. 'I am surprised to hear that. Mr Bowen wasn't one to join in with the activities. He was quite depressed after his stroke.'

'The stroke, yes.' Grace glanced back at Martin.

Martin came to her rescue. 'Grace's aunt gets a little confused with details.'

'We took her to his funeral,' Grace said. 'Such a lovely service, wasn't it, Martin?'

'Lovely. The carrot cake was –'

Grace dug him in the ribs. 'What an interesting life he'd lived. All those good causes he was so passionate about.'

'Good causes?' The agent looked even more bemused.

'The charities he supported. You know the ones.'

'Not really.'

'Children? Did his face light up when he saw children?' Grace trotted to keep up with the agent.

'Can't say we have many children in here.'

Martin drew level. 'Or animals? Did he indicate if he was more of a dog person or a cat person?'

'He was allergic to both, according to his medical records.'

This had been a mistake. Grace couldn't believe she'd agreed to such a harebrained scheme. The sooner they finished the tour and got out of this place the better. They'd have more luck drawing the names of charities out of a hat. And yet, she could tell Martin had scruples. He wasn't the kind of man to fritter away a fortune. What would he spend the money on, she wondered? Not sex, drugs and rock'n'roll, obviously. Though for all she knew, his nice-guy persona could simply be an act to gain her trust. She'd read about gullible women losing their life savings in friendship or romance scams. If Martin was a con artist, he was very convincing. She needed to keep her wits about her.

They'd all presumed Edwina was trailing along behind them, but when they paused outside the medical suite, which looked like the intensive care unit of a reasonably sized hospital, they realised Martin's mother was nowhere to be seen.

'Mother,' Martin called.

'She can't have gone far,' said the agent.

Grace wasn't so sure. Martin was carrying her walking sticks and the frail woman who'd climbed gingerly out of the car had given them all the slip.

'Wait here,' the agent instructed. 'I'll find the nurse on duty.'

'Quick,' said Martin when she'd gone. 'This is our chance to do a bit of snooping. I'll go this way, you go back the way we came. I'll meet you back here in five minutes.'

He headed for the day room where white-gloved waiters were serving morning tea on Willow pattern plates. Grace retraced their steps, pausing at an open door to snoop inside an empty room. The room was the size of her kitchen and living room combined, and decorated with sumptuous furnishings and tastefully arranged furniture. She felt an unexpected pang of pity for Raymond Samuel Bowen. He'd effectively spent his last days in a show home surrounded by strangers. What good were plush velvet curtains and designer cushions if you had no friends or family? All that wealth and not a single person to mourn his loss. Grace was more determined than ever to find a worthy home for his fortune.

Following the sound of high-pitched laughter, she poked her head into a spacious room with a large bay window overlooking the gardens. Inside, she saw a woman in a high-backed chair, stroking a sleeping cat. It took a moment for Grace to recognise Shirley Temple, and sitting in a matching armchair nearby, Edwina. A pair of half-empty martini glasses were resting on the mahogany table between the two women.

Martin appeared behind Grace. 'Here you are.'

'Darlings! Come and meet Felicity,' Edwina said, indicating the elegantly coiffed lady beside her who could have been anywhere between sixty and a hundred years old.

'Isn't it a little early to be drinking?' Martin said, curtly.

'Not according to my clock,' said Felicity, indicating the carriage clock on the chest of drawers. The hands appeared to be stuck at five past six. 'It's always happy hour in this place.'

Edwina folded over in laughter.

'Do you two know each other?' Grace asked.

'We do now!' The two women clinked glasses.

'Whoopsie. Time for a refill.' Felicity pressed a red button on the wall. An alarm sounded somewhere in the distance. 'I'd call this an emergency, wouldn't you, Eddie?'

'No one has ever called her Eddie,' Martin whispered to Grace.

Within seconds, a young man in a staff uniform materialised. 'Everything all right, Mrs Sherman?'

'Hello, handsome. Two more of these if you don't mind.'

Martin and Grace watched on, wide-eyed, as the young man placed the empty glasses on a tray. 'Certainly. Would you like gin or vodka in your martinis?'

'Vodka!' the two women shouted in unison.

'And make mine dirty, young man. You know how I like it.' When he'd gone, Felicity said, 'That's Gavin, our mixologist,' as if she was introducing the pharmacist or podiatrist.

All the excitement had woken Shirley Temple.

'Prepare for the hissing,' Martin said. 'She hates everyone except Mother.'

To everyone's surprise, the capricious cat stretched then snuggled in even closer to Felicity's bosom.

'I adore cats,' said Felicity, and to her credit she didn't seem in the least put off by the ginger hair embellishing her expensive-looking cashmere sweater. The feeling was entirely mutual judging by the contented purrs from her lap.

'That's that,' said Edwina. 'It looks like Shirley Temple has decided.'

Felicity's face lit up. 'Does that mean we're going to be neighbours, Eddie?'

'More than neighbours, I hope! No offence to my son,' said Edwina, 'but it's time I had somebody interesting to talk to again.'

Grace winced on Martin's behalf.

At the end of the tour, they returned to the main foyer dragging a now reluctant Edwina behind them.

'I do hope we see you again soon,' the agent said.

'We'll be in touch once we've talked to the bank,' Martin said, looking like a man who couldn't decide if he'd won or lost. 'There shouldn't be a problem with the finances. Mother did quite well out of the sale of her house last year.'

In the carpark, he left his mother admiring a yellow sports car, and pulled Grace to one side.

'Did you find out anything useful about our Raymond? Any potential heirs or favourite charities?'

'No, I was hoping you might have had more luck.'

'I spoke to one of the carers who seemed to know him quite well. She told me he'd won a fortune on the lottery some years back. Spent most of it on fast cars and fast women. By the time he had his stroke, he was down to his last couple of million. He was only in Ambrosia a few months before he died. The carer told me he never had any visitors. David Dyer was right, he didn't have any family. The last of his friends deserted him when he moved into the nursing home.'

'Perhaps he was hoping one of them might turn up to his funeral,' said Grace sadly. 'Did you find out anything more about him? Any clues about how we should donate the money?'

Martin shook his head. 'I'm afraid his interests were purely hedonistic. The only donations he ever made were to bookmakers and bartenders.'

They were no further forward on their quest to find a suitable home for the money, even if they had inadvertently found one for Martin's mother.

'One thing's for sure,' Martin said, 'Raymond Bowen would have spent every last cent if he hadn't had that stroke.'

'Where does that leave us?'

'Still disgustingly rich, I'm afraid,' said Martin with a sigh.

They were interrupted by Edwina who was stroking the bonnet of the yellow sports car like a promotions model. 'Martin! I've decided I don't want a hearse for my funeral,' she called over. 'I want to arrive in a Lamborghini.'

Grace considered the obvious difficulties of trying to secure a seatbelt around a coffin, yet Edwina had a point. People turned up to weddings in all sorts of vehicles: vintage campervans, horse-drawn carriages, and yes, Lamborghinis. So why not funerals? How much more fun than a black hearse. How much more Edwina.

'I'll investigate it for you,' Martin said.

He was so unbelievably patient with her. Beneath that stuffy, old-fashioned exterior, he was a big softy.

They said their goodbyes. Grace told Edwina she looked forward to seeing her again. Her own mother had been dead for years and she'd forgotten how much she enjoyed the company of older people, as well as children.

'What do you think about hiring a photographer for the day?' Edwina asked as Martin helped her into the passenger seat.

He gave Grace a look that said, 'What did I tell you?'

Grace smiled as she watched them drive off, the top of Edwina's red hat just visible through the rear window. She wondered when she'd see Martin again. Was it really wrong to hope there'd be another death in the parish very soon?

21

There's something about Mary

THE EVENING STARTED WELL ENOUGH WITH LAMB CHOPS and mashed potatoes – his mother's request – washed down with an excellent red. Edwina even complimented Martin on his mint sauce, then immediately complained that the lamb was undercooked. He couldn't win. He fared no better with the cat. Martin was convinced Shirley Temple weaponised food, using it as a tool to manipulate him by refusing to touch her dinner of expensive furball-control cat food. Then she failed to return from her evening constitutional. No amount of calling or rattling the food tin could entice the disobliging kitty back inside. In the end, he gave up and instead prepared for the remains of whatever nocturnal creature she decided to gift them in the morning.

Edwina retired early to watch a quiz show hosted by the world's most irritating comedian, leaving Martin to research local charities on his computer. Barely half-a-dozen clicks later and he was already overwhelmed. How could he possibly rank those in need? Was a homeless inner-city youth more deserving than a starving child in Africa? Was research into dementia more urgent than finding a cure for childhood cancer? Would he get more bang for his buck restoring someone's eyesight, or putting a roof over their head? No further forward, he switched to email. There, at the top of the inbox, from an address he didn't recognise was an email titled 'The Funeral Crashers Strike Again'. The body of the email was blank apart from the words, *I'll be in touch soon.* There was an attachment. Martin skolled his remaining port. He double-clicked and was confronted by a photograph of his own raised palm with his face clearly recognisable in the background.

Martin's first reaction whenever he panicked was to call Andrew. When Andrew answered, he sounded drowsy. It was barely eight o'clock.

'Sorry, did I wake you?' Martin asked.

'No. Bit of a headache. I took a pill and was having a lie-down. What's up?'

Martin told him about the email and the unfortunate incident with the photographer at the funeral.

'It was a misunderstanding. I was only trying to protect the poor woman from public humiliation.'

'Probably a freelance reporter who saw an opportunity and decided to make a quick buck. Vulture. What were you doing at Warwick Winthrop's funeral anyway? When I suggested getting out and meeting new people, I didn't realise you'd head straight for the upper echelons. You are a dark horse, Martin.'

It had been some time since their last chess night and Martin realised with a twitch of guilt it was the longest they'd gone without seeing each other in years. It was unlike either of them to neglect their friendship. He and Andrew had always had such an unconditional, uncomplicated relationship, and Martin wanted it to stay that way. Which was why he couldn't bring himself to tell his friend about the windfall. Andrew wasn't the jealous type and would no doubt be pleased for him, but it would change things between them. Because money always did.

'I'll give you the rest of the story over our next game of chess,' said Martin. 'In the meantime, what do I do?'

'Ignore him, Martin.'

'But what if he goes to the police saying I assaulted him? The photo is pretty damning.'

'And face being charged with blackmail? No, he wouldn't risk it. Delete that email and forget about it.'

'Thanks, Andrew. You are a true friend. What would I do without you?'

Once he deleted the email, Martin shut down his laptop. He poured himself another glass of port and put on some jazz, hoping the mellow saxophone and syncopating vocals might drown out the canned laughter coming through the floor. He swallowed the port in one mouthful and was about to pour himself another when he heard someone at the front door. Irritated by the intrusion at this late hour, he secured the braided cord of his smoking jacket and padded down the stairs in his moccasins. He could just make out the outline of a woman through the frosted glass of the front door. Expecting to find his next-door neighbour returning Shirley Temple with a lecture about protecting native wildlife, he opened the door a fraction.

'I've had enough of the old girl's drama. She can stay outside until the morning.'

'You really shouldn't be turning old ladies out onto the street at this time of night.' Professor Mary started to laugh and stumbled in through the open door.

'Mary, what are you doing here?'

'I brought you this.' She fumbled through her oversized handbag and produced a bottle of pinot noir. As if seeing him for the first time, she looked him up and down. 'You're ready for bed.'

'Yes. No. I mean no.'

'I do like your dressing-gown.' She fingered the red velvet collar.

'It's a vintage smoking jacket.'

'Very Hugh Hefner. Care to give me a guided tour of the Playboy Mansion?'

'Actually, this jacket was owned by Noël Coward. I bought it at auction.'

Mary wobbled on her high heels before discarding her shoes completely. One hit the wall with a thud.

'Please keep the noise down,' Martin pleaded, too late. On the other side of the wall the television had magically fallen silent.

On cue, Edwina called, 'Is that you?'

'Yes, Mother. It's only me.'

'Is there someone with you?'

'No, Mother. Go to sleep.'

Mary approximated her finger to her lips to hush herself. He could smell the alcohol on her breath and realised there'd be no getting rid of her in a hurry. Reluctantly, he led her upstairs to his makeshift sitting room. As much to shut her up, Martin opened the bottle of wine and poured two glasses. Mary sank into his feather-filled sofa cushions and let out a sigh. Wine sloshed dangerously close to the rim of the glass as she complimented him on his exquisite taste in furnishings. Luckily, before she spilled any on the hand-embroidered crewel-work upholstery, she swallowed the contents of the glass in a couple of throaty glugs.

'So, to what do I owe the unexpected pleasure of your company this late in the evening?'

'I've been to a drinks thing at the Town Hall and I didn't feel like going home to an empty house. Then I remembered you lived nearby.'

If Mary had turned up on his doorstep at this time of night, it probably wasn't to discuss the tutoring roster for next semester. Was this the moment he'd been waiting for? All his birthdays and Christmases rolled into one? His body certainly hoped it was.

Until now he hadn't been certain she shared his feelings. Her messages had been mixed. What had prompted her sudden change of heart? Andrew had told him not to overthink things. But overthinking was what Martin did best. Much as he willed his trousers to take over, he was suspicious. Perhaps Mary was only looking to reel him in because she knew about the money. And yet, Mary didn't seem like a typical gold-digger. She'd done well out of her divorce settlement and was on a good salary. If she was after money, why not go for Dominic Smythe? As vice chancellor of the university, he made a pretty packet, and he had the looks to go with it. But there was no mistaking the hungry look in her eye.

'I think this calls for nuts, don't you?' he chirped, stalling for thinking time. Nerves always affected his pitch. He was beyond counter-tenor and heading for castrato. He stretched out his jaw and in his best Barry White asked if she'd prefer pistachios or cashews.

When he returned a few minutes later, Mary was admiring a decorative bronze mirror he kept on the coffee table; the once shiny, reflective surface was dulled with age. He could have told her that she shouldn't need a mirror to tell her how exquisitely beautiful she was.

'New Kingdom,' Martin blurted instead. 'Fifteen hundred BCE or thereabouts. My father bought it in Thebes in the fifties. I have an alabaster perfume jar from the Old Kingdom that might interest you.'

'Very impressive, Martin. You're the dark horse, aren't you?'

This was the second time he'd been called a dark horse this evening and he still didn't know if it was a good thing or a bad thing. He refilled both their glasses to the brim, hands shaking so much that the wine bottle clinked against the glass like chattering teeth.

'While we're on the subject of antiquities, there was something I wanted to talk to you about.' Mary weighed her words. 'It's about your legacy.'

Legacy. The word seemed to be following him around, haunting him almost.

'In what sense exactly?'

'As in how you want to be remembered.' As it stood, if he dropped dead today, his legacy would be to leave behind a random collection of mismatched antiques, a pile of unmarked undergraduate essays and a looming assault charge. 'I'm talking specifically about your legacy at the university. It would be a travesty for all those years of work as a lecturer and researcher to go unmarked. None of us wants to be forgotten, to end up with our career as a mere footnote in history. Do we?'

'I haven't given it much thought,' he said truthfully.

'I have.' She lowered her voice and looked around, as if to check no one was listening. 'This is top secret, but with the other departments all moving to the new campus, the university have earmarked the old languages library for redevelopment. I am putting together a proposal to turn it into a museum of Ancient History and Antiquities.'

Years ago Martin had approached Prof Myers with a well-argued case for a small departmental museum. Ultimately the plans had stumbled at the first hurdle through lack of funding. The university wanted to attract more overseas students, or more accurately the fees they paid, and they wanted technology and modern facilities, not a museum of crusty old bits and bobs.

'Where is the funding coming from?'

'The vice chancellor is prepared to back my bid, if I can secure an endowment to cover the cost of the fit-out and acquiring the collection.'

Dominic Smythe. Of course. Anything to get into her pants.

Another of Mary's blouse buttons had mysteriously come undone, offering an unimpeded view of her cleavage. She inched toward him.

'I was wondering whether you might be interested.'

This had to be a dream. Mary – the gorgeous, unattainable Professor Mary Blake – was undressing him with her eyes and inviting him to curate the museum he'd always longed for. Any moment now he'd wake up in a sweaty tangle of bedsheets.

'Of course, I'm interested,' he replied. In being undressed and in curating her museum.

'Thank you, Martin. I can't tell you how grateful I am.'

It was soon obvious exactly how grateful Professor Mary Blake was. When Martin turned round after changing the CD, she was right behind him. Trapped against the bookcase there were only two places he could look, either straight into her eyes, or down at the lacy outline of her bra. Sweat trickled down his neck, soaking the quilted collar of his smoking jacket while Mary's manicured talons tugged at the knot in the satin tie around his waist.

'Wait,' he said, restraining her by the shoulders.

'What's wrong?'

How many times had he fantasised about this very scenario? His mother was right, he'd been sexually self-sufficient for far longer than was healthy. He'd already committed the cost of a rare amethyst scarab to this relationship, thinking he would one day marry her. They were two single, consenting adults who'd drunk a bottle of pinot and eaten half a bag of salted nuts between them. There were clean sheets on his bed and he had a Marvin Gaye CD in his hand. So what was wrong with him?

'Relax.' Mary's fingers touched the bare skin of his chest. He flinched as if he'd been stung.

'Mary,' he said firmly, containing her wandering hands in his. 'I really am very fond of you . . .'

He followed her gaze to a photo at eye level on the bookshelf. It was an old one of him and Andrew, arms around each other at a college ball. Judging by their glassy eyes and missing bow ties, it must have been getting on for dawn. He missed those long summer nights in Oxford that seemed to stretch out like a musical note held fermata. Andrew had framed the photo and given it to Martin as a token of their long friendship.

'Oh, I see.' Mary took a step backward. 'This is embarrassing. I didn't realise you were . . . Sorry, I completely misread the situation.'

'No, that's not it. Andrew and I are old friends from Oxford.'

'Is it me?' There was genuine confusion and hurt in Mary's eyes.

Martin shook his head. 'Of course not. You're absolutely gorgeous. It's more . . .'

What was it exactly? Why couldn't he simply relax and enjoy himself? Was he so unconsciously chauvinistic that he still believed that as a man he should take the lead? Was it performance anxiety, and the thought that news of anything less than one hundred per cent satisfaction could be all over the university by tomorrow lunchtime? No, the real reason did lie in that photograph, though not in the way Mary had assumed.

Martin could still see the woman behind the camera, wearing a strapless emerald dress that showed off her lovely shoulders, strands of hair escaping the carefully pinned chignon she'd started the evening with. He could still hear her tinkling laughter, smell her fruity shampoo, and feel the roughness of her hands that resulted from so much scrubbing-in for operations. She'd wanted to be a surgeon.

Mary huffed and crossed her arms. 'I should go.'

Martin hung his head. He imagined a panel of judges awarding him ones and twos for his performance so far.

'Please let me explain.'

'You don't need to.' Mary checked her phone. 'There's an Uber three minutes away.'

Three minutes to put things right otherwise he'd lose her. 'Don't get me wrong, I am very flattered, only we need to take things more slowly. I need time, that's all.'

From his front door, Martin watched the Uber's retreating tail-lights with a sense of déjà vu. He doubted she'd give him a third chance.

How long did it take to mend a broken heart? Perhaps it was time to face reality. Whenever he got close to anyone, he would always remember Jane. It was only fair that he should grow old alone. He didn't deserve to love or be loved again when she never would.

22

Hello, stranger

GRACE COULD HARDLY KEEP UP WITH ALL THE MAIL THAT had begun to arrive every afternoon. She'd never been so popular. In the past few days, the postman had taken to delivering the stack of cards and letters into her hands at the doorstep. Today, he'd even stopped for a chat, telling her all about his family. His son had won a football scholarship to the United States but was struggling to raise the money for the flight. His wife was living on soup because she couldn't afford the dental treatment she so desperately needed.

'I'd love to take my kids to see the snow, just once,' he'd sighed. 'Not likely on a postie's salary.'

Grace had made a mental note to tip him generously at Christmas.

It had taken her most of the afternoon to open and read all the correspondence, including one from a woman who claimed to be related.

I recently had my DNA tested and we're second cousins on your father's side! How amazing is that!!! I'd love to meet up and for us to get to know each other better!

Grace put the letter straight back in its envelope, on account of the excessive use of exclamation marks. Of the rest, most were asking for donations to various causes she'd never considered, like rehousing abandoned guinea pigs or providing warm coats for featherless chickens. There were the official-sounding societies that promised to end cruelty toward everything from donkeys in Morocco to monkeys in Thailand. Every second organisation needed a new minibus. Then there were the heart-rending stories of children needing experimental medical treatment in Germany or the US. The second-last in the pile had a familiar post mark. Her heart swelled at the sight of her nephew's wife's handwriting.

Do come and visit us whenever you want, Aunty Grace. We are your only family after all. Never forget, family is everything x

She hadn't heard from them in such a long time, and it wasn't even her birthday. How lovely, she thought, putting the card up on the mantle. How unexpectedly sentimental too.

The final letter, a meaningless circular, was addressed to Melody. Grace stroked the envelope against her cheek and heard a low moan, as if someone was in pain. Only then did she realise it was coming from her. She put the letter in a drawer with the other letters that still arrived for her daughter as if she might one day return for them. In the early days, she'd phoned the banks, credit card issuers, the electoral roll, and the various charities that Melody had supported to explain what had happened. Most had been sympathetic and removed Melody from their mailing list. Other companies persisted, and Grace had to brace herself every time she opened her mailbox.

Today's chat with the postman had been especially prolonged. Normally she would have welcomed the interaction but today was a trial run for what she hoped would become an ongoing arrangement. Grabbing her jacket and keys, she hurried out.

Waiting at the school gate was a new experience for Grace. Melody had always come to her classroom after school, meaning she'd missed out on the gossip and opportunity to arrange playdates. Grace knew several women who had met their entire social circle either through a mothers' group or by simply chatting to the other parents at the school gate. Many of these friendships had endured into later life, long after the children had grown up. Grace looked around the group, hoping to catch somebody's eye to open a conversation, but the cliques appeared impenetrable, or perhaps no one even noticed her. Then she noticed Stephanie, standing right outside the entrance on her own. Grace called to her but either Stephanie didn't hear, or pretended not to. She seemed on edge and when her twins emerged, she wrapped them in a tight embrace. Despite their insistence that they were too old to hold hands, she gripped each child firmly and led them away through the noisy huddle. Hudson was last out, trailing behind his classmates. Several parents cast disapproving looks his way. There'd be no playdates for this little guy.

Grace treated him to an ice-cream on the way home.

'Mum doesn't let me eat sugar before I do my homework,' Hudson told her as he bit into the choc-top.

'Why is that?' Grace asked, holding his sticky hand as they crossed the road.

'Dunno.' He shrugged.

'In that case, this will be our little . . . surprise. Only it's best if your mum doesn't find out about our surprise, otherwise it won't be a surprise anymore, will it?'

Realising she'd dug herself into a hole, Grace changed the subject. 'Have you seen anything interesting on TV recently?'

'*MythBusters* is my favourite show. Last night this guy Jamie tried to test if it was possible to survive if you got buried alive in a coffin. He only lasted thirty minutes.' The words were tumbling over each other as his mouth tried to keep up with his brain.

His enthusiasm for the science of the experiment, which he explained in detail – something to do with suffocation from carbon dioxide poisoning plus the crushing weight of soil pressing down on the coffin – was remarkable. He was still explaining the details when they turned the corner into Grace's street. A shiny black Range Rover was parked outside her house. A smartly dressed young man was leaning against the car scrolling through his phone. His bright blue suit looked cheap but had probably cost a fortune. He wasn't wearing socks, although that was increasingly the norm, Grace had noticed. The young man looked up from his phone, lifted his aviator sunglasses and greeted her.

'Oh, hi there,' he said, smiling to reveal a toothpaste advert. It was almost as if he was expecting her. 'Are you Leah Mackenzie?'

'No, sorry I'm not.'

'This is fourteen Wingallah Road, isn't it?'

'Yes.'

He consulted his mobile phone. 'That's the name and address my PA has given me. She must have written it down wrong.'

'I'm sorry. I don't know anyone of that name who lives around here.' Grace pictured Melody rolling her eyes at yet another unnecessary apology.

'That's a shame, I had an appointment with her at four.'

Hudson was already growing restless beside Grace, ripping the petals from her camellias. 'I hope you sort it out,' she said steering Hudson toward the front door. To her surprise, the man followed them.

'Can I use your bathroom? It's a long drive home and I had a couple of macchiatos after lunch with a client.' He named a fancy restaurant in the city.

Against her better judgement, Grace showed him to the downstairs bathroom and placed a clean hand towel next to the basin. She wasn't too worried. The worst he could do would be to steal the hand soap or the spare toilet roll.

Hudson complained he was hungry in a whiny voice. She led him into the kitchen and popped two crumpets in the toaster.

'Who is that man?' Hudson asked as he helped himself to milk from the fridge.

'I don't know. He's only using the bathroom.'

She gave Hudson a glass and watched as he poured the milk up to and over the rim. A few minutes later, while she was mopping up the spilt milk, Grace heard the toilet flush and water running in the sink. She poked her head around the kitchen door.

'Everything all right?'

'Yes, thanks very much.'

Instead of leaving, the man started looking at the row of Melody's framed music certificates on the wall in the hallway. Grace thought she'd been so clever, hiding the photographs from Rhondda on her first visit. Yet all along, Melody had been on full display. Her name. The musical connection. Her age would have been easy to guess too.

'I'm a bit of a musician myself. Nearly went professional,' the man said, reading the certificates. 'Drums.' He mimed the action of drumsticks, in case Grace was in any doubt.

'Who are you, exactly?'

'Simon Hicksworth.' He reached into his suit pocket and pulled out a business card.

'It says you're an investment advisor,' she said, scrutinising the card. 'What does that mean?'

'It's a little different to your ordinary financial advisor. I mean, those guys are all well and good, but they're only interested in the commission from signing clients up to mortgages, retirement plans or savings schemes. Okay for your average mum and dad investor but they can't offer the higher end, bespoke investment opportunities like us.' He preened his spiked fringe in the hall mirror.

The crumpets popped up, golden and steaming. From the hallway, Grace spotted Hudson's eager fingers hovering above the toaster.

'Watch out, love. They'll be very hot. Wait for them to cool.'

'When you have a significant sum to invest, you have a lot more choice, and more security. You can afford to invest with the top people in the kind of company that commands an exceptional return on investment. Do you see where I'm coming from?'

Hudson tried to poke a metal fork into the toaster to retrieve a crumpet.

'No!' Grace only just managed to intervene in time.

'We also do estate planning, if that's more what you're after,' Simon Hicksworth said as he followed her into the kitchen.

'Yes, no. Possibly.'

Grace now had an excellent idea of why Hudson wasn't allowed sugar before homework. She watched helplessly as he dragged a stool over to the high cupboard where she kept the peanut butter. Rhondda must be exhausted, looking after him as well as working at the nursing home.

'Why don't you put the kettle on, and we can have a proper chat,' said Simon Hicksworth. 'I can tell you more about a very exciting opportunity that has just opened up.'

Without thinking, and with most of her attention on Hudson, Grace agreed, deciding it was easier to make a pot of tea than to get rid of Simon Hicksworth. Plus, she was curious. She had no idea how to manage a large sum of money. Advice from a professional might make her life easier. It hadn't crossed her mind to consult a financial advisor and now, by happy coincidence, she had one sitting at her kitchen table. He couldn't possibly know about her windfall. Nobody did, except for Martin and the solicitor. All she needed to do was get Hudson started on his worksheet so she could concentrate on what Simon was telling her.

Hudson stared at the homework sheet as if he'd never seen one before.

'Can you help me?'

'Have a go yourself,' Grace encouraged. 'I'll help you if you get stuck.'

It was good to let kids try things first, have a stab at the exercise themselves and help where needed rather than hover. Hudson was a capable boy, and she was sure he could do well if he put his mind to a task. All he needed was a little patience and, she realised watching him dismantle a ballpoint pen, constant supervision. She watched in horror as he bit into the pen's cartridge, spilling black ink down his shirt and all over the bench.

'Hudson!' Grace shouted without thinking.

He flinched then cowered, eyes wary.

'I'm sorry, sweetheart. I shouldn't have shouted.'

Black inky saliva dribbled from the corners of his mouth, giving him the appearance of a word-thirsty vampire. Grace guided him to the kitchen sink and rinsed his mouth out with water. Then she set about cleaning him up as best she could with a roll of paper towel.

'I can still taste it,' Hudson said, opening his mouth wide and sticking out his comically discoloured tongue.

'Let me see.' Grace bent to his height and peered inside. Expecting to see a pair of giant strawberries, she was taken aback. His throat was stained black but otherwise looked entirely normal. Rhondda had told her he stopped breathing at night because of his large tonsils. Grace had written a cheque in good faith for his life-saving surgery. How strange that tonsils would miraculously shrink like that. Perplexed, she set Hudson up at the kitchen bench with his worksheet and a pencil.

Oblivious to the mayhem at the bench, Simon spread his information sheets across the kitchen table and launched into what Grace assumed was his standard spiel. There was no harm in hearing what he had to say, even if she was only half listening. She wouldn't commit to anything, not until she'd had a chance to read all the small print. She wasn't naive enough to fall for the usual sales tactics like a special discount for signing on the spot, or assurances of cooling-off periods. Raymond Bowen's money was quite safe in the bank until she decided what to do with it. The same couldn't be said for her chequebook, which was sitting on top of the dresser in full view. She'd been meaning to put it away in the drawer after Rhondda's last visit, only she must have got distracted. If she did it now, it would be too obvious. She couldn't be rude, even to someone who might be about to fleece her out of a fortune.

'You can see why this is such an incredible opportunity,' Simon said, pointing to a row of figures that meant nothing to Grace. 'The return on investment is unheard of in the current financial climate. And the best thing about this scheme is that you can withdraw your money at any time. It's a win-win.'

At the kitchen bench, Hudson kicked his legs under the stool and gazed into space.

'Hudson, sweetheart, how are you going with your spelling words?' she called.

'Good.' He was rubbing his eyes as if he'd just woken up.

'I'll need to think about it, Simon.'

'I can see you're hesitant.' He opened a glossy-looking brochure and showed her a row of smiling faces. 'Reading these testimonials should put your mind at rest.' When she didn't respond, he reached across the table and touched her arm. 'I understand you're cautious, Grace, but having met you, I feel as though I'm advising my own gran.'

OMG, Granny Grace. Melody would be laughing.

'Look, Simon, how about you leave the information with me. Let me read through it when I can concentrate properly. I'll be in touch if I want to go ahead.'

Simon drew his breath in through his teeth. 'I wish we had the luxury of time, Grace, but there's only one place left in this scheme. I know that Leah was super keen to get in before it closes. Once I make contact with her, she could beat you to that last spot. Just think of the return. All that extra cash to spend on your loved ones. You could take the whole family on a cruise, pay off your kids' mortgages, or pay your grandson's uni fees up front.'

When she turned round, Hudson's finger was bleeding and the tip of the pencil was missing. He'd only been in her care an hour and he was going to die of lead poisoning. She ran his finger under the tap and applied a band-aid.

'How about I pre-fill a few forms for you, Grace? To save time.'

'Can I have some cheese and crackers?' Hudson asked. 'I'm still really hungry.'

'Okay. Why don't you get your reader out and find the page you were up to while I fetch the cheese.'

'Did you say your last name was Cavendish?' Simon asked.

'That's right.' Had she told him her name?

'Mrs?'

It was easiesr to agree rather than to explain. Strictly speaking she was still a Miss. Out of propriety, the school had decided she should be Mrs Cavendish after Melody was born.

'I can cut it myself.'

Grace closed the fridge door to see Hudson brandishing a meat cleaver. 'Oh, no, no, sweetie. Please be careful with that knife.'

'It's okay, I know how to use a knife. Dad let me play with his flick knife,' Hudson said.

'Your dad let you use a flick knife?'

'He did before he went to prison.'

'Date of birth, Grace?'

She gave it without thinking.

'He's in prison?'

'Yeah. He says it was all a big mistake, that he only accidentally made those holes in the wall. Mum said we couldn't live in a house with holes in the wall so we had to move in the middle of the night. I miss my old friends but Mum says it's worth it not to have holes in the walls.'

Suddenly it didn't matter if Rhondda's supernatural powers were genuine or not. Grace had to look out for her and Hudson, even if that meant embroiling herself in a situation that might turn ugly. How long before Hudson's father was released from prison and came looking for them?

Simon was on his feet now, stuffing paperwork back into a folder.

'I can see this isn't a good time, Grace. I'll leave the brochure with you, and you've got my business card.'

After he'd gone, Grace closed the front door, fastened the security chain and exhaled her relief. She couldn't help feeling that she'd dodged a bullet. She had an overwhelming urge to phone Martin and relay the whole bizarre encounter. As for what Hudson had told her, she decided to keep that information to herself. No good could possibly come from reporting it to the school. She could still tell herself she had his best interests at heart. When she'd least expected it, she'd found someone to worry over. She would look out for him. She would keep him safe. When she turned around and saw that Hudson had lit the gas hob and was about to set fire to his reader, Grace wondered what exactly she'd let herself in for.

23

The Temple of Doom

THE BUREAU OF METEOROLOGY HAD PROMISED A FINE DAY. The weather had other ideas. Martin had checked the weather radar as he did every day before he left the house, and seeing nothing but clear skies had donned his tweeds. After the unfortunate incident with the chinos, he'd reverted to his usual attire. As he cycled through the surprise downpour, he drafted a strongly worded letter to the BOM. By the time he reached the university campus he was drenched and his soggy tweed jacket smelled like a Cheviot ram.

Martin locked his bike to the railing outside the department, noticing with dismay the first bloom of rust in the black paint. If it hadn't been so heavy and cumbersome he would have carried it inside out of the rain. For the first time he considered upgrading his beloved cycle to a modern lightweight number. He could afford to. But he didn't want to. This original Raleigh All-Steel gents' cycle with John Bull pedals was his last remaining link to Jane.

To Martin's relief, Mary's secretary Rita greeted him with polite indifference. Perhaps drying a senior lecturer's crotch with a hair dryer hadn't been that remarkable after all. He wondered if Mary would share Rita's insouciance after her late-night visit. Martin acted as if nothing had happened between them. To his surprise and mild disappointment, so did Mary. The only sign that she might have remembered turning up drunk at his house and then trying to seduce him was her offer of tea or coffee rather than the usual sherry.

'Neither, thank you,' Martin replied, preferring to play it safe.

Rather than moving to the comfortable chairs by the window, Mary sat down behind her desk and gestured for Martin to sit opposite her. Suddenly unsure of what to do with his arms and legs, he ended up looking as if he'd been cable-tied to the chair by intruders.

Mary consulted her laptop. The preamble started well enough.

'I called this meeting to discuss the latest student feedback forms. Firstly, may I say how grateful we are that you stepped in at short notice halfway through the semester.'

Martin picked at his cuticles. So far, so good.

'However . . .'

Here it came, the standard shit sandwich. Start off with praise, bury the bad news in the middle, and end on a positive note.

'I've collated the feedback and noticed a common theme emerging. I need to be honest, Martin.' Martin wished she wouldn't. 'One or two areas drew my attention.' Mary donned her sexy reading glasses. Martin had a flashback to her unbuttoned blouse. His face ignited.

'This week, two of your students have dropped out. One has swapped to data analytics, and the other has quit university altogether to train as a barista.'

His feedback on the latest assignment had been robust, admittedly. His intention had been to encourage self-reflection and improvement, not drive his students to sculpt flowers in frothed milk. Youngsters were so sensitive to criticism these days. A thought came to him. Could one of these disgruntled students have leaked the news of his inheritance as some kind of parting shot? Or revenge?

'The comments from the others don't exactly paint your teaching style in the best light either.' Mary proceeded to list his shortcomings, one for each of her scarlet-tipped fingers.

Tendency to ramble.

Doesn't get to the point.

Didactic.

Monotonous.

Uses too many big words.

Martin agreed these were valid observations, if not attributes, of his teaching style. It was only when the comments turned personal that he really took offence.

Smells fusty.

'Fusty or musty?'

Mary consulted her computer screen. 'Fusty.'

Whoever it was, full marks for consulting *Roget's Thesaurus.*

The cat hair on his jacket makes my allergies bad.

'All this puts me in an awkward position, Martin.'

Not as awkward as the position she put herself in only a few nights ago, he thought.

'I'm afraid if I don't see a significant improvement in student feedback, I will have no choice but to discontinue the arrangement. There's a young lecturer from the UK who is keen to lecture in ancient ceramics next year. It's always difficult to choose between experience and an exciting new face.' She tapped her talons on the desk. 'On a completely unrelated matter, I wonder if you'd given any thought to the museum proposal.'

'As a matter of fact I have. I'm all for it.'

'Really? Excellent.' She clapped her hands together happily. 'The Pottinger Building. It has quite a ring to it, don't you think?'

Martin hadn't envisaged that the university would name the building after him rather than some generous benefactor. He'd assumed his role would be purely administrative.

'Who would curate the museum?'

Mary appeared confused. 'Me, of course.'

Now he understood. This was a quid pro quo. What a fool he'd been to think that she was interested in a has-been like him when she had only seen their relationship as a means to build her museum.

'Thank you for spelling things out so clearly,' said Martin, standing to leave. 'Now if you'll excuse me, I don't want to be late for my tutorial group.'

What was left of it.

~

At the end of the lacklustre tutorial that followed, one of the boys stayed behind after the others had left. Leather-jacket boy. Khalid somebody-or-other.

'Can I ask your advice about something?' he asked.

'Of course,' said Martin as he wound his HDMI cable around his hand. 'What is it?'

'I've been looking at online auction sites and there's some cool antiquities for sale.'

'Indeed.' Martin appraised the boy, trying to see him anew. Here was someone who potentially shared his favourite hobby.

'My grandfather left me some money and I was wondering if you thought Egyptian antiquities were a good investment.'

'I'm not sure that antiquities will guarantee much of a return. The market is fickle. They go in and out of fashion. You can easily waste a lot of money on something that ultimately isn't worth much.' Martin thought about the amethyst scarab, about how carried away he'd been, simply because he'd been trying to impress Mary. What an idiot. 'If you want my advice, the only reason to buy something is because you love it. Because it makes you happy.'

'Your collection must be worth a bit by now.'

Taken aback by the presumption, Martin said, 'Not really. I have a few bits and bobs, mostly utilitarian objects. Nothing particularly valuable.'

'What about the pieces you inherited from your father?'

Martin pictured the half-dozen items his father had given him. Instead of the usual trinkets parents brought home from their travels, Martin's father returned with amulets, scarab ornaments and fragments of papyrus.

Khalid looked at him dubiously. Where was this going?

'Your father was in Egypt, right?'

'That's right. He took part in some of the big digs in the forties and fifties. Alexandria, Luxor, Kafr el-Haram, mainly. He died when I was six.' Sensing this was insufficient, Martin added, 'He contracted malaria in Cairo and died on the voyage home.'

'Ri-ight.'

What was the boy after? 'Any reason you asked, Khalid?'

Khalid pulled out a chair and straddled it backward.

'I'm confused,' he said, tugging at his barely-there goatee. 'I've been researching the illegal antiquities trade. I'm not particularly interested in digging up bits of worthless old pottery. In future I'd like to be involved in something a little more edgy. Like art fraud or the recovery of stolen antiquities. I'd like to travel. I can see myself working undercover for Interpol.'

He'd be perfect undercover, Martin thought to himself. There's no way anyone would suspect this grungy kid of working for Interpol.

'That's all very admirable, Khalid, but I'm not sure what your future career aspirations have to do with my father.'

'The name Pottinger, it's unusual. It piqued my interest, so I dug a little deeper, if you'll excuse the pun.'

'And?' Martin was suddenly aware of his heart.

'I came across a dealer by the name of Harry Pottinger. He was well known in the nineteen fifties.'

'A dealer? No, my father was a field archaeologist. Doctor Henry Pottinger. He might have bought one or two objects from legitimate sources for his own private collection, but he didn't sell antiquities.'

'Quite the coincidence though, to have two Pottingers, Henry and Harry, both active in the same area of Egypt at the same time, don't you think?'

Sweat ran down Martin's back. When he was a child, he remembered his mother calling his father Harry, a common nickname for Henry. 'You must be mistaken.'

'And that's not all, Professor. The Harry Pottinger I uncovered dealt in stolen and fake antiquities.'

Martin wasn't naive. He'd heard about the illicit trade in antiquities. Prior to 1983 when the Antiquities Service in Egypt finally cracked down on the illegal trade and export of antiquities, the systematic plundering of excavation sites was commonplace. The locals who worked at the sites, all desperate to make a little money on the side, often passed the finds on to dealers, who sold them to consular agents. The agents then used their diplomatic immunity to smuggle the pieces out of Egypt to collectors in Europe, America and Australia. Martin knew all this, and that there was a thriving industry manufacturing fakes, many of which were so convincing they ended up in reputable museums.

'My father would never have been involved in anything illegal. I don't believe a word of it.'

'I've made a list of references,' Khalid said. He handed Martin a USB stick. 'It's all here. You can cross-check the details for yourself. He's mentioned in a number of letters, travel diaries of legitimate Egyptologists, and was a regular in the local newspaper gossip columns. He made a lot of money in the late forties on the back of the post-war tourist boom. It looks as though he left Egypt because the authorities were on to him.'

'That's not true. He left because of the Suez Crisis.'

Khalid scoffed. 'I'm afraid not. The Suez Crisis began in 1956. Harry Pottinger left Egypt two years before, in 1954. And from what I read, he died from a head injury, not malaria. According to one eyewitness account he was drunk and fell down a stairwell.'

'No! You're making this up. I'll have you know my father was a member of the Royal Society. He was highly respected in his field. He had a doctorate for heaven's sake.'

'I already checked the database of the Royal Society. There is no record of a Henry Pottinger ever being a fellow. There is no record of him on any of the academic sites I checked. He must have faked his doctorate.'

If this had been an undergraduate assignment, Martin would have awarded Khalid full marks for documenting his evidence and arguing his case. But this was too close to home. If true, then everything Martin had told himself about his own father would be a lie.

'I'm sorry,' Khalid said, and to give him his due, he looked genuinely remorseful.

Martin waited until Khalid left before he crumpled. The revolting commercial-grade carpet turned to desert sand and his feet struggled for purchase. He surrendered to the floor and curled up in a ball.

The Royal Society's motto was *Nullius in verba*, meaning 'take nobody's word for it', and yet there was no need to plug in the USB stick. In his heart Martin knew it must be true. Something had always nagged him about his father's story. An archaeologist couldn't have supported the kind of lifestyle his mother demanded. After his death, Martin learned not to talk about his father. On the occasions he did push his mother for details, Edwina would become angry and defensive or brush away his questions with vague or ambiguous explanations. Over time, Martin had learned to live with the facts he'd conjured in his own head until they became his truth, one he'd never had cause to challenge. Until now.

Now he faced a new reality, and the uncomfortable possibility that his father was a grave robber. A tomb raider. A thief and petty criminal. The foundations of Martin's entire identity had been built on sand. He tore at his top button, released the stranglehold of his bow tie. His head ached.

Once word got out, he'd lose what little respect he was still clinging to.

He sat up, gripped the USB in his fist and sent it hurtling toward the bin.

It missed.

'There you go, potty head.' He laughed. 'That confirms what a total failure you are.'

Martin's mood had sunk so low that he doubted he would ever feel any better, like a low-pressure weather system that refused to move on. One that not even Andrew could have forecast.

Outside the department building the reflection of the sun in the puddles made Martin squint. At first, he assumed that was why he couldn't see his bicycle. Then something caught his eye. Hanging from the railing, in the spot where he remembered leaving his beloved bike, was his empty bike lock next to a discarded pair of bolt cutters.

24

The eye of the needle

DOROTHY BUCKLAND SMILED AT HER NEAREST AND DEAREST from the lid of her coffin. The enlarged photograph was propped up by a floral arrangement containing so many lilies that the front pews were already sneezing from the heavily scented pollen.

St Andrew's was larger than All Souls and far less inviting, Grace decided. The architecture that must have seemed cutting edge in its day was now dated, and despite the large windows, the interior felt gloomy. The yellow-tinted cathedral glass made everyone look jaundiced. There was music, of sorts. Apparently, the elderly pianist had fallen the previous day, and Dorothy's great-grandson, who was learning the keyboard at school, had stepped in to play at the last minute. Ten out of ten for effort, thought Grace, willing him through each painful note. She hoped Martin wouldn't be too disappointed. When she'd suggested they keep a low profile for a while after the debacle at Warwick Winthrop's wake, he'd sounded so disappointed and had suggested they try St Andrew's instead. At first Grace wasn't keen. What if the chemistry between them only existed when they were crashing funerals at the church where they'd met? Eventually her desire to see Martin again overtook any misgivings she had about the venue, and she agreed.

When Martin finally arrived, he had to squeeze past the earlier arrivals to the space on the pew next to Grace, which was barely adequate for one buttock, let alone two. Short of sitting on someone's lap, poor Martin was left no choice but to perch side-saddle.

'Sorry I'm late,' he whispered. 'It's not All Souls, is it?'

A woman in front turned round, did a double take, then gave him a filthy look.

'There's definitely a different atmosphere in here,' said Grace.

'Any news about Claire?' Martin asked.

'I've been so worried about her. Reverend Rod volunteers at a rehab centre attached to the hospital so he might be able to get her the help she needs.'

'Let's hope so.' Martin looked as if he was going to say something then thought better of it. He raked his hair with his fingers and puffed out his cheeks.

'Is everything all right, Martin? You seem a little agitated today. Is it this place?'

After his obvious discomfort at the first couple of funerals, Grace had been pleased to see him relax, and even begin to enjoy being at All Souls. She'd never asked him why he'd been so fearful, what had driven him to the verge of panic. Melody had battled anxiety too, despite having everything going for her. She was that rare triad of high-achiever, talented, and still popular with her peers. Sometimes these extreme emotions seemed to defy logical explanation. They were so ingrained that they could only have been triggered by a deep insecurity or long-buried shame. She'd never got to the bottom of her daughter's fears. Why should it be any different for Martin?

Mercifully, the keyboard fell silent. The service was about to start. 'There've been a few developments since I last saw you,' Martin whispered. 'I'll tell you all about it afterward.'

Whatever the developments were, he didn't look thrilled.

She opened her order of service. 'Look. "The Lord is My Shepherd", followed by "Lord of the Dance", and "Amazing Grace" to finish.'

'Excellent choices,' Martin whispered back, rolling his shoulders and stretching his neck in readiness. 'I'm particularly fond of "Amazing Grace".'

Cheeks ablaze, Grace studied her order of service. The visiting minister, who introduced himself as a friend of the Buckland family, welcomed everyone and sketched an outline of Dorothy's one hundred and three years. Despite being as poor as church mice, Dorothy and her late husband George had begat nine children, twenty-three grandchildren and fifty-one great-grandchildren. There were rumours of great-great-grandchildren on the way too.

'How very Old Testament,' Grace whispered.

'It'll be loaves and fishes at the buffet,' Martin replied behind his hand.

Grace chuckled in spite of herself, spawning another round of shushing.

St Andrew's was full to the gunwales with Dorothy's progeny. The numbers bode well for a hearty hymn or two. However, when the keyboard struck up the introduction to

'The Lord is My Shepherd' Grace felt as though she and Martin were the only ones singing. She reminded herself that this was why they were here, to encourage everyone else to sing. They let rip, soprano and tenor in glorious harmony, Martin adding his classic vibrato for effect. By the end of the first verse, Grace was feeling decidedly uncomfortable.

The qui-i-et wa-ters by . . .

At the end of the hymn, they kneeled to pray. 'Am I imagining it or is everyone staring at us?' she whispered.

More shushing.

'You're not imagining it,' Martin replied. 'The woman handing out the orders of service gave me such a filthy look that I checked to see if my flies were undone.'

It had never occurred to Grace that their singing might cause offence. Perhaps people thought they were showing off or that their exuberance was inappropriate for such a solemn occasion. Worst-case scenario, they'd been singled out as imposters and they would have to invent some tenuous connection to the Bucklands in the event of any awkward questions later. Seated again, they listened as one of Dorothy's many descendants read the perennial funeral favourite, 1 Corinthians 13.

'If I speak in the tongues of men or of angels, but do not have love, I am only a resounding gong or a clanging cymbal.'

Grace felt like a clanging cymbal. It must be their singing. Martin felt it too. The order of service shook in his hands and his deep sighs were attracting plenty of attention. The way he jiggled his foot and fidgeted in his half-seat reminded her of Hudson.

During 'Lord of the Dance', neither Grace nor Martin raised their voices above a murmur. It was almost a relief when the minister climbed up to the pulpit to deliver his sermon.

'We've heard about how much family and love meant to Dorothy,' he began. 'It is good to remember that money cannot buy either. As Matthew wrote in his gospel, *No one can serve two masters. Either you will hate the one and love the other, or you will be devoted to the one and despise the other. You cannot serve both God and money.*'

The minister painted Dorothy as a godly woman who'd eschewed earthly riches for the promise of a generous heavenly stipend. Grace heard whispers behind her. She didn't look round but could feel the judgemental looks fired like arrows into her back.

'Luke 16:11 says, if you have not been trustworthy in handling worldly wealth, who will trust you with true riches?'

Damp droplets rained down onto Martin's order of service punctuating the words of The Lord's Prayer with what Grace thought were tears. When she risked a sideways glance, however, she saw him mopping sweat from his brow with his handkerchief.

'*It is easier for a camel to pass through the eye of a needle than for a rich man*, or woman,' the minister added, and at this he seemed to look directly at them, '*to enter the kingdom of heaven.* And so, I call upon you all to take a leaf out of Dorothy's book. Do not become a slave to money. On that note, I'll end by reminding everyone that there will be a collection at the end for Dorothy's favoured charity.'

Grace didn't have the heart to sing the last hymn. Neither did Martin. Doris Day closed the service with 'Fly Me to the Moon'. As they shuffled toward the door, flying to the moon seemed like the only way to escape the collection plate.

Grace searched through her purse, finding only a handful of loose change in the seams. Darn it. The silver plate was already covered in ten-, twenty- and fifty-dollar notes. She could hardly deposit a handful of coins on top of all that paper money, nor could she walk past without giving anything. Martin had a fifty-dollar bill in his hand. She had ninety cents.

Suddenly the crowd parted around them. A woman, one of Dorothy's grandchildren, flanked by two great-grandchildren, stepped forward.

'I'm surprised you had the nerve to show your faces here,' she said.

Grace looked shocked. 'I beg your pardon?'

'I said, you've got a nerve. Did you think you might make yourselves a few extra bucks? Sorry, but you're going to go away empty-handed. My grandmother wasn't as calculating as you two. She worked hard all her life for everything she had, and what little she left behind is going to be split a lot of ways. So, you're out of luck, I'm afraid.'

'I don't know what you're implying,' Grace began.

'I've a good mind to report you to the police for what you did,' spat the woman. 'Scamming your way to a fortune like that.'

'We haven't done anything illegal,' Martin said.

'You preyed upon a lonely old man. You obtained a large sum of money by deception. Tell me how that isn't illegal?'

'We didn't deceive anyone,' Martin said, standing firm. 'It was pure chance that we were there on that day.'

Grace's legs wobbled beneath her. She reached for Martin's arm to steady herself. How did these people know about

Raymond Samuel Bowen's will? The letter and the email had been marked 'Private and Confidential'.

'Vultures,' said one of the great-grandsons with a sneer.

'Parasites,' said the other.

'Call yourselves Christians?'

'Hypocrites.'

'Gold-diggers.'

Luckily, the minister appeared, and the lynch mob dispersed.

'Come on,' said Martin, leading Grace by the hand. 'Let's get out of here.'

'That was awful,' said Grace a few minutes later, leaning against her car.

'Are you sure you're okay to drive, Grace? You don't look too well.'

She didn't feel too well. Her legs had turned watery and she feared she might vomit.

'That woman basically accused us of fraud. I don't understand how she knew about Raymond Bowen's will.' She searched Martin's face for answers.

He reached for her hands. Not long ago she would have welcomed his touch, the feel of his skin against hers. But something wasn't right. She pulled away.

'It's my fault,' Martin said, his head bowed so that all she could see was his bald patch. 'I should have told you straight away. I didn't want to worry you.'

'What are you talking about?'

'It was on the front page of *The Chronicle* last week. Somehow it got out about two unnamed strangers inheriting a fortune after being the only mourners at a funeral.'

Her thoughts scattered like startled pigeons. What was he talking about? She'd read *The Chronicle* cover to cover every day. Then she remembered. Every day except one. The day Martin came round to her house.

'Did you steal my paper?'

'I was trying to protect you.'

By keeping something as serious as this from her? How could he? She was a grown woman who didn't need protecting. How could she have been so gullible as to trust him? Her thoughts returned to the newspaper article. He'd said that it mentioned two unnamed strangers. If their names hadn't been printed, how did Dorothy Buckland's family know it was them?

'What else haven't you told me, Martin?'

She'd hoped it would be a rhetorical question, but the look of terror on his face told her there was worse to come. He swallowed hard.

'That reporter, the one taking photos at Warwick Winthrop's funeral,' he began.

'The one who knew your name?'

Martin nodded. 'He wasn't the one who broke the news, but our identities were no secret to those in the know. He thought he could make a quick buck by publishing a photograph of me.'

'What photograph?'

'The one he took just before I accidentally knocked the camera out of his hands. It looks as if I'm throwing a punch. I'm afraid you were in the background too. He tried to blackmail me. He must have found my email address on the university website. When I didn't respond to his threats, he went ahead anyway under the headline "The Funeral Crashers

Strike Again". It was in today's edition. That's what I was planning to tell you about.'

Grace was glad she was already leaning against her car. She felt like she could barely stand up. She pictured her rolled-up newspaper somewhere in the hedge. She didn't want to hear his excuses. In a way she was glad she hadn't seen the front page. Instead of reading the paper over breakfast as she usually did, she'd been up at the school volunteering with reading groups. Blissfully unaware of what was unfolding, she'd even detoured to check on her handiwork in the reserve. As she'd hoped, the little glade was full of light and the native flowers were thriving since she'd cleared the weeds. Inevitably, it only took one rogue seed to germinate out of sight for all her hard work to be undone. The begging letters suddenly made sense. The postman's friendliness. The card from her nephew. Simon Hicksworth appearing on her doorstep. Hudson's mysteriously shrinking tonsils.

Tears were close as she fumbled for her car keys. Martin tried to stop her but she dodged his touch and opened the car door as a barrier between them.

'Please don't go,' he pleaded. 'Let me explain.'

Grace reversed out of the space and drove away with a skid, leaving him standing in a cloud of dust.

She was so confused.

If she couldn't trust Martin, who could she trust?

25

Opening Pandora's trunks

HOWEVER MUCH MARTIN WISHED HE'D IGNORED ANDREW'S advice and paid the reporter off, he couldn't blame anyone except himself for making a hash of things. It was his own fault that Grace wasn't returning his calls or replying to his texts. He deserved to be ghosted. Luckily Edwina had been so preoccupied with Operation Ponte Vecchio and the imminent move to Ambrosia Lodge that she hadn't noticed him moping about the house. When she'd asked about her missing newspapers, Martin told her the delivery boy was on holiday. She'd believed him, yet it was only a matter of time before she discovered the truth about her son, the notorious 'funeral crasher'. Until then, he planned to lie low.

While tidying his desk one afternoon, Martin came across a yellow Post-it note on which he'd written the account number and password for his mother's bank accounts. The deposit for her room at Ambrosia Lodge would need to be paid any day now. The proceeds from the sale of the family home had been safely gathering interest in the bank. The freedom Martin craved was tantalisingly close. A couple of simple transactions would see both him and his mother living their best lives. Separately. No more catching his shins on the electric bed. No more cat hair clogging the vacuum cleaner. The snug would once again be his sanctuary. With his mother's wooden crates finally gone, he'd even had thoughts about converting his attic into a library and reading room.

At first he thought he must have logged in to the wrong account. He tried again. He removed his glasses and rubbed his eyes, not quite believing them. However many times he logged in and out, or whichever browser he used, the balance remained the same.

Fifteen dollars and forty-five cents.

Martin scrolled back through the transactions. Over the past month, in a series of transfers, the account had been all but drained. In total, a little over a million dollars had been withdrawn. What had she been doing?

He didn't bother to knock on his mother's door. His heartbeat was so loud she would have heard him coming. He found her on the chaise, pasting a picture of a vintage caravan converted into an ice-cream van onto her mood board. The glue stick, minus its lid, appeared to be stuck to the velvet seat cover.

'I thought ice-cream would be perfect at my wake. Late November can be warm,' Edwina said without looking up. 'What do you think?'

'You're planning your funeral for November?'

'If I wait until December, people are already booked up with Christmas things.'

'Mother, we need to talk.'

Edwina put her scrapbook aside and sighed dramatically. 'If this is the beginning of a boring conversation, Martin, I'm not in the mood.'

'Nevertheless, I have some rather disturbing news.'

'Have you broken up with your girlfriend?'

'I told you Grace is just a friend.' Or as it stood, an ex-friend.

'I'm talking about the one who was here the other night. The one with the perfume.'

His smoking jacket still reeked of Mary's overpowering peony, tuberose and orange blossom eau de toilette. He waved away the mental image of Mary's inviting cleavage and put on his most serious face.

'I've been going through your bank accounts. There's a problem.'

Edwina turned pale. 'What kind of problem?'

'The money has gone. There's nothing left in the account. I think you've been hacked.'

Her colour returned. 'You're such a worrywart, Martin. I can explain.'

It was Martin's turn to blanch. 'Go on.'

'Pat's husband's sister's friend promised me it was a sure thing.'

'What are you on about?'

'I was talking to him at the funeral the other week, and he told me how he'd made half a million profit in a couple of months.'

'Doing what?'

'Investing in kryptonite.'

Cryptocurrency? 'Please don't tell me you've invested in Bitcoin.'

'He told me everyone's doing it. He has a friend who's in the know.'

'Exactly how much did you give this friend?'

Luckily, Martin was sitting down on the edge of his mother's space-age bed when she told him.

'All of it? Every last cent?'

Edwina nodded.

'He told me not to worry, that he'd handle everything. So I wrote down the details from that yellow sticky note. By the way, Martin, you really shouldn't leave confidential information lying around where it could fall into the wrong hands. Anyway, Pat's husband's sister's friend said not to be alarmed if I saw multiple smaller withdrawals rather than one large one. Apparently the bank are less likely to put a stop on the account that way.'

Martin collapsed backward onto the bed. The intelligent mattress emitted a sigh as it deflated under him. He covered his face with his hands hoping it would all go away. He didn't know whether to laugh or cry.

'And how much have you made so far?'

She gave a nervous laugh. 'Well, that's the funny thing about kryptonite, Martin. Apparently, the price can go down as well as up.'

It could also disappear into thin air.

Several phone calls later, Martin's worst fears were confirmed. The only consolation, not that it was much of one, was that Edwina wasn't the only one to have fallen foul of the fake get-rich-quick scheme that targeted vulnerable old ladies at funerals. The police were looking into it but warned it was unlikely any of the investors would see their money again. For Edwina, it meant no dirty martinis with Felicity in Ambrosia Lodge. For Martin, it meant the unthinkable. He was going to have to install a cat flap.

They sat in mutual despondence as the full ramifications sank in.

'Felicity WhatsApped me to ask when I was moving in,' said Edwina. 'Apparently, they've started a Pinot and Picasso night on a Thursday.'

'You've always hated Picasso, Mother.'

'Yes, but I really like pinot,' she responded, miserably.

The solution was obvious. A little too obvious. All Martin had to do was reveal that he'd inherited the cost of a room at Ambrosia Lodge from a virtual stranger. He'd buy her the unit, and with it, his liberty. And yet, there was something too neat about it. His mother had always landed on her feet. She had always put her own needs ahead of his. Why should he forfeit his opportunity to do some real good in the community so that she could get sloshed every night with her new pearl-wearing friends? And there was Grace to consider too. What would she think of him if she knew he'd used the money that was destined for good causes to turf his mother out of his bachelor pad? His first thought was to phone Andrew. His second thought, a sad one, was that after falling foul of the blackmailer, he could no longer rely on his friend's advice. From now on, he needed to trust his own instincts. That way, he'd only have himself to answer to.

Martin sat up. His mother had stopped speaking, her head lolling awkwardly to one side. For one dreadful moment, Martin feared the disappointment over the pinot had triggered a fatal heart attack or stroke. It would be a neat, if ironic, solution to his dilemma. He watched her back and shoulders, waiting for her to take a breath. Then without warning, she sat bolt upright, like something out of a Boris Karloff movie.

'Mother! You gave me a fright.' Martin clutched his chest to stop his heart from leaping out.

'I want you to go into the attic,' she said as calmly as if she was asking for sugar in her tea. 'I don't know why I didn't think of it before.'

'The attic. What for?'

'The wooden trunks. I want you to bring them down. But be careful, what's inside is very valuable.'

Martin remembered feeling inadequate beside the burly Islanders who barely broke a sweat when they hauled the old storage trunks from Edwina's house up the steep ladder into the attic. 'Trunks' might be glorifying what were essentially wooden packing crates. Each box had been carefully labelled in his mother's elegant handwriting, but the contents – dinner service, tea service, clothes, ornaments, blankets and kitchen utensils – were of little interest to him.

'If you want rid of me,' Edwina continued, 'do as I ask.'

'Whatever you say.' Martin agreed, as much out of curiosity as obedience.

He donned a hat, gloves and his sturdiest brogues to protect him from spiders, and with Edwina watching from below, climbed the rickety ladder into the roof space. Inside, the air was hot and Sahara dry. The only light was a single electric bulb that swung like a ghostly lantern in the breeze from the open hatch. Dusty cobwebs hung from the roof tresses, disintegrating on the slightest touch. He imagined this must be what it felt like breaking into a sealed tomb.

'Is everything all right up there, Martin?' Edwina called.

'Fine,' he squeaked through a building sneeze. The third sneeze made his eyes water.

'Lower the trunks down. I'm here when you're ready.'

It had taken the combined muscle power of four prop forwards to get the heavy wooden trunks up here. There was no way a frail old woman like Edwina could catch them, even if he did manage to push them to the hatch. The only way this would work would be if he unpacked the trunks first. His mother had said the contents were valuable. Was it too much to hope for three trunks full of gold bullion? More likely, he'd find knick-knacks his mother had paid a fortune for that were now worthless.

Taking care to only step on the boards and rafters, Martin knelt in front of the first trunk. He rattled the lock that secured the catch. The others were similarly padlocked. The rusty locks and hinges looked as if they hadn't been opened in years, or decades.

'Where are the keys?' Martin called down.

'That is a very good question,' Edwina replied, her voice fading as presumably she went to search.

Five minutes passed. Growing impatient, Martin looked around for something to jemmy the lock. He settled on a cast-iron poker from an abandoned fireplace set. His first attempt failed, the chisel end of the poker skidding over the rusty lock and narrowly avoiding the palm of his left hand. By now, Shirley Temple had appeared at the hatch. She watched his efforts disdainfully. He tried again, levering from a new angle. The lock remained fastened but the wood gave way around the catch.

'What's happening up there?'

Martin didn't answer. With every sense heightened, he registered only the crack of splintering wood, the exotic scents of pine, cedar and myrrh, and the salty tang of the sweat that trickled onto his lips. He carefully removed the lid and propped it against a joist, then scooped out the dusty packing straw to reveal half a dozen or so parcels wrapped in old newspaper. The print was faded but he could still make out the name of the newspaper and the date on the sepia pages. *The Egyptian Gazette*. June 1954. The year his father died.

'Well?' Edwina called.

Ignoring her, Martin unwrapped the first parcel, his knotted stomach urging his all-too-eager fingers to take their time. He would not be rushed, either by his own burning curiosity or his mother who was suddenly so impatient after all her years of silence. The outside of this crate had been marked *Tea Service*, in his mother's handwriting. It took a moment to register what was really hidden inside. The apple-green amulet in his hand was made thousands of years before Wedgwood or Spode. Martin recognised the likeness of the goddess Mut but there was no time to marvel. He placed the amulet aside carefully. He unwrapped the next parcel: a wooden shabti. One by one, he removed the wrappings from a stone seal, a fish-shaped palette carved from green schist, and an amulet in the shape of a ram's head.

Martin collapsed back onto his haunches, breaths so shallow he felt light-headed. Was he hallucinating?

'Can you see anything?' Edwina called from below.

Martin recalled Howard Carter's famous reply when he first shone his light inside the sealed tomb of Tutankhamun. 'Yes, wonderful things.'

'You need to be more specific, Martin. I'm getting a knot in my neck down here.'

He rolled his eyes. Had Lord Carnarvon been this impatient?

Martin focused on the next trunk, which contained more treasures, similarly wrapped and stored. A fragment of linen bandage inscribed with lines from the *Book of the Dead*, once used to wrap a mummy. Gold earrings in the shape of dolphins. Strings of glass and stone beads set in gold. A tiny bronze scorpion. Three ancient papyri, fragile and damaged but still intact. This haul could only have come from a burial chamber.

Hungry to see what was inside the final trunk, marked *Miscellaneous Ornaments*, he wrenched off the lock with a single twist of his wrist. Inside he found more rolled-up papyri. Placing them to one side, he dug deeper until he discovered a bundle, this time wrapped in simple brown paper, held together with string. He untied the knot and removed the paper. His breath hitched as he looked straight into a pair of painted eyes. The blue and red mummy mask in his hands was made from linen and resin and gilded in gold. Shirley Temple, who'd been watching from a distance, arched her back and hissed. Overhead, the light bulb flickered.

'What *is* going on up there?' Edwina called.

Martin couldn't have responded if he'd wanted to. The final item in the trunk was something special. He sensed it, even before he'd removed the wrapping. While his fat fingers fumbled at the knot, an uncomfortable memory returned.

It had been his birthday, his sixth or seventh. Edwina had insisted he invite the entire class to his party, including the boys who seemingly went out of their way to make his life a misery. They played pass the parcel and Martin recalled the thrill when, with the parcel down to its final layer, the music stopped and the parcel was in his hands. He'd never won anything at school. He was invariably last in every race. Last to be picked for every team. Academically, he fared better, and if it hadn't been for a boffin appropriately named Nigel Smart, he might have won a prize. When his mother whipped away the parcel and passed it on to the next boy, a sadistic classmate who always taunted Martin by calling him 'potty head', he burst into frustrated tears. The prize had been a cap gun that all the boys coveted. When Edwina had turned her back to light the candles on the cake, the winning boy aimed the gun's barrel at Martin's heart and smiled as he pulled the trigger.

There was no passing this parcel along. Martin had waited a long time to open his prize. And what a prize! A set of blue faience flasks of the kind used to store anointing oils. The four fragile containers had survived completely intact. They were perfect, museum-worthy. To think that Martin's holy grail had been lying undiscovered above his head while he slept.

Edwina had been right. The contents of the trunks were indeed valuable, potentially thousands of dollars. Whether the auction price would meet the cost of his mother's dream home at Ambrosia Lodge, he wasn't sure. Even though they were priceless to Martin, it was hard to put a figure on what they might fetch on the open antiquities market. The real mystery was why his mother had kept them a secret from him all this time.

He made one final sweep through the straw in the empty trunk before he closed the lid. To his surprise, his fingertips brushed over something else hidden at the bottom of the trunk. At first, he assumed the ordinary-looking cigarette packet must have been packed by mistake. Who would bother to hide cigarettes among all these treasures?

Before he understood why, Martin felt the hairs rise on the back of his neck. One eye began to twitch. He stared at the camel, the palm trees and pyramid on the yellowed packet. Every nerve cell in his body begged him not to open it.

'That's it. I'm counting to ten, then I'm coming up, Martin. One . . . two . . .'

At arm's-length, Martin released the flap and tilted the pack to look inside.

'Three . . .'

He crumpled, knowing he could never unsee what was in his hands. Hadn't he always known what was hidden inside? Hadn't his frightened body always known?

'Four . . . five . . . six . . . seven . . . eight . . .'

Khalid had been right. No legitimate archaeologist would smuggle something like this out of Egypt.

'Nine . . .'

Martin hid the Camel packet in his pocket. He turned off the electric light and lowered himself down the ladder with Shirley Temple under one arm. When he reached the bottom, Edwina was waiting for him, ashen-faced.

'You weren't joking,' Martin said. 'There's a small fortune sitting up there.'

'It's your small fortune, Martin. Your father wanted you to have it all. Everything in those crates belongs to you.'

'Why didn't you tell me?'

'Please don't be cross with me,' she said, wringing her hands. 'It was for your own good.' She looked so frail and vulnerable. He couldn't be angry with her. If anything, he felt disappointed. Betrayed.

Back in the snug, he made them tea and added a nip of whiskey to each cup.

'Mother, dearest,' he said, sitting down beside her. 'I think it's high time you and I had a little chat.'

26

God's answering machine

IN AN EFFORT TO DISAPPEAR, GRACE HAD UNPLUGGED HER landline and turned her mobile to silent. She deleted messages as they appeared and threw the unopened mail onto a growing pile on the Welsh dresser. Martin had been trying to contact her. She'd heard his excuses already. It was best to make a clean break, draw a line under their brief friendship.

Money corrupted even the most decent people in the end. If she had the physical banknotes in front of her now, she'd be tempted to take a match to them. If only she could get her head together and work out the best way to get rid of the money once and for all. She needed to think, somewhere she was safe from the scammers and the leeches, the manipulators and the sob stories. In order to make sense of what had happened, she needed to return to All Souls.

The moment she set foot inside the empty church, she felt calmer. The cool air and silence soothed her jangled senses. Judging by the cars parked outside, she was not alone, as she'd hoped. It was only a matter of time before her peace was interrupted. In the quiet space her sneakers sounded like clodhoppers. Halfway down the aisle she switched to tiptoes. It was too late. Moira materialised like an apparition.

'Here again?' Moira's face was flushed and a strand of her usually perfectly set hair had broken free. She looked so unexpectedly tousled that Grace apologised.

'Sorry, the door was open. Rod doesn't usually mind parishioners coming inside for some quiet reflection.'

'Well, poor Bernard can't concentrate with people wandering in and out willy-nilly.'

Grace glanced up at the silent organ bay.

'If you'll excuse me,' Moira said, 'I have to get back to work.'

Exasperated, Grace called after her, 'I've offered to help, Moira. Many times. I'd love to be more involved in the church, only I get the impression I'm not welcome.'

'Don't be ridiculous. It's a church. Everyone is welcome.'

Except when Bernard is concentrating.

Moira thought for a moment. 'If you really want to make a difference, you need to dig deeper.'

'Spiritually, you mean?'

'No, financially.' Moira turned to face the huge stained-glass window. 'Do I really need to spell it out to you? St John isn't going to miraculously sprout a new head.'

Grace hung hers. 'I want to help, and I will. Rest assured St John will get his head back.'

So, Moira knew about the money too. Apparently satisfied with an IOU, she disappeared into the vestry.

Grace headed to her favourite pew. The dark wood was cool against her back as she searched the jewelled window above the altar for a sign. When several minutes passed without any kind of revelation, Grace wondered if she should announce herself. She was always impressed by the ability of receptionists to ignore people standing right in front of them.

'Excuse me,' she said out loud, though hopefully not loud enough to disturb Bernard. 'My name is Grace Cavendish. Perhaps you remember me. I've been a regular here at All Souls since . . . well, you must remember my Melody. I don't know why I keep coming back. For the company, I suppose, and the hymns.'

What did God think of the hymns sung in His name? Did He think 'Abide with Me' was slow and boring? Did He prefer more uplifting hymns like 'All Things Bright and Beautiful'? Or was He more of a Coldplay fan, like Melody? Now that Grace thought about it, 'A Sky Full of Stars' would have been perfect at the funeral. If only she'd paid attention to what her daughter had been trying to say.

Grace picked up a Bible and opened it. Someone had drawn a cartoon caterpillar in the bottom right-hand corner. At first, she was horrified by the desecration of the holy book, but when she flicked through the pages, the caterpillar turned into a butterfly and flew away. She slid down from the pew and kneeled on the tapestry cushion, lacing her fingers together to pray like she had when she was a child.

Dear Lord . . .

Where to even begin? She should have thought about this before, prepared an agenda. There was so much to say. So much to ask forgiveness for. Was there a limit to how much ground she could cover in one sitting? Maybe she should do a quick Lord's Prayer to let Him know she was here. Like ringing the bell at reception.

Our Father . . . Who art in Heaven . . .

When she opened her eyes briefly, she caught sight of a dust bunny hiding under the pew. For all Moira's claims to be rushed off her feet at All Souls, most of her hard work seemed to be behind the scenes, out of sight. The resentment curled Grace's praying fingers into two fists. Then she remembered where she was.

Hallowed be Thy name . . .

What came next?

It was no good. Her mind was everywhere except on the words of the prayer. Perhaps she really was a lost cause, and her faith had died with Melody. Grace pushed herself back onto the pew and kicked the kneeler under. She was about to leave when she heard her name. Had she imagined it? She looked up at the east window.

'Yes?'

'I've been trying to reach you. I think you've been avoiding me.'

The voice was heavenly, though not exactly holy. Grace turned to find Martin standing in the aisle. Not quite the divine presence she'd been hoping for.

'Mind if I join you?'

She shrugged as if to say, *please yourself.* For a long time, they sat in silence, both staring at the hole in the stained glass.

Something had been bothering Grace about the window and she'd finally worked out what it was.

'Did St John the Baptist keep rabbits?'

'What?'

Grace pointed to the headless body. 'He has a rabbit under his arm. And there's a bird on his shoulder. I think Moira's been raising money for the wrong saint. Unless I am very much mistaken, that's St Francis.'

'Are you going to tell her, or shall I?'

Their chuckles summoned Reverend Rod, who stuck his head out of the vestry to see what was going on. They apologised for disturbing him.

'No, carry on. It's good to hear laughter in this church again,' he said. 'There've been far too many funerals recently.'

When they were alone again, Grace turned to Martin. 'What are you doing here?'

'Same as you, I imagine,' Martin replied. 'Sneaking in to steal the communion wine.'

She smiled in spite of herself, realising how much she'd missed him. There'd been other men, after Melody's father. But none who'd made her laugh like Martin did. None who had stayed. She'd come to believe that the better she got to know someone, the more likely it was that they would let her down in the end.

'I was hoping to find some answers here,' Grace said. 'There's so much I need to sort out in my head.' She knocked her skull with her knuckles. 'I didn't know where to start. Thought the Lord might offer up a solution.'

'Has He?'

She shook her head. 'Not yet. I keep reaching the answering machine.'

Martin shifted and made some noises in his throat, as if he was working up to something. 'I thought I might find you here. I came to say sorry. I should have told you straight away that we were front-page news rather than trying to hide it from you. If you'd known, you could have prepared yourself better. I made a mistake in thinking I knew what was best for you. I fear I've ruined what was a wonderful friendship.'

Grace turned toward him. 'I know now you were only trying to protect me.' It was impossible to stay angry with someone who looked so contrite.

'Do you forgive me?'

'Of course I forgive you. Your intentions were honourable. But by the same token you must have heard the saying, no good deed goes unpunished.'

Martin ran his fingers through his hair. She'd noticed he did this whenever he had something profound to say.

'The honourable intentions thing must be a family trait. I recently discovered that the father I'd always idolised was nothing more than a drunken grave robber. It seems that in trying to secure a better life for his wife and son, he did things that were both illegal and immoral. As if that wasn't bad enough, my mother lost her life savings to a scammer because she wanted to leave me well catered for in her will.' He bowed his head. 'Oh, and to prove that the apple never falls far from the tree, I should tell you now that the girl I loved died because I was trying to make a grand gesture.'

She'd never seen a man cry before. The next thing she knew, she was crying too. They reached for their handkerchiefs at the same time, each offering theirs to the other.

'Martin, I had no idea. Do you want to talk about it?'

'There's nothing much to say about my father, and, well, you've met Mother.'

'What about the girl?'

'One day I'll tell you all about Jane.'

They sat in silence until their tears dried. When she pocketed Martin's damp handkerchief and he did the same with hers, the act felt surprisingly intimate.

'Want to hear something funny?' One of them had to lighten the mood. 'Someone has stolen my chequebook from right under my nose.'

Martin looked anything but amused. 'You still use a chequebook?'

'I'm taking a stand, but that's beside the point.'

'Are you sure you haven't simply mislaid it?'

She bristled at the implication. 'Positive.'

To be fair, Grace had also assumed she'd mislaid the chequebook at first. She'd emptied her handbag and searched the dresser drawer to no avail. Then she remembered seeing it on top of the pile of begging letters and feeling anxious when Simon Hicksworth sat at the kitchen table filling in his stupid forms within arm's reach of the chequebook.

'Has any money been taken from your account?'

'Not yet.'

The last transaction on her statement was Rhondda cashing her cheque for Hudson's surgery.

'Have you been to the police?'

Grace shook her head. 'I'm going to ask for it back first.'

Martin raised his eyebrows but didn't pass comment. What a mess they'd both found themselves in. So far, Raymond Bowen's bequest had brought them nothing but trouble.

'Do you think there's any such thing as an honourable thief?' Martin asked, his mind clearly miles away.

'All I know is that things aren't always as clear cut as they appear,' Grace replied.

As Martin himself had proved, good people could sometimes do the wrong thing for what they believed was the right reason.

27

The camel's curse

MARTIN ALMOST DIDN'T RECOGNISE THE WIZENED FIGURE walking toward him. The weather was perfect for a game of outdoor chess in the city's main park and Martin had been looking forward to seeing Andrew again. He'd even stopped at what was now his favourite patisserie for what was fast becoming his favourite sweet treat.

Andrew's eyes widened as he peered inside the white cardboard cakebox. 'I haven't had carrot cake in years!'

'Don't worry, I won't tell Maggie. Besides, you look as though you could do with feeding up.'

Maggie's paleo obsession clearly wasn't suiting Andrew. His normally round cheeks were caved in and his neck looked almost too thin to support his head. He'd aged too, if that was possible in such a short time.

'Your turn to open,' Martin said. He'd already set up the painted metal pieces on the concrete chequerboard in the dappled shade of a large tree. The previous players had deserted their game, leaving the pieces in an unresolved battle scene. Kids probably, thought Martin, although he was prepared to forgive any youth who chose to play chess rather than throw stones at stained-glass windows.

In a couple of moves, Andrew was out of breath. The pieces he'd always moved with ease now seemed too heavy and cumbersome for him. Rather than watching where his own pieces were moving, Martin was watching his friend. Something was wrong. Very wrong.

'Tea break?' Martin suggested. Andrew readily agreed. They sat either side of the cakebox, on the wooden bench near the chessboard. Martin poured tea from a flask and cut the carrot cake with a knife he'd brought in his bag.

'You want to be careful, carrying a concealed weapon like that,' Andrew joked. 'Worried someone is going to mug you for that ancient pile of rust you ride around town?' He looked around and frowned. 'Talking of which, where is the old penny farthing? Don't tell me you've finally joined the twenty-first century and bought yourself four wheels?'

'Someone pinched it from outside the archaeology building. Probably didn't want to walk home in the rain.'

'Shame. I know how attached you were to that bike.'

'I always thought I'd be buried with it. Which reminds me, I hope you don't mind but I've appointed you executor of my will.'

When Andrew didn't answer, Martin worried he'd overstepped the mark. Perhaps he should have asked first. Andrew was staring off into the distance. He'd barely touched his carrot cake. He returned a half-eaten slice to the box. 'Sorry, it's bit rich for me, I'm afraid.'

Martin wanted to ask him what was wrong. The words were poised waiting for a starter's gun that never came. The longer he went without asking, the longer he'd go without hearing the answer he was dreading. Instead, they recommenced their game, though clearly neither had their hearts in the contest. The pieces fell in rapid succession following silly error upon silly error. Black bishop, White rook. Black knight, White queen. Pawns of both colours piled high. When Martin moved his queen into position, and declared checkmate, he was almost disappointed. He'd beaten his friend for the first time. It was a hollow victory, like beating a man who was unable to defend himself.

'Well done,' said Andrew, magnanimously.

'Are you sure you didn't let me win, to even things up after last time?'

'I wish. No, you beat me fair and square.'

With the game over so quickly, and neither particularly wanting a rematch, Martin suggested they go for a walk in the park. They paused to let the little tourist train pass then headed toward the arched windows of the nearby conservatory. Once inside the bright, humid building, surrounded by plants and flowers, Martin relaxed a little.

'So, any more blackmail threats?' Andrew asked, examining a hanging basket of orchids.

'No, although I trust you've seen my face on the front of *The Chronicle*?'

'I was going to ask you about that,' said Andrew in his typically understated manner. 'I take it you didn't pay up.'

'I took your advice, as ever.'

'If I'd known . . .' Andrew shook his head, clasping Martin gently by the shoulder.

'It's not your fault. It was the right thing to do. My father taught me never to give in to bullies.' Martin remembered how he'd tried to cover up what was happening to him at school, out of shame. He desperately wanted to be the son his father deserved: brave, strong, popular. After his father died, Martin did stand up to his tormentors, by using his brain rather than the brawn he lacked. 'It's time I told you the whole story, Andrew.'

Outside, sitting on a bench, while they watched a young family picnicking on the grass, Martin told Andrew about meeting Grace, the funeral crashing, and how he'd accidentally ended up the beneficiary of a stranger's fortune.

Andrew whistled. 'You have landed on your feet, haven't you?'

'That's one way to put it. I'm beginning to see my good fortune as more of a yoke around my neck.'

'Then why not give the money away?'

Martin sighed and buried his face in his hands. 'I am trying. Believe it or not, it's a tricky thing to give away a large sum of money. It's a moral minefield trying to decide which organisation is the most deserving. Philanthropy is stressful, Andrew.'

Andrew smiled. 'Then spend it on something wild and frivolous.'

Martin shook his head. He'd already done that. Buying the amethyst scarab had clouded his already cloudy judgement about Mary. Besides, he'd had to save up for all the other antiques he'd collected. The yearning and the delayed gratification made each piece precious and therefore so much more valuable. From now on, whatever he bought with Raymond Bowen's money, however rare and expensive, would feel shallow and worthless.

Martin opened the cakebox and offered it to Andrew. When his friend refused, Martin helped himself to another slice anyway. He'd found surprising comfort in food lately, and it showed. Without the daily exercise that came from cycling across the city, and with the extra calories from the buffet food he ate at funerals, Martin's waistband was feeling snug.

An idea came to him. What if Doctor Lowe was right and there really was nothing wrong with him? Physically speaking. What if there was something else going on, some other darker force at play? He thought back to his most recent doctor's appointment, the one he'd convinced the receptionist was an emergency after finding a suspicious mole on his chest. Doctor Lowe had taken all of twenty-five seconds to decide the brown mark was benign.

'Martin.' The name fell out of the doctor like a sigh. 'It's time we talked properly about your symptoms.'

It was time, Martin agreed, having been afflicted with odd bodily sensations since childhood. Flickering lights in his vision, pins and needles in his fingers, and fleeting pains in every part of his body. Yet against all the odds, he'd survived.

'I'd like to suggest a referral to a specialist. A psychiatrist.'

Martin had told the doctor he would think about it. But in the meantime he had a theory for why he was always suffering from some ailment or other.

'Do you believe in curses?' he asked Andrew.

His friend looked at him sceptically.

'The Mummy's Curse.'

'What does that have to do with anything?'

'Remember the story about what happened in 1922 after Howard Carter discovered Tutankhamun's tomb in the Valley of the Kings?'

Martin went on to tell his friend what he probably already knew about how the excavations were funded by the 5th Earl of Carnarvon, a keen amateur Egyptologist. Carnarvon, along with several other members of the excavation team, died within weeks of opening the burial chamber, sparking rumours of an ancient curse.

'Didn't Carnarvon actually die from an infected mosquito bite?' Andrew said.

'True. All the deaths were purely coincidental. Howard Carter died years later from Hodgkin's lymphoma. But . . .' Back in their Oxford days, Martin used to enjoy this kind of intellectual debate while sipping port in Andrew's study. It was a rare subject that Andrew didn't have at least a little knowledge and a strongly held opinion about. 'Carter's curse was that he ended up sad, lonely and unloved. Wealthy but unhappy. His obituary in *The Times* called him a "great Egyptologist", and yet Carter never received any official recognition of his work, no honours back in his homeland. In contrast to the lavish burial of the pharaoh he'd discovered, surrounded by all that gold and treasure, only nine mourners attended Carter's funeral.'

'And?'

Martin removed the Camel cigarette packet from his jacket pocket. 'I think this might be my curse.'

'Have you tried nicotine patches?' Andrew laughed.

Martin opened the lid, as if offering his friend a smoke. A brown leathery object protruded from the box.

Andrew recoiled. 'Good grief. Is that what I think it is?'

'A mummified finger, yes.'

'I didn't think mummies were your cup of tea, Martin. You used to be quite squeamish about dead bodies. I thought that's why you specialised in pottery.'

Not far from their park bench, a father was kicking a ball with his young son. When the little boy aimed it between the makeshift goalposts of discarded jumpers, the man scooped him up and blew on his stomach, eliciting squeals of delight. Even this man would disappoint his son in years to come.

'How did you get your hands on a human finger then, if you'll excuse the pun?'

It was time for Martin to own the truth. 'My father probably stole it from a burial site in the fifties. I think it was meant for me. He knew I was being bullied at school, though I did my best to hide it from him. Maybe he thought it would bring me some much-needed cachet among the other boys.'

'Either that or he thought you could scare them all to death with it.' Andrew examined the fingertip protruding from the packet. 'What does this have to do with your supposed curse?'

'If the sins of the fathers are visited upon the sons, then the only way I'm going to find peace is to get rid of this thing.'

'That sounds like an excellent plan.'

The father and son had packed up their things and were walking toward them now. Martin shoved the cigarette packet back into his pocket out of sight.

'I've got cancer,' said Andrew. 'Stomach. I don't have long.'

The bottom fell out of Martin's world. Even though he'd been half expecting something like this, the thought of not having Andrew in his life brought physical pain. There he was going on about all his bad luck, whingeing about how he didn't know what to do with his fortune, and how the doctors couldn't find anything wrong with him. All the while, his best friend was dying. Once again, he'd failed to see what was in front of his eyes and join the dots.

Bloody cancer.

There'd be time for promises later. For Martin to promise Andrew he would stay by his side. For him to promise to write his eulogy, and to always look after Maggie. By the time the man and boy reached the bench, the father was on his phone. The little boy stared as he walked past, perhaps at the unlikely sight of two old men sitting on a park bench holding hands.

28

Who wants to be a millionaire?

EXPECTING THE FRIENDLY POSTMAN WITH ANOTHER TALE of financial woe, Grace was surprised to find her neighbour Stephanie standing on her doorstep holding a bunch of what at first glance looked like weeds.

'Hello, Grace. I hope I'm not disturbing you. I thought you might like these.'

On closer inspection, the weeds turned out to be fresh basil, mint and coriander.

'Thank you.'

'My kitchen is overrun with herbs. They seem to like the windowsill.'

'Lovely. That's very kind of you.' Grace braced herself for what might come next, suspecting the herbs might be a Trojan horse for another sob story that needed money. What Stephanie actually said next was so out of the blue that Grace needed to steady herself on the doorframe.

'I didn't realise you'd had a daughter.'

Over the time that they'd been living next door to each other, their conversational portfolio had consisted of the usual neighbour-to-neighbour small talk. The weather. Bins. The hedge. Missing car keys. No one asked people Grace's age about their children anymore. Grandchildren were always valuable conversation currency. Adult offspring less so. Stephanie had never asked if Grace had children, and realising what a potential conversation killer it might be, Grace had never mentioned Melody.

While Grace searched for a response, Stephanie continued.

'As you know, Reece and Annabel moved to Parklea Primary this year. I was in the school office the other day and I noticed the words to the school song, and that it was composed by a Melody Cavendish. It's not a common name, and well, I put two and two together. I'm so sorry, I didn't realise. Dee told me what had happened.' Stephanie fiddled with her handbag strap. 'I have an idea what you must be going through. My son Thomas died when he was four. It was awful.' She shook her head as if to disperse the memory. 'I still have two lovely healthy children, but the pain never goes away. I just wanted to say that if you ever feel like a cuppa and chat, my door is always open.'

Mute, Grace nodded her thanks. By the time she'd regained her senses, Stephanie was gone. Poor woman. To lose a child at any age was a tragedy, especially one who'd barely had a chance to live. *Thomas.* Such a strong, sensible and perennially popular name. She'd taught many Thomases. So why did the name suddenly ring a bell? Grace didn't have time to dwell on it. There was something very important she needed to do, something she couldn't put off any longer.

She'd passed this particular apartment block many times. The uninspiring red-brick building was a well-known landmark, though usually in directions to other places. Number 103 was instantly recognisable by the dreamcatcher pinned to the front door. Potted geraniums guarded the threshold, and spa-type music wafted from inside through an open window.

Grace hated turning up at people's homes unannounced, especially when a potential confrontation was on the cards. Taking a leaf out of Stephanie's book, she'd brought along a tin of homemade shortbread, in case things turned awkward. The door opened before she'd had a chance to ring the bell.

Ten grubby fingers grabbed the biscuit tin and were gone again, leaving Grace standing uncertainly on the doorstep. Eventually, a woman appeared, a towel round her shoulders, her head plastered in hair dye.

'Grace! What a lovely surprise.'

'Rhondda?'

'You'll have to excuse me, I wasn't expecting visitors.' Rhondda ushered her inside. 'Come in. Put the kettle on. I won't be a minute.'

Rhondda disappeared into the bathroom while Grace found the kitchen and filled the kettle. The flat was clean and comfortable, with the level of untidiness anyone would expect for the home of an eight-year-old boy.

Hudson came into the kitchen carrying the almost-empty biscuit tin.

'Thank you for the shortbread,' he said, spraying crumbs across the patterned floor tiles.

'I'm glad you enjoyed it,' said Grace.

Rhondda reappeared, rubbing her wet hair with a towel. 'It's getting harder and harder to hide the truth,' she quipped. Seeing Grace's puzzlement, she added, 'My grey roots.' She scooped some exotic blend of tea into a pot and covered the leaves and dried flowers with hot water.

'I apologise for turning up out of the blue like this,' Grace said. 'I should have called first.'

So far Rhondda hadn't asked how Grace knew their address. Perhaps she'd already worked out why Grace had persuaded Hudson to write his address in the front of his exercise book, in case he lost it.

'Nonsense. It's a lovely surprise.' Rhondda's gaze shifted to somewhere beyond Grace's left shoulder. 'And you brought Melody with you, how lovely.'

She led the way out to a tiny balcony that was just wide enough for a table and two chairs. The first floor was level with the tree canopy, as though they were sitting among the birds. Overhead, a windchime tinkled in the pleasant afternoon breeze. If the circumstances had been different, this would have been perfect. The flowery tea wasn't what Grace was used to. She sipped it politely, her thoughts turning to weeds. It had been too long between weeding projects and she was feeling that itch again. She longed to unwind a tangled creeper or tug at a rogue plant, experiencing the rush of pleasure that came as the roots broke free of the soil. If only painful emotions were as easy to uproot.

'I've found Tommy's mother,' she announced, for want of a better opener.

Thomas. *Tommy.* It was too much of a coincidence. Grace told Rhondda about the conversation with her neighbour.

'Melody will be relieved,' said Rhondda. 'She's taken it upon herself to look after him. I suppose even angels need guardian angels.'

When Rhondda didn't offer to mediate a quick chat, Grace was disappointed. She supposed this meant she'd finally bought into the illusion. Was it possible to believe in the supernatural and still have faith in God, or were the two mutually exclusive?

'I think I know the real reason you're here,' said Rhondda.

'You do?'

'I understand. He can be a handful at the best of times. Don't worry, I'll find somewhere else for him to go after school.'

'What? No, I love having Hudson at my place.' Grace tried to calm her staccato heart so she could concentrate. 'This is a little awkward, so I'd best come straight out with it.' 'It' would put an end to contact with her daughter, and the after-school arrangement with Hudson. But she had to say something, however much she wished she could simply ignore the evidence. 'I can't find my chequebook. I think Hudson might have it.'

She'd chosen her words, been careful not to accuse him of theft. Grace told Rhondda about the day that Simon Hicksworth had turned up, and how everything had pointed to him as the culprit. It was only later as she was going through the drawers and piles of papers as Martin had suggested that she had a flashback to seeing the chequebook on the dresser after Simon Hicksworth had left.

'I remembered feeling relieved, thinking what a close call I'd had.'

Rhondda's reply was more weary than defensive. 'Let's go and ask him, shall we?'

They found Hudson curled up on his bed reading a book.

'I need to ask you something, Hudson,' said Rhondda calmly, 'and it's very important you tell the truth.' He sat up. 'Did you take something from Grace's house?'

A shadow passed over his face. The drawn-out silence was agonising. Finally, he nodded. Without a word, Hudson climbed down off his bed and opened his desk drawer. He rifled through the debris and pulled out the chequebook.

Rhondda's hand flew to her mouth. 'Oh, Hudson. Why did you take it? You know that stealing is wrong, don't you?'

'I only borrowed it,' he said, handing it gingerly to Grace. 'I was going to give it back. I promise.'

'Borrowing without asking is stealing.'

'It's all right, Rhondda.' Grace put a hand on her shoulder.

'No, it's not all right. Why did you do it, Hudson?'

'It was meant to be a surprise for your birthday,' he replied miserably. He returned to the drawer and pulled out what looked like a homemade card. The front of the card was decorated in drawings of flowers that looked very similar to the weeds Grace had taught him about in the reserve. Rhondda opened the card. A single cheque fell out. He'd written Mummy on the payee line. Below, in childish font, he'd written one million dollars. Quite a birthday gift.

'It's so you can stop working all the time, and stay at home with me,' he explained.

'That's not how it works, my sweet,' said Rhondda.

'But you took that other cheque to the bank, and they gave you the money.'

Rhondda slumped onto the Spiderman doona cover and buried her head in her hands. Hudson flung his arms around his mother's neck and tried to comfort her.

'I think this calls for more shortbread,' Grace said. 'Hudson, could you go into the kitchen and fetch the tin?' Knowing he'd become distracted, Grace sat down next to Rhondda and Spiderman. They'd have a few minutes until he returned.

'I'm so sorry, Grace. I feel terrible.' Rhondda was crying now. 'I've made such a mess of things.'

Grace handed her a clean handkerchief. There'd been so many tears lately that her supply was running low. 'Don't say that. He's only a child. He was trying to help you. He's obviously a very caring boy.'

'It's what I've done too. I've taken advantage of your kindness and generosity. When I read about the inheritance, I told myself that because the money wasn't really yours, it didn't matter. A victimless crime if you like. I lied about Hudson's tonsils. I needed the money because I'm behind with the rent, and although this flat isn't much, it's the only stability Hudson has right now.'

'You don't need to explain. Hudson told me about his dad, and about you having to move away. It takes time to find your feet again after something like that.'

'I was planning to pay the money back. Once my dad passes away and probate is granted. But Dad's still hanging on and, despite me doing extra shifts, my job at the nursing home doesn't cover the bills.'

Grace squeezed Rhondda's hand as she sobbed.

'What kind of parent teaches their kid that it's okay to take money from innocent people?' Rhondda whimpered. 'I'm supposed to be setting an example, teaching him right from wrong. I'm a failure.'

'No, you're not.' Grace put on her stern schoolteacher voice. 'Now you listen to me. A mother will do whatever she can to protect her little ones. You should never apologise for that instinct. I know what it's like to be a single parent, having to be both mother and father. It's doubly hard. Every parent does the best they can with what they have.'

Rhondda swallowed. 'What if Hudson takes after his father? I'm worried that he'll grow up thinking that it's his right to take what he needs from other people, regardless of the consequences.'

'Trust me, Hudson is a great kid. He'll work it out for himself. If anything, you're teaching Hudson a valuable lesson. If children never see their parents struggle and occasionally fall short, they grow up thinking that the world is always fair. When life throws obstacles in their path, they simply can't cope. They never learn resilience.'

The tears were gone. Rhondda pulled an action figure onto her lap and began to rearrange its limbs. 'I hate myself when I think how much easier life would have been without him,' she said. 'I chose to keep my baby, but that meant staying with his father.'

'We are all faced with impossible choices at some stage in our lives.'

Grace thought back to the white-walled clinic and the form on the clipboard. Nobody would have been any the wiser. She could have risen to the top of the career ladder, perhaps later met a man who wanted children. But her body had chosen to create this tiny life.

'Melody says she knew about her father. She'd always suspected. She wants you to know that she never felt the need to go searching for him. You were all the father she ever needed.'

Grace's insides plummeted. 'That's impossible. I deliberately left the "name of father" blank on her birth certificate. I wanted to save her the disappointment, and potentially the hurt of rejection. I was only trying to protect her.'

This was an echo of Martin's excuse for not telling her about the newspaper article, she realised.

All the emotions arrived at once. Disbelief, anger, regret, sadness, and with them, relief.

'I'm sorry,' Grace said to Melody.

Rhondda squeezed Grace's hand. 'Your daughter says there's nothing to forgive.'

A gust of wind ruffled the leaves that almost touched the balcony. A startled bird took flight. Grace watched a feather see-saw down from the branch, the bird blissfully unaware that its wing was missing a feather. As much as Grace wished she could hold on to Melody, she needed to move on. It was time for Grace to live among the living once more.

Grace was hit with a sudden clarity that both thrilled and terrified her. 'I'd like to help you both,' she announced. 'I think Hudson has a lot of potential. There's still time for him to turn himself around before he goes to high school. With regular tutoring and support, he could go to university and beyond.'

'The teachers have all given up on him.'

'Not all of them.' Grace turned to a blank cheque and wrote the date. 'To start, I'd like to pay your rent arrears. And don't you dare argue.'

Hudson burst back into the room. Instead of the cake tin containing the shortbread, he thrust a sketchbook into Grace's hands. He flicked through to the very last page and a drawing he'd made in coloured pencil. At first, Grace thought it was another of his homemade flyers. When she looked closer, however, she recognised a woman, presumably Rhondda, holding the hand of a little boy with cartoonish ears. He was smiling, his mouth a long eclipse filled with dozens of tiny rectangular teeth. Holding the boy's other hand was a round-bodied woman with grey hair, carrying what looked like a bunch of weeds. At the bottom of the page, Hudson had written, *My Family*.

For a moment Grace was worried she'd lost her voice again, until she realised her throat was clogged with tears. She swallowed, and the tears were gone.

'It's to say sorry,' said Hudson.

'Thank you.'

She studied the picture again, noticing something she hadn't seen on first glance.

'Who's this?' Grace asked pointing to a man next to a black bicycle.

Hudson shrugged. 'Dunno.'

'Is he part of the family?'

Again, the boy shrugged.

'What made you draw a bicycle?'

'Someone told me to.'

'Who?'

He looked sheepish. 'An angel. I don't know her name.'

'Hudson . . .' Rhondda cautioned. 'Are you telling the truth?'

'Cross my heart and hope to die. There really was an angel here. We were talking and everything. Only she said it was time she left.' He looked directly at Grace. 'She said to say goodbye.'

29

Provenance and fate

PROFESSOR MARY'S ICY TENTACLES WRAPPED AROUND Martin's hand in a curt handshake. So, this was how it was going to be. The overpowering perfume that Martin had once thought so intoxicating now seemed cloying and sickly, and her thick make-up only emphasised the large pores around her nose. Had he really once thought her irresistible?

'Sherry?'

'It's a little early for me.'

She poured herself a mid-morning tipple. 'To what do I owe the pleasure of your company?' She eyed the cardboard box under his arm.

'I've come to talk about the museum.'

She perked up and ushered him to the special armchair by the window. He placed the cardboard box on the coffee table.

'Is this for me?' Mary gestured to the box.

'All in good time.'

'I hope this means you have good news for me, Martin. After the other night, I don't think I could handle any more disappointment.' She crossed her bare legs seductively. Was this all part of the game? 'Well?'

'I have good news and bad news.' He'd promised himself he wouldn't draw this out. At the same time, he'd waited patiently for this moment, and for once in his life he wanted to feel as though he had the upper hand. 'The bad news is that I will not be funding the building of the new museum.' She sucked in her cheeks, adding ten years to her face. 'However, I'm sure that your friends in high places will persuade the university to underwrite the building works.'

Mary's mouth hardened. She clearly didn't like being turned down a second time. 'Naturally, I'm disappointed you've chosen not to leave a meaningful legacy to the university. I thought that you of all people would recognise the importance of the museum to future generations of students and academics. It's rather sad to think your academic tenure will end on such a sour note.'

She stood and straightened her skirt. 'Rita will see you out.'

Martin didn't move. He'd steeled himself for her rancour. So accustomed to being on the back foot in relationships, the novelty of the situation almost went to his head. He gave the cardboard box a tap with all the flourish of a magician setting up a trick. 'If you'll let me finish, Mary. The good news is here in this box.'

She was playing it cool, but Martin could tell she was itching to see what was inside. She'd once called him a dark horse. Perhaps that's what he'd been all along.

'May I?' Mary's eager fingers hovered over the lid.

'Be my guest.'

When she lifted the lid from the box, her eyes widened in disbelief, then greedy delight. She removed the first item as if lifting a baby from a crib.

'Oh, Martin,' she murmured as she unrolled the fragile papyrus. Breath quickening, she returned to the box for the next item and unwrapped the dolphin-shaped earrings with a gasp.

'There's more,' said Martin.

With perfect timing, Rita appeared at the door. 'Some undergraduates to see you, Mary.' She stood aside for a procession of Martin's students who filed in, each carrying a similar cardboard box.

'What is all this?'

Martin rose, and thumbs in the armholes of his five-button waistcoat, enjoyed the performance he'd rehearsed.

'Allow me to explain. My father Henry Pottinger was a renowned Egyptologist and a prodigious collector of antiquities in the nineteen fifties. He was considered outstanding in his field.'

'Infamous' was more accurate than 'renowned', and 'dealer' rather than 'collector', but Martin settled on a narrative that lay somewhere in between the truth and the myth.

'He bequeathed his personal collection to me, and since I have no heirs, I want these objects to form the foundation of the new museum's collection. As my legacy to the next generation of young archaeologists.'

There'd been plenty of time to think since he'd opened the chests. Enough time to consider the options and decide how best to dispose of Raymond Bowen's poisoned chalice. During the long overdue conversation with his mother, Martin had finally learned the truth about his father and it was as though a fog had lifted between them.

As a child, Martin had never questioned how an archaeologist's salary could have supported his comfortable upbringing. As an adult, he knew that it couldn't possibly have paid for the private school and his mother's expensive wardrobe. The fortune his father had made by illegally trading in Egyptian antiquities finally explained it.

'I begged him to leave Egypt and come home, find a proper job,' Edwina had told Martin. 'None of it sat right with me. He kept promising he'd come home but there was always one more dig, one more deal. So I gave him an ultimatum. By then your father knew he was running out of time. The authorities were catching up with him. He fled Egypt but couldn't resist smuggling out one final cache,' Edwina explained. 'Unfortunately his luck ran out on the way home while he was celebrating. I suppose having lived in a Muslim country for so long, he couldn't handle the alcohol.'

Martin knew the rest. Edwina rocked back and forth. He'd never seen his mother in so much pain, not even when she'd tripped over Shirley Temple's scratching post and fractured her femur. She'd loved her husband, yet for Martin's sake she'd built a carapace around her grief.

'What I don't understand is why you kept what was in those trunks a secret for so long.'

'I forgot about them.'

'No, Mother, you forget where you left your reading glasses, you don't forget that you have the contents of an ancient Egyptian burial tomb sitting in the attic. Why didn't you hand them over to the authorities here?'

'And have your father's name dragged through the mud? I was trying to spare you more hurt and humiliation. You were having a hard enough time as it was just being you.'

'You could have sold them and invested the proceeds,' Martin persisted. 'Why leave them festering in the attic?'

'Because they weren't mine to sell, Martin. Those trunks belong to you. Before he left Cairo, your father wrote telling me he was on his way and that what he was bringing with him would secure your future. It's all yours, Martin. Yours to do with as you see fit. Keep, sell, hand back. It's your decision now.'

Now Professor Mary was examining the mummy mask in the final box. 'I don't know what to say, Martin. This is beyond generous.'

'My students have catalogued everything,' Martin said. 'You can't beat good old hands-on archaeology.'

The students grinned. He'd got to know them well over the past weeks and was proud of all the extra hours they'd volunteered to help him catalogue the items in his father's collection. It had started when he'd decided to bring a few props along to his tutorial.

'Today, I thought we'd do something a little different,' Martin had announced to the group. He'd emptied half-a-dozen newspaper-wrapped parcels onto the table. 'I want you each to pick one, open it and tell me what you think it is, using the techniques and principles you've learned this semester.'

The rustle of paper had given way to gasps as the students unwrapped their object. Shona had picked a small mummy-shaped figure inscribed with hieroglyphs.

'What is it?' Martin asked.

'Is it a shabti?'

'Correct. And what does it signify?'

'A shabti is a miniature servant placed in a tomb to perform manual labour for the deceased in the afterlife.'

'So, basically a minion. In the biblical sense rather than the movie,' Martin translated for the rest of the group, who laughed.

Taking turns, the three other students unwrapped the seal, the palette and the ram's head amulet. He quizzed them about their object's age and use. They'd been so engrossed in the task that the tutorial ran an hour over, and only ended when a group of impatient anthropologists knocked on the door. Then, instead of sloping away, Martin and his students continued to discuss the objects, chatting on the steps and even suggesting a WhatsApp group to share their findings.

'The catalogue is digitised,' Martin told the still speechless Professor Mary. 'I'll send you the files. Khalid has cross-checked everything against the Art Loss Register and Interpol's register of stolen antiquities, and none of the items are listed.'

Martin winked at Khalid. Of course they weren't listed. Nor were they ever likely to be, given how skilled Martin's father was at covering his tracks. Henry Pottinger had been outstanding in his field, if not quite as upstanding. In years to come, Martin hoped the items would find their way home to Egypt. That would be up to today's undergraduates. For now they'd be part of the conversation about the ethics of foreign museums displaying the 'finds' of previous generations.

'Thank you,' said Martin to the students. 'Coffee in ten?'

'See you there, Prof,' said Khalid.

'This is incredibly generous of you,' said Mary when they were alone again. 'I can't tell you how perfect all this is for the museum. It goes without saying that we will reference the exhibits as the Pottinger Collection.'

Martin waved away the suggestion. 'I'd rather you didn't. I'd prefer "Anonymous donor" if you don't mind.' The sooner he broke free of the family connection, the sooner he could move on with his life.

Mary fetched her laptop and sat in the armchair opposite Martin.

'I owe you an apology. I wasn't completely honest with you about the student feedback the other week. I was annoyed. I'd read the newspaper and I knew you were in a position to help me financially. It felt like another rejection.' She looked out of the window at the sunny quad. 'I was embarrassed about what had happened between us, or rather what didn't happen. It wasn't my finest hour. Anyway, what I didn't tell you was that the student comments weren't all bad.'

She opened a file on her laptop and turned the screen toward him. Was there anything that could redeem being labelled smelly and boring? He could take the romantic defeat – he'd had plenty of practice – but being failed by his own students hurt more. Adjusting his reading glasses, he scrolled down the spreadsheet.

Knowledgeable and interesting.
The personal anecdotes and real-life examples brought the subject to life.
His passion for glazed ceramics was inspiring.
Will definitely be enrolling for this tutor's classes in future.

A grin hijacked Martin's face as he read the last comment. Especially when he saw her name.

Professor Pottinger has inspired me to apply for a Master's in archaeology.

'Please stay,' said Mary.

He told her he'd give it some thought. It was good to feel appreciated, and wanted.

'I nearly forgot,' Martin said, reaching into his jacket pocket. 'This is a gift for you. It's not part of the collection. It's yours to keep.'

He handed her the amethyst scarab. She caressed it in her palm, beaming in recognition. Dominic Smythe must have told her about the auction.

'It's incredible,' she said, holding it up to the light. Then her face fell. 'I'm not sure I deserve it after how I've treated you.'

'You absolutely deserve to own it,' said Martin. 'It's as perfect as you are.'

He didn't tell her about the lively debate the amethyst had sparked in his tutorial group. They'd examined the engraved hieroglyphics under a borrowed microscope, an exercise in translation that had turned into a competition for which Martin promised the winner a bottle of vintage champagne. Shona had been the one to point out the minute flaw, something that Martin hadn't noticed in the catalogue photographs. Even when he'd examined the scarab up close after the auction, he'd missed the tiny extra stroke among the engraved symbols.

A quick internet search by Khalid brought up an article from an academic journal on forgeries in the world of antiquities. Sure enough, this kind of mistake was a hallmark of a modern forgery. The stone may well have been an amethyst, but it was not what it claimed to be. As a piece of decorative modern jewellery, it had a certain value, but in terms of provenance, it was about as genuine as Professor Mary herself.

Martin took the stairs two at a time on his way out. He was feeling lighter and more energetic than he had in years, as though he'd purged a heavy load. All he had left to do now to break the curse was dispose of the mummy's finger.

30

In flagrante delicto

GRACE HEARD REVEREND ROD BEFORE SHE SAW HIM. HE was tidying the parish noticeboard in the vestibule, his chainsaw voice tearing through a private rendition of 'What a Friend We Have in Jesus' in a key that defied all traditional musical conventions. She paused at a distance and smiled as she watched him, engrossed in his task. He was a handsome young man with charm and charisma, who could have been a success in whatever field he chose. And yet he'd dedicated his life to the church. Grace couldn't help but admire him.

'Hello, Grace,' Rod said, noticing her. 'What are you up to this fine day?'

She inched forward. 'I came to see Moira actually. I have something for her. Do you know where she is?'

He shook his head. 'Her car's in the carpark but I haven't seen her yet. I've only just arrived.' He turned to the noticeboard. 'Thought I might tackle the notices this morning. Most of them are out of date. I know it's Moira's job to write the notices and publish the newsletter, but I wonder if it's getting too much for her. What do you make of this?'

He handed Grace a notice in which Moira had thanked visiting 'monster' Reverend Hedley for leading the group in an enlightening session of 'B.S.' instead of Bible study.

'I see what you mean.'

Grace enjoyed organising things, she was reliable, and most important of all, she always read aloud whatever she'd written before sending it. But she didn't want to be the one to suggest turfing Moira.

'Let's pray the Lord shows us what to do about the Moira situation.' Rod looked up hopefully. 'In the meantime, can I help?'

'It's for the east window.' Grace flashed the sealed envelope she'd been carrying.

'Fundraising is Moira's department. I hope her maths is holding up better than her English. Try the vestry. She might be in there.' Rod smiled genially. 'You'll have to excuse me. I'm meeting a young couple who want to get married here followed by a visit to a parishioner who's in hospital.' He looked doubtfully at the notice once more. 'And then I have to write a letter of apology to our visiting monster.'

Grace wished him luck. 'By the way, how is Claire? We've been worried about her.'

We. It was becoming increasingly difficult to think of All Souls without thinking of Martin.

'She's doing well.' Rod smiled fondly. 'Although I am not sure where she will live when she leaves rehab. I'll mention it next time I speak with our Heavenly Father.'

There was no sign of Moira in the vestry, nor the flower room. Thinking she'd find her in the church hall, Grace slipped out the side door and walked along the narrow path, noticing how overrun with weeds it had become. She picked up a discarded McDonald's Happy Meal box along with a whole armful of rubbish she found scattered between the headstones, and dropped it all into the bin outside the church hall. Inside the lights were on but there was nobody around. The grille was down over the kitchenette and the bathrooms were empty. When Grace called out, there was no reply. How strange. Moira must be here somewhere. It was unlike her to leave her post unattended. What if she'd collapsed or had a fall? She could be lying unconscious somewhere, or worse. How typical of Moira to be martyred on holy ground, thought Grace uncharitably.

'Moira, where are you?' Grace called again, irritation now outweighing concern.

Grace was just about to leave when she heard something. It sounded like moaning. She listened again, wondering if she'd imagined it. There it was again. Muffled voices and groaning. As if someone was in pain. The only place she hadn't looked was the storeroom where the Sunday school stored all their play equipment. She pictured Moira drowning in coloured balls or crushed under a pile of crash mats. For all their disagreements, she couldn't let Moira come to such an ignominious end.

Grace tried the handle. To her surprise the door was unlocked. How strange. Moira was very particular about this room, insisting it was out of bounds to mere mortals. Grace fumbled for the light switch. She flicked it on. Then quickly off again. She closed the door and retreated.

She'd found Moira. She'd also found Bernard.

Grace was still deciding what to do when Moira came bustling out of the storeroom.

'It's not what it looks like. Bernard was giving me a hand to fold the parachute.' Seeing Grace's disbelief, she said, 'He's a very lonely man.'

And you're a lonely woman, Grace thought. They were two single, consenting adults. The choice of venue for their tryst might be questionable, but really, where was the harm? Actually, it was quite sweet that love should blossom here of all places. Rod had been right when he said that it was good to hear laughter again, that there had been too many funerals recently. Perhaps it was time for wedding bells at All Souls.

'I came to give you this.' Grace handed over the envelope. 'It should cover the rest of what you need to repair the window.'

Moira handed it back.

'The appeal is closed.'

'What? I don't understand. The last time I was here you still needed to raise thousands.'

'Somebody beat you to it.'

'Who?'

'I'm afraid I am not at liberty to disclose that information.'

Grace exhaled her disappointment. What an anticlimax. She'd so wanted to give St Francis a new head, and in doing so tick the first worthy cause off her list. Second, if she counted helping Rhondda and Hudson to stay in their apartment. There was still far too much money left in her account. Really, how difficult could it be to give away a fortune?

'How about new hymn books, a new tea urn? Or play equipment?'

They both glanced toward the storeroom.

'That won't be necessary.' Moira tried to conceal her cardigan buttons, which Grace now noticed were done up all wrong. 'I know you and I haven't always seen eye to eye,' Moira continued, 'but I was wondering if I could ask a tiny favour?'

Moira, asking her for a favour? This was a turn-up for the books. 'Of course. Anything for All Souls.'

'I was wondering if you wouldn't mind not mentioning to anyone what you just saw, with Bernard. I'd hate for people to judge.'

'Naturally. You can count on my discretion.' Grace saw her opportunity. 'And could I ask something in return?'

Sensing she was backed into a corner, Moira pursed her lips. 'Yes?'

'It's more the other way round, really. I'd like you to do me a favour by letting me do you a favour. I'd like to take over the parish newsletter. And help with the flowers. The catering too, if you'll let me.'

Moira conceded. 'Anything for All Souls.'

On the way out, Grace hummed to herself. 'Onward Christian Soldiers'. She'd won a battle though perhaps not the war where Moira was concerned. Someone, and she had strong suspicions who it might be, had beaten her to the headless saint. Thinking of Martin made her smile, as it always did. She'd assured Moira of her discretion over the tryst with Bernard. However, she couldn't promise not to be appallingly indiscreet when she next saw Martin. She couldn't wait to hear his take on the Moira situation.

Martin.

He wasn't like the other men she'd known. He was charming. Thoughtful. She loved the endearing way he always stifled his sneezes. He was a good listener, and only spoke when he had something worth saying. Martin was the first person who'd made her laugh since Melody had died, and not feel guilty for doing so. He'd helped her rediscover the fun in life; helped her rediscover life. Grace could no longer deny her feelings for him. That left the question of whether he felt the same way about her. She'd never know. Her bruised heart simply couldn't cope with the possibility that he didn't.

Grace paused to say hello to Alice Bailey, letting her know she wasn't forgotten. Near the end of the path she spied a ragwort covered in cotton-wool seeds obscuring the adjacent headstone. She couldn't let the wind spread those seed heads over the rest of the churchyard. She leaned over, plucked out the offending weed and shoved it, seeds and all, into her handbag. It was followed by a self-seeded camphor laurel which was too big for her bag. Standing back to admire her handiwork, she realised what she'd uncovered.

Agnes Mabel Bailey. Born twenty-two years before Alice, and died aged eighty.

This had to be Alice's mother. Grace did a quick calculation in her head. If so, this woman had spent the same number of years grieving her daughter as she'd known her alive. How had she survived that long so irreparably damaged? How many times had she, like Grace, longed to lie down among these quiet neighbours and let the weeds consume her body too?

People had told Grace the pain would end. She'd waited and waited. But the agony was still there; it would always be there. The secret was to keep moving in spite of it, just as her chiropractor had instructed her. The day would come when she no longer feared the pain and could once again do the things she enjoyed.

There were three cheques left in her chequebook. With the bank refusing to issue a new one, she'd need to embrace online banking sooner rather than later. For now there was something magical about signing her name at the bottom of a piece of paper that could literally change someone's life. More importantly, Grace had learned that a person's life could be changed forever in ways that didn't cost a cent. Trust could not be bought or sold. You couldn't put a price on forgiveness. Loving, and being loved, were priceless.

Something caught her eye as she searched for her car keys among the weeds in her handbag. It was part of a wheel poking out from behind a headstone. Thinking it was an abandoned supermarket trolley – she wouldn't put anything past the kids who hung around the grounds after dark – Grace scrambled between the overgrown graves and found an old-fashioned bicycle. It was the kind of utilitarian bike that people used to ride during the war, with a leather seat and curved handlebars. Only it was clearly well loved and well maintained with surprisingly little rust on the frame. The tyres were still firm too, considering its age. Someone, somewhere would be missing it. She had a strong suspicion who that someone might be.

When Grace parked the bicycle against the fence she noticed something else. High above, in the branches of the lightning tree, a green haze of new leaves. To Grace's delight, the tree was starting to grow again.

31

Night at the museum

Trapped in a tedious conversation with a notoriously dull anthropologist, Martin's heart did a happy dance when he saw Grace across the crowded room. What a relief! Having tried to make the invitation to the museum fundraiser sound relaxed and casual he feared he'd totally undersold the event, or worse, made it sound as if he was only inviting her out of politeness.

'You'd be more than welcome to come. If you haven't got anything else on. I mean, it will be a bunch of dull academics boring each other to death, but there'll be sausage rolls and I've put in a special request for carrot cake.'

'What's your opinion, Martin?' the dull anthropologist asked.

'Sorry,' Martin stumbled, having forgotten the man's name already. 'Would you excuse me?'

Martin quickly wove between the other guests to reach Grace. The sight of her out of context took his breath away, as if he was seeing her for the first time. Instead of her usual funeral attire, Grace was wearing a blue dress that showed off her soft curves. She'd done her hair differently too. When she smiled, Martin's cheeks flamed.

'This is Hudson,' she said, introducing a young boy. 'He's been beyond excited to see the artefacts.'

Not accustomed to greeting small children, Martin extended his hand.

'How do you do, Hudson.'

'How do I do what?' The boy sized him up warily.

'Do you know how to shake hands, Hudson?' Grace prompted.

'Like this?' Hudson twisted Martin into an arm wrestle. It was sweet, if a little awkward.

'I'm so glad you came,' said Martin, offering Grace a glass of champagne.

'It's so kind of you to invite us both.' She took a cautious sip, out of politeness he suspected. Meanwhile, Mary was way ahead, laughing like a bagpipe at something Dominic Smythe had just said. He was wearing a tight-fitting designer suit and was swigging a fancy beer straight from the bottle. The fact that he wasn't wearing socks with his suede loafers merely confirmed the kind of man he was.

Hudson tugged Grace's arm. 'Where are the mummies?'

She smiled apologetically at Martin.

Martin cleared his throat. 'There is a lot more to Egyptology than mummies, young man.'

'Why aren't the male mummies called daddies?'

'That is an excellent question.' One, that in over fifty years as an archaeologist, Martin had never been asked before.

'Let me find someone for Grace to talk to then I'll give you a guided tour of the display.'

Martin ushered Andrew and Maggie over and introduced them to Grace. His oldest friends meeting his newest. When he'd introduced Grace to his mother at Ambrosia Lodge, he'd assured her they were 'just friends'. What a curious notion. It implied that friendship held less currency than a romantic relationship, devaluing the three most important people in his life after his mother. He left them all to get acquainted and led Hudson to the first of the display cases. The boy was conspicuous among the adults, mainly because he was more interested in the exhibits than the free drinks. He pointed to a large earthenware jar.

'Is it true they scooped out all the body's insides and put them in a jar like that one?'

'That is correct. It's called a canopic jar. Everything was removed from inside the body except for the heart and the kidneys.'

'Why not the heart and the kidneys?'

'The heart was considered to be very important. The kidneys . . .' He waved his hand about, wondering how best to describe the technical difficulty in removing kidneys from deep inside the abdominal cavity. That was for another day. 'Afterward the body was dried in natural salt, covered in resin to preserve it, and finally wrapped in linen bandages.'

'I had to have a bandage once,' said Hudson, skipping to the next exhibit.

Martin never heard why Hudson had needed a bandage because, at that moment, Mary tapped the side of her champagne glass. She welcomed guests and prospective donors alike, remarking on the uniqueness of the occasion. She thanked Martin and his students for preparing the collection, and officially announced Martin as the Deputy Director and Assistant Curator of the museum. It marked the beginning of a whole new chapter in his career and, in his mind, a way to atone for what his father did by allowing him to research the exhibits further and liaise with the Egyptian authorities over the right to display them. Mary continued her speech, intermittently glancing at Martin. The museum was still a work in progress, she said, but hopefully tonight's event would secure the remaining sponsorship it needed.

'It is widely held that the Ancient Egyptians were obsessed with death,' Mary said, approaching the end of her speech. 'On the contrary, they were obsessed with life.'

The applause was accompanied by a hearty, 'Hear, hear!' that Martin traced back to Edwina. He'd parked her on a comfortable chair away from the champagne, with Shirley Temple on her lap, and naively hoped she'd behave. His mother was as much part of this story as Martin was and it was only fair she should be part of the evening. There was no need to spoil the dignity of her remaining days by telling her the truth behind the miraculous return of her lost savings. What mattered was that Edwina would end her days a happy woman, drinking bottomless martinis with her new friend Felicity.

With the applause finally dying down, Martin looked round for Hudson. He wanted to show him a papyrus inscribed with the *Book of the Dead*, only the boy had disappeared. It was just as well Martin had never had children of his own. He'd been responsible for this one for less than ten minutes and had already lost him. Martin surreptitiously checked under tables and behind display panels, eventually finding him talking to Edwina.

'Are you going to turn your cat into a mummy so it can live forever?' he asked, stroking Shirley Temple's fur the wrong way.

'What an excellent idea,' said Edwina. 'Since I'd quite like to live forever, I think I might do the same.'

Martin needed to nip this one in the bud. Before she added mummification to her mood board.

'Mother, this is my young friend Hudson.'

Edwina, dressed to the nines as usual, basked in the sudden attention.

'How do you do,' she said, holding out her hand.

'Like this.' Hudson went straight in with his signature handshake.

To Martin's surprise, the two were soon deep in a conversation. Spying Grace in the clutches of the dull anthropologist, he left them to it.

'Thank you,' she said when Martin rescued her. 'Andrew apologises for leaving early. Maggie took him home because he wasn't feeling well. They said to say goodbye.'

Martin looked toward the exit. It was good of Andrew to come at all, given how rapidly he was deteriorating.

'What a lovely couple,' said Grace. 'I'm not surprised you and Andrew have been friends all these years.'

'He is the best,' said Martin. He swallowed a lump of sadness. 'I hope this evening isn't too boring for you.'

'Not at all. It's nice to have an excuse to go out.'

Her face and neck were fetchingly pink from the alcohol. This was the perfect opportunity to ask her out on a proper date. He didn't want to wait until someone else died to spend time with her. But could he risk it? What if she wasn't interested? What if she was interested, but their relationship only worked at funerals?

They made intermittent eye contact in the awkward silence. He could almost hear Andrew coaching him from the sidelines. At least say how nice she looks. Compliment her dress, her shoes, anything. The moment passed, unfulfilled. She looked over his shoulder, her attention on the other side of the room. He'd lost her.

'I don't know if you've noticed, Martin, but Professor Mary Blake keeps looking over here. Is there something going on between the two of you?'

'Good lord, no.'

Grace narrowed her eyes. 'Are you sure?'

'Mary and me? Never. We hardly know one another outside of work.'

'Martin.' He started at Mary's voice, spilling champagne down his front. 'You've been avoiding me all night.' Mary moved in for a peck on the cheek but in his haste to avoid the gesture, Martin turned his head and ended up with her sticky scarlet lips on his. Before he could regain his composure, Mary had introduced herself to Grace.

'I have enjoyed working closely with Martin on this project. We've been practically living together.' She stroked his arm possessively. 'All those dinners at the bistro, the meetings over sherry. It's about time we switched to champagne, isn't it?'

'Dinner, singular,' Martin interjected. 'It was only the once, and I'm not a huge sherry fan.'

Grace gave him the side eye before turning her attention back to Mary. 'I must say, that's a stunning necklace you're wearing.'

Mary fingered the amethyst scarab which was mounted on a gold chain around her neck.

'A present from Martin,' she said, running her freshly manicured fingers up the back of his neck. 'He has quite the eye for bright shiny things.'

Grace inhaled deeply and exhaled with, 'I need to find Hudson.'

Martin watched helplessly as she disappeared into the crowd.

Mary kept talking to him but Martin barely heard her as he watched Grace making polite conversation on the other side of the room. She was the real treasure in this collection. The greatest find of his career.

Dominic appeared. 'Been to any more auctions recently, Martin?' he sneered.

'No, not recently.' Nor did he intend to. He'd even deleted the online auction app from his phone. The past had held him back for too long. It was time to look forward.

'Just as well. You can't win every time. There are some things that will always be beyond your reach.' He placed a possessive arm around Mary's waist.

'I know when to stop bidding,' Martin said. 'It's important to know the value of something.'

'No hard feelings?' Dominic held out his hand.

'None whatsoever,' said Martin.

'Mary, I want you to meet someone important,' said Dominic leading her away. 'I think he's good for a couple of mil.'

Mary resisted for a second. She leaned in and whispered, 'Grace is a lucky woman.'

Remembering he'd left his mother entertaining Hudson, or possibly the other way round, Martin made a beeline for them.

'I was just inviting Hudson to my funeral,' said Edwina. She turned to Grace who was hovering nearby. 'You too, my dear.'

Hudson bounced like a young kelpie. 'Can we, Grace? Please can we go to Edwina's funeral.' He tugged on Grace's sleeve, glancing hopefully between the adults.

Martin tried to rescue the moment.

'Hudson, how would you like to see a real mummy?'

'Cool. Can I see it now?'

As Martin led Hudson away, he caught the tail end of his mother asking Grace to take her shopping.

'I need to choose something special for my funeral, and I want a woman's opinion. No offence to Martin, but you've seen the way he dresses.'

Accessing the department's main storage room out of hours was a privilege of the new Deputy Director and Assistant Curator. Inside, he pulled a chair up to the bench for Hudson to stand on, and fetched the age-stained cigarette packet from a labelled drawer.

'Now, don't get too excited. It's not a whole mummy, only part of one.' A little under one per cent in fact. It wasn't unusual for mummified body parts to turn up in unlikely packaging. Sydney University's antiquities museum had been given two Arnott's biscuit tins, one containing a mummified hand, and the other a foot. They were often collected as gruesome souvenirs by World War I soldiers stationed in Cairo.

Martin handed the withered digit to Hudson. Showing no fear or hesitation, the boy silently inspected the finger from every angle. Only his wide eyes gave away his awe.

'Can I take it into school for show and tell?'

'Best not.'

'What happened to the rest of it?' Hudson asked, suddenly less impressed.

The horrors of what past generations had done to these ancient remains in the name of science or entertainment could wait until he was a little older. 'We'll never know for sure,' Martin said. 'But soon this finger is going home to where it belongs.'

Martin had arranged to surrender the remains to the Egyptian embassy. From there, the finger would be repatriated to its homeland.

'I think that's the right thing to do,' said Hudson, putting the finger gently down again. 'With great power comes great responsibility. This is my gift. This is my curse.'

What remarkably profound words for a child, thought Martin.

'Who said that?' he asked, assuming he was quoting from one of history's great thinkers.

'Peter Parker.' Seeing Martin's confusion, Hudson clarified. 'Spiderman.'

32

Weeding a stairway to heaven

GRACE WAS AMAZED AND DELIGHTED BY THE transformation in the reserve. Her hard work was paying dividends. Native grasses were growing tall and lush in the space she'd cleared and, freed from the creeper's stranglehold, the she-oak was once again standing straight, reaching for the sunlight. Nature was doing a good job of erasing the makeshift bike track too, with the recent downpours flattening the hillocks and filling in the gullies. The council's new skatepark was proving far more popular with the local kids anyway. Buoyed by her success in the reserve, Grace had decided to turn her attention to the overgrown jungle at All Souls.

In a dramatic change of heart, which may or may not have been prompted by the incident in the storeroom, Moira had finally delegated responsibility for the parish noticeboard and the newsletter to Grace. The board was now filled with grammatically correct notices advertising a variety of activities at All Souls, all designed to bring the community together. Hudson's hand-drawn poster calling for volunteer 'Weed Warriors' to tackle the neglected churchyard featured a host of hovering angels, who all looked suspiciously like Spiderman, and had proved irresistible. The turnout was impressive.

Wielding his very own pair of miniature gardening gloves and fork, Hudson appeared remarkably at ease around the gravestones. Claire had re-emerged clear-eyed and coherent from her time away. Grace could only imagine her reaction when handed the set of keys to a small apartment nearby. The anonymous note in the envelope explained that a year's worth of rent and utilities had been prepaid on her new home. It was signed 'A little gift to help you get back on your feet, from someone who is finally back on theirs'. Bill was also enjoying a stroke of luck in the shape of a year's worth of gas and electricity, and a weekly delivery of ready meals. In these and her many other anonymous acts, Grace had discovered a new sense of purpose. According to the New Testament, *'It is more blessed to give than to receive.'* There was a long way to go, but recently Grace had found herself flicking through her Bible and finding comfort and truth in the ancient passages.

There were projects that couldn't remain anonymous, however. She could hardly have expected a random stranger to set up the Melody Cavendish music scholarship at Parklea Primary School, nor to have arranged for the school grounds to be landscaped to match the bush beyond the gates. New shade cloths had been part of the project so that children could escape the lunchtime sun, and Grace had paid for the library to be updated and restocked with books, many of which were chosen specifically to appeal to reluctant readers. Airconditioning had been installed in every classroom. Much as she'd enjoyed her time as Fairy Godmother, sprinkling her gold glitter far and wide, she was looking forward to being utterly unremarkable again.

The inaugural Weed Warriors working bee took place on a sunny Saturday morning. After the damp start to spring, summer was finally in the air. And so was love. Moira and Bernard were well past discretion and were virtually inseparable. Once she'd realised that the community only wished the couple well, Moira had softened, especially toward Grace. She'd even apologised, claiming she hadn't remembered Grace as the grieving mother from Melody's funeral.

'I feel awful for the way I treated you,' Moira said. 'I didn't put two and two together when you turned up wanting to help out. I didn't recognise you.'

'That's all right,' Grace had replied. 'I hardly recognise myself these days.'

Moira and Bernard weren't the only newly fledged lovebirds. Grace wondered if she was the only one to notice Claire and Rod working shoulder to shoulder on the far side of the churchyard. Rod had taken more than a casual interest in her journey to recovery. Sobriety and security had transformed Claire, and Claire had transformed Rod. On the downside, falling in love hadn't improved his singing. Even Rhondda was dating again now that her divorce was finalised. Everyone had someone. Sadly, that included Martin.

Prior to the museum fundraiser, Grace had wondered if Martin might have been her someone. Then she'd met Professor Mary Blake and realised what a ridiculous notion that was. Why would he look twice at Grace when he had a woman ten years her junior with impressively long legs and a string of academic qualifications that put Grace's teaching qualifications in the shade? Why would a man of Martin's charm and intelligence look at her as more than a friend anyway? He was an attractive man. And attractive men only looked at attractive women. She was happy for them. Happy for all the couples. She was too busy for romance anyway.

With the team assembled, Grace assigned everyone a task. There was only so much a single day of weeding, trimming, raking and mowing could do to reverse the years of neglect. If all went well today, hopefully this might become a monthly event.

'Isn't it wonderful to see so many youngsters here?' Grace commented to Rod, as she did the rounds with the wheelbarrow. Moira had even roped in her teenage nephew and several of his friends to help.

Rod smiled knowingly. '*Whatsoever a man soweth, that shall he also reap.* Galatians, 6:7.'

The truth dawned on her. 'You mean Moira's own nephew was one of the youths causing trouble in the churchyard?'

'Let's just say that he has a strong right arm and a particularly good aim.'

Well, well. No wonder Moira had been so focused on repairing the window. At her age she couldn't afford to leave any sins, her own or her kin's, unrepented.

With so many sharp implements and potential hazards around, supervising Hudson was a job in itself. Rhondda was constantly distracted by her phone, exchanging messages with her new beau, leaving Grace to show Hudson which plants to leave and which needed to be cut back or dug out. She wished Martin was here. He and Hudson had got on so well at the museum. But she knew he was busy moving his mother into her new home and his last message explained that he might not be able to attend today. There were plenty of other volunteers; it wasn't as though they really needed the extra pair of hands, and yet every time anyone appeared at the gate, her breath snagged in her chest.

As the morning progressed, Grace channelled her growing disappointment into teaching Hudson how to push the wheelbarrow, and then how to empty it into the skip she'd hired for the day. They'd only been going an hour, and the skip was already half full of rubbish and vegetation. Hudson, being Hudson, soon lost interest in the wheelbarrow and turned his attention to a plantain growing at the side of the path.

'Grace! It won't come!' His face was pink, tongue protruding from the corner of his mouth as he struggled to uproot the recalcitrant weed. She watched his efforts with all the pride of a grandparent. He was far more capable than anyone gave him credit for. All he needed was encouragement, and for other people to believe in him.

'You can do it. Keep trying,' Grace called, as she pulled a thin, herby weed from a patch of soft leaf mulch. With their shallow, fragile roots, they were easy to pull out, unlike the tenacious little plants that grew tough and resilient through the cracks in the inhospitable concrete.

'Come on, you bastard!'

Grace stifled a chuckle as Hudson swore at the weed. Rhondda was on the phone, and Rod pretended not to hear while he dealt with a rogue clump of agapanthus.

'Here, use this.' Grace turned so quickly she almost lost her balance. It was Martin. 'It's all about having the right tools if you want to dig successfully,' he said to Hudson.

He handed over what looked like a large barbecue fork with a wooden handle. Hudson dug deep into the base of the plant and, with a look of satisfaction, levered it out, roots and all.

'I didn't see you arrive,' Grace said to Martin, wiping her sweaty face on her sleeve, smudging the make-up she'd spent way too long applying for a day of gardening.

'I hope it's okay that I brought Mother.' He pointed to where two women were sitting together on a memorial bench. 'She had FOMO.'

'Is that Felicity with her?'

'They're joined at the hip. Or more accurately, hip flask.'

Edwina called to Martin and gestured to a patch of bare grass at the far end of the churchyard.

'She's reminding me to pay special attention to that grave over there.'

'Whose is it?'

'Hers.'

Grace recoiled.

'She wants it to look pristine for the big day.' He toed the ground. 'I hope young Hudson wasn't too upset about the invitation to her funeral. Mother hasn't had much experience with kids.'

'I think it's healthy to talk to children about death. We've become so constipated about it.'

He laughed. 'That's one way of putting it.'

Hudson dragged Martin away to help him find the oldest grave. Grace watched them search through the Ediths and

Sarahs, the Arthurs and Georges, noticing that Martin didn't talk down to him, instead addressing him as he might an academic colleague, and answering his endless inquiries by asking searching questions of his own. She smiled at them pontificating, each unconsciously mirroring the other's body language.

'Can we dig up these graves to study the skeletons?' Grace overheard Hudson asking.

'That would be illegal, as well as immoral. These are real people who should be allowed to rest in peace.'

'The Ancient Egyptians were real people too.' Hudson scraped a furrow on the dry ground with his new tool. 'Why is it okay to dig them up?'

'That's different. They died a long time ago and we need to study them.'

'Why?'

'To understand their culture and how they lived.'

'By putting them in museums for people to take selfies with?'

'Yes. I suppose . . .'

'Why not put . . .' Hudson read the name on a nearby headstone, 'Samuel Thomas Jones in a museum?'

'That's not the done thing.'

'But it's okay if it's a body from another country?'

'Now that you put it like that . . .'

Grace went to the rescue. 'Hudson, good job with that weed. How about you do another circuit with the wheelbarrow?'

He didn't need to be asked twice. Weeds spilled over the sides of the wheelbarrow as he banked sharply into the first corner emitting fighter-jet sound effects.

'Sorry about the bombardment,' Grace said to Martin.

'I wish some of my undergraduates were that curious.'

'You're wonderful with him. He's clearly very fond of you.'

Their eyes met fleetingly. Only weeks ago, they'd been able to have entire conversations while looking at each other. Now it seemed that neither could hold the other's gaze.

'Best get to work,' said Martin. 'Although you've done a great job already without me.'

It will be even better now you're here, she wanted to say. Instead, she handed him a scraper and led him to a mossy headstone.

'How about you start by excavating this one.'

She left him to it, smiling at how fastidiously he worked to uncover the engraved letters on the weathered stone. One by one, the names of the long-forgotten were reappearing. Whether it was with a grand pyramid, a simple headstone, or a sapling in a woodland, everyone deserved to be remembered. Sitting back on her haunches, with the sun on her face and the smell of earth and trees scenting the air, Grace surveyed the scene. She remembered one of her daughter's many existential crises that always seemed to coincide with bedtime.

'What is heaven like, Mummy?'

'No one really knows,' she'd answered truthfully.

Melody's smooth forehead had wrinkled. The chances of her falling asleep now were slim. She didn't cope well with uncertainty and was on the cusp of a full-on meltdown.

'That's the great thing about it,' Grace backtracked, stroking her daughter's hair. 'It can be whatever we want it to be. My idea of heaven is somewhere very beautiful, with sunshine and trees and birds. And it's filled with all the people we love.'

Melody thought, forefinger on her chin. 'In that case, my heaven is the reserve.'

'Mine too, darling.'

Her little body relaxed. Grace pulled the flowery quilt up to her chin. She kissed her on the forehead and turned off the light.

Melody called out. 'Mummy, if mermaids live in water, are their fingers always wrinkled?'

Grace let the bittersweet memory fade away. She couldn't hold on to Melody forever, even though there would always be a Melody-shaped hole in her heart. She remembered losing her car keys when Melody was a toddler and eventually finding them inside the plastic shape-sorting toy. The keys had not matched any of the shapes – a square, a circle, a star and so on – but they'd found their way inside all the same. Martin was a different shape from Melody yet he fit perfectly.

'When you've finished,' she shouted to Martin, 'plant some of these on Alice.' She threw a bag of daffodil bulbs for him to catch. He missed.

'Bulb sports are not really my thing,' he joked.

'I nearly forgot,' Grace said, springing to her feet. 'I have a present for you.'

She led him to the skip, now full to the brim with rubbish and weeds.

'I found this in the bushes.' She wheeled the old bicycle out from behind it. 'One of the kids must have dumped it. I remember you saying your bike had been stolen. Is this it?'

She'd cleaned up the frame with a bucket of soapy water and polished the saddle with beeswax. However, his reaction wasn't what she expected. He was rooted to the spot. She wished he'd say something. Yes, or no. Thanks, or no thanks, it didn't matter. When she noticed the tears spilling down his face, Grace was as confused as she was worried. He mopped his cheeks with a white handkerchief.

'I never thought I'd see it again,' he said.

'So, this *is* your bike, the one that was stolen?'

He nodded. 'I know it's not very fashionable, but it has sentimental value. I wouldn't expect anyone else to understand.'

'Does it have anything to do with Jane?' When his face crumpled, she knew she'd hit a nerve.

'I promised I'd tell you about her one day. I suppose now is as good a time as any.'

They found a quiet spot on a wooden bench under a sprawling yew tree.

'Did you know the druids regarded the yew as a natural emblem of everlasting life?' Martin gazed up into the dark green canopy. 'They are amazing trees. Yews can live for thousands of years and regenerate from their own branches or roots. That's why Christians see them as a symbol of resurrection, renewal and the circle of life. There's even a powerful cancer drug that was originally extracted from the bark.' He looked horrified. 'I'm sorry, that was insensitive of me.'

'Please don't apologise, Martin. The more we avoid talking about things like cancer and death, the more hold they have over us. We need to name the beast and take away its power.'

'You're right. That's why I need to tell you about Jane. Until I do, she will always be the third person in any relationship I try to have.'

Grace swallowed. Was he talking about Mary? Martin told her how he'd met Jane during his fellowship at Oxford. Grace tried not to be jealous as he described this perfect woman. They'd met when their bicycles collided on a blind corner and he'd mended her puncture. They were in the same college choir. Their fairytale courtship had taken place against a magical backdrop in the city of dreaming spires.

'I'd planned the night of the proposal down to the very last detail,' he said. 'I wanted everything to be perfect: the best table in the best restaurant, a bottle of the finest champagne on ice, and a ring I'd spent all my money to buy. It was supposed to be a surprise.'

Grace examined him as he told her what had happened. His gardening clothes were older, tattier versions of the tweeds he always wore, and instead of gumboots, he wore laced black shoes. He'd probably worn the same uniform all his life, as though his emotional clock had stopped when he was a young man in Oxford.

'Jane was supposed to come straight from her hospital placement. She sounded annoyed when I insisted she cycle all the way into town from Headington. She was tired after a long day and would probably have preferred a bath and an early night. She wasn't to know that I was planning to propose to her that night on the one-year anniversary of our bikes colliding.

'Anyway, seven o'clock came and went. It had started to rain outside. I knew she'd be soaked through by the time she arrived but it was too late to call her a taxi. At eight I borrowed the restaurant's phone and called her house. Her housemate said she hadn't seen her since breakfast. I knew she could have been held up at the hospital. It wasn't as if she could scrub out of an operation to have dinner with her boyfriend. Eventually, I had to accept that I'd been stood up, that she'd come to her senses and had decided to save us both the pain of separation. Or she'd found someone better. I paid the bill and left.'

'That must have been hard.' Grace turned a fraction toward him. He was shaking his head.

'I could have handled rejection. What happened was much worse. By the time I left the restaurant, the rain was belting down. When I crossed the road I noticed an ambulance parked a little way up the hill. A crowd of people had gathered and, although the lights were still flashing, no one seemed to be hurrying. I didn't think anything more of it until I got home.' He gave a wry laugh. 'I remember being annoyed that my best suit was soaking wet and my new shoes were ruined.' His laughter turned into gasping sobs. The horrible truth was spelt out in capital letters all over Martin's face. Before she could offer any words of comfort, they were interrupted by shouting.

'Grace!' It was Rhondda, running toward them. 'Hudson's fallen into the skip and cut his head open. He needs to go to hospital.'

33

Dearly beloved

MARTIN WAS ALMOST RELIEVED WHEN THE BIG DAY DAWNED with perfect cloudless skies. He was exhausted. Whatever the funeral equivalent of a Bridezilla was, his mother had turned into one.

'I suppose you're going to tell me next that I can't have Christmas carols either,' she'd pouted.

Hands raised in resignation, he'd replied, 'Okay. It's your funeral.'

The skirmish over the hymns and processional music was only the start of Edwina's outlandish requests. Fireworks, doves, face-painting, gift bags. Every bell and whistle. Including bagpipes. And a man in a kilt. Deep down he knew she was only trying to make his life easier. Or perhaps she still didn't trust him.

Edwina had moved into Ambrosia Lodge only a few weeks before the funeral, the size of the congregation packed into All Souls testament to her instant popularity.

Her martini-drinking prowess had endeared her to the other residents. Less so to the care staff. Today, Edwina's partner in crime, Felicity, had claimed pole position on the front pew, the space usually reserved for family. She'd enthusiastically adopted the dress code – *Ladies dress to impress, gentlemen dress not to disappoint* – and was wearing a feather boa.

'Wouldn't it be easier to ask everyone to wear your favourite colour?' Martin asked when they'd discussed the invitations.

'Too boring.'

'What is your favourite colour by the way?'

'Impossible to say. That would be like trying to choose my favourite child,' she'd replied.

Given her predilection for nudity, the dress code could have been worse. The real challenge was accommodating Edwina's musical tastes since Bernard's limited organ repertoire didn't include anything by Edith Piaf. Instead, proceedings kicked off with a recording of 'Autumn Leaves'. It was a surprisingly demure choice considering Edwina's taste for mischief. Unfortunately, the falling leaves had barely drifted past the recently repaired east window when Edith Piaf was silenced by a loud boom. Sparks followed, accompanied by the acrid smell of an electrical fire. The guests in the pews closest to the speaker were left clutching their chests and wondering if this was all part of the show. Where Edwina was concerned, anything was possible.

After Edith Piaf's premature finale, Reverend Rod took to the pulpit to the undisguised delight of the ladies from Ambrosia Lodge, several of whom had brought opera glasses.

'A very warm welcome to All Souls on this special day,' he began, flashing his best Hollywood smile. 'We are here to celebrate the life of Edwina Frances Pottinger. I am delighted to see so many of her friends and loved ones joining us for what promises to be a unique commemoration.'

Unique was one way to describe it. Edwina had wanted her funeral to be memorable, and with All Souls filled with sequins and sparkle, kilts, ballgowns and even a Spiderman suit, no one was going to forget this day in a hurry. All Souls was also dressed to impress in streamers and bunting. Edwina didn't want the church to look too 'churchy'. When Martin turned briefly to take in all the glitz and glamour, he couldn't fail to notice his mother's helium-filled face floating en masse several feet above the second pew. The balloons were Hudson's idea.

'You get balloons on your birthday, so why not on your death day?'

Under strict instructions not to let go of the Edwinas, Hudson had tied the strings to his wrist. The cut on his forehead had healed weeks ago but he still wore the large surgical dressing as a badge of honour. Apparently having stitches had vastly increased his kudos with his schoolmates.

'From what I know about Edwina,' Rod continued, 'she would have hated to miss out on the party. Which is why we're delighted that she could be here today to enjoy her own *living* funeral, or as she prefers to call it, her *fun*-eral with the emphasis on fun. Edwina wants you all to enjoy yourselves and hopes you will join her in the church hall afterward for the *a-wake*.'

Edwina beamed from the plush armchair she'd ordered especially for today. The chair, which wouldn't have looked out of place in Elton John's house, was angled toward the congregation rather than the altar. As guest of honour at her own funeral, Edwina was wearing what would have been the perfect camouflage if she'd been trying to blend in at a zoo. She was dressed head to toe in animal print: leopard, cheetah, zebra and, unless Martin was mistaken, giraffe. Her ensemble was so busy it should have come with a warning to migraine sufferers. Shirley Temple was on her lap and wearing her best pink tutu. Even in his best paisley waistcoat and matching bow tie, Martin felt underdressed.

Andrew and Maggie were sitting toward the back, Andrew having reluctantly conceded to a wheelchair. Martin gave a little wave. Andrew gave him the thumbs up.

'As a concession to me dying, Maggie's letting me eat all the cheese I want to,' he'd joked the last time they spoke. 'The irony is that now I can't face the stuff.'

'In that case, I'll be sure to eat your share,' Martin had said, making an excuse to end the call before his voice cracked.

There was no sign of Grace in the congregation. He couldn't help feeling she was avoiding him. He'd blown it. Again. After his throwaway comment about the rain ruining his best suit and shoes on the night of Jane's accident, perhaps she'd finally seen him for what he was. Self-centred. Pathetic.

Rod announced the first hymn. 'We're going to start by singing "Oh Come All Ye Faithful".'

Nods of approval. No one seemed bothered that it was still only November. The organ's pipes burst forth. The All Souls regulars braced for Rod's customary vocal assault. But his nails-down-the-blackboard rendition was no match for the enthusiasm of the Ambrosia Lodge ladies' choir who'd come along to support their newest member. Then one voice rose above the others, a soprano as sweet and pure as spring rain.

She was here.

It was too late for them to go back to being friends who crashed funerals together. Too much had happened between them, and at the same time, not enough. All he could do right now was concentrate on giving his mother the send-off she deserved.

The hymn finished and, taking his place at the lectern, Martin waited for the coughs, murmurs and general shuffling to die away. He unfolded his speech and adjusted his glasses. Or what he'd mistaken for his glasses. He must have picked up Edwina's pair by mistake. Overcome with vertigo, he grabbed the lectern for support. He ditched the glasses and the spinning stopped. Holding the speech at arm's-length he could just make out the title of what looked like an article he'd printed out some weeks ago.

Is your doctor missing eosinophilic oesophagitis? Five symptoms to look out for.

He cleared his throat, and refolded the sheets, tucking them away inside his jacket pocket. He'd ad-libbed his first tutorial; there was no reason he couldn't do the same with his mother's eulogy. Gripping the sides of the lectern, he began.

'For those of you who don't know me, I'm Martin, Edwina's second favourite child.'

Polite laughter. Edwina hugged the cat.

'According to my mother, who did not want a eulogy, this is my opportunity to say nice things about her.' He peered around the room. 'It will be a very short speech.'

'Oh, Martin, really,' Edwina said.

'She also made me promise not to mention her age today, not because she's ashamed of being ninety-four, but because she thinks it's too old to be a cougar. As you can see from her outfit today, she still lives in hope.'

This wasn't going so badly. The audience were warming to him. He continued reciting the all-important biographical details.

'Edwina was born in India while her father was serving with the British Army between the wars. The family later moved to Singapore, Burma and finally to Australia.'

Edwina nodded approvingly, as though he'd passed the test. Martin realised how little he actually knew about his mother, or she about him. Children were notoriously incurious about their parents' early lives. Conversely, the offspring that parents knew so well in childhood became virtual strangers in adulthood. By the same token, spouses rarely knew their husband or wife as children, and friends were only privy to the edited highlights of a person's life. Loyal pets were with their owners for their entire lives, yet were only a chapter in their owners' lives. None of Shirley's predecessors had enjoyed more than a few years with Edwina.

'My mother met my father, Henry, at university.'

Martin had wrestled with how to word that she'd abandoned her modern history degree to travel with him. Edwina looked nervous, obviously wondering where this was leading. Martin smiled reassuringly. The family secrets were safe with him.

'Theirs was a whirlwind romance that took them on many exotic adventures in Egypt and the Middle East. It was a glamorous life. Until I came along, and wrecked her pelvic floor.'

He waited for polite laughter. Someone filled the silence with a throaty cough.

'Sadly, my mother was widowed when she was only thirty.'

Edwina had been a widow for most of her life, just as he'd been a bachelor for most of his. The longest and closest relationship of his life had been with his mother, and vice versa. They'd fought and bickered like a married couple, claimed each cramped the other's style, and yet all these years, they'd clung to each other to stay afloat.

Martin felt his body turn down the old, well-trodden path to panic. His vision tunnelled, as if he was looking through the wrong end of binoculars. Then Grace came into focus, hers the only features he could decipher in the morass. As long as he could see her, he could continue.

'No one deserves that kind of loneliness. Humans have a basic need to love and be loved.'

Grace, graceful Grace, was hanging on his every word.

'I lost who I thought was the love of my life a long time ago. She'd gone before I could tell her how I really felt about her.'

The church was silent, as though the entire congregation was holding its breath.

'What I've learned is that we cannot avoid grief in our lives,' Martin continued. 'To love someone means opening yourself to the possibility of losing them. Pain is a normal part of the human existence.'

All too soon his mother would vanish completely into his past, joining his father. And Jane. And too soon, Andrew.

Felicity leaned over and, loud enough for everyone to hear, said, 'I thought you said this was going to be fun, Eddie. I was promised bottomless martinis.'

'What I'm trying to say,' said Martin, 'is that we shouldn't wait until someone has died to say nice things about them. How much better to say those things to their face, while they're still alive to hear how much they are loved.'

Murmurs of agreement.

'And Edwina is still very much alive. It's easy to take someone for granted when you face them every morning across the breakfast table. It's easy to see only what's in front of you rather than the person behind the familiar facade. We may only be a small family of two –'

'Don't forget Shirley!' Edwina interjected.

'Sorry, three, but we have a found family large enough to fill this church. The fact that so many of you came along today is testament to how much Edwina is loved and admired. By the way, rumour has it that Mother is going into business as a funeral planner.'

It wasn't such a bad idea. She'd have a ready-made clientele at Ambrosia Lodge.

'One day, we are all going to miss Edwina very much.'

In truth, he already missed her. Having spent the last twelve months wishing she'd magically disappear, Martin was feeling surprisingly alone in his own house. He missed the soap operas, the infernal gameshows, and the bed that had a nervous system all of its own. He even missed his mother's knick-knacks, her creepy doll collection, and the way she policed his tea-making. He still listened for the 'Is that you?' in the silence that greeted him when he came home. He'd never admit it, but Martin missed Shirley Temple too. Although there was still enough cat hair inside the vacuum cleaner to convince him she'd never left.

When the emotion threatened to choke him, Martin used his last breaths to thank the minister and invite everyone for cake and cocktails in the church hall. This was greeted with murmurs of eager anticipation, and not a little relief all round. He was about to hand over to Rod to announce the final hymn when Edwina ditched Shirley and struggled to her feet. Martin tried to support her elbow. As usual she brushed him away and tottered alone toward the lectern in her kitten heels.

Edwina's speech began with a list of thank yous. Thanks to the minister, the caterers, to all her friends for coming. She paid tribute to Shirley Temple and all her feline companions who'd gone before. She thanked Moira for the flowers, Bernard for playing the organ, and Hudson for suggesting the balloons. Martin wasn't expecting to be lauded exactly, but as the Oscar-winner speech went on, his mother expressing gratitude to the carpark marshals, the printers for the invitations and the Weed Warriors for sprucing up the churchyard, his heart sank. A simple acknowledgement would have been nice.

When she'd run out of people to thank, Edwina paused and took a deep breath. 'And of course, it goes without saying that I am grateful to Martin for helping me organise my dream funeral.'

Where he was concerned, it always went without saying.

'Every mother boasts about their children, and my friends will vouch that I have never missed an opportunity to bore them with Martin's latest achievements.'

He looked around and found the smiling faces of his mother's new friends all nodding in agreement. Edwina continued, reeling off his accolades and the various academic posts he'd held. Her speech sounded like the LinkedIn profile for someone much more impressive than him. He was, she concluded, an inspiration to generations of young archaeologists and a man his father would be proud of.

'The ancient Hawaiian practice of *ho'oponopono*, which translates as "making things right", consists of four statements of reconciliation: I am sorry, please forgive me, thank you, and I love you.' She turned to face Martin. Were those tears in her eyes, or simply her glittery make-up?

'So, to my son, I say, "I am sorry. Forgive me. And thank you."'

Yes, those really were tears. Before Martin could hand her his handkerchief, she produced her own.

'I love you.'

Martin wasn't sure he'd heard correctly. She'd never once told him she loved him, even when he was a little boy. Saying it to an audience of over a hundred was apparently easier than saying it to his face. Martin didn't hear the rest of the speech. He'd heard all he needed to hear; everything he'd longed to hear.

'Thank you, Edwina,' said Rod, reclaiming the lectern. 'What a joy to see such affection between a mother and a son. Now would everyone please kneel.'

Rod led the prayers, thanking God for Edwina's extraordinary life, and for the anonymous donations that had restored St Francis's head. Martin smiled to himself. At least some of Raymond Bowen's money had gone to a good cause. The rest of his half would have to wait a while to work its magic. Who knew how long?

As he bowed his head, Martin thought about his mother's speech. He closed his eyes and summoned his favourite memory of Jane. They were punting on the river and, in his eagerness to impress, he'd pushed a little too hard with the pole. When it became stuck in the mud, he clung to it while the punt slowly floated out of reach. He remembered Jane's belly laugh as she watched him slide down the slippery pole into the murky water of the Cherwell. He loved the way she laughed. Loved to make her laugh. It didn't matter whether she laughed with him or at him.

Martin whispered a *ho'oponopono* to Jane.

I'm sorry I tried too hard. Please forgive me for not saying goodbye properly. Thank you for the precious time we shared. I love you. I will always love you. Goodbye.

He tuned back in as Rod was finishing the prayers. '. . . in the sure and certain hope of the resurrection to eternal life. Amen.'

Hudson took this as his cue to let go. Edwina's giant faces floated up into the rafters high above the congregation, where she was joined by half-a-dozen panicked doves released prematurely from a cage at the back. For a moment, there was chaos. Edwina had never looked happier. While the white feathers rained down like snowflakes, Martin nodded to Moira who was waiting in the wings with a spare Bluetooth speaker.

Je ne regrette rien.

Edwina spread her arms and sang along. Martin had never listened closely to the words before. The song was about having no regrets, about leaving the past behind and moving forward. That his 94-year-old mother, at her own funeral, could express such optimism about the future, was the lesson he'd waited his whole life to learn.

34

The Sphinx and the mummy

MARTIN BOWED. 'I HOPE I'M NOT TOO EARLY,' HE SAID, handing her a bottle of wine. He was still wearing his bright blue bicycle helmet.

Grace curtseyed and stood aside to let him in. 'No, you're perfect,' she said. Perfectly on time, she'd meant to say. It was too late. 'It's so good of you to give me a hand.' She hadn't expected wine.

'The pleasure is all mine. Thank you for asking me.'

Was the whole evening going to be like an Edwardian tea party, the easy conversation and entertaining banter confined to funerals? Now they'd shared their painful secrets with one another, there was apparently nothing left to say. At Edwina's a-wake, Martin had been monopolised by a steady stream of female admirers, every one of them over eighty. And who could blame them? His eulogy was a beautiful tribute to his mother. It had taken courage to bare his soul like that in public.

'Right then. Where are these curtains?' Martin was already rolling up his sleeves.

'Upstairs. Follow me.'

It was perfectly possible for one person to hang curtains without assistance, yet it was the first excuse that had popped into her head when she said goodbye after the funeral. Martin had jumped in with his offer to help. Grace suspected he would have volunteered just as readily if she'd asked for help to move the entire house six inches to the left. Now, as she led him up the stairs toward the bedroom, the whole thing felt too intimate. Too clumsy.

Hudson appeared at the bedroom door in his Spiderman pyjamas and shot them both with a web from his wrists.

Martin didn't hesitate. 'Excellent timing, young man. We're in need of a superhero for a very important job. Do you happen to know any?'

'Can I really help too?' he offered.

'Of course. They're your curtains, Hudson,' said Grace.

A task that would have taken Grace twenty minutes on her own, took an hour and a half with Martin and Hudson helping. After much cogitation, a pair of simple blue gingham curtains hung in place of Melody's floral ones. They didn't match the Spiderman doona that Hudson had brought with him for the sleepover, but he was more concerned with his new PlayStation than the aesthetics of the soft furnishings.

'Can I game for a bit before bed? Please, Grace.'

'Half an hour then. No more.' He was so excited to see Martin that Grace feared he'd never go to sleep. Playing a video game might help him unwind.

'I see that "to game" is now officially a verb,' Martin remarked when Hudson had his headphones on. 'I game, she games, we game, they game.'

Grace laughed. 'I had my doubts about keeping a game console here. I found one second-hand and the man in the shop said the games we chose were age appropriate. I checked with Rhondda first and she said it was okay. For once I agree with that "all the other kids are doing it so why can't I?" argument. Hudson has struggled to fit in with his peer group. I want him to be able to relate to the other boys, and if that means playing video games, then so be it.'

'I struggled to fit in at school too. I had nothing in common with the other boys. I was no good at sport and I was only interested in museums.'

A wave of pity broke over her. A teacher's sympathy for the odd little boy he must have been, and undeniable affection for the man he'd grown into.

'I've become very fond of him,' Grace said. Perhaps a little too fond of him. 'He's having a sleepover tonight. Rhondda has a hot date.'

'That's marvellous,' Martin said. 'She seems like a lovely woman. Not at all what I expected.' Not at all what Grace had expected either, in the best possible way.

In the kitchen, Grace found two glasses while Martin opened the wine. She imagined Melody teasing her.

'Looks as if Rhondda's not the only one on a hot date, Mum.'

Martin poured the wine and offered her a glass. 'You were miles away.'

'I was thinking about my daughter.'

'You were smiling,' he said.

'Was I?'

There was a time when thoughts of Melody brought only anguish. The memories would crash over her like breaking waves, the seventh in the set always the most likely to drown her. She'd always taught the kids in her classes that if they were caught in a rip, not to try to swim against it. Now, Grace was riding those waves rather than sinking beneath them. Everything felt possible again.

'Are you hungry?' She hadn't mentioned dinner when Martin offered his help with the curtains. He would probably have refused out of politeness anyway. Knowing how much he loved his food, she'd decided to ambush him with a roast instead, Hudson having eaten his favourite dinner of pasta earlier.

'I am indeed,' Martin replied eagerly. 'Since Mother moved out, I've not been bothering to cook much for myself. I thought it would be the opposite, that I could finally enjoy something more exotic than meat and two veg.'

Grace bit her lip. Thinking Martin was rather a traditional sort, she'd cooked a shoulder of lamb, with roast potatoes, peas and beans. There was still a lot they didn't know about each other.

She was just about to suggest they order a Chinese takeaway instead, when Martin said, 'Turns out I'm not as adventurous as I thought. Whatever is cooking smells delicious.'

Hudson bounded into the kitchen, a red-hot fireball of energy.

'*Minecraft Legends* is such an epic game,' he explained, mostly for Martin's benefit. 'It starts in a cave but the piglins have invaded the Overworld so you have to defend the villages then destroy three Nether outposts. Then, when you've destroyed all the portals and defeated all of the piglin bosses, you get to fight the Great Hog.'

His mouth could barely keep up with his words. Martin listened intently as the boy described the game. Grace watched in amusement as Martin tried to follow Hudson's story.

'Fascinating,' said Martin.

'You can play with me if you like,' Hudson offered. 'I also have a game called *Sphinx and the Cursed Mummy* which you might like.'

Grace intervened. 'It's getting late, and you have school tomorrow, Hudson. How about we invite Martin to come over at the weekend to play instead? That way, we can all take our time.'

Hudson looked to Martin, full of anticipation. 'Would you play with me at the weekend?'

'I'd like that very much.'

With the meat resting and the potatoes still in the oven, Grace invited Martin to set the table while she tucked Hudson into bed. She lingered at the top of the stairs, taking in the warm glow from Melody's old bedroom. For too long, that door had been closed, her daughter's essence sealed inside along with all her precious things. Grace hadn't wanted to disturb a thing, as if she could hold on to her by stopping time. Now, with its fresh paint, new blue curtains and a bookshelf full of books suitable for a keen eight-year-old reader, the room was no longer a mausoleum. With Hudson in bed and Martin downstairs, the house was alive again.

When she crept in, Hudson was already asleep, his butterfly eyelashes fluttering as he dreamed. Grace pulled the doona up over his shoulders, trying not to wake him. He stirred and grasped her arm.

'Grace,' he said sleepily. 'Can I still be an angel if I've been naughty?'

'Oh, my dear boy. Of course you can.' She stroked his hair, hoping he wouldn't see her glistening eyes in the dark.

'Grace, can I ask you something else?'

'Anything.'

'When I grow up, do you think I could be a famous archaeologist like Martin?'

He was asleep again before Grace whispered that he could be whatever he put his mind to.

Downstairs, Martin had laid two places at the dining table and lit the dusty candle she only ever used as an ornament. Melody had given her the candle one Mother's Day. She'd saved up her pocket money especially, and Grace had always considered the candle too precious to burn. When Melody eventually noticed the pale wax gathering dust on the mantle, she threw a teenage tantrum, accusing Grace of being ungrateful. She'd behaved appallingly now Grace thought about it. A grieving brain chose only to remember the good parts. Melody had not been perfect. No one was. She'd been even better than that. She'd been human. They'd continued to use the candle as a surrogate for all their disagreements, until it became a joke. Even when Melody was dying, Grace refused to light it. Once it had burned down, the flame would be out forever.

'I hope it's not too presumptuous of me to light a candle,' Martin said sheepishly when Grace stared at the flickering light.

'Not at all. It was long overdue.'

She carried the plate of sliced meat, potatoes and a dish containing the shiny greens to the table. Martin's features looked softer in the golden candlelight and, judging by the way he was looking at her, so did hers. Even the simple meal looked exotic in the flickering glow. From now on she would use her best china and light a candle every night of the week. Melody would surely approve.

'Here's to us being a million dollars poorer than we were a few months ago.' Martin raised his glass to Grace's.

'And a million times happier.'

'Cheers to that.'

Martin tucked into his lamb roast with undisguised relish. She smiled when he paused and, with an intense concentration that reminded her of Hudson, used his knife to scrape gravy from his tie.

'Martin,' she said. 'I realise this might be a bit forward of me.' The wine had gone to her head and she felt flirty. 'Would you do something for me?'

He put his knife back on the plate. 'Yes, of course. Anything.'

'Are you sure?'

'Absolutely positive. Assume your request is already fulfilled.'

He was such a funny fish. She couldn't help but smile.

'In that case, Martin, would you please take off your bicycle clips before we have dessert.'

He bent down and fiddled about under the dining table, removing the matching pair of silver-coloured trouser clips. 'Will that do?'

'Better.' She smiled.

Grace found a bottle of champagne, a leaving present from the staff at Parklea, that had been languishing in her larder. Martin's eyes widened when he saw the bottle and the pair of flutes she brought to the table, but so did his smile.

'Allow me,' he said, popping the cork and pouring the champagne. 'Here's to us.'

'The Funeral Crashers.' They clinked glasses.

They both took a sip, the peppery bubbles forcing Grace to squint.

'How do you know when enough is enough?' Martin asked unexpectedly.

'There are plenty more potatoes if you're still hungry.' Grace offered the dish.

'I'm not talking about potatoes, delicious as they were. I meant funerals. How many before the debt is repaid in full?'

Had he really seen through her facade?

'There's no scoresheet, Martin.'

'For you, maybe not. But I fear my penance will never end.' The playful Martin disappeared behind a cloud.

'I don't understand. Is this to do with Jane? I thought what happened to her was an accident.'

'It was, and I've finally come to terms that her accident wasn't my fault. It's what I did afterward, or rather what I didn't do that still haunts me.'

He told her the rest of the story and the last piece of the puzzle fell into place. On the morning of Jane's funeral, Martin had woken with nausea and stomach pains. By the time he'd arrived at the hospital, the pain was so severe that he was wheeled straight into the operating theatre to remove his appendix.

'By the time I woke up, woozy and sore, it was too late. I'd missed the funeral.'

'You couldn't help that, Martin. You had appendicitis.'

He hid his face in his hands, as though he couldn't bear her to look at him.

'The worst thing was feeling relieved that the funeral was over. I wouldn't have to see her coffin, nor face her parents. I wouldn't have to say goodbye. It was the most cowardly thought I've ever had, and I'm still ashamed of myself. To make matters worse, when the surgeon came round later he told me my appendix had been completely normal. They couldn't find a cause for my symptoms. Turns out my body had given me an easy way out.'

His anguish was palpable. No wonder he'd been so tense at that first funeral.

'As the days passed, it became harder and harder to pick up the phone to Jane's parents. When I eventually plucked up the courage to speak to them, they didn't even know who I was. Apparently Jane had never mentioned she had a boyfriend.

'I was utterly lost after that. I tried to forget and move on. Unfortunately, my body has an excellent memory and tortured me whenever I thought about Jane or death. Eventually, I landed a place on a dig in Saqqara, which I was hoping would be a new start for me. But most of the work was excavating burial sites and I started having panic attacks. An archaeologist who can't handle death doesn't last long in the field. I contemplated giving up altogether and retraining as an accountant.'

'But you didn't.'

'I switched to the less glamorous world of ceramics instead. I found studying the objects ordinary people used in their everyday lives brought me unexpected comfort. The rest as they say is ancient history.'

Grace searched for the answer in her glass. 'You asked me a question, Martin, and I presume that means you respect my opinion. Here's my answer. The number of funerals you need to attend is seven.' She counted them off on her fingers. 'Cynthia Preston's. Sandra what's-her-name's. Joan Sweeney's. Raymond Samuel Bowen's. Warwick Winthrop's. Dorothy Buckland's. Seven if you include your mother's. That's enough. Your penance is paid in full.'

He looked relieved, then his brow wrinkled. 'Does that mean our funeral-crashing days are over?'

'Not necessarily. But I think we could shake things up a bit and crash a few weddings and baptisms too. We could even rope in a few more and start a choir at All Souls. What do you say?'

'That is an excellent idea.'

Grace's head was weightless, her arms and legs not quite under her control. Before she realised what she was doing, her hand had slid across the table. Martin's slid to meet it.

'It's my turn to suggest something,' Martin said. 'Have you heard of the temples of Abu Simbel near Luxor?' She hadn't. 'They were built three thousand years ago by the pharaoh Ramses the Great. He dedicated one to his wife Queen Nefertari.'

'Why are you telling me this?'

'Because it is the most romantic place in the world and one day I'd like to take you there.'

'I'd better renew my passport then.' Grace laughed, in case it turned out to be a joke. When she could see he was serious, she added, 'I thought you said you weren't one for grand gestures, Mr Unglazed Ceramics.'

He smiled bashfully. 'That's why I need you to keep my feet on the ground.'

'How about we start with a kiss instead?' Grace said. 'And see where we go from there.'

At their age, there was no point in beating about the bush. When their lips finally met, the kiss was tender and unhurried, as if, having waited so long, neither wanted it to end.

35

When Ramses met Nefertari

CONFOUNDING HIS MOTHER'S PESSIMISTIC PREDICTION, Martin arrived at All Souls without a single mud splatter or oil stain on his new suit.

'I can't believe you wanted to cycle,' she chided after adjusting his tie and checking he had a clean handkerchief. 'And wearing gumnuts in your buttonhole . . . whatever next?'

'I think he looks very handsome, Eddie,' said Felicity, sipping a sneaky livener from her hip flask. 'He reminds me of someone. What's that film? You know the one.'

'Indiana Jones?' Martin smoothed his hair.

The two women squinted at him. 'If you wore a false beard and a hat, then you might pass for Indiana Jones's dad.'

He'd take even a passing resemblance to Sean Connery as a compliment.

'Well, you both look lovely,' he said, ignoring his mother's multi-coloured fascinator that made it look as though she'd been dive-bombed by a kamikaze lorikeet.

It was good to see his mother happy again. Her old spark had finally returned after Shirley Temple's sad demise. The sour puss had literally been loved to death at Ambrosia Lodge. Edwina had spared no expense in giving her the send-off she deserved, although Martin suspected most of the mourners were only there for the open bar. A taxidermist had bestowed immortality on Shirley and she was now enjoying her tenth life in pride of place on Edwina's bookshelf.

At the church, the ushers encouraged the guests to sit wherever they liked. Martin watched from behind the stone pillar in the north transept, stomach lurching and with a mouth drier than the sands at Deir el-Medina in high summer. Once again, he had some serious nerves to control. This time they were good nerves, the kind the body took for fear but were really excitement and anticipation.

'Good luck,' said Rod as he passed on his way to the vestry.

Martin nodded thanks, still barely believing that he was getting married. This whirlwind romance had been a long time in the making.

Moira grumbled under her breath as she hurried by on some totally unnecessary errand.

'I've been running around like a blue-arsed fly all morning. I can't believe I have to do everything myself.'

Bernard popped up from the organ bay and winked.

'Make sure Bernard gets an extra slice of wedding cake, won't you, Moira,' Martin called after her. 'He'll have worked up quite an appetite by the end of the service.'

'Bernard does have an extremely healthy appetite.' Moira paused and blushed. 'I don't know where he finds the stamina at his age.'

As well as the choice of buttonholes, the choice of cake – carrot cake with cream cheese icing, naturally – had met with Edwina's disapproval.

'Root vegetables in a wedding cake? What is the world coming to?'

Next to disrupt Martin's quiet reflection was Hudson.

'Excuse me,' he said. 'How long do you think you're going to live for?'

By now, Martin was accustomed to Hudson bowling conversational googlies. The boy's brain was a marvel.

'I don't know, Hudson. None of us know.'

'That's not true. There's an app that can tell you what day you're going to die.'

Not so long ago, Martin had been convinced that day was close. His body had faked illness so convincingly that he'd wished he would hurry up and die, simply to get it over with. But his brain tumour had miraculously disappeared, and he hadn't had a heart attack in weeks.

'I'd rather not know,' said Martin. 'I think I'll take each day as it comes. Any reason you ask?'

'I'd like you to be my new grandpa. Only I don't want to get too attached if you're not going to be around very long.'

Hudson was an old soul and Martin couldn't hide his growing affection for the boy. When invited to be a pageboy, Hudson had agreed on the strict condition that he wouldn't be required to hold hands with any girls. When told he'd have to dress smartly, he'd assured everyone he'd wear his very best Spiderman costume. And here he was, a four foot tall superhero carrying a basket of native leaves and flowers.

With time running out to calm himself, Martin tried some deep breathing exercises that made his fingers tingle. By now, the church was full. He marvelled at how such a recently lonely couple had managed to attract so many well-wishers. Rhondda was the last to ambush him, her arms around him as she kissed him on the cheek.

'That's from an old friend. She's happy for you.'

Jane? Martin had remained politely sceptical of Rhondda's mystical powers.

'You'll be pleased to hear your father is here. There's someone else too. Someone who's only recently left us. He wants to make sure you have the rings.'

'They're here.' Martin patted his pocket.

The rings had come from a second-hand jeweller. They weren't rare pieces, not even antiques. With so many good causes to support, there was no point wasting money on frippery.

'He's sorry he couldn't hold on for your big day.'

'I'm sorry too.'

Martin had seen Maggie slip into one of the pews earlier. She was doing well, considering. After Andrew's funeral, she'd thanked him for delivering such a moving eulogy. It was the least he could do for his friend, fulfilling a promise they'd made each other as young men.

'Spare no words in describing my greatness,' Andrew had said, the last time they'd seen each other.

'Nor you for me, old man,' Martin had replied with faux cheeriness.

'I won't be here to give your eulogy, and we both know it. Which is why I've prepared this.' He'd handed Martin a folded piece of paper. 'It's my best man's speech. You can read it out at the reception.'

'So you approve?'

'Of course! Maggie and I adore her. You're perfect for each other. You've been in love with a ghost for most of your life, Martin. We both know Jane would probably have dumped you for some hunky rower eventually.'

It would have been wrong to punch a dying man. Instead, Martin had hugged what was left of his closest friend and thanked him.

'What for?'

Martin smiled. 'For being my better half all these years.'

The last of the guests hurried to their seats.

'One more thing,' said Rhondda. 'This friend of yours wants me to tell you he only let you win that last game to even the score between you.'

Bastard, thought Martin, affectionately. A draught whipped through, as if someone had opened a door, then closed it again. Then, before he knew it, the moment he'd been waiting for all his life was here.

As an archaeologist he was used to not a lot happening very slowly. This time his patience had been rewarded. Or was it luck? The greatest finds were always accidental; chanced upon and easily overlooked. After all the disappointment, Martin had stopped searching for buried treasure. And that's when he'd stumbled across Grace. He'd taken care to uncover her little by little, with a trowel edge here and a dust of his brush there, until he'd revealed her in all her glory. Grace was the discovery of a lifetime. The most exquisite artefact of all.

36

All things bright and beautiful

SHE HADN'T SLEPT AND RISING EARLY GRACE DECIDED ON the spur of the moment to drive out to the Woodland burial ground. There was something she needed to do, something that had been on her mind all night. With the wedding only hours away she needed to hurry.

It was only the third time she'd visited the burial site in nearly three years. Every time, she'd leave disappointed, not quite finding the peace she'd been searching for.

Today Grace hardly recognised the spot. The woodland was so lush and green. Melody's tree had grown into a fine young specimen with symmetrical branches and silvery green leaves. Tiny birds, fairy wrens, flitted in and out of her branches and the leaf litter at the base of the tree was alive with insects and geckos.

'I'm getting married today,' said Grace. 'I wish you could be there. I think you'd approve. He's a good man.'

Grace took a small cutting from one of the lower branches with her secateurs. She stroked the cool, smooth bark of the trunk. For all the natural beauty and tranquillity of the place, Melody wasn't here. Her atoms might be in this tree but her soul, her essence were not. She was wherever Grace was. A mother's body never forgets.

By the time Grace returned home, she was way behind schedule. Luckily, she wasn't one for elaborate preparations, and there was no wedding photographer to capture her sipping champagne in a fluffy white bathrobe as she primped and preened. Determined to avoid the usual bridal rigmarole, Grace did her own hair and make-up wearing her old pink dressing-gown. Instead of a traditional wedding gown, she'd found a lovely cream suit in a second-hand designer store in town. The matching skirt and jacket were a bargain and still had the original tags attached. There was no point wasting money on a fancy wedding car either, now she was back to living off a pension, and only buying petrol on a Tuesday. But when Stephanie had heard she was planning to order a taxi, she'd insisted on driving Grace to the church. The two women had grown close over the last few months, and although Grace would be moving to her new home soon enough, she knew they would always be bound by loss.

At the church door, Moira cast a judgemental eye over Grace's bouquet, made using foliage from the reserve and the spray of young gum leaves from Melody's tree. She'd incorporated a loop of trailing ivy that had started to grow back over Alice's grave.

'Ivy,' Moira tutted, rolling her eyes. A smile followed. She wasn't such a bad old stick after all, thought Grace.

Rhondda was waiting in the vestibule with Hudson.

'When can I start throwing the weeds, Grace?'

'Very soon.' His mother looked unusually frayed. 'Are you okay, Rhondda?'

Perhaps it had been too much to ask them to be pageboy and matron of honour, however symbolic the roles were meant to be.

'Headache,' said Rhondda, rubbing her temples. 'It's the heavenly host. They're all fighting to get my attention. There's even a cat here. Turns out you two are very popular.'

It was comforting to know that the spirit world wished them well too.

Moira gave a thumbs up to Bernard who launched into Handel's 'The Arrival of the Queen of Sheba'. Hudson raced down the aisle lobbing the flower petals as if they were tiny hand grenades. His sound effects were so convincing that several guests ducked. By the time Grace reached Martin at the chancel step, her cheeks ached from smiling. When their eyes met, any lingering doubts evaporated.

Rod welcomed everyone, saying what an unexpected joy it was to see love blossom between two strangers who'd met at a funeral, here at All Souls.

'Our first hymn is a favourite of both the bride and the groom,' said Rod. 'In fact, it is how they first met.'

In the nave, the members of the new choir were poised with their hymn books, ready to do their duty.

Bernard played the familiar introduction. Martin cleared his throat. Grace gave the choir a nod. The weeks of choir practices were rewarded with a sudden explosion of sound. Gracious in defeat, Reverend Rod closed his hymn book after the first line and lip-synced the rest of the hymn.

Acknowledgements

FIRSTLY, THANK YOU TO THE EXCEPTIONAL TEAM AT Hachette, including publisher Rebecca Saunders, editors Karen Ward and Deonie Fiford, cover designer Alex Ross and the many hard-working folk in sales, marketing and publicity. Thank you for not baulking at the idea of a novel about funerals.

Thanks to my agents at Curtis Brown, namely Tara Wynne for being my champion and for shrinking every mountain into a manageable molehill, and Lucy Morris for that first brainstorming session over G&Ts and the invaluable feedback on what emerged. Liz Dennis, my books couldn't be in better hands.

To my Ink Well buddies, Michelle Barraclough, Laura Boon, Rae Cairns, Pamela Cook, Terri Green, Penelope Janu, and Angella Whitton: how did I end up with such a wonderful group of smart, witty and talented women in my life? Terri and Michelle, thank you for your reassurance and suggestions.

I am grateful to Professor Sahar Saleem, Professor of Radiology at the Faculty of Medicine at Cairo University and a member of the Egyptian Mummy Project, for answering my queries about handling mummified remains. My gratitude also to Dr Melanie Pitkin, Egyptologist and Senior Curator of Antiquities at the University of Sydney Chau Chak Wing Museum, for holding her lecture 'Unravelling the Ethics of Antiquities' at exactly the time I needed to hear it. To Mahmoud Nour of Egypt Portal Tours, thank you for bringing ancient Egypt to life.

Writing is a solitary activity, so I'm grateful to the wider writing community for their generous support and friendship, including the selfies, 'shelfies' and shout-outs. Thank you for turning up to events and listening to stories you've probably heard a dozen times. My heartfelt thanks go to our booksellers and librarians, the unsung heroes of the book world, for matching each book with its perfect audience. Which brings me to my lovely readers. Whether for you this is the first or sixth of my novels, thank you for reading *The Funeral Crashers*.

To my IT guy, barista, martini shaker and loudest cheerleader, John: thank you for being the best support team a writer could wish for. Will and Charlotte, you might technically have flown the nest but it is a privilege to be part of your exciting new lives. To my daughter-in-law, Yanina, welcome to the Nell family.

Margot, it's been a lonely year without you snoozing under my desk. I miss our 'plotting and planning' walks, the ever-growing pile of sticks at the front door, and even the double coat Labrador hair between the pages of my manuscript. This book is for you.